continued . . .

"Douglas Clegg is a writer who knows how to tell a great story with characters that any reader can empathize with . . . The vampires are not the typical creatures of the night but have weaknesses that make them vulnerable objects of pity. It will be hard to wait for the next book in this bloodcurdling series."
—*The Best Reviews*

"Clegg's evocative, vivid medieval setting is every bit as appealing as the vampire lore in this promising series starter."
—*Booklist*

"[An] extravagant tale of fantasy . . . thrilling . . . Clegg also shows his ability to write exciting prose."
—*Garage Radio*

"Clegg's unique interpretation of vampire mythology makes for a page-turning, bone-chilling adventure. Vampire fans and horror aficionados will relish this tale."
—*Romantic Times Book Reviews*

PRAISE FOR DOUGLAS CLEGG

"Douglas Clegg has become the new star in horror fiction."
—Peter Straub,
author of *In the Night Room*

"Douglas Clegg is a weaver of nightmares."
—Robert McCammon,
author of *The Queen of Bedlam*

"Clegg delivers."
—John Saul,
author of *The Devil's Labyrinth*

"Clegg is one of the best."
—Richard Laymon,
author of *Cuts*

Ace Books by Douglas Clegg

The Vampyricon Trilogy

THE PRIEST OF BLOOD
THE LADY OF SERPENTS
THE QUEEN OF WOLVES

—THE VAMPYRICON—

THE QUEEN OF WOLVES

DOUGLAS CLEGG

ACE BOOKS, NEW YORK

THE BERKLEY PUBLISHING GROUP
Published by the Penguin Group
Penguin Group (USA) Inc.
375 Hudson Street, New York, New York 10014, USA
Penguin Group (Canada), 90 Eglinton Avenue East, Suite 700, Toronto, Ontario M4P 2Y3, Canada
(a division of Pearson Penguin Canada Inc.)
Penguin Books Ltd., 80 Strand, London WC2R 0RL, England
Penguin Group Ireland, 25 St. Stephen's Green, Dublin 2, Ireland (a division of Penguin Books Ltd.)
Penguin Group (Australia), 250 Camberwell Road, Camberwell, Victoria 3124, Australia
(a division of Pearson Australia Group Pty. Ltd.)
Penguin Books India Pvt. Ltd., 11 Community Centre, Panchsheel Park, New Delhi—110 017, India
Penguin Group (NZ), 67 Apollo Drive, Rosedale, North Shore 0632, New Zealand
(a division of Pearson New Zealand Ltd.)
Penguin Books (South Africa) (Pty.) Ltd., 24 Sturdee Avenue, Rosebank, Johannesburg 2196,
South Africa

Penguin Books Ltd., Registered Offices: 80 Strand, London WC2R 0RL, England

This is a work of fiction. Names, characters, places, and incidents either are the product of the author's imagination or are used fictitiously, and any resemblance to actual persons, living or dead, business establishments, events, or locales is entirely coincidental. The publisher does not have any control over and does not assume any responsibility for author or third-party websites or their content.

THE QUEEN OF WOLVES

An Ace Book / published by arrangement with the author

PRINTING HISTORY
Ace hardcover edition / September 2007
Ace mass-market edition / August 2008

Copyright © 2007 by Douglas Clegg.
Cover art by Judy York.
Cover design by Judith Lagerman.
Interior text design by Kristin del Rosario.

ISBN: 978-0-441-01620-4

ACE
Ace Books are published by The Berkley Publishing Group,
a division of Penguin Group (USA) Inc.,
375 Hudson Street, New York, New York 10014.
ACE and the "A" design are trademarks belonging to Penguin Group (USA) Inc.

PRINTED IN THE UNITED STATES OF AMERICA

10 9 8 7 6 5 4 3 2 1

For Mick and Anne Schwartz

For readers of my novels:
   Please be sure to subscribe to my free private newsletter at www.DouglasClegg.com and get access to free exclusive screen savers, behind-the-scenes news, e-books, book trailers, and more—plus you'll get updates on my upcoming books.
   I want to thank all the readers of the Vampyricon for coming along with the story of Aleric, Falconer through the three books: The Priest of Blood, The Lady of Serpents, *and* The Queen of Wolves.

◆ CHAPTER 1 ◆

The Wolf Key

◆ 1 ◆

A small key made of carved bone, kept secret, hidden away—this was the only object I kept from Natalia Waterhouse within our resting place. I wrapped it into an old, leathered pouch, and placed it in some worthless pottery amidst the debris of my tomb that no one should find it—and if they did, they would not know how to use it.

Even the vampyres who had been with me for the past several hundred years did not know what lock existed that fit such a key—made from wolf bone, and missing one piece.

Natalia herself had brought me the one bit of wolf bone that had been missing from the key for centuries.

It was a long, curved tooth, taken from a mahogany box—with a silver clasp in the shape of a wolf's head—which her mother had delivered to her only in death. A wolf's tooth with a tiny hole drilled into it that fit perfectly into a groove of the bone key.

The key was now complete in its hiding place.

When she stole it, I knew it was nearly time for me to show her the lock that waited for the key.

◆ 2 ◆

IN this twenty-first century, as the storms of war poured around us from beyond our hidden fortress, I spent long nights showing Natalia Waterhouse the treasures of Alkemara. Beyond our tomblike sanctuary, jets blazed their paths across the sky, and the blasts of bombs could be heard even at a distance of a hundred miles. A city across the desert was under siege, and its districts set afire. At night, the distant billows of smoke enshrouded the stars. You could not exist in the tomb at daylight without dreaming of the red skies of battle, and of ancient nights when the torches set the woods ablaze and the burning arrows showered the sky like a thousand falling stars, when the sword and axe hewed the flesh of memory.

Within the necropolis beneath the hollow of the mountain, I shared with my mortal guest the years of the lost century of humankind while the dark hours of earth passed over us. At daybreak, we slept side by side, or in an embrace, in the crystal bier that had once held the Priest of Blood, far below the heavy stone floors of the Temple of Lemesharra.

I showed her much of the evidence and writing of my early life and resurrection as a vampyre, but there was one thing I held back.

The wolf key.

I knew the night would come when I would take that key and lead her to the one secret chamber—hidden from even the others of my tribe—and reveal to her why she, of all her bloodline, had found Alkemara at all.

I did not expect her to steal it, and yet mortals sought knowledge and power at all times and could be tempted to their own destruction with this seeking. Even my tribe of vampyres—the Fallen Ones of Medhya—had stolen secrets and sorcery from our Dark Mother, who—in turn—had stolen from the Great Serpent who brought us immortality.

I was sure I could trust her by our twentieth night together. She had given me no reason to mistrust her, and
Natalia had revealed a keen intellect and an apparent lack
of the need for power over anyone.

When I awoke in darkness, I felt heaviness within me as
some unrestful thought preyed upon my mind. *She found it.*

As certain as the doom of sunrise, the news awaited me
in the form of Vaspiana leaning over me. Vaspi had grown
possessive of me since Natalia had come to us—my first
thought was that Vaspi herself had done something to our
mortal guest.

Vaspiana grasped my shoulders to shake me out of the
day's rest. I smelled dusk in the damp of my tomb. My
eyes quickly focused and brought up the ambient light
within the darkness. Instinctively, I sniffed the air, for—
upon awakening—the threat of mortal hunters hung over
us like a sharpened blade at our hearts.

Beside me, in the tomb-bed, the blanket and the pillow
untouched as if Natalia had not slept there at all.

"No one's hurt her?" I glanced about my chamber. I
briefly took in the clothes that were missing—her tan
slacks, her shirt, her sandals.

"She escaped." Vaspi pointed to the lid of my chamber—
a round stone doorway above us, from which a staircase
descended. It was meant to be sealed daily, with a vampyre
on guard, above, at all times. She looked back toward me, a
sly grin on her face.

"You've done nothing to harm her?"

She offered me a look of offense, raising her eyebrows
and nearly sneering. "I don't stoop that low."

"You've checked the city?" I looked about the room—
an urn had been upturned, broken, its bits swept beside a
stack of unrolled scrolls. When I found the leather pouch
and strap that had been hidden in the urn, it was empty of
its small occupant: a key.

I imagined her hand clutching the key, moving toward
the door over which the winged serpent sculpture stood—a
place where none could pass without my consent.

Vaspi eyed the broken bits of pottery. She might have guessed its contents, given that many a vampyre wished to go into that secret chamber with me.

She sniffed the air. "She can't go far. Someone will catch her, I am certain of it. Mortals are easy to find. Her stink alone will leave a trail like a comet."

"She's not an ordinary mortal." I rose, and checked my other belongings to see what had been disturbed.

"If she were, you would have shared her with us," Vaspi said.

I ignored her comment. These young vampyres with only a century or two to their existences were full of themselves. In the early nineteenth century, Vaspiana had been preparing for her execution in some Baltic backwater for stealing a horse, but I saw potential in her when I gave her the Sacred Kiss of vampyrism.

Nearly two hundred years later, she still had the urges of arrested adolescence; I could barely trust a word from her mouth. Yet Vaspi had saved me from my Extinguishing on more than one occasion. Without a quest of some kind—without a reason to guard the mortal realm—these young ones grew lazy and fought among themselves simply for entertainment.

All this would change. I was the only one to feel it in the air, but each night that I rose, I sensed the slightest weakening of the Veil, and had felt it for several years.

Something sought to come through again, and one of the signs of this was Natalia Waterhouse herself, though she did not know it.

"Of course, she's so special, she might have fooled even you. She may be out along some road, approaching a settlement," Vaspi said as she began climbing the steps.

"Natalia Waterhouse is still here," I said. "She would not leave. If she had, my heart would be staked, and I doubt very much you'd be standing before me, either."

"I'd have cut her throat first," the vampyre said, glancing back at me, a gentle snarl on her lips.

"Where's Daniel?"

Daniel had been our guard, who was to sleep above us, at the doorway itself.

"Hunting, I suspect," Vaspiana said.

"Don't lie to me, Vaspi. Where is he?"

I closed my eyes briefly, feeling for Vaspi in the stream that connected all vampyres to one another. If it was a web, I was the spider of my tribe—I plucked at the stream, drawing her close to me that I might read her thoughts.

When I opened my eyes, I said, "If she's dead, you will answer."

"If she's dead," Vaspi said, "I will be the first to applaud. But I won't be the only one."

She reached the floor above, and I rushed after her. I leapt through the round opening of my tomb to see the gathering of the tribe along the arched doorways of the Temple of Lemesharra.

They all watched me with indolent and empty expressions upon their faces. My tribe of vampyres did not appreciate the strange mortal allowed to live among them and not serve them or, at the very least, feed them.

They, in fact, were made to serve her—to bring food from the outside world, to cook and clean, and to treat her as if she were above them in some way.

I snarled at them with fury—though I did not have time to take on their foolishness. To say that all who occupied this fallen necropolis were under my command would be the ultimate in self-deception. They served me from an oath of loyalty, but this could mean nothing when they became a gang of ruffians—they did not like serving mortals, whom they considered mere vessels of blood.

Leading these vampyres was like herding saber-toothed tigers at times. Their instincts were too rooted in the next sip of life force and not in their duties.

I glanced up and down the halls, sniffing the air for the smell of mortality.

Outside, on the steps of the temple, I glanced along the two-story flat-roofed dwellings that had not been occupied since the Priest of Blood ruled the city. I had lived for centuries, and knew the double-dealings of mortal and vampyre. For all I knew, Natalia Waterhouse might already be dead.

Vaspiana had tacitly agreed to Daniel's taking of Natalia, as had any of the others who had been witness to it. If I had told them why she was important to me, my own tribe might have torn her limb from limb.

I should have known it would be nearly impossible to allow a mortal to live among us as she did—freely and without obligation or offering—not as our protectors did, who were also mortal. The protectors lived along the boundaries of the city, guarding our resting place from the living. Only a handful of them acted as house servants who slept nights within the ruins of the old city, though they were not allowed into the temples or the tombs. These mortals took care of matters of cleanliness—difficult among a pack of vampyres who did not always notice where they left the vessel's bodies or care if their sleeping quarters grew filthy. The protectors who entered Alkemara rarely escaped with their lives, nor did they wish it. They were addicted to our tribe, and often begged to be bled so that they might experience the heightened pleasures that our bleeding them provided.

Only Natalia had entered the Temple of Lemesharra, and had sat at the table in the Great Hall, feasting on the finest food and drink. No other vampyre or mortal shared my tomb as she had.

Daniel may have been the most offended by her presence. He was barely more than a boy, and to me, he was a son. But as a son, he desired to be an only child and could not stand having a rival, in friendship or love.

Natalia was a threat to him—I should have recognized this. Yet, in all her nights with me, I had watched him. I had believed him, based on his demeanor. Daniel had been nothing but helpful. He had made sure that her food and water were fresh, and her wine was among the best of the cellars of the earth.

And yet, I should not have completely trusted him—for he had been too solicitous of her.

Daniel was a jealous youth, not more than a handful of years from his resurrection into the tribe. Even when I had drank from him in the alleyway where I had found him, I sensed a dangerous nature. I was blinded by his resemblance to someone from my own youth, someone who had extinguished long ago. I could not resist bringing him the breath of vampyrism and resurrecting him from the dead.

I had put too much trust in him. Now, I would pay the price of this trust. If Natalia had been murdered, all of my existence would be for nothing.

All I had dreamed, and all I had done, would be as the fallen statues of gods in some dig of an ancient city—the dust of the past and no more.

I shouted to Vaspiana and the others to find Natalia and Daniel. "No harm shall come to them, but you must bring them both to me. She must be alive. If you have hurt her, or drunk from her, you will be drawn from the grave at morning's first light and left beyond Alkemara's protection!"

I pulled Vaspi to my side, using the strands of the stream. She resisted, fighting against the pressure she felt at her shoulders and back. Like a fly caught in the silk strands, she struggled against the pull, but eventually gave in and stood before me. Her long, thick braid of hair came undone, and her dark tresses fell across one side of her face.

Her eyes were like a wolf's as she glared at me.

"You know where they are," I said, as calmly as I could. "Tell me now, and I will forgive you. If you wait but another moment, I will set the protectors upon you at tomorrow's sunrise, and you will feel the fire of Extinguishing."

She spat. "You love mortals too much, Falconer."

"Vaspi," I said.

She curled her lips downward as she said, "The cave, above the serpent stair."

"She *will* be alive," I said as if in warning.

I drew wings out from my body and rose in the great hollow mountain. I saw other vampyres rise from their tombs, their beds, their dark places. Like falcons, they flew out into the night sky, high above—and if I were to call any of them, they would return swiftly to my side.

I would find Natalia—and Daniel—myself.

I followed the tunnels and wormholes and caverns that snaked and curved beyond the city. I crawled across the great boulders that jutted out from the rock cliffs—they formed the serpent stair, a series of ledges that led to narrow caves. I sniffed the air—the faint mortal aroma seemed to linger there. I sensed Daniel very close—and then saw movement in one of the narrow mouths of a cave on the ledge above.

Yes, he is here, I thought.

• 3 •

AS I drew myself up to the cave, I saw his muscular, pale back—a rippling of alabaster—and his red hair like a beacon in the dark.

He leaned over Natalia, his face buried at her throat.

He was too busy with his task to sense my arrival. I only hoped I was in time to stop his thirst from taking her life. My heart seemed to beat too slowly. My fears overcame me. If she were dead, all was lost.

If she were dead, it would be too late.

I scrambled over to him, and wrapped my arms around his neck, and drew him from her. I knocked his head against the jagged rocks. I glanced at Natalia—she pressed her hands to her throat.

Daniel let out a keening wail as I dragged him out of that cave, onto the ample ledge beyond it. I threw him down at my feet.

His shirt was a brown-red and his face shiny from her blood. He growled like a mad dog, and I struck him with the back of my hand. He tried to rise, but as he did so, I grasped him by the collar and threw him down again.

"After all I did to take you from your miserable life in Prague," I said. "Begging for death in an alley. I made you a guardian of this world."

"This *underworld*!" He spat at me. "We could live in palaces. We could rule over men, and they would sacrifice to us, Falconer. You made me a wolf but hold against me the nature of wolves."

"Spoken like a foolish young man." I slapped him across the face. "You are no wolf. Why did you do it?"

"She tried to escape," he whimpered.

"Did she?" I asked. "Or did you plot for many nights, and imagine that you might lure her up just at twilight, before I would rise. Risk the last of the sun, perhaps, and drain her, as you have done to others before?"

"That wasn't it! She . . . she . . ." He wiped his bloodied mouth against his sleeve as he tried to come up with a lie that might convince me. "She's a deceiver!"

"You had to drink from her," I said. "The one person I told you was not for any here. The one person all the tribe knows they are not to bite."

"They all wanted to. They did. Ask Vaspi. Ask any. They longed for her blood. I held them back. I fought them, for you. For you." He nearly smiled, and his eyes gleamed. "I can see why you keep her for yourself. Private stock. Her blood . . . it's rich. It's not like other blood."

"I would stake you for such an act," I said.

"You taught me such acts," he snarled, and when I moved toward him again, he flinched.

"Jackal," I said. "I should have expected this."

"A dog perhaps," he whispered. "But a loyal dog, my master."

"Get out! Get out and hunt, before I . . ." As I determined what his punishment might be, he crawled to the end of the ledge to be farther from me.

He turned around, pointing an accusing finger at me. "I know why she is here! I know what you will do!"

"Quiet," I said, almost softly. I stepped toward him, crouching to be closer to his level.

"I want it," he said, glancing about as if afraid someone might hear him.

"I should never have shown it to you."

"It should be for me," he said. "I could have it. Not her. Not a mortal like her."

"It would destroy you," I said. I reached my hand out to him. He looked at me as if confused by my sudden gentleness. He could be both a tiger and a lamb. When he took my hand, I pulled him closer to me. "You cause me so much pain."

"Sons do that, I guess," he said.

"Did you intend to kill her?"

"No," he whispered. "I swear. She promised me blood. Each dawn."

"Dawn?" I asked.

"Before the sun, but after morning's twilight. When the sun had not quite reached the rift. After you had closed your eyes. She bribed me with her scent. I could not . . . I could not resist."

"You have drunk from her before?"

"Only a taste," he said, pitifully. "Before this. Only a drop or two. Her taste is worth many vessels of ordinary blood."

"Is this the truth?"

I felt him shiver as I held his throat in my hands.

He nodded. "I would not lie. Not to you."

"How many days has she had her freedom?"

His eyes narrowed, and he counted it out on his fingers. "Since her twelfth night here."

"Go," I said, feeling as if I had lost my bearings. Why had she done this? Why had she not obeyed? Why had Daniel betrayed me in this way? I could trust no one, and did not want to risk Natalia's life to these flying jackals that surrounded me. "Do not touch her again. Do not drink from her, nor make bargains with her, fool. Do not ask about those things you know are not meant for you, Daniel. I will not forgive you if this happens again."

I watched as he flew off the ledge, upward toward the great rift in the mountain above, toward the open sky.

I returned to find Natalia clutching her neck. I took her

into my arms, and whispered, "Don't be afraid." I touched the wound at her throat, sensing the warmth. "The healing has begun. You will need rest and food, I think, to recover your strength."

I managed to close the wound, though two small pinprick marks were left to remind me of Daniel's betrayal.

She held out her fist and opened it to reveal the wolf key in her palm.

"A thief," I said. "I allow you access to the treasures here. I feed you well. My tribe would rather cut your throat than allow you these freedoms. I punish them for such thoughts. I guard against their worst intentions toward you. Is this how you repay my generosity?"

Natalia looked up at me, fear in her eyes. "I saw you put it in the urn once. Sometimes you keep it at your waist or at your neck. I was . . . curious. When I examined it more closely, I noticed a missing part to it, as if it were a puzzle. And this." She drew the wolf tooth off the key, then set it back, nestling it along the carved ridge of the base of the key. "You had been waiting for me to bring this tooth. It had been put away for . . ."

"For centuries."

She held the key to her eyes as if trying to read the tiny glyphs scrawled upon it.

"*Let she who finds, know,*" I said. "It was engraved in the eighteenth century. A master craftsman in Florence who had a special magnifying lens that allowed him to write such tiny words."

"Am I the 'she'?"

"I can't answer that for you."

"What box does this open?"

"If I showed you what this key fit, you would not understand. Not yet," I said.

"I'm sorry for taking it," she said. She passed it back to me.

"As you took a key years ago and found a crushed dried flower and a wolf's tooth among your mother's possessions," I said. I could not help smiling, thinking of all the things that had been passed down through the generations in her bloodline, secrets kept, promises held, oaths sworn. "Theft. It is what began my tribe of vampyres, for the priests of Myrryd stole immortality and more from Medhya. She in turn had stolen these secrets from the Great Serpent."

"All power begins with a theft," she said. "Prometheus stole fire from heaven to bring to mankind."

"By legend, he is punished eternally for it," I said. "As we are, here, cursed by our Dark Mother to drink blood and never to cross the threshold of Death. Power itself is cursed. We must exist alongside such punishment."

• 4 •

"YOU are not safe here anymore," I said, as we walked down the road that led to the gates of the city. "There is a place even these vampyres will not go. Within the city. A bedchamber fit for a mortal queen, untouched for hundreds of years."

"It must be very dusty," Natalia said, and I smiled at this show of good humor.

"We have protectors who take care of it," I said.

"The human cattle," she said.

"Protectors. They have their benefactors among our tribe."

"And lovers," she said. "So, does the key fit the lock of this room?"

"No, not this bedchamber. But you will have your own key to it, and lock it from within so that no one may enter unless you wish it."

THE torches had been lit along the fields of bones—and among these dead, the flower of the Flesh of Medhya twisted and turned, grown over the years into a bramble of thick vine and blossom. The statues of the old gods seemed to shine gold and onyx in the wavering fires. The great statues of the bulls of the Mithrades had been brought long ago to the walls of the city, and stood as enormous guardians of the Dal-Bas Gate, the main entry to the Temple of Lemesharra.

Alkemara, abandoned after dusk, seemed new and fresh. I enjoyed the city like this, emptied.

I led her along the streets, through a vaulted doorway, beyond which was a courtyard with a marble floor. Slender columns rose to a terrace, and we climbed the stairs. Several apartments led from the terrace to an interior house of sorts, which was empty of feature and furnishing.

At the end of a hall, there was the silver door with designs of the second kingdom of Alkemara upon it. Beside it, two middle-aged women slept upon cushioned benches. "Inside, there are no windows, yet air enters through a system of slender pipes. The door is silver so that no vampyre may breach it."

I called out to one of the women by name, and she awoke. When she saw me, she reached into the pockets of her shirt and brought me the key. I passed it to Natalia. "You must open it. None but you and these protectors may do so."

I followed her to the door, feeling that vibrating pain of the silver aura as I drew close to the door. She unlocked it and pushed it open.

I heard her gasp as she glanced inside.

"Go on," I said. "It's for you. This way, you may come and go as you please. You won't have to bribe a guard with your blood."

• 5 •

WITHIN, a great bedchamber meant for a noble-woman. It had exquisitely carved posts along the bed, and its light source was several candles in sconces. She went in and lit each one. Though it was kept clean and well attended, no one had slept in it for nearly a thousand years.

A toilet of an old kind as well as a rectangular bath—the size of a small swimming pool—was cut into the marble floor, and steam rose from its waters.

"You may bathe here, if you like. Rest. I will guard you

tonight. I can entrust your care to no one but myself. My tribe is not good with matters of temptation."

"It was my fault." She looked about the sumptuous room, avoiding my gaze. "I wanted to explore. I couldn't rest. I told him he could drink from me if I would be allowed the freedom to wander."

"That is what you wish?"

"Yes. When you sleep, I . . . want to see Alkemara in the daylight. I want to go about without vampyres watching me. I want to see more than you show me each night. You know I won't try to run from you. Look at me. You know this is the greatest treasure I could find. Right here. This is more than I ever hoped for in all my studies. All my *dreams*."

"You have been out during the day without my knowledge?"

She shot me a defiant glance. "You do not own me. You do not dictate where I go. What I do."

"It's a dangerous game you've been playing."

"No vampyre threatens me during the day. Do you think I will destroy you and your kind?"

"Perhaps," I said. "You have reason to do so. It is easy enough for mortals to send us to our Extinguishing when the sun is high above us. We are vulnerable during those hours. During times of plagues and famine, we were hunted like wolves—scapegoats for every crime of the earth. We were devils. There are hunters who seek our treasures."

"You have given them freely to me," Natalia said. "I do not wish the end of your tribe. But . . . Aleric, there is so much . . . It might take me a lifetime to decipher the scrolls here, to see each frieze and painting, and to pore over the works. As long as I am here, I want to explore all of it."

"You have a great hunger for this."

"I've spent my life dreaming of finding a place like Alkemara," she said, and something in her voice reminded me of another voice I had heard centuries before. "I am here. Now. I don't know for how long. I know people will search for me—at some point. I know that some night, you may . . . you may take my life."

Never, I thought. I did not answer her, for to do so might reveal what I sought to offer when I had told her of my past.

"The wars," I said. "They grow closer with each passing night. I can't risk you to any of this."

"Will you give me my freedom here?"

"But the dangers," I said. "I trusted Daniel, though I should not have."

"He adores you," she said. "And he's terrified of you."

"You can say this . . . after he . . ."

"He wouldn't kill me. He's afraid of me, as much as he wants to destroy me," she said. "You are not so easy to decipher. I cannot read this much in you. In the papers and scrolls of your first century, I have begun learning so much. I want more. I want the lock for the key made of the bone of a wolf. Is it a box, or a room?"

"It's in a room. Forbidden to all."

"All but you."

"Are you my Bluebeard?" she asked. "If I find a way into that forbidden room, will I find all your dead wives?"

I could not lighten my demeanor when it came to this chamber. "You must not even search for it," I warned her. "I will take you to it when I know you will understand what is there. Come, my friends have laid out a feast for you."

"After supper? Will I see this forbidden place?" she asked.

• 6 •

THAT evening, we sat in the Great Hall of the Temple of Lemesharra within the buried city of Alkemara. She was in a sullen mood, and I, too, had grown moody. She wanted too much too fast. She needed to know all that had happened, and yet there was much of the journey of my first century to tell.

All around us were the gently curved ceilings where—in centuries since my first discovery of this city—I had brought the young apprentices who had worked with Michelangelo himself to create a similar heaven and hell upon the walls of Alkemara.

Above us, the paintings of angels and demons, the creatures of the Veil and of Myrryd—including the Lamiades, the Akhnetur, and the Myrrydanai themselves—told a story of the visible and invisible world around us. The lizardlike Lamiades seemed to chase each other's tail; while the Akhnetur—those flying scorpions with the faces of maidens—spun their webs and swarmed along a white tree that produced golden fruit at the center of a garden deep with the purple Veil flower. Other creatures, from harpies to gryphons, guarded the corners of the ceilings—each rendered so clearly as to seem drawn from life. A portrait of the vampyre Pythia watched us from the far end of the room.

Closer to our table, Enora's portrait adorned the smooth wall. She glared at us, but the painting did not capture her ferocity.

Surrounding her in the portrait were her Chymer wolf-women, some vaguely in the middle of a transformation from wolf to human, others complete. All of them crouched at Enora's feet.

I glanced up at the ceiling—to the magnificent falcons of my mortal life—and the words returned to me from many hundreds of years previous: "The falcons hunt the skies."

As I spoke it, Natalia also glanced up from where she sat at the table. "You were a falconer as a boy. You flew as a falcon as a vampyre."

"I was called Falconer, and did not understand for many years why the name remained with me," I said. "Those birds . . . from my childhood . . . from the teachings my grandfather gave to me of their language and their nature. I did not know that my own nature was of a flying predator. The falcons became like spirit guides to me, although it took me until the first battle against Taranis-Hir to understand this."

Upon our long table, laden with the scrolls, the maps, the debris of the past, all sprawled about amidst the generous repast my companions had brought for our mortal guest: grapes, dates, flatbread, spiced goat meat stewed in steamy tarjines, and chicken roasted to a tender brown-yellow. A flagon of red wine, a heavy bottle of white; a pitcher of warm jasmine tea; lentil samosas; and various other tidbits and tastes that they had gathered from flights to the cities each night.

The smell of sweet spice was in the air. The room, filled with a thousand candles, shimmered with the light, almost giving movement to the portraits and images on the walls. Between the flickering lights, the shadows.

"You haven't eaten much this evening," I said. I pushed away a scroll Natalia had unraveled and offered her some bread dipped in warm, yellow hummus. "Try something."

"I'll grow fat here," she said, but took the bread from my fingers. Tasting it, she made a gentle sound of satisfaction. "This is heaven for me."

"Heaven? Many mortals would call it the opposite."

"This room, this temple. The entire city," she said. She reached for a goblet, and I poured wine from the flagon into it. She took a sip. "All these scrolls. All this lost . . . lost history. Lost knowledge."

"The world seems no worse without it," I said.

"No better, you mean." She glanced over at the painting of Enora. Enora, in her wolf-pelt robes, her hair dyed red for battle. Beneath the robe, a long gown of pure white. In her left hand, the Nahhashim staff; in her right, what looked like a great claw thrust on the end of a half spear. "She was the mother of your children."

"When she was Alienora," I said, not bothering to look over at the painting. "The Myrrydanai took her over. She invited them into her. She sought the lowest form of magick—power over others. The destruction of others. Anyone can destroy. Even a child may wipe out a colony of ants with one well-placed footstep. She was nothing but fury . . . at the end."

I closed my eyes for a moment, trying not to remember the last time I saw Enora, as she stood along the balcony of the tower of White-Horse. I did not yet wish to recall her words, or remember what her final act had been.

I opened my eyes and directed her attention to the far end of the table—the portrait of the Pythoness. "Pythia—a Pythoness of an ancient age. Daughter of Merod, child of Alkemara. She enjoyed power as well. A trickster, a deceiver, a liar, a betrayer. Despite all these qualities, she rescued me and led me from certain Extinguishing in Aztlanteum, risking her own life—for she had become mortal then."

"The mask that leached immortality from her, yes. The Gorgon Mask."

"Medhya's Mask, the mask of Datbathani—the mask has had many names, for it has passed through many hands until it reached Pythia herself. Some legends say that the mask was stolen from the god of the sun and given to a tribe of men that slaughtered all other tribes in those years when men lived beneath the ground. Others, that the mask was stolen from the temple walls of a conquered god. The mask brought immortality to its first wearer, who then became a god. It has since leeched immortality or mortality from whoever wore it. Nezahual called it the mask of the Ketsali, and claimed ownership. I think he loved the mask more than he loved Pythia."

"You loved her."

I nodded. "Perhaps this love was forced upon me when she brought me into vampyrism. She was avaricious. Lustful. Lazy. Sneaky. Bloodthirsty. How do you love a betrayer? A seducer? A creature who brought her own father to misery? She could not see gold, but she had to steal it. She could not find a beautiful youth, but she must seduce him. That love is like a firestorm. In the centuries that have passed, all love seems . . ."

I could not finish the thought. I felt the old pain at my heart. I had three loves in my early life, and I could not think of any of them without experiencing regret and sorrow. "Yes. I loved her, and others."

"I think most people would not believe a vampyre capable of love," Natalia said as she reached to the middle of the table to pluck a handful of grapes from a wooden plate.

"Some vampyres cannot love," I said. "There is a love between us, even so. The stream is a kind of love—it flows as if telepathically between all vampyres. We feel the sorrows of those we cannot even see. We understand those who have committed atrocity. We forgive the vampyre his flaws, because to feel what the other feels is to understand completely. That is a kind of love. But I suspect love doesn't interest you tonight. Or does it?"

"What about your children? You had two with Enora."

"Lyan, my daughter. Taran, my son," I said. I did not like to think of them anymore. It had taken me centuries to want to recall their young faces.

"Surely you had not given up on them? Even their mother—I can't believe you had given up on her."

"A vampyre? Care about mortal children?" I grinned.

"You are not like the others here. I know that. You loved Enora once. She was the mother of these two children. Did you truly give up that love?"

"Despite all she had done? I had watched her eat the heart of her youngest brother, his blood along her lips and chin. She was more the monster than I. How could I love her then? When she destroyed vampyres and burned many of the Forest women—could I love her, despite this? When she . . . did all that she could, using bog sorcery and the old magick that the Myrrydanai taught her . . . No, I could not feel that pure love again for her that I had felt when our world had still been a place of innocence and purity."

"But she was a prisoner of Medhya herself—a hostage to the White Robe priests."

"Yes. A hostage. I could be blamed for her transformation, for it was my death at Pythia's hands and my resurrection from the Sacred Kiss that brought about her descent into darkness. When I professed my love for her, and we took our passion into a chapel, beneath the gaze of the stone virgin, did either of us truly understand how love could turn to daggers in a heartbeat? We conceived our twins that night, and I was sent to war soon after. What war taught me was mortal waste and the inability of humankind to value what is within its grasp, and instead to value what others hold. Wars are for wolves and scavengers.

"So, I grew to hate the world. While Pythia drank my blood in a tower of Hedammu, my beloved Alienora received news of my death, and then rumors of my damnation. Yes, the Myrrydanai priests began to dominate her. Yes, she turned to bog sorcery to learn my fate, and to try and bring power into her soul that she might—perhaps—save me. The taste of the magick of the Forest turned her to a darker magick, to the bogs where the hounds of Medhya whispered to her of ancient sorceries, of plagues to be born, of dreams brought as a Disk into the world. It was her decision to spill the blood of our children to call up shadows from the bog. It was her decision to murder her family that she might become baroness after her father's death. She sought power, and showed her true nature—a nature that is hidden when we're young and untested."

"You drink blood," Natalia said. "You have sipped from my throat for many nights. You have murdered many men. Don't pretend you're not a monster. Perhaps you are more monster than a vampyre like Daniel, who is honest in his bloodthirst."

I nodded. "I am no hero of mortals, I know this. What seems brutal is instinct to me. What seems bloodthirsty is merely . . . survival."

"You could hate Enora for her crimes," Natalia said. "You could love Pythia, despite hers. And your friend Ewen. He, too, murdered. The stain of murder and slaughter is also on your hands. It must be difficult to separate the good from the bad."

I felt fury rise up in me from her mentioning of names as if she understood who these people had been to me. I stood up, kicking my chair backward. "Do you say such things to drive a stake through my heart? How many nights will I tell you of these things? How many nights will you listen and not understand?"

I turned away from her, grabbing the flagon of wine. I

threw it at Enora's portrait. It smashed against the wall, just at Enora's throat. A red stain dripped across Enora's wolf-pelt cape and the robe beneath it.

"You must see with the eyes of the immortal to know. You cannot look at mortal life and see the difference between the way of the vampyre and the way of humankind. You all think us monsters! I have had companions hunted by human wolves who—in their blind ignorance—believed that annihilation of my tribe was for the good of all mortals. I spent years during the inquisitions in Europe, rescuing witches and gypsies—and when my kind was caught, we were beheaded and burned, extinguished as devils. Who were the devils? The inquisitors? The accusers of these innocents? Or the vampyres who drank blood for existence, but spent nights guarding those who had no guard left to them upon the earth?"

I turned to face Natalia. "And you! The man you intended to marry when you were young would have destroyed you as he had destroyed others. I saw in his eyes what was to come, and I tasted it in his blood. He was a killer, a rapist, and a thug. He wanted your death, and he lied and cheated you to draw you into his web."

"Vampyres only kill bad men?" she asked, defiantly. "Your servants here killed people who had accompanied me. Those people were not murderers and rapists."

My wings drew out from my shoulders, and I flew upward to the curved ceiling. There among the harpies and gorgons, I roosted on a wide ledge that separated ceiling from wall. "Do not question this, Natalia. Do not. You are here as my guest. That you even live is a testament to what I speak of. No creature is pure in thought or deed. No mortal, no immortal. The instinct of a lion cannot be compared to that of a lamb. When one creature kills for survival or protection, you cannot compare that to those who kill for pleasure and power."

She stepped around my fallen chair and went to the portrait of Enora. She glanced from the portrait to me. "You two were not so different, Aleric." Then she looked up at me with ferocity in her eyes. "She thought she was doing what was necessary for her survival, as well."

Then, she put her hand up to Enora's face, as if looking for life in the portrait's eyes. "Am I . . . is she my ancestor?" Her voice had softened. "Am I descended from her? From Lyan? Taran?"

"You must wait. For if I told you now of your bloodline, you would not yet understand."

"I'm not an idiot," she snapped back, and pointed at me. "You watched me for years. You knew I would find you here, eventually. You've withheld the truth from me. Tell me now. Show me the secret place. The place where the wolf key fits the lock. If you must, drink all my blood. Bring the breath of vampyrism into me."

I felt what seemed a fist tightening at my chest. I willed my form to shift, as I had learned to do centuries before. I showed her the monster that I was—my canines grew to a size like a lion's. I drew off some of my glamour that she might see the rotting corpse beneath my skin. I spread my wings wide, and revealed the kind of graveyard creature she had read of in fairy tales and horror stories.

"Is this what you wish for yourself, Natalia?" My eyes went white and yellow, and my skull showed through the thinning hair. "This is what exists beneath the beauty you see. Do not forget it, for I never have. I have seen it in mirrors, and know that while others may see and feel the flesh of a youth, I am this. If you wish to be both beautiful and hideous, then, come to me. Give up your life. Die for immortality, and become the blood-drinker you despise."

• 7 •

IN a moment, I returned my visage to its former glory—a youth, barely past nineteen, thick hair at the scalp, the skin of a man of twenty—some have said, like an angel of the alleyways. Each was an illusion—both the corpse and the young flesh.

"I did not choose my fate. It was smashed against my

soul. I chose the path of guardianship, rather than that of wholesale slaughter of innocents. What I do, I do to guard your realm. When I murder, it is within my instinct to do so—as the lion must chase down the antelope. What mortals do—when they slaughter and murder and war—is destroy their own kind."

I swooped down to her, standing before her. "You may judge me as you wish—only wait until my tale is ended. You have reminded me of the brutality of that world of my past—and of this one, beyond this city, full of the avaricious and the self-destructive."

"I'm sorry," she said. She raised her arm and upturned her wrist toward my lips. "Drink from me. Show me the secrets that you've kept to yourself."

I grasped her wrist and drew her into my arms. My wings unfurled, and we rose in the air. I carried her out of the temple, to the fields of bones beyond the walls of Alkemara. There, where the flowers of the Veil grew thick in vines along the ancient ones, I drew out a vine, plucking two flowers from it.

"Am I to get a lesson again about this flower?" she asked, crossing her arms before her.

"If you need one, yes. If I squeezed the juice at the center of this small, sweet petal onto your tongue, you would cross the Veil and understand all. You would die, also. No mortal can drink of this and not breathe her last," I said.

She tried to reach for a blossom, but as soon as she neared it, it pricked her finger, and she withdrew it. She was about to thrust her finger in her mouth, and I reached over and grabbed her hand.

"I must withdraw the poison," I said.

I drew her hand to my own mouth, and sucked lightly at the pinprick wound. I tasted the copper of her life, and a slight essence of the Veil itself.

When she withdrew her hand, the wound had healed. She reached for my left arm, and drawing up its sleeve, she said, "Will you tell me what this marking means?"

There, like a tattoo of pale blue, just below my elbow,

there was a jagged line that encircled my arm. "An old wound."

"Your arm was cut?"

"Torn off, clean," I said. "But there is sorcery that regenerates the flesh within me."

"Do all vampyres have such power?"

"Many do," I said. "Some do not. Some who have been maimed remain so, and others will draw back such limbs in a day's rest." I flexed my hand.

"Was it cut off in battle?"

I drew my sleeve back down, wishing to speak of other things, for I did not wish to remember the night when this scar had been new. She was insistent in her questions, and I told her that much of the Veil had touched me over the centuries, and I had seen many wars, and much peace; I had fought hunters who came to my tombs to destroy me, and had guarded those who were preyed upon by the world's wolves.

"I would love to see the Veil," she said.

"Perhaps, one night, I will cross it with you," I said.

"But not yet?" She looked down at her finger, then at the petals in my hand, and finally up to my face again. "How long does the poison take?"

"To kill a man? I have seen one die before dawn, having ingested the flower at dusk. Others may die swiftly. It depends on the dose."

"Is there an antidote?"

"None," I said. "Do not worry. No poison flows through your bloodstream."

She turned her attention to the many statues of the gods of death and of rebirth that had lain for centuries along the outer walls of the city. "It is still hard to believe that these treasures have been buried for so long."

"Mortals have only recently found harbors and cities of the ancient world in the past several years that have been there for all to see for centuries. Sunken cities of Kah and Rohendris, the scrolls of Canuris, and the temples at Aztlanteum, with the bones of that prehistoric dinosaur that can be none other than Ixtar herself, extinct these many centuries. Yet no one looked before. The tribe brought our protectors here. Yet, if they were abandoned by us two hundred miles in the distance, they could not find their way here again. Only you found your path here. Myrryd has yet to be rediscovered."

"It still exists?"

"A vast red city."

"Where is it?" Natalia asked. I saw her eyes flash with desire, as if knowledge were a pleasure kept just out of reach.

"You must wait, for there is much to show you. I will tell you before dawn. The following night, again I will tell you more of those times. Each night until the telling is done."

"You must tell me more of this now. I want to see the forbidden room. I want to know what has been waiting for me all these nights, Aleric. Tell me of the city of Myrryd. The battles. What happened to Pythia? Where did you go when you escaped Aztlanteum? She stole Ixtar's orb, didn't she?" Natalia shot the questions at me like the excited scholar that she had become. "There was someone— some stranger—following you in flight from that burning kingdom?"

Could I have told her that I had waited centuries for her to come to me—for the man or woman from this bloodline to find these secrets of the medieval age in which my fate was determined? For there was no scroll for this, no leathered pages. I had left the last tale of my first century as a secret, which only she and I would know.

The wolf key itself would unlock the final secret.

"The orb was known to me as the Serpent's Eye, although it had a far older name that I would learn much later. Some called it the Lamp of Death. It was the size of Pythia's fist." I made a fist, remembering how Pythia's hand had fit into mine. "Pythia clung to it as if it was the greatest of prizes, yet even she could not unlock its power."

"She was pregnant," Natalia said, recalling the events we had not long ago spoken of. "A mortal vampyre, because of

the mask. Who pursued you from Aztlanteum? What of Calyx and the Akkadites, and Taranis-Hir?"

"You must wait for this," I said. "Come with me to those
ancient days of my first century when war descended like a
storm of dark angels across many lands, and my path was
illuminated by the Dark Madonna herself, the Queen of
Wolves and Plagues and Shadows . . . when the fires of
Nezahual's city burned bright, and I followed Pythia
through the billowing smoke."

BOOK ONE

THE PATH
OF SERPENTS

I

THE FOLLOWER

• CHAPTER 2 •

Escape from War

• 1 •

I watched the skies when I escaped Nezahual's besieged kingdom for a sign of the new moon's birth—for it was the solstice that had become my target, the bomb lobbed at me by those who understood the Veil and its fragile nature during the shortest night of the year. These ancient sorceries were rumors to me, for I did not understand the importance of the season, nor of the solstice night. Though I had been claimed Maz-Sherah by the Priest of Blood called Merod, I did not feel as if I were anything more than a tool in the hands of some larger force.

• 2 •

WHEN Pythia and I left Aztlanteum, on a continent far from my homeland, the moon no longer reigned over the black of night.

We had fled another war in an obsidian city when the vampyre king Nezahual was besieged by his brothers and sister in a battle for supremacy, for the blessing of their mother, Ixtar, and for the lands that had once been divided among them. Jealousy and envy divides all families, mortal and immortal, and the want of power—and the ignorance of its corruption—destroys many kingdoms.

The city of Ixtar burned and raged, and below us, vampyres fought in the air, tearing at each other like wolves, while fires consumed the walls of their temples and palaces, while priests fought against invaders, and mortal men died for their gods. The cries of mortal and vampyre alike seemed to ride with us as we moved beyond its territories.

In the stream, we knew that someone pursued us through that blinding darkness.

Within an hour of our escape, I glanced back, briefly, and spied a gray shape in the whirling black smoke.

· 3 ·

I was still weak, and did not think I could fight any of the vampyre guards who had trailed us from the burning city. I knew why this guard had followed us—it was not merely our escape, it was that fist-sized orb of black stone that Pythia had tied in a pouch around her throat as we flew.

She had stolen the sacred relic, and I had no doubt that this had awakened Nezahual's ire, even as his city perished. Perhaps it held some secret power that only he could access, or perhaps it was simply that it belonged to Ixtar herself, and Nezahual's existence depended upon its return.

At first I thought it was one unseen vampyre who followed, and then I felt many coming for us, but at a great distance. The stream felt strange to me, alive and yet confusing, and this follower seemed a disruptive influence. Perhaps, I thought, I only sensed those vampyres fighting many leagues away, amidst fire and smoke.

Below us, the smoke met a haze of mist out upon the sea. I was not going to be able to fight the pursuer off in midair, and Pythia was now mortal—she would easily be captured by a vampyre. I felt our only hope to deflect any pursuing guardians of Ixtar was to throw them the orb.

I flew toward Pythia and reached for the strap at her throat.

She hissed like a snake, her fangs bared toward me. The strokes of her wings increased, and she shot ahead.

If my sense of the stream was correct, I could not outfly the guard who followed. I turned in midair to face him, remaining motionless in the sky, my wings spread apart as if to glide downward.

"Show yourself!" I shouted. I glanced down toward the ragged land as it dipped several miles ahead to the sea. The thick smoke blinded my view.

I was sure I saw a movement in the clouds of gray and black, yet no one came forward from them.

I waited another few seconds—still feeling something in the stream—just a vibration there. If one of Nezahual's brethren had been hiding in the ash-clouds, he easily could have leapt out and subdued me—though I would give him a fight he might not forget.

Finally, I turned again toward Pythia, who had almost reached the edge of Nezahual's lands, a mile or more ahead. I flew along, catching up to her, but I could not shake the feeling that some vampyre stalked us.

The smoke of the burning kingdom swept across the sky, and held back the dawn.

• 4 •

TOWARD the western sea we soared, beating our wings against the tides of the wind. The stink of sulfur and ash attacked our lungs and seared our flesh, as if the inferno behind us reached up to draw the two of us back to earth, two demons escaping Hell.

Pythia flew slightly ahead of me, like a dragon on the air, the spines of her wings flexing up and down as the eel-skin stretched across them like those of some angel of the deepest pit—beauty and terror bound up in her form.

The world below us burned and spat fire into the sky. Lamentations rose from among mortals of that land, and they sang of the immortals whose mother, Ixtar, had given birth to them. The songs that came up through the rumble of falling stones and the cries of war seemed like those hypnotic chants of the monks from my own country: beautiful and somber and not of the death of a city, but a mournful prayer to the gods for swift passage from this world to the next.

The whorls of clouds around us seemed endless tunnels within the night sky, and I followed my guide—Pythia—as she ascended farther upward, until the red ember of the burning city and countryside below us seemed a distant hearth.

The cold, dark sea lay below us now as we left sight of land. Still, I sensed our pursuer, but now his form barely touched the stream. He had fallen back, and yet I could not help but think that he still followed.

• 5 •

I began to form—in my mind's eye—a figure of a male vampyre, but without a face and without human form. That corpse-reflection of myself I had seen in the mirrored hall on the way to the torture device that the alchemist Artephius had devised.

It was the stream that brought this to me, and yet in it, I almost felt as if it were myself—my dead mortal body—somehow in pursuit.

As a vampyre, I knew that physically I had the beauty and vibrancy of a youth of twenty, for my hair was rich and thick, and my body sinewy and strong, a musculature built in my mortal life from war and its practice. My flesh renewed itself with each day of sleep and night spent hunting for mortal blood.

I had seen myself in that mirror—for a vampyre does reflect, yet we reflect upon ourselves alone and those who have died at our hands—and the truth of my body was there before me. I was a corpse, and yet even this was an illusion of the trickery of the silver mirrors, for I was neither the dead nor the living—but between these states of existence. The mirror lied; and my body lied. The truth was neither, and yet it was all I knew.

I was, as all vampyres of my line may be, a shadow of

my own self. Neither in this world nor the next, the children of the Serpent and of Medhya are on the borderline, the threshold between.

In my mind's eye, I could see my dead self—that nineteen-year-old youth, bled by the Pythoness of Alkemara, rotted—my own shadow pursuing me to remind me of what I truly was beneath the beauty of vampyric glamour.

The feeling did not pass, but as dawn threatened us at our backs, Pythia dived through a smoky cloud toward the sea, as if falling to her death. I followed behind her, and saw her goal: a place where we might sleep the night.

◆ 6 ◆

WE spent our first night on a small island barely larger than the grave we dug from its dirt and rocks for our rest. Just before the sun rose above us, Pythia and I had to huddle together so that no ray of its light cut through the pile of rocks beneath which we slept. She was wonderfully icy against my flesh.

She took the stolen orb from the pouch at her neck and strapped it around her waist. I felt its small, hard roundness between us. She whispered only in my mind, *If you try to steal it, I will return to Nezahual. I know that's not what you want. Not with your child in me.*

I would kill you, mortal vampyre, before you did this.

You would kill your child? For when I die, your son within me also dies. I could practically hear her smile as she drifted into deep sleep, knowing how these words would be like daggers to my heart. My bond to her had not yet loosened, and though I could not trust her, I also could not risk losing her.

When the sun sank below the horizon, and twilight darkened, I opened my eyes.

She sat above me, looking down as if studying me. "You and I are so different," she said. "Still, I feel as if you know me more than anyone has."

"It is the breath of the Sacred Kiss," I said, sleepily. "It binds us."

"No," she said, her mood darkening a bit. "It is something more."

She had already drawn off all the rocks and dirt that had covered us in the day. The night was thick with clouds and silence. I smelled rain as if at some distance.

"We could return," she said.

"What?"

"A night's journey to the shore. Not to Nezahual. There is a country deep to the south of Aztlanteum. Emerald jungles rise up along twisting brown rivers, where none know the paths, but many mortals live. Abandoned cities from the first age of the Great Serpent still stand, carved from cavern walls lying deep in hollowed wells. You and I would be gods there, Falconer, as our tribe was in nights long past. Our child would be born, untouched by these pains and prophecies. He would grow to be king. I would grow old, but I am not jealous. You could take other lovers."

I sat up and grabbed her at the shoulder, wishing to shake her. "You would say anything to save your own skin."

She tugged away from me. She flashed a sullen look like a scheming child and pushed herself up. She stood over me, as if about to say something, and then thought better of it. She walked to the edge of the rock shelf that jutted out over the sea and pointed back to where our journey had begun. "It is not so far. You can hate me there as well as here."

"You know what I must do."

"How do you keep a dream from becoming flesh?" Pythia asked. "Medhya is a dream all vampyres know of, yet few have known her. A phantom. The darkness of night itself, held back by the Veil. She whispers like her Myrrydanai jackals."

"Like the Great Serpent," I said.

She half smiled as she looked at me, watching my face as if I might betray some knowledge. "You have never seen the Serpent?"

"In visions, I have seen a statue. I have felt his power in the stream."

"My father spoke with the Serpent, as did the Nahhashim priests, and the Myrrydanai before their souls became corrupt. He is all around us, they tell us. I don't believe it. I was a priestess—a Pythoness—and only felt stirrings of him. To make us guardians of mortals. These are stories priests use to control us. I think the Great Serpent has been vanquished, a dream disturbed. Medhya will come into this world in flesh. It is you—and this ritual— that will bring her to flesh and blood. Do you think I will live through this? Your child? Will he be born if you do this? You cannot understand how the mortal world exists until you have watched lifetimes pass, Falconer. When you came to me, in the tower of Hedammu, I did not know you were anything other than a young soldier, ready to be bled. When I brought the Sacred Kiss to you, I saw where your journey will end."

"I saw this, too," I said. "On an altar stone. You wear this mask."

She glanced back at me. "I did not see the mask in my own vision. I saw you, looking at me. I saw a curved blade in your hand, like no other—it was jeweled and made of a burning gold. All around us, I felt her. Medhya. Standing near. Waiting for the Veil to tear. I heard the first whispers of the Myrrydanai priests, for the Sacred Kiss had awakened them. You—coming to Hedammu—to my towers—to my arms. This brought them."

"You can't be afraid of this," I told her. "You can't run from what you see in visions. Not everything that has been foretold will come to pass."

She shook her head, closing her eyes. "*You* came to pass. I had a vision of you long before we met."

"Why did you run from me then?"

She closed her eyes and in opening them scanned the darkening sky. "Let us not argue. We can cross a thousand miles or more if we fly swift and true." Her wings spread from her shoulders, and I remembered how she had been terrified when she had given me the kiss that brought the breath of immortality into my lungs.

I grabbed her by the wrists. "Why did you run from me if you knew these visions?"

"Let go of me," she snarled, shaking off my hands. "I saw your destruction. I saw my own death. A terrible shadow descended upon the earth, a terrible cry from the earth itself. I saw your doom. Mine, as well. That is where your journey takes you, Falconer—Maz-Sherah—to your Extinguishing."

"Is this yet another game of yours?"

Her eyes lit up in anger. Her lips curved downward as she spoke. "Yes. I am playing games. A liar. Thief. Betrayer. Believe that, if you like. It will serve you well when you watch them murder your child that grows within me. When they kill me."

More softly, I said, "There are others who suffer. I would not save my own flesh and know that I leave them to die in torment."

"They are mortal. They will die whether tomorrow, or in a thousand tomorrows."

"Some are of our tribe."

"Like the youth named Ewen who was like a ewe, tagging after you as if you were the great vampyre lord."

"He . . . I could not have survived without him."

"Yes, you love him. You with your mortal traits still intact. After more than a hundred years or so, those instincts erode."

As I remembered Ewen, something struck me. "How could you know about him? You had fled when I brought him back to life." In an instant, it came to me. "You . . . followed us?"

She moved away from me, never letting her glance leave me. "Did you think I just vanished? When the breath passes from one vampyre to another, the stream between them grows deep."

"How long did you follow?"

"Until I saw you and your companions heading toward

your capture," she said. "I could not follow you there. But I have felt you since. I sensed you. I hid from those whispering shadows of the Myrrydanai. When the plagues came, I saw the ice of Medhya's breath. But I knew you existed. Even in the obsidian city of Ixtar, I knew you would come to me."

"You left us there, all those years."

"What is a decade among my many thousands of years?" She narrowed her eyelids, as if trying to judge what to reveal and what to keep secret. "The mask called to me. You do not understand because you have not felt its call. I wished to put the seas of the earth between us that I might never see you again. You are my destruction, Falconer. I know this."

She ran toward the shoreline, leaping into the air, as her wings bore her aloft. I followed after—the creature that had killed me, and brought me to this existence, was my only hope—for our fates were bound together.

We soared upward. The heaviness of night drew close in a quiet mist that descended across the sea.

◆ 7 ◆

As we flew, hour by hour, I did not see anything but the dark of sky and sea and the ghost-light of the stars beyond the mist.

After many such hours, when the wind had stilled, I felt the slight warmth of a slow daybreak like a soft warning behind us, in the east, hours away, yet it bothered me to know it would come. My breath began to feel ragged. Thirst tore at my throat and dried my mouth. The pain of it had begun to grow intense, but I did not want to drink from Pythia again, for it would weaken her more than it would strengthen me.

Pythia did not fare much better. She began flying low, almost down to the waves themselves, as if expecting to dive below them should the sun reach out with its fire toward her.

The sky went from blackness to a rich purple, and we both knew the sun would burn the skies behind us within a few hours.

I saw vague shapes as if great luminous beasts lurked in the depths of the sea—serpents and tentacled creatures, behemoths and leviathans roaming the wide ocean; some I would later come to know as whales and dolphins and large schools of squid, others vanished from the earth before mortals could observe them.

I saw what seemed to be human faces of creatures as they swam, clinging to the backs of rays and long narrow fish as they moved along the surface of the water.

As we soared farther, the sea calmed as if dead. It grew heavy and impenetrable with weed and grass at its surface.

This made me think there might be some island nearby. As we went into the fog that thickened around us, I had nearly lost hope.

The stillness of the mist, and the quiet of the water—not twenty feet below where we flew—gave me an ominous sense that we had somehow left the sea itself and had crossed the Veil.

After an hour of flying through this, I began to feel the hackles of panic along my wingspan. Within the stream, I felt Pythia's movements draw me from the moonless sky, to a great ship with its sails slack, a prisoner within this silent calm sea.

Here was our island for the morning.

We would have extinguished in the sunlight above the great sea to the west of Aztlanteum had Pythia not seen the ship, still in the middle of the sea, as if docked.

With less than an hour to sunrise, we dived down as if falling toward the vessel.

◆ CHAPTER 3 ◆

The Storm Dreamer

◆ 1 ◆

THE ship had seven masts, and was longer and broader than any ship I had ever seen. In my youth, I had sailed on wide vessels off to the Holy Land for war, but these seemed like little more than planked log boats compared to this magnificent trader. Its sails were not square, but turned to the side, and hanging like rolled mats. It smelled of spice and the sea and rot. The wood of it was a deep, rich earth color and with a ruby-throated prow. The craftsmanship was of a wealthy nation—for all around it were carved wooden statues of sea gods and doglike dragons and fish and even turtles. This trading vessel looked as if it would contain the wealth of its country of origin.

At its prow, the red-painted statue of some goddess who seemed the very image of Medhya herself—for she seemed to have the aspect of a dragon, with spines along her back and arms, and what might've been wings in the sails that drooped along her shoulders. Her breasts were bounteous, and the smile upon her face was as fierce and dazzling as

Pythia's. The banners along the quay poles bore a cuttlefish with a warrior in armor upon its back, a spear in his fist. It was outlandish, this ship, an alien presence within the mist. As we descended I saw what might have been several masts of other such ships thrust upward in the dense atmosphere, similarly stuck in the silky waters.

During the lost century, ships often foundered on the sea as swift ice storms descended, and at other times, the wind died for many days and nights, and the sea calmed as if it were no more than an enormous lake. Days grew short, nights long. Such were the signs of the rips in the Veil, and of Medhya's hunger to return to this earth in flesh and blood.

Despite the size of this craft—for surely it contained many decks beneath and could have housed a village if not a small city—I did not see many men guarding its decks. Evidence of warriors lay strewn about the forecastle deck, which curved upward in a bow—armor lay heaped there, and piles of crossbows as well as shields.

Out of some hidden place, a stream of arrows shot out at us—Pythia went back up into the mist, but I was struck at the arm by one of these darts. I grabbed one of the topsail masts and clung to it. I drew the arrow out, sealing the wound quickly. I glanced down along the decks, and spied what seemed a huddle of men-at-arms, their spears and bows at the ready. They scanned the sky, but the mist covered me. To Pythia, I streamed a thought, *I will deal with them, wait above until you hear my call.*

Leaping the length of the mast, I landed upon the deck, among these warriors, their armor made of wood and cloth. I broke many spears, and tore the throats of men quickly that they might not surround me and hold me like dogs hold a deer until the great hunter—the sun—would arrive to slaughter me.

One after the other, the men scattered, and I killed those who remained with spear drawn and crossbow at the ready. Yet even these I pitied, for I saw the starvation in their sunken faces as I drew off their helms and finished them quickly.

I felt the prickly heat of the sun—unseen, but known to me—and soared upward to the flat board that served as crow's nest of the ship. I called to Pythia in the stream, and soon enough, she dropped down from the gray night.

I took her to one of the dying men, and she drank the last of him. Then, while men shouted along the ship's edge in their terror, I led Pythia—nearly dragging her for I feared the sun's approach—down through the maze of corridors beneath the ship's deck. To say I felt dread is to make light of it—for the ship had many chambers beneath it, bedrooms and bunkrooms and those that were salons for drinking and gaming—but it was the smell of death in the air that puzzled me.

As we went to the depths of the foreign ship, I saw in some of these rooms the bones and carcasses of dead men. The merchant trader had been here for more than a few nights—it must have sat in these waters too long, for I smelled no salted pork or wine—only those who had died. When I passed the empty storeroom I understood what had happened aboard this ship—the men had begun devouring each other.

For here, in place of meat and bread, there were men hanging from the low ceiling by great hooks, their bodies heavy with chunks of salt, and some of their limbs had been cut. How long had they been marooned here without wind, without food? How long had it taken them to turn to cannibalism?

A ship of this size might hold a thousand men, and yet I sensed fewer than twenty on board, and these moved furtively in the chambers above us. They did not wish to pass the larder in these dark hours, but remained above, on the decks, despite the threat of the flying demons that had descended and already killed several of them.

I drew Pythia into a room full of barrels—we had only outraced the sun by seconds. I rolled the heavy barrels—and did not wish to think what they might contain, but I knew they must be filled with their sustaining meat—and blocked the entrance to this dark, icy chamber.

I wrapped my arms around Pythia, and told her they would not dare follow us, though she had grown fearful with the coming sun and her vulnerability as a mortal. I kept her warm with the last of my heat until we went into the death sleep, beneath a long shelf, guarded on all sides by the great barrels of the dead.

When the night came again, we rose up and went hunting.

◆ 2 ◆

I saw the splintered evidence of someone's attempt to break down the door to our sleeping chamber, but they had been unsuccessful. We were met with empty corridors beneath the ship's upper decks. As we emerged into the chill air above, I saw two men upon the rigging, and others in armor.

Pythia found a young sailor immediately, but when she held him down, I warned her. "We will need these men. We do not know how far the next landfall may be. We need them to want to protect us."

She allowed him to run off. "Why? We will leave tonight."

"How far is the next island?" I asked. "How far until we reach those distant lands beyond the ocean?"

She dismissed my fears. "Did you not notice how it grows darker as we move west? The sun cannot catch us if we move swiftly. We traveled farther in the dark of night than I thought possible. With these men, we may drink our fill. Watch how we will soar with such strength in us."

"No," I said. "Until we know how far land is to the west, I will not risk it."

"If this ship has been here long enough for these men to begin salting each other's corpses, do you think the wind will suddenly pick up?" she asked, then went flying to the man in armor and leapt upon him with what seemed the piercing growl of a lion.

I had no time to follow her—two men jumped me as I was about to spring into the air. When I had shaken them off, I leapt onto a raised trunk at the edge of a doorway along the forecastle deck. The men had drawn short but stout swords.

The smaller of the two wore what must have been the simple garb of a sailor, while the other—a large man with close-cropped hair—wore fine heavy clothes that suggested great wealth—a merchant, no doubt.

The sailor came at me, lunging forward and leaping as if he would pierce my skull. He stabbed first near my throat, but I knocked his arm away, and then he pressed the blade into my gut. I grasped the dagger and twisted it from his hand, though it cut at my palm, and threw it across the deck.

The nature of my tribe is cruelty. I wish this were not so, but the power that comes with the bloodthirst is not power over appetite—it is an unleashing of appetite with ferocity as I can't myself fully understand. It is something to be controlled, and yet—in the grip of it—it is uncontrollable.

I was sure I could take him quickly and be done with both of them, but the other one—the scrappy sailor— jumped on my back again. I dug my teeth into the shoulder of the merchant and shredded a thin layer of flesh, all the while trying to shake off the other. My teeth sharpened quickly, the effect of fresh blood in my mouth.

When I brought the muscled man to his knees, he passed out, knocking his head on a block of wood. I pressed my hand quickly over the wound at my belly to help stop the bleeding. In seconds, the healing had begun—my strength returned with the blood, and the glamour of the body closed up the wound and turned the pain into a sharp memory that faded within seconds.

I turned and grabbed the sailor, wrestling him down. When he spoke, mainly gasping curses upon me, I began to decipher his language. Once I understood it—for the vampyre mind works quickly through mortal tongues—I realized that he was begging me for his life.

He fought, but was too weakened by the conditions on the ship, and was easily overcome. His curses grew softer, and I had to hold his mouth shut with one hand while I brought his wrist to my lips with the other. I gently pressed down upon his skin until I tasted blood. I watched his face as I drank from him. I did not wish to kill him, or his friend. But mortals had difficulty understanding this need.

In the mortal blood, much of the vampyre's own mortal life is remembered—but the mortal host also recalls pleasure in some part of his brain. I saw his eyes light up slightly, then roll back into his head. His face flushed in the pleasures that are private to all mortals, and when I released him, the young man begged me to drink more.

I asked him of the numbers of men left alive on the ship, and he confirmed my thoughts—there were no more than nineteen, barely enough to man the ship should the storms come.

"Storms?"

"We been here two full moons, Sir Demon," he said. "But storms always come—even the sea grows tired of quiet."

"This calm is unnatural here. How are you sure there will be storms?"

"We got a . . ." Next he said a word for which my mind found no translation, but I began to understand that they had a seer of some kind on board who had not only predicted a gale that would come through, but had also predicted the arrival of demons. I asked if I might meet this seer, and the sailor did not wish me to do so.

With both promises and threats, I managed to get him to take me into the bunk area, where several of the men lay only half-sleeping, many of them watching as I entered with their mate. He took me to an old man who lay on his side, his head shaved, his body wrapped in a heavy blanket, but I saw the hint of red silk with gold embroidery on his shirt beneath.

• 3 •

THE old seer looked at me with fierce eyes—so unlike the broken and sunken eyes of the handful of men who lay nearby.

"You have come with a she-devil," he whispered. "I know you. I have seen you in dreams, my good demon." He glanced about at the others, barely lifting his head to look. "They are afraid of you."

"But you are not?"

The old man nearly smiled. "Afraid of demons? Many generations ago, it was said a demon king guarded the lands of my ancestors. I am named—Illuyanket—for such a demon, a warlord who is my ancestor. Yes, there were times when demon and woman might bring forth children." He paused a moment, his eyes narrowing, and what seemed a lightening of blood beneath his flesh occurred as if he felt a sudden inspiration. He touched the edge of my hand, and turned it over so that my palm turned upward. "You have a child who is mortal and a child who is demon."

"Two mortal children," I said, nodding. "A third child grows within the lady who helped me escape from a prison far to the east."

He nodded, patting my hand beneath his, then letting it go. "Why would a demon care for his progeny? Does the snake watch the young asps as they leave the broken nest?"

"I do care for them, the one unborn and the two who live beneath a terrible shadow," I said.

"Yes, as my ancestor who was demon loved my ancestor who was not, and the children brought into the world by them. Why do you love these children? For mortal they are, and enemies of demons they may become."

"I suppose . . . I suppose because they give me hope."

"More than hope," he said, his eyes gleaming. He pointed at my face. "They give you a reason to fight the shadows that these children may have a better world than that world you know. They are your dreams, your prophecies, in flesh. I know of demon half-breeds, for my ancestors were such. Many of them were outcasts because of their demon blood. Yet I met a demon in my childhood, and met with no harm. There are demons that protect, and demons that destroy. I do not believe you are here for destruction. These men who watch us as we speak, they would destroy each other . . . They are willing to eat the dead. Perhaps even kill the living—to survive. I would not do this. I would rather die without a full belly than die with human flesh at my tongue."

He had refused food, which was why he lay in such a state, barely moving, only sipping from a small pitcher—the size of his hand—of water. He told me of their journey—they were sent by an emperor of their country, with several other ships, and had not yet reached the foreign lands for their trade. They had been at sea several weeks when they hit the calm, where the ship now sat.

"I had felt this my first night," he said. "The earth has changed. Plagues spread from the west, like the shadow of a great bird that hunts the world itself, covering all lands, touching all men. Illness and pestilence follow, and the sea grows ice upon the edge of some lands, and in the oceans, a stillness waits for the storms as if the waters are dead. There is some deep peril at work, and I feel the growl of a dark goddess in my dreams. Yet, from the depths of the earth, treasures will come—I believe this—and much may change. Demons such as you bring fortune, though you frighten many, as you may see if you look about this room. You, good demon, I have seen before, though in another guise.

"When I was young, there were such demons in our lands—I was a poor child of a village without hope. The smallest insects were our food when droughts came and crops failed. When the demons came, much fortune changed. One such as you touched me upon the forehead. From this touch, such a fire grew inside me as if igniting a small spark of the bloodline within me—and it is from this that my dreams come. I grew in fame—a child of eight!

Many districts and many farmlands sent me those who sought knowledge of the future. But one day, warriors came to our village, and to my home. They bought me from my mother and father, and took me to the palace of my emperor. There, I grew in honor and charity, and even the holy men consulted me in times of trouble. I was called the Storm Dreamer, because I felt the brothers of the wind before they had swept back their clouds. I knew when drought came, and when even the storms of war—and its victors—might descend. I became the palace favorite—in my youth—and predicted the outcome of many battles and many wives for my emperor. As I grew older, he allowed me to become a guide for his fleet in both war and trade. So it was upon this voyage—the *Illuyanka*, named for me, but also for the demon who had many centuries ago taken one of my ancestors for a bride—that I agreed to go, though many wished to dissuade me from such a journey."

"But you did not dream of what would happen here—in the dead sea?" I asked.

He raised his eyebrows. "You will make me laugh with such questions, my demon. I dreamed of much that was bad, but also of much good. You run from one trouble; you find three more. You hide from your fate; it is angry when it discovers your hiding place. When a vision of the future is of such interesting times, one does not shrink from it. I saw my death in this ship, and I did not wish to run like a child. The dream cannot be murdered in sleep, good demon. It can only be known so that we are aware when it comes to pass in the waking from it. I am ancient now—although to demons I am certain I must seem young. But I will reach one hundred years soon. I know that before we return home, my death will come like a sweet child grasping at my hand to take me into those places unspoken of by the dead and unseen by the living. When I heard you and your lady companion had come to us, I knew all would be right for the men who remained here."

"Tell me, what have you seen in your dreams of demons?"

He smiled broadly, showing small brownish yellow teeth. "You would bring us food. You are harbingers of good fortune as well as bad, though my shipmates do not understand this. They think in only dark and light, they do not understand the shading of the brilliance within the dark, or the spot of darkness in bright sunlight. If one stares at the sun, one will see night soon enough. You are the deep light in darkness, my demon friend. Your coming tells me that the great storms will seek us out, as they did in my dreams of what-will-come, where the sisters of the sea slap at the brothers of the winds. We will be set free from this stillness." He nodded, remembering his dream. "Oh, some will die, I am certain, for demons take a price. But good fortune, nonetheless, shall be—for you are both dragon and demon."

"How will we bring you food, my friend?" I asked. "For we are blood-drinkers, but have no supplies for you."

He brought his frail hand up to my face and brushed his fingers along my features as if it would allow him to see me more clearly. "Yes, you are the demon and the dragon and the bird that brings shadow. But you are the deep light in the dark, as well."

He reached across for his small pitcher and took barely a drop from it. He savored this a moment, his eyes closing with the momentary pleasure, his parched lips smacking slightly as if a flagon of sweet wine existed within a single drop of water.

He opened his eyes and set the pitcher down beside him. "We have two sister ships, also in the quiet water. Abandoned. We heard the shouts of the men leaving them on small boats to find a shore. Many of our own men left on the boats—many hundreds of them, and did not leave any boats for those who remained. The *Illuyanka* did not have so many boats after the storm tossed us here. Many of us could not leave. Many died within the first days after our storehouse emptied. But the other ships remained in the mist with few men aboard.

"Yet those who left their ships—many days ago—would

not live long upon the waters, for it is too far to the nearest land. Nor did any return, and it has been too long to hope for their success. Thousands set out from those ships, our companions. There will be food there, and freshwater, where ours dwindled over the months. In my dream, you flew several miles to one of the ships and returned with these supplies." He said this all as if he had known of the will of the universe well before my arrival, and I had fit in perfectly with it. "There is a nettle's leaf, ground to fine powder, stored in small red boxes I would like, also." He pointed to a shelf by his head, and there was a horn-shaped pipe with a round blue bowl at its tip. "It is good to burn it in the bowl and breathe it into the throat. Old men enjoy such things."

I glanced at the men who squatted near us on the floor, listening intently. Each looked at me with a dreaded curiosity, as if expecting me to shoot fire from my mouth and bolts of lightning from my eyes.

I returned my attentions to Illuyanket. "Your dream included bringing you a burning leaf for your bowl?"

"My dreams are very particular," he said, a wan smile upon his face.

"You are a wise man," I said, chuckling a bit at his ingenuity. "Perhaps your dreams may be true."

"Always," he said. "They are. Since the demon touched my brow when I was a child. Now, please let an old man rest for the night. When I see you again, I would like a bit of salted pork and a larger bowl for drinking water. Do not forget the small red box with the turtle engraved upon it—it is the size of your hand, no larger."

I told him I would bring what I could find from the nearest ship. "Tell me, how far is it to land?"

"To the east, too far. To the west, too far," he said. "You fly like a bird, but even a bird must rest. You must wait, for when the storms come, we will find our way homeward, far to the west of this unhappy spot, just as the storms flung us across the ocean. Within no more than two nights, you will fly from us and seek your landfall. As you fly to the west, the night will stay with you many hours. Beneath you, islands large and small will welcome you and your lady. This is my dream."

"In your dreams, you have seen these storms come again?"

He nodded. "Demons are the bringers of storms, my friend. When the demons come, the sisters of the sea grow angry. The brothers of the wind chase them. You will see, my friend. You will see."

His eyes shifted slightly as he glanced at the other men, crouching nearby. "Do not fear them. They will do as I say, though I could not keep them from devouring their own kind. But they fear you more than you need fear them. After you have brought us good meat and drink, I will show where you and the lady demon may sleep in comfort and not fear these ruffians. They believe you have the power to watch them while you sleep. I know the secret of your kind, my friend. I know that in the day, you . . ." He then spoke in the barest of whispers—"are vulnerable"—then resumed his soft but audible tone. "But you are a demon of terror and blood. You will kill us if we do not do as you say. We will protect you while you rest during the brief hours of sun that burns beyond the mist. You shall fear nothing from us, so long as you do not murder any more of our men. Do you understand?"

I nearly grinned. "What a bargain this is, for if I do as you say, I become your servant. If I disobey you . . ."

"While you sleep, it would be terrible for a blade to reach your heart," he whispered. "For even an old man might stick a small knife into the flesh of the dead."

I wished then that such men could live as long as vampyres, for the world needed more of them. "You seem a thousand years in wisdom, not a mere hundred," I said. "Will you dream of what destiny awaits me?"

He closed his eyes and was silent—so quiet that I grew afraid he had died. But after several moments, he let out a snuffling snore as if coming up from the depths of sleep. He opened his eyes, and said, "Your fate is beyond my understanding. All I can see of it is a magnificent fire and a terrible place—vast and intricate—beneath the earth. But this does not mean you will meet with misfortune, my friend. It is only a brief sip of the future dredged up within the wells of dreams. The water of what-is-to-come too often is muddy and deep. But do not fear your nights ahead, for I see in you more than demon. I see a noble falcon whose prey is the wolf. Do not let any emperor or warlord dissuade you from your path, though it would lead you to the end of your nights. It is yours and yours alone and must be taken, this path, even if it burns as you walk it. Now, please, my friend, hunger gnaws at me, and I have not much more than appetite left. The red box—do not forget!" He made a stabbing sign with his fist, as if to threaten me, grinning the whole time.

◆ 4 ◆

I rose and turned to the gathering rabble. "Did you hear that? I will bring meat and drink from the distant ship. I will kill no more of you. I will tell the lady also that this is the law of the ship. You will give us sleeping quarters where we may rest at dawn undisturbed. Further, you will protect and honor this Storm Dreamer as if he were your emperor—no—your god. For if, as he says, the storm comes soon, and your ill habits are replaced by salted pork, you owe him much. May I have your oath?"

"If we have yours, Sir Demon, that you will not murder us in our sleep. And that you will but drink a little from us that you may live, but not enough for our deaths, as well," came a voice from the doorway. It was the sailor I had drunk from earlier.

"You have it," I said. "Is it agreed?"

As I spoke these words, grumbling and arguments broke out, but the old man raised his arm up to silence them. When they had quieted, he spoke with that melding of softness and firmness, and it seemed as if his voice projected far beyond his small mouth.

"You have eaten of the dead and dying," he said,

admonishing them with a well-pointed finger. "Do not begrudge the demons your blood, for they will suck out the poison of your deeds. Those whom you have fed upon will forgive you. The ancestors you have dishonored will pray for you to the spirits. Many demons are omens of ill fortune, but these demons that come to us are from the blood of my own ancestor, called Illuyan the Fierce, who waged war against the enemies of our people in the kingdoms before memory. These bring us good fortune—this demon called Falconer, and the one who is called Pythia."

I felt a vague clutching at my throat. *Pythia*. I closed my eyes for a moment to feel for her in the stream. Her movements were overpowering. I felt her abovedeck as a mouse might feel an ox lumbering atop its nest.

I rushed out of the bunk area and wandered the corridors to emerge in the fresh salt air.

• 5 •

I found her moments later. She had murdered two men who remained abovedeck. She had drunk too deeply from them. Their corpses lay beside each other, and she had just pushed herself off the most recent of her kills.

"You fool!" I shouted. "I have just this moment bargained with those men on board to keep us safe in daylight but took an oath not to kill them."

"I have never taken such an oath," she said haughtily. "Nor would I allow mortals to govern me as you do."

The gold mask of her face turned black-red from the life force she had drunk, her hair stained, her breasts shiny and soaked, I remembered how she had taken me in a tower once. How she had loved the slowness of death in mortal man.

She was everything I hated in myself, in the world, and among vampyres. Even as I had these thoughts, I remembered her naked, her breasts high and heavy, and the slight swell of her belly as emerald and ruby snakes swarmed about her in Nezahual's kingdom.

I could not erase this from my mind. I could not keep

from wanting her, yet she was promiscuous and devilish. She could not be trusted, and yet she had saved me. She had made me feel love the way that my companion Ewen had with his goodness, and Alienora had once—all too briefly—with her purity before the dark had descended.

Wiping her chin as she approached me, Pythia gave a guttural laugh, and said, "Do not feel for him. He was a cannibal. No better than the worst of all men. Do you know what they called me? Demoness. Like a princess of Hell. They prayed for their speedy deaths. I blessed them as they went to sleep. They think they are headed for Heaven because of me, so do not lecture me. I need more blood than you. I drink for two."

Reading my thoughts, she leaned into me and pressed her lips to mine. I tasted the warmth of mortal life there, with the tinge of blood on her tongue. She drew back, laughing. Was she mocking me? Did she feel the same bond with me that I felt with her? For surely, we were bound together in some way as if we'd been chained to each other.

"Throw the bodies to the sea," I said. "For the men below do not need to see the evidence of your cruelty."

"Throw them yourself."

Not wishing to argue the point, I dragged the corpses to the side of the boat and let them drop. The splashes were loud, and echoed. I could only imagine what the men aboard would think of such noise.

Pythia came up behind me as I looked out across the curtain of mist. She pressed her body against my back, wrapping her arms about me. "Death truly is a blessing for them," she said. "They will die of terrible hunger here. You know that."

I turned toward her, holding her at arm's length. "There are fewer than twenty men here. They need to live in order to guide the ship—for us. There is a storm on its way, and it is too distant to the nearest land to attempt flight across the sea."

"How do you know such things?"

"A seer," I said. "A vampyre had brought second sight to him when he was a boy. He is a descendant of vampyre and mortal, though many generations removed. Our child may be like him: mortal, but with the inner dark of our tribe." A cloud seemed to cross her golden face, and I guessed that she was thinking about the child. Did she care deeply for it? I felt she did, but this lady was as volatile as the mask itself. I could not read her from expression or words. I had the sense that she always spoke from two understandings—the one that was evident in her words, and a hidden meaning far beyond my own mind's grasp. "Illuyanket is his name."

She nodded as if understanding. "It is a name from the old worlds," she said. "It must have been passed to him from his ancient ancestor, for it was a name of a vampyre whom mortals considered their god."

"The ship is named for him—*Illuyanka*—for this elder gained fame in his country for his storm dreams and prophecies. He is nearly a century old, and predicted our coming—and the storm, as well. I believe him."

The sneer within her voice returned. "Mortal prophecy. As good as mortal promises."

"You are mortal, Pythia. Our child may be mortal, as well. You were once a seer among mortals," I said. "Was there truth to your visions? Is there truth to mine? I have met this man, and I believe him. You will do this—if not for me, then for that child you claim to care so much for. You are in more danger than I am—for they could kill you now with sword and arrow. Do not forget this. You are more like them than like me. If you do not kill them, they will allow us to drink from them as long as necessary. We do not know if we will have to remain here one night or three. I promised them this."

"I promise them pleasure followed by peace." She smiled, exuberant with the mortal blood inside her, bringing a glow of strength and vitality with it.

I did not even wish to argue with her. "I need to find the other ships nearby," I said. "There may be more men, and food for these who will protect us in daylight. Do not kill again here. Do you understand?"

"I do not take orders, even from the Maz-Sherah," she said. "If we drain them of their blood, what do we need protectors for?"

I controlled my fury. "We are in the middle of a vast sea. You cannot tell me where land lies. We do not know how many nights we will be here. We cannot take flight in the dark if we do not know that there is an island or a continent before sunrise. These sailors can head toward their lands when the wind picks up, to the west—our destination. We murder them; we meet a watery grave. Which oblivion would you prefer? Death at the bottom of the sea, rotting, or deep in this ship until its boards give way and it is torn by a gale? These men may save us, if we promise them life."

"You care too much for these mortals. Their deaths are sweet to them."

"Sweet?" I asked. "Will yours be so sweet? For as you kill them, remember what you will face when your own death comes." I regretted these words as soon as they left my tongue, for I saw the stricken look in her eyes, and the slight flinch of her body as if I had slapped her. Then, weary of the argument, I said. "If you wish it, fly now. I do not need to go with you. Save your skin—fly away, little bird."

Her eyes seemed to burn with fury. "Do not test me, nor tempt me, Falconer. I made you. I brought you from the tomb of Ixtar. Do not forget this. You belong to me. In me your seed grows, and in my death, it dies."

I sighed, doing what I could to let go of my feeling of exasperation. "If you will not fly away, golden face, then you will come with me. We will find the food and water these men need. We will see if the wind picks up as the seer has predicted. If it does not, tomorrow night I will go with you to our deaths out over the dark sea, if need be."

"If you call me 'golden face' again, I will leave you," she muttered.

"Pythia, then," I said. "Now, come. There is a ship not

more than a few miles from here, and another beyond it. Gather what food and water you can from the closest one, and I will find the distant vessel."

Feeling the power of new blood in me, I opened my wings to their fullest and leapt from the ship. She flew after me, but I sensed her cursing within the stream. We communicated in our minds as I told her to fly toward the nearest of masts, while I flew beyond it, seeing a phantom of a ship at some distance against the blanket of fog.

◆ 6 ◆

WITHIN the quarter hour, I had located one of the sister ships of the *Illuyanka*. I landed upon it, and heard only the sounds of my own movements. The wall of fog all around created a kind of cave, encircling the ship with a stony silence.

The first thing that met my eye was the fresh kill on the deck.

◆ 7 ◆

A sailor of this third ship had met a terrible death at the hand of one of my tribe, and based on the quivering of his fingers, the vampyre who had done this had departed just moments before.

I put the man out of his misery, for he was not going to regain consciousness again. The brutality of the act was evident from the multiple bites along the arms and shoulders—the skin had been shredded as if the vampyre's jaw had locked in place when he'd bitten down.

This kill was not like that of the vampyres I knew—and I began to worry that several guards from Aztlanteum had followed us. I looked about the ship, among its ropes and barrels, and I found more evidence of these vampyres' handiwork—always too vicious and inexact in the bite, which would have been unusual for even Nezahual's tribe. I closed my eyes to feel the stream, and in its strange dark light, I neither sensed nor had a gut feeling that the vampyres who had committed these acts still lurked.

I heard a human moan that was nearly a whistling sound—I will never forget it, for it chilled my blood just to hear it. I had still not gotten used to the worst of killing—when the death was slow and painful. I did not think then I would get used to it in a thousand years, for it reminded me too much of the sorrows of mortal existence.

I followed the sound of the strange noise, and as I did, I began to get a vague sense in the stream of at least one vampyre feeding. I moved swiftly through the warren of rooms beneath the deck, following the stream, tuning my ears to the sound of the man who seemed to be dying.

As I turned a corner, there was the victim of the vampyre—a man whose face had been obliterated by the attack, and blood everywhere around him. The strange sound from him had come because of the damage to his face and throat. Feeling pity for him, I closed off his breathing, and quickly sent him to the threshold of death.

I felt a tug in the stream, and turned to the left, and saw a brief flash of movement.

"Wait!" I called, but the creature moved swiftly along the low, narrow corridor that twisted suddenly to the right. All I saw of him was a cape and hood, and in his arms, he carried what seemed to be a boy—perhaps a kitchen servant on board, for the boy had left his handprints on the wall, the dust of flour upon them. By the size of the hand, the boy was not yet thirteen, and I knew what the vampyre meant to do with him once he had him in some quiet place.

I rose to my height and bounded after him, following his scent all the way to the upper decks. There, I saw a ship's boy whose head had been shaved as if to ward off lice, and whose flour-dusted tunic had been torn at the throat as if the vampyre had just begun feeding upon him when I caught up to him.

The boy glanced at me, wide-eyed.

"Do not be afraid," I whispered. "I will not hurt you."

I reached for the shredding of skin at his shoulder, but the vampyre had not had time to bleed him much.

The boy tried to speak, but instead took deep gulps of

air, one after the other. His face was pale, and the terror in his eyes did not diminish as I tried to comfort him.

I felt at his throat the too-quick beat of his pulse. His mouth opened as if in a scream, and then his jaw went slack.

Dead, from the fright of it.

I felt a cold wave of nausea go through me. Movement in the stream.

The creature that had terrified the boy stood behind me.

Without turning around, I knew that the vampyre leaned over me—as I crouched by the boy—and nearly tapped me on the shoulder. Challenging me to turn and fight him, probably for the boy's blood.

I slowly twisted my head to the left. For a quarter second, I saw a vampyre as if in the mirror—a skull with long dagger fangs and the white of bone where his lips and chin should have been, yet with leathered skin held tight to the skull, and strands of thin hair dangling over his sunken eyes which were red and soulless.

· CHAPTER 4 ·

The Corpse-Vampyre

· 1 ·

I could not move as I beheld him, though it was a mere second or two of time—and the creature seemed also to react as I did, as if seeing me at all was a shock to him.

His hood fell down over his eyes. He moved like a wriggling worm upon a hook, a blur of motion as he leapt from a crouching position into the air. His cape seemed to billow out from him, and I heard a screech like an owl as he shot up through the mist.

After I laid the dead boy down upon planking and covered him with a torn bit of the sail's matting, I looked up into the mist. No trace remained of this vampyre—nor did the stream reveal his presence to me.

· 2 ·

THE ship had been mostly abandoned, but a dozen or so men and boys had remained behind. The vampyre had worked quickly. I had not known any vampyre—except perhaps Pythia—to slaughter so well, so indiscriminately. One vampyre could not possibly have drunk deeply from all the men on board—his only object was to kill them. I wondered if he intended to use this ship as his sleeping quarters, and then had decided that he could not trust those on it to be protectors during the day.

He was a throwback in vampyrism to some age when vampyres were truly nothing more than the rotting undead. He had no glamour, no semblance of health. The blood did not bring back his youth.

In some respects, he reminded me of the alchemist Artephius—one who held the essence of immortality, yet could not keep his flesh from falling away over the centuries. But Artephius was not a vampyre. He had stolen some of the secrets of the immortals, but not all.

A vampyre without youth?

The drinking of blood and the glamour—which was our youth and beauty—was part of our tribal energy. How could a vampyre have none of this? Surely, such a vampyre would have extinguished long ago.

Why did a member of my tribe follow us, and yet not reveal himself?

• 3 •

I went in search of supplies for the other ship. I found salted meat and barrels of water stored belowdecks. I poured some of the water into wineskins I found in the galley and carried as much of the salted pork as I could. There were bags of grain, also, which I tied at my waist. As I was about to leave, a flash of red along an upper shelf caught my eye. It was the beloved red box full of dusty leaf for smoking. I sniffed at it and found the aroma intoxicating. I grabbed two of the boxes, tucking them beneath my arms, above the sack of pork.

When I returned to the other ship, I took these supplies to the young sailor and told him to give the red boxes to Il-luyanket alone. "I am sorry that my friend has killed two of your men," I said. "It was beyond my control."

"Sir Demon, we did not mean to offend her. Nor you,"

he said, a tremble in his voice. "She brought us food and water from a ship, as well. I will not talk of the spirits of the dead, for they may lurk nearby." He drank greedily from one of the wineskins, and tore off a chunk of the salted pork, chewing it as I spoke to him.

"This will be good for all of you for several days, if you ration it carefully. The water, too. Tomorrow night, we will bring more of it. What they have in storage there might last another month or more."

"All the men are dead?" he asked. "None survive?"

I tried to block out the face of the boy who had died from fright. "The ship is abandoned. I found no one." I searched for Pythia within the stream and felt her presence far belowdecks.

I went with him to the old seer, who wept tears of joy as he lit his bowl and sucked the yellow smoke from the stem. Pythia crouched beside him, and I gathered he had been regaling her with stories that had bewitched her, for she was genuinely caring of his condition. I wanted to draw her to one side to speak of the vampyre who had followed our flight and now hid upon one of the other mired ships, but it was not the time to do so.

She glanced up at me, and in that brief look I saw another side to her—the aspect of this Pythoness that had been missing beyond our night of passion. I dread to say it, but it was her mortal side—and when she returned her attention to Illuyanket, she seemed not like a terrible vampyre who had slaughtered many, but like his granddaughter, sitting by his bunk, listening to stories and legends of another country that she had heard once as a little girl.

"Yes, Illuyan was the name of the great ancestor demon." He nodded as he puffed on the stem. "There are many statues in the hills of my homeland of him dressed as a warrior, with sword raised so." He lifted the pipe up as if it were a weapon and gave a fierce scowl. "He saved our people and drove back the enemy. These are ancient fairy tales, but in my family, it is believed, for we are his bloodline. In those ancient days, demons and mortals mated, though when the demons were driven away, those of us with even a drop of demon blood were stripped of property and honor, driven to a life of hard work, and early death. Yet it was this same demon blood that awoke in me the dreaming. This Illuyan, my namesake."

"I have known Illuyan," Pythia said, resting her hand on his shoulder. "He was a great ruler in the nights before the night and day had parted."

"Yes." The old man nodded, grinning a smoke gust. "Before the moon held shadow, and in the days when the trees spoke of the treasures of the deep earth."

He asked us both to try the burning leaf. Pythia refused, but I cupped the bowl in my hand as he had and sipped at the pipe stem until smoke filled my mouth. It was sweet and strong and seared my throat with its heat. Then, I coughed it out, for it was too much like inhaling fire itself.

He laughed, though the other men were silent while they passed water and meat and boiled grain among themselves. One of them began singing a high, beautiful song of distant maidens and lovely flowers while more sacks of grain were poured into black pots and set to cook over the fire.

I began to love these men, despite their rough circumstance, and particularly Illuyanek, the Storm Dreamer, for his wisdom and respect. He did not fear me, nor had I given him reason to fear; but better than this, he treated me, a demon to his kind, as an equal—even as a son.

As if reading my thoughts, Pythia came up behind me as I stood in the doorway, watching the men enjoying their repast.

"You know this vampyre, Illuyan?" I asked.

"He ruled Myrryd, and founded many cities. But as with all the old Myrryd kings, he extinguished. All who wear the crown are hunted by those who wish to take the crown, yet no one wears it long." She looked at me almost lovingly. She took my hand in hers, drawing me along the corridor, past the many rooms to the steps that led above. Once on the deck, she let go of my hand and went to look out over the deep mist. I followed her there and stood a few feet behind her.

"You are like my father." She sighed. "You believe mortal man is worth saving."

"And you?"

"This one man, Illuyanek, is worth the world," she said. "But to care for the prey . . . it was the downfall of my father's kingdom. It is like taking a soft rabbit into your arms and keeping it safe . . . until the hunger for it outweighs the love of the creature. My father protected many rabbits, but few vampyres."

"You have rarely spoken so kindly of Merod."

"What is there to say? He fulfilled his prophecies. In the end, that is all he cared for—he was a guardian, he told me. Not a wolf, but a shepherd—as if a blood-drinker who lives off the wine of man could also care for mortals beyond the thirst itself. He nearly ensnared me in his delusions."

"Ensnared?" I faced her, shaking my head. "It was you who trapped your father."

"Were you there? Did you watch me trap him?" she asked. For the first time, I genuinely believed I had hurt her in some way. She was not as invulnerable as she seemed. "You cannot pretend to know what I have done. Or what has been done to me."

"No, I cannot know any of this, other than what you tell me. You have kept much from me. You spent years in Nezahual's kingdom. Tell me of those times now. Was there another vampyre of our tribe there? A vampyre who had no glamour, no beauty? A vampyre whose eyes shone red with the blood that pulsed behind them? A vampyre whose skull jutted from rotting flesh?"

The golden mask rippled slightly on her face, and her eyes would not meet mine. "Why do you ask this?"

"I have seen him. You must have sensed him in the stream. He follows us from Aztlanteum."

• 4 •

PYTHIA grabbed one of the hanging ropes, drawing herself up to the edge of the ship, swiftly leapt from it, and soared off into the mist. I tried to reach her through my mind, but it was as if I had hit a wall with my thoughts. Then, she dived back down, crouching along the ropes of a nearby mast. I reached her seconds later, grabbing her at the waist before she could flee again.

"This is no time for anger and games. He slaughtered a dozen men on the other ship. I caught a glimpse of him. He looks like a ghoul—a walking corpse. Did you see him in the prisons?"

As I said this, her eyes betrayed some knowledge, but she remained silent. She withdrew her wings, and I took her down to the quarterdeck of the ship. We sat among ropes and trunks, and she looked out at the mist.

"There were many prisoners in Nezahual's city," she whispered, as if it were dangerous to say.

"He wears a hooded cape, and I did not detect any feeling from him," I said. "Just a pure and utter chill."

"He didn't attack you," she said.

"He seemed . . . terrified of me. He did not want me to see him."

"Nezahual and his priests imprisoned many—some creatures who crossed from the Veil itself and others from the nameless territories of the deep earth."

"Tell me what you know of this vampyre," I said.

"Nothing," she said. "If he did not harm you, perhaps he is merely following us to escape from Nezahual's reach."

"Are there vampyres who look as we do in the silver of mirrors?"

"I have never looked into a mirror, nor gazed in deep water to see my reflection. It is forbidden. You should not do so, either." She gave me a look—from eyes that flashed fire beneath the gold mask—that made me want to rage against her, yet I knew this was her bait for me. I grinned, which only made her angry. "If you seek answers, go to the Veil and tear it again."

"You will tell me of this vampyre."

She would not look at me. "I do not know this creature."

I knew by her tone she lied, but at that moment the young sailor found us on deck and told us that Illuyanek had commanded him to show us our quarters for the coming of day.

• 5 •

THE sailor led us along the deck to the captain's quarters, which had but one small window that could be easily covered with heavy drapes to block the sun. We did not need a deep grave for our sleep, but darkness without sunlight—for it was the sun itself that would burn us.

I was not used to comfort in sleep—I much preferred a tomb to a palace, a rock-strewn cavern to a bed. But Pythia liked her comforts, and when she entered the room ahead of me, she cried out in delight.

I glanced about the quarters—vials of perfume littered the room, no doubt gifts for mistresses or wives, collected from outlandish places, tossed about by the men who had murdered their leader—and fine silks and heavy cloths, torn and drawn as if the men on board had gone mad and sought to destroy any finery their captain had gathered for himself. Reds and blues and vibrant yellows in the cloths, and woolen and silk rugs, made by expert craftsmen.

There was treasure here for me and for Pythia—fine linen and silk clothing, like the perfume, gifts from foreign princes or bought in exotic marketplaces.

Because I had traveled much, my clothes were caked with the filth of earth and air, and I gladly undressed. I tore off the nasty tunic I wore and the ragged trousers and all manner of clothes that had seemed to become one with my body.

Naked, I took up the water bowl at the door and washed myself clean, though this was not something my kind seemed to do—nor was it necessary, for each dawn, our flesh renewed, fresh and clean, and only covered with the dirt of our resting place. Bathing was a habit I missed from my mortal years, and so I relished the scrubbing of my arms and legs. Water was considered our enemy, but this was simply because being immersed in it, we would have no strength, no magick. Who cared for power when one could be clean?

Pythia sat on the bed and watched me. She questioned my need for such cleanliness, mocking my mortal ways. "The day's sleep will refresh you enough," she said. "Although I am enjoying seeing you scrub."

"Do not laugh," I said. "You are next. You still stink of Nezahual's snakes."

Once I was clean, I tossed tunics and trousers and mysterious leggings and various cloth bindings that I did not quite know the use for—all across the enormous bed. "Tonight, when we rise, we will dress as the Lord and Lady Demon that we are. Now, you, my lady."

I beckoned her to the bath.

"Come to bed," she said as she drew off the rags she had worn since our escape.

Reaching for the bowl of water and the rag within it, I said, "I feel no sun yet. Here, wash."

"A daughter of Merod does not wash like a mortal. Water would . . ."

"Hurt you?" I asked. "Perhaps we grow weak in a river, or a lake. Perhaps we would drown if in the sea. But the rain does nothing to us. A good bath will help you rest."

"I rest well enough. Vampyres have no need of baths."

"In more than a thousand nights, you have not bathed? Not ever? You forget yourself, Pythoness. You live in a prison of mortality now. You reek of life," I laughed as I threw the cloth over to her.

She seemed to rear back, her eyes burning, a snarl curving her lips. The cloth landed on her shoulder, and she shrugged it off to the floor. "You vile snake, reminding me of this . . . insult . . . this parasite!" She reached up to the mask, raking her fingernails into its golden flesh. "I wish I had never put this upon my face. I wish now I had remained with Nezahual and ruled his kingdom beside him and left you to your fate in the jaws of Ixtar."

"You hated him," I said, feeling anger rise up. "He would have tormented you until your Extinguishing. He would have destroyed you, my sweet Pythoness. You have bad taste in men. For the most part."

"He loved me," she said. "He would not have sought my destruction."

"You have been loved by many, and you have loved them," I said.

"As have you. What is good for a man is also good for a woman," she said. In those nights of that century, I had an old way of thinking of maidens, although the fierce vampyre women had changed this swiftly enough. "I have even loved my prey when it has taken my fancy."

"Did Nezahual keep the mask from you?" I asked, ignoring what was surely a barb aimed at me. "Or did he take you to it and show you its glittering beauty? Did he allow you to feel its seduction? Did he tell you where it was, knowing that you would not stop searching for it until you had it on your face?"

Her eyes widened, and she froze, as if remembering. The gold mask rippled at her brow. When she spoke, her voice had altered; it was lower and deeper, as if she had gone into a trance merely by recalling her first sight of the mask of Datbathani. "It called to me. It sought me. It is a creation of a deep place, where sorcery still holds power over us. It is beyond even Medhya's touch. You would not understand unless it called to you. I slaughtered many of Nezahual's priests to steal it. It had been locked away, this beautiful mask—so lovely—like a beautiful creature, a bird of rich and vibrant plumage held against its will, selfishly imprisoned so that none might bask in its glory. It had been laid upon an obsidian statue of some demon of Nezahual's choosing—a youth with many arms, a god long forgotten to even that world of the Ketzal. The mask was a whisper in my mind as I beheld it. Will you come to me, Pythoness? It asked. I am your fulfillment; I am power beyond dream, it whispered. I am meant for your face. I trembled at its sight, Falconer. I shivered as I touched the smooth edge of it. When I held it in my hands, I saw beauty and hope, as you can only dream. I saw sunlight reflected in it—light that I had not seen in millennia, and it did not burn me. This beautiful gold mask. Its power. I felt it. When I wore it, when I could not remove it, I felt its lies, its deception. I felt my power being sucked from my flesh and blood just as we drink from mortals. I must bring nourishment to myself and my child—but also, to this. *This*."

She reached up and tore at the gold of her face, pulling at the mask as if it could come off, but instead, she only tore at her own skin—for the gold was within and on her skin, and could not be separated from it until death.

She began weeping, and I felt the heat of her pain. I set down the bowl and went to her. I crouched down to pick up the moistened cloth, and then I took her in my arms.

"I do not understand this world," I whispered. "Nor do I understand the destiny to which we are drawn. I have hated you. I have loathed everything about you. Yet, here we are. At the edge of the world's oceans. For whatever gods or demons have called us to this earth, I know that your fate and mine are bound together."

She fought against me, but I drew her close to me that she might weep upon my shoulder. I felt her mortal heartbeat as I held her.

"I will not leave you," I said.

"How can you say that?" she whispered through tears. "I will destroy you. I know this."

"In visions of prophecy?" I asked, amused by her fear. "What if our vision has been faulty. No, I do not believe you will harm me—not in that way. You brought me back from death as a fulfillment. No, Pythia, you fear that I will destroy you. We have both envisioned this. Even this dream, I do not believe."

Within a few minutes her sobbing had ended. I carried

her over to the bowl of water. I took the washcloth, dipped it, and brought it up to her face. I wiped the tears from the mask, from her lips, then washed her throat clean of the foulness of her journey.

I kissed her throat, feeling the throb of the stream between us, smelling that delicate aroma of mortal skin. I had an urge to drink from her—it was both the scent of life and a feeling of wanting to get beneath her flesh, to be part of her, to ease her pain by the passing of blood.

Remembering those I had loved, I pressed myself close to her as I washed down her slender belly, following the curves of her body. I reached for the pouch she had still had wrapped about her waist, the only modesty that remained on her. The orb was within the pouch, and when she felt me touch it, she drew her hand down to remove mine from it.

"I felt its pulse when I touched it," I said.

"You must not take it from me. I do not understand its power, but it is of some great worth. I will not lose it."

"Nor will I take it unless it is given to me," I said. I dipped the cloth into the bowl, and wiped the warm water below the binding of the pouch, where its strings hung across the light hair where her thighs opened.

Thin rivulets of water ran along her legs, and I brushed the cloth at the back of her knee and down to her calves. Finally, when I reached her feet, I took special care and massaged them with my hands to try and warm them.

She pressed the sole of her foot against my chest. I felt the now-familiar pleasure rise as she brought her left foot downward, playfully brushing it lightly between my legs. I drew a dry cloth from the wardrobe and began drying her skin, daubing at the droplets of water that remained.

She closed her eyes, smiling, moaning softly as I brushed the cloth down her belly.

I laid her down upon the soft bed and grabbed a vial of perfume. Opening one, I smelled the petals of sirus-blossom, one I had known well in my youth, for in those years this blossom grew the world over. I dipped two fingers into the aromatic liquid and rubbed it along her ankles and daubed her shoulders with it. I took the scent and gently caressed her thigh. I held her feet until she parted them, slipping back the cord at the top of my trousers as I drew her knees away from her center.

I slipped between her legs and embraced her, bending toward her face, kissing the last of her tears back, and rocking the two of us slowly together. My lips wandered her pale flesh, and I remembered those I had loved, and how fleeting love could be—and yet, how the fires of lust and love rekindled easily between two souls to whom all others were enemy.

I thought of her sorrow and my need to sweeten it with closeness and warmth. I brought her some pleasure before the vibrations of the sun's light closed our eyes within the darkened room.

◆ 6 ◆

IN a vision during the day's sleep, I stood before my friend Ewen. He sat upon a large round stone, like a millstone, chained to it from a brace at his neck, and along his arms and waist were more chains, moored to the stone.

He looked up at me with terrible, accusing eyes, and opened his mouth in an agonizing wail.

When I tried to comfort him, it was as if I were a ghost, and he could not see me. I tried to glance around his prison, but it was vague like morning mist, with a terrible burning sun beyond it, blinding me. I heard his voice cry out, *"You abandoned us!"*

◆ 7 ◆

WHETHER in dreams or during my waking hours, I was haunted by a sorrow I could not express, and such visions burned into my soul.

I had failed. I had left him there to his terrible fate, and instead, I lay next to Pythia in a room of wealth and luxury, full in my belly, sated in my desires.

And Ewen—I could not stop imagining the torments visited upon him.

The last moment I had seen him, he had been painted with silver. A metal band had been drawn about his teeth and jaw to keep them locked in a trap so that he could not bite. Glass tubes had run from his body to crucibles and cups, drawing out his blood slowly, as the alchemist sought immortality's essence. In Ewen's eyes, I had seen a glaze of tears.

That moment would only be the beginning of his torments. I knew what the Red Scorpion machine would do. It would flay him and pierce him. It would take his last shred of human memory from him and leave a hollowed shell to be filled with the voice of Artephius himself, or worse, the Myrrydanai White Robes, who would use Ewen as their attack dog, a Morn.

I had failed him whom I had sworn to save. I had failed Calyx, and those of the Akkadite Cliffs and of the Forest.

My children, whom I did not know, raised by their wolf-mother, Enora, counseled by the White Robe priests who were Myrrydanai in disguise.

I was no Maz-Sherah. There was no savior of my tribe.

We were the damned.

Everyone I had ever loved, destroyed.

Gone, I thought. *All gone.*

I pushed away these thoughts. I could not seek my grief, for it would bear down upon me as the heaviest of burdens. I could save no one with worry, with fear, with doubt or heartache. I could only save Ewen, and my tribe, and perhaps even my children, who did not know me, if I kept focused on our journey.

Dusk arrived, with its cooling fingers on my skin. I awoke, and Pythia stood over me, beside the bed.

"We haven't moved?" I asked.

"The sails are slack," she said. "You worry about your friends. You call to them in your rest."

"I fear I have failed them. I have lost what Merod offered me. I no longer hear him in my sleep, or feel him in my blood."

"All we can do is survive," she said. "Until our doom finds us."

• 8 •

IN the red-wood wardrobes and trunks of the spacious cabin, Pythia discovered the ladies' gowns and the jewelry that the ship's captain had no doubt gathered as gifts on his journey.

She stood before me in a beautiful pure white tunic that seemed made of the thinnest of material, trimmed with blue and gold bands. Though I considered her beauty as athletic and wild, the garment softened her and brought out the pink glow of mortality on her skin. About her waist, a corded belt, and her feet were bare, as she had only just begun picking through the elegant slippers.

She glanced over at me. "I feel like a lady in some nobleman's court." She laughed and spun as if she were a young maiden discovering a gown for the first time. She drew up the long, draping white sleeves, nearly transparent in the candlelight. "Like angel wings."

"In my home country, the great ladies all wear such things," I said.

"It must take hours for such ladies to dress. This is only the first garment. There are sleevings and wrappings and coverlets. Look, look at all of this."

She threw other clothes she'd found about the room. "Here," she said, reaching her arms out for me. "Take my hands. Come here."

"What is this madness? Has that mask made you a fool?"

"It is mortality." She laughed. "It makes one . . . frivolous. Come on, even an Anointed One can dance."

"Not when I remember why I am here. Why I need to return."

"Tonight it is impossible. You may suffer, or you may . . . dance."

I bounded up out of bed and stood before her.

"Draw your trousers back on." She laughed, and when I returned to her, dressed from head to toe, she took my hands, and said, "Look at you. Let me be the mirror of your beauty."

I felt happily embarrassed. "Men do not have beauty as women have."

"Men have beauty. You know this more than most. Your friend Ewen is beautiful. I doubt I am the first to notice it," she said. "In you, I see a beautiful youth who is a prince of the earth. You have the muscles of the youth I took in Hedammu and made my own. You have the glow of skin of one who has not yet touched loss or lack. Your glamour is strong, Falconer."

"In you, I see a queen being born."

"A mortal queen," she said. "You will still be young a thousand years from now." She reached up and touched the edge of my face. "Your warmth will exist when many other fires have gone cold. I see you as you are, Falconer. Perhaps this is the only good of the mask—it allows me to see beyond my own desires. Look in my eyes and see yourself. Do you see? Hair long and tangled from the day's sleep. Leather trousers, tight about him, and a captain's boots upon his feet. His eyes, bright with life—the lie of our tribe. You remind me too much of my earliest life. In my first life, before the Sacred Kiss, we had beautiful festivals where the youths and maidens would dance until the world spun and all fell to the earth from the need for sleep."

"But we have no tune," I said, offering her my hand for a dance. How could I feel so light and free? A vampyre had followed us, my friends suffered halfway around the earth, and I did not know when my own doom might strike. Despite all this, Pythia had reawakened some youthful energy in me that I had nearly forgotten. What was there to do, stuck on a ship in the middle of the greatest of seas—but dance?

"I know a dancing song. It was a shepherd's tune I heard once. Sad, but lovely. It makes me think of one shepherd boy who made me laugh."

"One of your seductions," I said.

She began humming a slow, haunting melody. It reminded me too much of the kinds of old songs my mother would lull me to sleep with when I was too young to know words or meanings. It was not the same tune, but had the same peaceful quality.

I took her in my arms and we moved about the bedroom, clumsily and without a sense of rhythm. The room spun slowly about us, as if it were unwinding, and I felt as if we stood still in an embrace while the earth circled us.

Then, she drew back from me, breaking off the tune, and turned away.

"What is it?"

"I have not thought of that melody since I was a child," she said

"In your first mortal life," I whispered.

"In all these centuries, I had not remembered such music. Simple music, the kind the shepherd boys would play, and we would . . . we would dance." She clutched her head as if trying to tear the mask from her face. "This abomination has brought this to me. This terrible cursed thing!"

I embraced her from behind and grasped her wrists in my hand. "You will only hurt yourself."

"I had several years of freedom as a child. I would have become a priestess of the great Python of Pergamos, one day. I would have remained a virgin until such a time as the oracles ceased speaking through my tongue. I would have then bound myself to a man, and had a life . . . a short life, with a husband and children. I loved a boy who tended the flocks. His name was Micahel. He had promised we would bind our lives together when he no longer worked for others but had his own goats and sheep. But then . . . before my twentieth year, after serving the Serpent as a guide for those men and women who wished the blessings of the gods, my father heard strange words of prophecy as the grasses turned in the wind. His journey took him and my mother and sisters to those cities that even I have not seen, though I have dreamed of them."

"Myrryd?" I asked.

She nodded, as I released her hands.

I stepped back from her, but she remained facing away from me. "You know Myrryd?"

"I was not long there." Her voice trembled as she spoke. "A terrible place, a vast labyrinth of crimson towers, dug deep into the chasms of the land, and then rising up, titans of a lost earth, as mountains beneath the sea rise up. Mortals call it the place of the fire-colored sea. It is a red place, and a nest for creatures that never know the sun or moon. It is a place of doom and despair. A fitting grave for the vampyre kings and their priests. It is a city of bones and empty streets, and no mortal who has entered has left, and no vampyre dares pass its gates, for it takes their magick and power, and none return from it since the fall of the priests."

"When did you go there?" I asked.

"When my mother passed me the Sacred Kiss," she whispered. "She, a queen of many lands, wife of Merod, pressed her mouth over mine as she slit my throat. I fled the city as soon as I could, for in its depths . . . A terrible ancient sorcery burned beneath it. It was to Pergamos and Alkemara I went to live, and rule as Pythoness in the temples of Datbathani, Our Lady of Serpents. But Myrryd is in my nightmares. Artephius has been there, for he sought its magick. He has told me of the riches and lore found in its deepest vaults, in those places where even vampyres do not go. Yet, Myrryd stole much from him, and he barely escaped. It is where he stole the grimoire, with secrets of Medhya within it. The words of blood on pages of human skin. My father had once read these as well. Artephius bound the scrolls of Medhya's blood and flesh, and the sinew of the gray priests of the Nahhash bind it— and it is from this grimoire that he learned much of his art."

"He would destroy us both, given the chance. You should never have allied yourself with that alchemist."

"Your *father*?" When she saw the blank stare I offered at her words, she shook her head. "But you know it is true. He loved me. He loved you, though he might sacrifice us both. I cannot blame him for what he seeks—all wish for immortality on this earth."

"It is for his own vanity he seeks it. He would destroy all

vampyres . . . and mortals, as well . . ." I began, but did not continue the thought.

"Yes," she said. "But if he found the essence of immortality itself, he would bring Death to her knees. I have seen Death herself when I was a priestess—she is a child, blinded by the storm ravens, who wanders where there is suffering, attended by her handmaidens, who guide her to those who suffer most. I do not wish to see her. I do not wish to know the taste of mortal death again."

"I do not believe the alchemist would serve the good of the mortal world with this knowledge," I said. "I believe he would create gods and terrors to enslave the kingdoms of men."

"As we have done?" she asked, without expecting an answer. "Sometimes, when I go into the day's sleep, I think I deserve a terrible death. Mortality has put me in mind of the crimes I have committed. As an immortal, they were no crimes for me to grieve. But as a mortal woman, I have done such things as monsters dream of. My instinct is to murder, to drain the mortal of blood, and to love the act."

I wished to take her mind from such troubling thoughts. "The tune you hummed moments ago, that your shepherd boy taught you—are there words?"

She nodded, and began singing:

> *Upon a hill, beyond the fields,*
> *A maiden lives with sorrow gray*
> *And I shall go and catch her tears*
> *For greater than gold are they.*
> *And I shall make of them a crown*
> *To rest upon her lovely head*
> *And it will shine above her brow*
> *Even after she is dead—*
> *And when she dies I, too, shall go*
> *To fields where the dead remain*
> *To make a crown of sorrow*
> *That she might wear it once again.*

She broke off suddenly. "It is a song of mortality. You will make a crown of sorrow one day. I have not thought of death for thousands of years. It has not concerned me. I did not think a mortal vampyre could exist. I will begin to grow old, as well, for I can feel the pull of the earth upon me."

She drew the drape from the small window at the door.

Looking out, she said, "I have not felt mortal concerns before. Even in my mortal life, I did not think of death. Even when the Sacred Kiss was bestowed upon me, I had no fear, though my body grew cold in the grave for three nights. My mother brought me to this existence, but with my father looking on. My sisters, too. We were more than his children. We were his slaves. Do you understand what that means? Yes, I believe you do. We were slaves to his will and his whim and his ambition. He was not just a Priest of Blood, of the Kamr priests. He was a king of Pergamos and of Alkemara and of what remained of Myrryd itself, though other rulers sat upon the thrones of their palaces. I ruled my people in my provinces. Yet, I hated him for how he had cursed us with the Sacred Kiss. And yet . . . to be immortal again . . ."

She turned back to face me and clutched her belly. "A child grows here, where none should. You—the only vampyre who could plant a seed within a mortal woman—have done this to me. I see my death, Maz-Sherah. I see it in your love. I have no love in my heart, but you . . . you are close to your youth, even now. You are but a short time from the end of your mortal life. Love still lives within you. I own a mortal heartbeat now, but I have no heart within me. I have done terrible things in my long existence. I cannot undo them, nor do I believe they were against my nature. When I first brought you the Sacred Kiss, and the breath of immortality, the terror I felt . . . of knowing I had awakened a new Maz-Sherah. That all the terrible visions I had of my own destruction would come to me through you—and I was the instrument of your becoming vampyre. If I had but killed you . . ."

"You must not look at the past in this way," I said. "What is done is done. We cannot grieve those footsteps in the mud behind us, for to retrace them is not to wipe them clean but to set ourselves deep in the clay and be unable to move forward."

"Your words bring no comfort," she said. She touched the edge of her upper lip, at the border of the mask and her flesh. "This has stolen my immortality. This, too," she said, again pressing her hands into her belly. "This child will steal my mortality. I have felt it. My body is not made for this birth." Her eyes glistened with tears. "I am weak from mortality. I am heavy from it. I grow sick when I awaken, and it is the illness of the lowliest maid whose child grows within her."

"It is life, within you," I said.

"Or death. This is the fulfillment of all the prophecies I know," she said. She approached me and put her hands against my face. The gold mask shimmered as she approached me. "It is you who breached the Veil, and brought the Myrrydanai through—by your presence alone, and by your taking of the Veil's juice into your blood. You burned the stream, nearly destroying it, when you allowed another vampyre to drink of your Veil-tainted blood. I felt this even across the sea. Within you, my father lives—for you fulfilled a prophecy when you devoured him. It is not his body that is within you, but his soul. He seeks a way out from you, as well. But you polluted my body with the creation of this child. I do not know if this child is monster or mortal, vampyre or goddess, but it is a door for the Dark Madonna who wishes our destruction—and the enslavement of the mortal realm. But even against all this, I have that terrible mortal instinct to protect this child, though it is a passageway for Medhya and the end of our kind—and the destruction of much that exists on this earth."

"I have learned in these years that all that is prophesied by the ancient ones does not come to pass."

"I have lived longer, and I have seen too many prophecies made flesh." Saying this, she reached up and sliced a fingernail against my cheek, drawing blood. She held her bloodstained hand to her face. "If I were to kill myself, the child would die with me. If I bled, I would pass away as any mortal."

I grabbed her wrist, drawing it from her face. "What if our child is the reason we are both here? What if there is another prophecy, unknown to you? What if all that was once written is dead, and all that we write, here, today, lives for the future? What if I prophesy that our child will grow in daylight, and will become a great mortal, and will be part of a world that Medhya cannot touch?"

She tried to strike me with her hands, but I held them tight. "When you have lived as I," she spat at me, "then you will understand. When you see a thousand times a thousand mortal lifetimes pass, then you may begin to know how these prophecies come to light. For you, I waited through the ages, and when you came, I knew you, for I had studied such things and found scrolls you could not hope to decipher. I worshipped gods that were like you, Falconer. But I watched those gods break like fragile stone against the trembling of time itself. You learn through visions, Maz-Sherah. You have seen many. But have you seen the vision of the priestess who wears the gold mask?"

As she spoke, I felt something clutch at my throat. I did not want to remember such visions.

"On a bleak plain," she said, her voice growing soft as she spoke, cold and soft, and lulling me into a memory I did not want to recall. "Wearing ceremonial robes. Holding a curved knife, meant to be used for sacrifice. Do you remember such a thing? Yes, I see the light in your soul as it flickers with the memory. My father showed you that moment. He revealed the objects necessary for such a sacrifice upon a great altar stone. He is there in that vision, is he not? With his tattoos coming alive upon his body? The Nahhashim staff. The curved blade. The mask of Datbathani upon the maiden's face. But did you notice the swelling of that maiden's belly? Did you notice the sky on fire all around? The beasts of the Veil beginning to come through? Did you hear the whispering of the Myrrydanai at their great moment of becoming? This was not some dream you have had, nor some idle unspoken prophecy.

"Shall I tell you what will happen? I have shared this vision, too, and read of it in the ancient scrolls. I saw it when I brought the Sacred Kiss to you. It is the last day of light in the world, Maz-Sherah. It is the day when the Veil tears, and those beasts of Hell draw Medhya into the world upon their backs. The plagues sent from the Veil are but harbingers of this terrible night to come. The earth slowly turns to an age of winter, and even now, famine reaches across the seas. Soon ice will cover more than the sea beyond Taranis-Hir. Plagues have come from the Myrrydanai and the bog sorcery, and spread on the winds. Mortals grow weak, and the dream of the Disk has persuaded them to accept the words of the whispering shadows. What my father called the Myrr—that invisible boundary—a glass that fueled the city of Myrryd, brought from the Veil by the first priests—will cover the earth in darkness. We are the instruments of this. My father held the gate closed to Medhya within his own body, and he could not be destroyed by ordinary means. Only the Maz-Sherah could take him into his flesh, and only you—only you, Falconer—contain that locked door, behind which Medhya may come through. I tell you, I know this will destroy you, and you will break like those statues of heroes and gods that are broken along the walls of Alkemara. We have both had the vision of the altar. Altars exist for sacrifice. You and I are there, and I am shackled as the victim of this ritual."

We both went silent.

"We have both failed," I said, after several minutes. "The vision I saw of the maiden at the altar was not fulfilled in sacrifice, though it seemed it. Nor did I see terror in her face. It was a mystery put before me—and before you. It is something that cannot be spoken of in words, but must be lived, I think, for in visions, all is not as it seems. If this is you, in this vision, perhaps it may yet be undone. We will not know if we do not continue our journey. I believe our child may grow into a great leader, and should we fail in this quest to destroy the Myrrydanai, and to mend the Veil that Medhya and the leviathans and behemoths of this other world do not cross into the world of mortal men and women, perhaps our child will have the strength to be more than a daughter of Alkemara, and a Maz-Sherah. For I have heard that many Maz-Sherah have failed over the centuries, and if I join them, I believe what you and I create in this child may overcome our failings."

At first I thought she intended to attack me, for she rushed to me swiftly, and embraced me as if to choke me into my Extinguishing. She did not weep, nor did she speak, but she held me for a long moment, and only released me when we heard the shouts of sailors on the decks.

When we had gone out on deck, a youth pointed up to the mast and shouted, "There, we see a beast from hell!"

Without a thought, I unfurled my wings and shot upward, catching my hands on the limp sail.

The night's mist was heavy, but through it, I made out the vague shape of a creature like a crouched gargoyle clinging to the top of the mast.

• 9 •

I crawled toward it, as quietly as I could. It must have sensed me, and it took off into the mist, crying out like a gull as it went.

I tried to follow it, but could not find it in the haze.

When I returned to Pythia, I spoke of the corpse-vampyre. "It is like us, but without glamour. Why it has followed us, and yet not attacked—or spoken—I cannot understand."

"Nezahual had many dungeons and prisons in his temples, and a menagerie of creatures I could not bear to look upon," she said. "This may be some beast sent to spy upon us."

"To retrieve what was stolen," I said.

Instinctively, she clutched the pouch at her waist. "If it has flown off, it is probably on one of those other ships mired nearby," she said. "I do not feel danger from it. Do you?"

I shook my head. "Not danger. In the stream, I felt its weakness. What if that orb calls to it? For it has followed us too well. I do not like this, for we have burden enough without this stranger stalking us."

"We will hunt it after we have drunk our fill," she said, but within minutes, an alarm sounded across the ship's decks. The sailors on watch cried out, and I sniffed the air.

"Do you smell it?" Pythia asked.

"It's the wind," I said. "It is coming from the east."

Even as I said these words, there was a great, terrible creaking sound, as if every board of the ship groaned in pain. The *Illuyanka* shifted restlessly in the now-moving waters, and I heard the crack of thunder in the mist that moved like a broom, sweeping across the sea. Flashes of lightning in the dark clouds overhead tore at the fabric of the fog, and I thought of Illuyanek and his dream of the brothers of the wind as they agitated the sisters of the water itself—for this is what it seemed like as the squall came upon us all of a sudden.

I saw it—the rising waves in the distance that had cleared of mist—and the cries of the remaining men as they took their posts. The rain came like a sheet of shattering jewels against the deep early morning, before the sun, before the warm vibration of dawn. The waves rose up and slapped across the decks so that some went below, though others shouted for them to return.

I flew to the highest mast, feeling the wind whipping at my wings as if trying to shred them. I clung to the mast as the sails shifted, turning first left and then right as the men at the rigging drew them to and fro with their skill at handling the roughest of winds. With the sun threatening a pale light beyond the darkening storm, I joined Pythia belowdecks, away from the comforts of the upper cabin, and remained far beneath in the depths of the ship, until we awoke in the night to hear the cries of men far above, and that endless groaning of the ship—and the cracking of one of the masts as it broke far above us.

II

OPHION

◆ CHAPTER 5 ◆

The Distant War Cry

◆ 1 ◆

FIVE nights had passed since Pythia and I fled Aztlanteum's fall, and before the sixth night ended, the ship had been thrown into the maelstrom of a storm, battered and bloodied. Fewer than a dozen men aboard survived—the sea had claimed several men. Two of the seven masts had broken—one smashed the captain's cabin down its center after midnight, damaging the deck below. Men lashed themselves to masts and wheel, and some hid belowdecks with the Storm Dreamer. Pythia could not rest in the night, nor would she drink the blood of the remaining men, for she feared their strength would be gone if the gale continued. I took orders from one of the sailors who knew the ship as well as any captain might have, and managed to draw at least one man back from the brink of death as waves washed across the foundering ship.

The storm also brought blessings, for the men who remained were able sailors and believed in the prophecies of their Storm Dreamer. The *Illuyanka* had been shot by the storm like a stray arrow, and yet the ship had traveled many more leagues than it would have been able to under passable weather.

Despite the damage and loss, in the day and half the night, the vessel sped along as if propelled by engines, for the fierce storm did not abate, and pushed us halfway across the ocean.

I consulted Illuyanek in his bunk. He thanked us both for the "demon blessings," and for bringing food and water and the burning leaf from the abandoned ships. "You must fly now, my good demon," he said. "For as you pass through the layers of night, you will see that the dark remains ahead of you, even while light comes from behind. If you move swiftly, you will reach such islands where you may find a day's rest, with many mortals to quench your thirst."

I did not wish to remind him of his own death, which he had dreamed of, nor could I ask him of the fate of the remaining crew, for fear that he would tell me of some misfortune. Yet, as if understanding my silent thoughts, he raised his eyebrows and smiled slowly. "Oh, these men will reach their homes, good demon. But I will pass to the halls of my ancestors before my foot touches the threshold of my own doorway. Yet, do you not understand such prophecy?" He chuckled. "For if I never return to my house, I will not die soon. Instead, I will go to the emperor's palace and live out my days. I will think of you, my friend. I hope we will meet once more before my last breath comes."

"This is my hope, as well," I said, clasping his hands in mine.

"Tell your lady demon that I have dreamed of a child, a boy, who will one day remember this journey his mother has taken, and will thank her for it," he said.

♦ 2 ♦

PYTHIA wept as she left the ship, for the old man had touched her heart deeply. When the worst of the gale had ended—with several hours until dawn—we departed the *Illuyanka*, and the wind was with us as we spread our wings and passed across the still-roiling seas. Illuyanek had been right—as we traveled, if we kept up a swift flight—it was as if the night grew deeper. The wind pushed at our wings, sending us faster into the dark, and though I thought dawn would come soon, it seemed as if it lingered far behind us.

As we approached several islands, I saw again the line of frozen sea along their edges, for the terrible winters of the plagues had touched that edge of the world.

We spent two nights traveling, sleeping during the short days in caves and in the broken tombs of the dead—for we passed through cities and villages, just long enough to drink blood and sleep, and then take off into the sky again.

After we had crossed many thousand miles, Pythia found her way toward that poisoned city where she had first taken my life—and so we came again to Hedammu, upon the great cliffs above the sapphire sea.

I did not sense the following of the strange vampyre, nor did I know if he had survived the storms as we had. A sensation had taken over the stream, interrupting my feel of it, as sometimes happened on long journeys.

Yet, as we came to the towers of Hedammu, I did not believe the vampyre had left us.

The towers of Hedammu were nearly as I remembered them. I had barely been more than a boy when I first approached the poisoned city. Now, many years after death, I felt that another life had been lived between the youth I had once been and the creature I had become. The gates of the city had been both torn and held tight by ropes, locked as if to keep the devil in and those called by the devil out.

I crawled like a spider along the side of the jawlike gates and looked across the empty courtyards. Pythia called to me from one of the open chambers at the top of the northernmost tower, and I flew to her. She had gone to the place where many vampyres had extinguished, but found no guard, no one left of our tribe here.

As I stood beside her, I glanced back, scanning the night sky for the vampyre who I was sure still followed us.

"I had hoped that some would be here," Pythia said. "For this is the birthplace of many of our tribe."

I shook my head to her hopes. "Kiya had raised her army and fought when I lay imprisoned. They were defeated, and many went to their Extinguishing. Others were captured and have become the mindless servants of Enora and the Myrrydanai." Even as I said these words, I understood what we would have to do, even here, in Hedammu.

I leaned across the tower spur and looked out across the sea, and then toward the mountains.

I saw some small speck of darkness moving along the mountaintop. Though it might have been a beast of some kind, I suspected it was the vampyre I had seen on the *Il-luyanka*. I did not like this creature following without speaking, without showing what threat he presented. I was sure that if I flew out to that distant mountain, he would have already flown many miles from me.

I could not spend my nights chasing a flying corpse. So I ignored the distant threat and instead focused on what we would need to do next before returning to Taranis-Hir. "Both you and I have the breath of the Sacred Kiss within us. There may still be battles waged in the cities along the shores of this land. We need warriors—and we shall gather them from these Crusader wars. If you are not with me, you are against me. Choose now, Pythoness. We have loved, and we have despised each other. You murdered me, and you resurrected me. We bring a child to this world. But you and I both know the vision of the end of this. It may be our doom. I cannot predict the future, nor can you, despite visions and omens. There is more at stake than the forest of my childhood or the friends I have left in their prisons. You know of these things—for you fear Medhya and her Myrrydanai dogs as well. You have helped me escape, you have brought me here. But it is not enough. We must raise the dead now. We must bring warriors to the war. Will you help me?"

When I did not hear an answer, I turned to her, expecting her rage or disdain. I could not help but wonder at the vast depths within her form—the fury, the unbroken will, the torrents of passion, the steel, the heat, and the fierce mind. Pythia was a magnificent vampyre, and if she had decided those centuries ago not to follow her own passions, she might have become a great priestess of her tribe—or a queen of the world.

"Yes," she said, resignation in her voice, and smoldering fury in the mask upon her face. "I will help you raise the dead."

• 3 •

I spent the last hours of the night hunting the fortresses to the north and the south looking for signs of war, and did not have to fly far or fast to find them. The men of my country and of many others had increased their attacks on the Saracens and those armies of the east in those years since I last fought as a mortal. No doubt the Veil plagues had fanned the flames of religious ardor and the hunger for blood sport among fighting men. I found three cities under siege, and one fallen; still others had captured the invaders. Within the walls of these garrisons, fights broke out like small battles among the market stalls and courtyards. But the closest siege raged several miles to the south, just over the next mountain range.

A hundred ships were in the port, and Crusaders had taken over the towns of the harbor, all bearing the banners of those lands and provinces near my homeland. I saw both the Knights of the Temple and Knights of the Hospital among the garden of tents and mean shelters built in that fervor of war that still held my countrymen in its grip. Miles inland, across a scorched plain made empty by war and drought, a fortress loomed, as imposing as any of the Saracen strongholds.

Siege towers stood like mute giants, tall as the city walls, great ugly beasts of construction, to be dragged toward the fortress come dawn, with the battle beginning before the afternoon. Some of these machines lay in ruins, destroyed by rock and flame in a previous day's fight. There were piles of the dead from a recent battle just outside the tall citadel of the Saracens.

When I returned to Pythia, she had already gone to her day's rest. Before sunrise, I lay down with her, wrapping my arms about her.

I touched the black orb in its pouch at her waist and felt that slight pulse of life within it. In touching it, I wanted it, though I did not yet understand its hidden secrets. I watched her gentle breaths as she slept, her eyes fluttering lightly in a mortal's dream. The gold mask rippled slightly. For just a moment I felt I was not looking at Pythia at all, but at that Dark Madonna's face on the gold mask itself, a third eye painted at her forehead, scorn upon her brow.

I fought sleep, but finally gave in as my mind turned to the darkness of oblivion.

• 4 •

A vision of Medhya came in my sleep:

The Dark Mother crouched, her weight pressing upon my chest, making my breath slow and laborious. The skin of her face was like an opal darkness. Through it, I saw the strange ghostly orbs that somehow carried her life force through her body. Her face was hideous—not the noble face of statues, not the beautiful Queen of Myrryd—she was monstrous in her deformity. Every part of her skin from her throat to her brow wriggled with life as if thousands of small shiny maggots moved, in a rapid mass, over and around each other—a city of tenebrous larvae, constantly moving, creating the impression of facial features—a gaping mouth, two holes for nostrils, and her eyes, empty and dark as if all light had been sucked from them, with a third eye painted across the wriggling mass at the center of her brow.

Her hair was wild and seemed a nest of vipers and brambles. Her wings were her outer cloak, which drew back to reveal the rose-flesh robe of human faces as if sewn into cloth, covering much of her body. What was revealed from her waist to her breasts seemed to be a series of teeth, strung as an undergarment.

"Maz-Sherah," she whispered, her voice a burned whisper. She sniffed at my face. "I smell Merod inside you. You are good to bring him to me."

Her mouth was empty of teeth, and the teeming maggots dropped from her ragged lips as she spoke. She reached down, and with the curved blades of her fingernails, gently felt between my lips for my own teeth, reaching for my incisors.

"Oh." She seemed to shiver with pleasure. "You were born to tear the Veil. I have loved you, Maz-Sherah, and felt your presence. My breath is in you and gives you great power. You are not like the traitor priests, my child, my boy. You are to be my lord and master, and I will come to you in the flesh of love that you may know me." Her fingers pushed farther into my mouth. The larvae and beetles that crawled along her face began to drop down onto my tomb's bed, and as they did, I saw the emptiness behind their wriggling mass—she was a hollow darkness, clothed in the creatures of the grave. "It is nearly the solstice, my love, and you are far away from me. Mortals from the cliffs seek to destroy Myrrydanai and their earthly queen who rules the wastelands since the burning of the Forest—but you are not there to help them, Maz-Sherah. Why are you not there? Has Pythia misguided you? I hear the cries of your lovers and your children, even now, even here within the Veil. The ashling calls to the elementals for news of your destruction or return. A vampyre of great beauty cries out to you from his torment. Your son wails for mercy, and your daughter weeps, but they shall be my little mortal rats soon."

A shadow of three dimensions, she pushed her hand farther into my mouth, to the back of my throat. I no longer felt a woman's hand there, but the slick moist skin of a fish of some kind—an eel or a pike—choking me as she pushed her forearm farther down my throat.

"My breath and my blood are in you," she said. "But so is a traitor. *Merod of the Kamr.*" She spoke his name as if it were a curse. "Stealer of sorceries, betrayer—priest of mud, and he will forever be in mud and muck when I come to you, my love."

I could not breathe. It felt as if wriggling parasites swam in my blood and encircled my heart as the hollow darkness watched me and whispered. "I will find the priest in you, my sweet youth, my liberator. I will burn his soul from your blood. You have come to bring me to flesh. I desire this mask stolen from my priests, and this fire sword. You will bring them to me, for I will reward you greatly." I felt a tearing at my heart, a white-hot pain that shot through my very being.

◆ 5 ◆

I came out of the vision, gasping for air. My heart pounded rapidly, and my throat was dry.

Fire sword. Merod had told me, in the silver mirrors at Taranis-Hir, of such a weapon. *A sword made of fire.* A weapon against Medhya.

Pythia stared down at me. "You went into the Veil," she said. "Its venom is in your blood." She said this as if she had not fully understood it before. "You are opening the Veil, Falconer, even as you exist, as you breathe. You are allowing it to tear."

"No," I said, catching my breath as if I had come up for air from deep water. "I am going to close it. The war of the vampyres will be brought down upon the Myrrydanai."

"If it is too late . . ."

I refused to consider this. "In the Forest—on the cliffs called the Akkadites—elemental spirits told me that the solstice was the time when Medhya would come through. We are still several nights from it. We must return."

"Do not believe such things," Pythia said. "Medhya cannot come into this world without you. I lived many lifetimes before you came to me, Falconer. I once believed in heroes. In what could be done. But I have met heroes greater than you. Though I feared you once, I no longer have fear *of* you. I fear *for* you. We cannot stop a force as great as Medhya from breaking through the Veil. She will have her vengeance. Her Myrrydanai are more powerful than the Kamr priests. The Great Serpent once walked the earth, but now hides from his children. I know where the sorceries of Medhya were born, for I have heard the legends. They are from the nameless depths beneath Myrryd itself, from a sorcery older than the magick of our tribe. This mask—the rituals—were not created by the priests of Myrryd, but by an ancient race of those depths. These things cannot be fought, cannot be changed. But you and I have created a child between us. I am mortal. My child is mortal. We could return to Alkemara and rest there until my child is born. If you avoid the fate set for you, Medhya may not gain in power—for her power is linked to yours. She would not have this mask. You know this. The Myrrydanai would fade in some distant year. The plagues would end. The Veil would heal on its own."

"When? Next year?" I asked.

"Many years. But a short time in . . . in your existence."

"When you are dead, will it heal on its own? Will the plagues that have ravaged this world also fade? Will the frozen seas thaw?"

She closed her eyes. "Our son would see life. Does that mean nothing to you?"

"What of my other children? My friends? Our tribe? We would hide for years and let them suffer? What of the darkness that will come to the earth if you are wrong? Your child will be enslaved to such priests as the Myrrydanai."

"You do not understand her power. She needs you there, for she draws power from you. Do you not understand? She draws her own breath from yours. If we fight her—we are lost."

I touched her shoulder gently and looked into her eyes, as if trying to find the Pythoness who had once shown no fear.

"You will extinguish," she said.

I turned away from her.

"We need to raise an army," I said. "Tonight. Soon, for they will not resurrect fully for three nights. I need at least a hundred warriors with us. I will not abandon those I have promised to rescue."

◆ 6 ◆

WE reached the mountain ledge that overlooked the battlefield. The roar of the warriors was like the howling of jackals on the hunt. I saw the trails marked by the rising dust where they had retreated, and another line of men had advanced. Siege engines burned along the dusky plain. Huge gouges had been taken out of the fortress's heavy walls from the trebuchet's onslaught. Fires were lit among the tents and town at the shore. The Saracens sent showers of burning arrows down into the Crusaders' midst, while the soldiers of my country rattled their shields and threw spears at the enemy who had come on horseback from towns beyond the fortress to slice sword and ax into the invaders' flesh.

"Do not take great risks," I told Pythia. "Be cautious. Only approach those who have fallen. If a man draws his weapon, leave him. But find as many strong men as you can, and make them vow to serve us before you give the Sacred Kiss. Not all will take the oath, but many will. These men love war."

◆ 7 ◆

THE constant sounds of horn and hew and the endless battle cries arose like calls from Death herself. The dust rose along the darkling plain as a thousand men or more raced toward the walls of the battered citadel.

Thirteen horsemen led the most recent charge—knights of England—and behind them, those servant-soldiers who had dedicated their lives to the recapture of Jerusalem, to the hands of Heaven itself, and to the spoils of war promised by their masters. A storm of arrows flew from their outer flanks, many of them breaching the sand-colored walls, while the sky seemed to rain with fire as their enemy—the Saracens, as my people had called them— poured oil and lobbed burning bundles over the towers upon the aggressor below. Their allies had drawn off the invaders at the north and south, and were driving them back to the sea, a journey of many miles.

The spears raised, the battering ram held high as shielded men ran with it to the chaste gates of the Saracen strong-hold. Horses keened terrible sounds as they were struck down, and many knights fell as arrows and great stones from the walls themselves rained down on them. The fury of the soldiers quickened, and I could sense the white-hot fire in their hearts as the swords clashed and horns blew.

A new Saracen army of thirty or more came around from the north on horseback to attack those who laid siege to their city. Mortal courage was great that night, and the slaughter seemed equal to both sides. A standard-bearer led the charge to the city gates, and the remaining siege machines were run by dozens of men pushing them hard into position, even while their enemies shot arrows into their midst and hacked at those who guarded them.

Fires brightened the city walls, and from these heights, burning logs dropped down upon the soldiers below who had begun ramming the gate to the city. A man caught fire and ran through the midst of the others, his final cries fad-ing as he fell to the earth.

The siege engines groaned as they released their cargo—great fallen slabs and burning bundles, some of them clearing the high wall, others slamming into the stone and falling down upon the soldiers whose army had sent the missives.

I saw the great leader of the Crusaders—a man in a mud-died white robe beneath which a white tunic carried the long cross of crimson. His shield took much battering as he drove his horse against the tide of the oncoming Saracen. His dark horse, shot with arrows, still pushed through the slashing of sword and spear and ax, and did not fall.

The general on horseback—a prince, no doubt—slammed his shield against the heads of some men, while thrusting his blade into others. Those closest to him, on foot and on horse, proved themselves brave and able men as they fought the impossible odds of this terrible fight.

Many went down to the earth, their limbs shorn from their bodies; many retreated, deserting the others. But there were those whose swords glimmered like stars in the night, who raised torch and weapon against the Saracen lord whose army poured forth from the broken gates, pushing back the invader, back across the plain. Fires had broken out from the siege engines, and many boys and men lost their lives to an idea of conquest that would bring no victory.

✦ 8 ✦

PYTHIA turned to me, her voice was uncontrollably excited and held a monstrous deliciousness, as if the delight of mortal bloodshed brought a sexual thrill. "Do you smell it? Ah, blood, it is so wonderful. The flow is sweet, and smells of springtime. Hundreds lie there in death throes!"

How could I be so enthralled by such a creature? The moments of warmth and affection we shared in private did not seem to have changed her love for the blood sport. Yet I would be a hypocrite not to understand this, for the scent of fresh mortal blood brought a thrill beneath my skin, as well; yet her unabashed excitement filled me with dread for our tribe. Blood was good, and it truly was sweet. While I could cling to my mortal memories, in which I would be repelled by such thoughts, the raw animal of vampyre in me longed for the taste of newly torn flesh and its liquid bounty.

She pointed to the scene below us, to a clutch of warriors who lay together, victims of arrows shot from the yellow towers.

Through the dark and smoke, I saw soldiers, and horses—and the knights who had failed in their siege—all lying amidst the wreckage of wagons and shields and swords and spears—many of them gone to the threshold of Death, but some still breathing.

Among them, the strippers—young boys of eleven or twelve—who skittered among the dead, gathering weapons and armor from those who no longer needed them. Now and then, an arrow would sing through the air, and catch one of the boys as he lifted shield or ax—the Saracens did not wish for the invader to recover weapons for the next onslaught of fighting.

I did not love watching this carnage, for it reminded me too much of the battles I had fought—watching my own brother be cut down for the vanity of the knights on horseback, many of whom could ride away to their camp when retreat was necessary—but not so for the foot soldiers, who often would be mowed down.

Pythia stood upon the ledge and stretched her arms up to the sky. "Perhaps I am mortal, but I feel the power of our tribe in me. It has been too long since I have been able to hunt like this!" Her wings spread out, narrower and bonier than mine—they had thinned a bit since mortality had overtaken her flesh. The wings seemed made of fine dark silk, taut against the arch of bone that held them aloft.

She crouched again as if ready to swoop from the crag into the valley, but glanced back at me. "I want a young one. One like you when you came to me. Beautiful and fierce. I want him to struggle against my jaws. I want to feel that again—that love. That taste."

"Go down there now, and you're dead," I warned her. "We must wait until they have given up for the night. Only then do we seek the dying from among the bodies. It's one thing to grab a lone traveler, or a laundress carrying her bundle before dawn. But there, you will surely be slaughtered."

Pythia had not quite grasped mortality. To know a vampyre with full powers, with the ability to spread the great dark wings, to grow sharp teeth at the moment when touching the throat's flesh, and to bring the greatest of vampyric gifts to the mortal—the Sacred Kiss—and yet, still to be subject to mortal death—this seemed to go against every law of our tribe she had known. She had spent years invincible to harm, and now—the Gorgon Mask upon her face, leaching out her immortal essence— she might be killed. An infection might send her to a slow, painful death. Yet, she still had vampyric energy within her, and she still craved blood, and would only survive upon its flow.

"Then go grab me the most beautiful youth," she said, surveying the men far below. Could she see them, individually? For her remaining powers would still be stronger than mine. "A French boy. With yellow hair. A servant-soldier, perhaps, but one with blood upon him from the many he has slain."

"Like me," I said, "When I was in a valley like this one, not more than an hour's flight from here—fighting to the death."

"Like you. Look!" she cried out, pointing into the distance as a rabble of soldiers took down a great Saracen lord and his horse, and swarmed over him like locusts after grain.

I sat upon my haunches along the distant mountains, a demon watching the folly of mortal men. "When you have passed the breath to your intended," I said, "raise him up and bring him to these caves, for they must be prepared for their first night as vampyre."

"I am not new to this." She grinned at me, and her mask seemed a great blank of flat yellow rock. "I have brought many to our tribe. We will give them a bed within the dark and bring them mortal vessels to drink on their first rising."

After several hours, when many fires had died, and many men had fallen; when the horns at the gates sounded, and the Saracens withdrew; when the rallying cries of the Crusaders had gone mute, and the dead outnumbered the living, the remaining knights gathered their soldiers and returned to their camps, leaving behind their dead and those who were left for dead; after all this, with but four hours until sunrise, we leapt from the mountainside, and like the death-birds themselves, circled the dying below.

• 9 •

AVOIDING the strippers who ran about quietly drawing off armor, lifting shields, grabbing poleaxes, I crouched down among the men whose legs had been torn from them, and those whose faces had been battered in by cudgels and axes, and skulked along the periphery of the dead, listening for the sound of life. As I drew close to a fallen knight, his helmet drawn off his head and most of his armor already stolen, I saw that small bubbles of blood moved from his lips. His own men had left him for dead, and he lay there in mail and a tunic, even his shoes taken from him.

I tore off a bit of cloth from my shirt and wiped his lips clear of blood. I pressed my head near his mouth and heard steady but troubled breathing.

"Can you hear me, sir?" I asked him. I did not see a response in his eyes, which stared up at the stars. I took his hand in mine and squeezed. He squeezed back, lightly at first, and then with some strength.

I brought my lips near his left ear, and whispered, "You are near death. But you may live again, if you desire. If you would become a creature as I am—a vampyre, you would regain your strength, although blood would be your sustenance, and you would be hunted my mortal men. I will save you if you swear an oath of loyalty to me. Squeeze my fingers if you will follow me. Let your hand go limp if you would rather die."

Even as I spoke these words, I thought of the torments of my existence, and was certain this knight—a man of holy orders, perhaps—would accept his death.

But I felt his tugging at my hand, and he gripped it so tightly that I winced.

"I must drink from you first," I said. "Then I will breathe immortality into your lungs." Swiftly, I leaned into the wounds at his side and drank of him.

Afterward, I pressed my mouth over his, and as I did so, he began to fight me, but with little strength left to him. I felt him squirm and try to close his mouth against mine, but the Sacred Kiss was too strong, and he could only yield to it. The burning breath poured down his throat, and as I let him go, his body went limp.

I lifted the man up, spread my wings again, and rose into the darkness, unseen by the mortals below, save for one stripping boy, who cried out and called, "Devils! Devils!" as he saw me. He went running back to the distant camp, dropping what he had gathered as he went.

I found many of these dying warriors within the next few hours, and each of them swore loyalty to me. I had not expected so many of them to wish for vampyrism, for I saw none of the advantages of this existence, only its curse and burden. Yet these men gladly wished for eternal youth, and immortal life, over their fear of the touch of death.

Pythia, too, had brought several corpses to the caves high in the mountain peak. An arrow had singed her shoulder, and I grew worried for her safety—but she told me she felt stronger for the passing of the Sacred Kiss. "I did not think I could carry one of them, but bringing the breath up from my soul, I felt that surge of power I thought I had lost when my immortality passed. Then, that *resistance*. It is as if Death herself is nearby, furious at me for bringing the dying back to this world."

We placed the bodies as far back from the cave's mouth as we could, and although we did not gather one hundred men on that first night, still, I counted nearly fifty before dawn.

The following night, again, we waited until the last of the battle was through, and again, the Crusaders had been fought back to the sea, leaving their dead and those believed dead along the dusty roads and plain.

◆ 10 ◆

OUT of concern for the Saracen arrows, I accompanied Pythia the second night. Eagerly, she went to those who still had breath in them. We found two friends clasping each other's shoulders as if wishing to enter the next world together. Both still breathed—one had open wounds upon his chest and legs, and the other had been stabbed in the ribs, the broken spear still stuck in his side.

As she leaned over one of them, whispering of oaths and immortality, I noticed that the pouch hung low at her waist. I reached over and stealthily drew the small globe from it. She did not notice, and I held the orb up, feeling its pulse in my hand.

It was a living rock, shiny as obsidian.

Alive, in my hand. A pulse.

Beyond this pulse, I felt a tingling sensation at my wrist. This shot upward along my arm and elbow, and became a kind of burning along my shoulder as it moved in a lightning bolt toward my throat. I gasped, trying to cry out, but I barely made a sound. I felt the earth spin around me, as if my mind had been thrown into a whirlwind. I dropped to my knees from nausea and the force of the burning at my throat and along my jaw.

A strange light that was another blackness—as if a lantern of night itself, cast upon the night—came from the orb. It was as if light were reversed to darkness, yet still illuminating the path of its beam.

In dark light, I saw strange figures moving among the dead, which had not been there before. These phantoms were robed in white, and at their center was a child, a little girl, with a blindfold upon her face. The women with her guided her among the bodies of the dead. I noticed that each of them held an object that was very much like the orb I also held.

Suddenly, one of the robed women turned her head and looked directly at me.

She was a ghostly image against that strange blackness that projected outward from the orb. It was as if I had startled a doe in the woods, for she gave an impression of panic, yet she stood completely still as if she did not understand what threatened her. Her face was a blur, and I could not see features other than the general impression of eyes and mouth.

She stepped out from among her companions and began to move toward me. She stepped over many bodies, although it was as if she floated upon them. The ghost came to me, her robes like a nun's habit, but made from fabric of blurred white light.

"You have something that belongs to me," she said, her voice calm and sonorous, and were I mortal, I might have fallen into deep sleep from such a lulling tone.

"Who are you? Are these your sisters who tend the dying and sick? Why do you wander the field of the dead?"

"You see me?" she asked, and even as she said this, I saw the contours of her eyes and brow and nose and lips more clearly. Her face was an oval of tan, as if she spent long hours in the fields, a laborer. Although she was young, she had a careworn look. Her robe began to show the stains of the blood from those she had tended on the battlefield.

"What sisterhood are you?"

One of her companions noticed us talking in that orb light and moved along the paths between the bodies until she reached us.

"You have something that belongs to us," the first woman said.

"This?" I asked, turning the orb in my hand. "This is not yours. We brought it from across the sea."

"You're an undead," she said with some disgust. "This was stolen from my mistress's home, long ago."

"Your mistress? Who is she?"

She pointed to the child who, with blindfold on, leaned over, and touched a dead man's forehead as if she knew him.

"Is the field of battle a place for children to play their games?"

"She plays no game, unclean one. She is a reaper of the earth, for the harvesttime has come, and many must be gathered."

I looked at the little girl. She seemed common enough, even though I knew she must be Death herself. She did not seem royal or noble, but had the look of my own sisters when they had been young—and as I watched her in that orb's shadowed light, she seemed to glance over, although without seeing from behind her blindfold.

"Give it back to us," the woman said as she reached for the orb. I pulled it out of the way, and Pythia, having finished passing breath to the dying man, and noticing her stolen prize was the object of interest, came over to us.

"It's mine," Pythia said. "I own it."

"What is it?" I asked. "For this is the first we have seen of this unearthly light."

The robed woman's face seemed to shimmer for a moment. "It is an Eclipsis," she said. "A lamp of deathlight."

"It is my . . . orb," Pythia insisted, and made a grab for it, but I drew my hand away from her reach.

"Unclean creature," the woman said. "You stole it from thieves. The Eclipsis was given to us at the Threshold of Death's house, a gift from those of the depths. All belong to the handmaidens, for these were made to guide us in unfamiliar places."

We looked at the other hooded women, each of whom held a small black orb in her left hand, in front of her as if the orb guided her steps. "It pains Death to lose one of her lamps."

"It is lost to her," Pythia said. "It has been for many centuries. She could not have missed it so much. It had been with the vampyre goddess Ixtar in those lands forgotten by many, and may have been there since time began. Why did you not go to her for it?"

"We would not steal back what has been stolen from us, for we are ruled by the laws of the houses of the dead. Unlike your kind, who have no authority or law," the stranger said, her voice calm and firm. "You must give it freely."

"Is this how we see you?" I asked. "Because of its light?"

"It is not light itself. It is the absence of both light and dark. The deathlight is a living creature. It comes of its own desire, when it is near a secret place, or when we have lost our way upon the earth. It is a color that few may know. But you are not an ordinary undead," she said to me. She put her hand upon my wrist. I tried to draw it back, but her grip was strong. "Yes. You have the Veil within you. You have crossed where even undead do not often trespass. The Nameless touches you, as it once touched the child you see."

"She is Death?" I asked, looking at the girl who wandered with the other robed and hooded women.

"A child of Death. We are her handmaidens," she said. "We guide her to those who seek the relief she offers them."

"How can she be here, and in many places? For surely, men and women are dying in other lands at this moment?"

"Death has many children, and many handmaidens."

"Why does she wear a blindfold?"

"She must know their souls without sight, for sometimes, those who seem to be dying are not, and those who seem to be alive are on the edge of death at that moment. The souls of the dying call to her. We are here to help guide her. The Eclipsis"—she nodded toward the orb—"guides and protects us."

"Tell me, does Death ever return the dead?"

"*You*—an undead—ask me?"

"We extinguish, which is worse than death."

"All who walk this earth may be revived," she said. "So long as the soul has not left on its journey."

"What happens in death? At the Threshold?" Pythia asked, so quietly I barely heard her. "Tell me these things, phantom, if you ever wish to possess the . . . Clipsis again."

"It is called an Eclipsis, and you are not worthy of it," the handmaiden said, her face erupting in a sneer. "I have seen you before, Lady of Serpents, daughter of Merod. You have stolen many souls from Death's dominion. Why should I answer this question?"

Pythia lunged forward, scraping her hand through the mist that was the handmaiden's body. "Ghosts, spirits, that is all you are," she said. "Answer me—for it is said that those who see spirits must be answered."

The handmaiden ignored her, returning her radiant gaze to me.

"Would you answer her questions for me?" I asked.

"The Eclipsis honors you. If you wish, I will tell." The handmaiden smiled slightly, and a humming sound came from the glow of light around her. "When mortals die, they go to the Threshold. Beyond it, Death welcomes them into her halls. But beyond this, we do not know. Some ask us at their last breath if there is a heaven or a hell. We have seen nothing beyond the doorway where Death comes for us and leads us into the places of slaughter that we may help her children gather the souls of many. But I have known of souls who return and are reborn."

The handmaiden beside her whispered, "Quiet, sister. These are bloodsuckers."

The one who had spoken to us, turned to me, smiling. "Your tribe shames us, and ruins the crop of souls. We are not meant to speak with you."

"Reborn? In flesh?" Pythia asked.

The other handmaiden took her sister's elbow, tugging at it. "There are souls that need harvesting. We must relieve their pain with the spice."

I glanced at the other handmaidens across the dark field. I saw in the deathlight that there were dozens of them, bending as we had over the dying. The Death child held her hands in the air as if calling up the souls through ritual.

One of the handmaidens was near a boy who groaned in pain not more than six feet from us. The handmaiden cupped her hand near the boy's lips.

As I watched, the handmaiden nearest me held her palm out, showing me the yellow-brown spice. "If you would like to see what it can do to you, just taste it."

"I'd rather not."

"It was mined in the quarries of the underworld, where all ancient sorceries were born," the handmaiden said. "It dries the pain and draws out the soul as salt draws a snail from its shell."

"Do you know of other such treasures of the depths of

the earth? For there is something I seek. It is a sword that burns with flame," I said.

The handmaiden considered this question, then something strange overcame her—a haunted look as if she had once seen the sword itself. "It is hidden from all, this sword, though once the great queen of your tribe wielded it. But it is lost to all and cannot be found. It belongs to an ancient race, and must never be sought, for it curses all who touch it."

I was about to ask more of this, when Pythia tried to grab for the handmaiden's cowl.

"Tell me of this rebirth," Pythia demanded, impatient for an answer to her earlier question. "I thought Death took all mortals."

"Not all," the handmaiden said. "You, my lady, are mortal, with the sorcery of your tribe. Few like you have existed, but one night, yes, we will find you, in your suffering. Perhaps you will taste the spice before you close your eyes. Or perhaps we shall withhold it."

Pythia grew insistent. "Answer me, servant of Death. Some may be . . . reborn?"

The handmaiden's face transformed into a terrible aspect, her eyes burning with yellow fire, her lips peeled back to reveal a black chasm mouth. "Do not test the patience of one who reaps souls, for we may press the spice to you now and take you and the child you carry!"

Then, calming swiftly, she spoke more quietly. "There are those souls who spend many ages in Death's halls, but we see them again in this world. It is mystery, my pretty devil, and though we serve Death, we do not know her secrets." She returned her attentions to me, and said, "Give me this Eclipsis, for if you do not . . ."

Pythia grabbed the Eclipsis from my hands and quickly thrust it back into the leather pouch at her waist. The death-light vanished, as did the phantom creatures that had begun to surround us, as if a candle had been snuffed. "You see? Phantoms. Nothing more. Some trick of the light of this . . . Eclipsis."

Pythia and I stood there in the midst of the battlefield, abandoned by the living, haunted by the dying, the dead, and the undead. Stunned and silent, we stared across the smoky expanse, the whirlwinds of dust blowing along the distant land, the moans and cries of soldiers, the strange emptiness as if we still imagined the handmaidens and their blindfolded child—pressing the spice to the lips of the dying—only seen in the deathlight of the Eclipsis.

"You must never touch it again," Pythia warned me. "You bring the orb to life. Its power is vast, or those ghosts would not seek it. Those handmaidens have no power over the living. I will fight again with her for this orb at the hour of my death and not a moment before."

She went to lift the dead man into her arms and take him to our lair.

I stood, staring into the black night, wondering if the handmaidens gathered around me still, or had returned to their night's labor. The earth was full of invisible spirits. While Pythia knew this from her centuries of experience, it filled me with dread and amazement—for how many of these phantom handmaidens wandered about every village and city and castle and hovel? Had one of them been there when my mother burned—and did they bring comfort to her when the flames licked her flesh? Had they held my brother Frey as he died on a battlefield like this one?

I began to see the earth as more than the domain of mortal and vampyre, but as infested with secret histories and beings that interacted with us and yet did not reveal themselves. As a boy I had heard of the angel of Death, and I began to think of these handmaidens as these beautiful and terrible angels—gentle to mortals, unyielding to those of us who shunned Death's house.

When the night was over, I lay down with Pythia, who kept her back to me.

"You must never touch the Eclipsis again," she whispered.

"If you had felt it as I did, you would not say that. It brought me strength, and it took strength from me. It is a breathing rock, Pythia. Its deathlight may help us when we fight the Myrrydanai."

"You must never touch it again," she repeated.

Beyond our cave, the sun rose, its light touching the mouth of our lair, but going no farther. Around us, the corpses of soldiers and knights who had fought bravely and accepted the Sacred Kiss from each of us. In two nights time, we had drawn together almost seventy such men.

Pythia went deep into her sleep, clutching the Eclipsis in her hands.

I nearly went to the deep oblivion of day, but I felt some movement in the stream, as if another vampyre had entered our lair.

The lurking one moved from rock to rock, spindly—like a spider—quickly scampering, yet with a graceful movement. I felt a strange tingling along my spine as if it had feelers of some sort that touched me.

I felt the slight chill of its shadow over my face, and I fought against sleep, but finally, darkness took me.

◆ CHAPTER 6 ◆

Maz–Sherah

◆ 1 ◆

WHEN the brief day had passed, I opened my
eyes.

In a moment, I saw the most loathsome of the undead
that existed upon this earth.

The gauzed skull of Artephius himself was not so repul-
sive, and my own undead semblance in a mirror with rotting flesh and torn bone was not so vile to me as this *thing*.

This abomination.

When I had been a boy, I had heard the priests speak of
unholiness, and though I was the kind of demon they might
mean, I felt that thing looking down at me was the essence
of the unholy.

I felt the pathos of the beast—a man who was not a
man, a creature who was unlike any other, a vampyre who
had no glamour of youth or beauty.

I recognized kindred in its glance, and in its movements. It was one of us—but without the gleam of youth
and vitality.

The remaining dried-leather skin was pockmarked with disease, and its eyes were small and yellow—sunken into their sockets with just the barest of skin to provide an unblinking eyelid over each. He had the dagger teeth of a vampyre, though larger, and each one sharp and biting, and thrusting from his lower jaw like tusks. Truly, he seemed to be more teeth than face, his scalp and eyes an afterthought, extending upward from those long fangs.

Half his scalp had been torn, and hung like a fallen hood behind what had once been ears, now mere dark holes at the sides of his jaw. The hooded cape he had once worn, when I had seen the vampyre aboard the ship, was in shreds and tatters, hanging from his shoulders.

In surprise, I gasped.

He, too, gasped, spewing a breath of foulness upon me that would best have come from a nether region than from between the lips.

He leapt from me, wings snapping outward, torn and tattered though they were.

His wings fluttered slightly as he jumped from me, and he hung suspended above me in the air.

Pythia sat up suddenly, startled by the sounds around her. She did not speak, but pushed herself against the cave wall, her mind adjusting to the night-rise, and to this intruder's presence.

I leapt up into the air, grabbing the creature. We tumbled to the earth. He fought me like a cat about to be thrown into a drowning bag—claws and talons sliced at my throat and face and nearly took my eyes. I wrestled the abomination to the earth, and drew the dagger from his own shoulder strap, pressing it over his heart, if he had one at all.

The thing spat yellow bile at my face and cursed in languages that were not familiar to me. Yet there was no doubt by his expression—for the skin at his lips tore as it snarled and hissed the words.

"Why do you follow us?" I asked. I demanded of him every question, every possible answer supplied by me—was he a spy of Nezahual? Why did he follow us? Was he after the Eclipsis? The mask? What had he come for? Pythia told me to extinguish him then and there, and began snarling like a tiger as the corpse-vampyre began shrieking in tongues of a language that Pythia immediately understood. She began spewing words of this tongue back to him, and so they argued between themselves while I tried to decipher the words.

When I began to understand the language, the intruder screamed, "You must not kill me, for I am like you! I am Maz-Sherah!"

♦ 2 ♦

HIS name was Ophion, and he told me that he was a vampyre. "But I have no glamour to speak of, no fine flesh, nothing but this rot. Youth was stolen from me, my brother."

"He is not your brother!" Pythia snarled, and grimaced as she turned her attention to me. "The vile ghoul is some spy of Nezahual. Or of the Myrrydanai. The vampyre glamour cannot be stolen."

Ophion glanced sidelong at her, and then at me. His teeth made a grinding sound, and then he snapped at the air as if wishing to attack her. I pulled him back and made him face me. "It was stolen and torn from my bones! You she-bitch, you know of the place I speak—the nameless deep, where your mask was first forged!"

Pythia, almost instinctively, reached up to touch the gold mask, feeling its contours. "Why would he tell us this? Why did he follow us?" Her voice growled as she spoke. "He lies. He wishes to destroy us. He is a spy of Nezahual. Of Ixtar."

"Is this true?" I asked.

"Ask her," Ophion said, like a cat who had caught a mouse. "The she-bitch knows."

Pythia leapt upon him, and nearly tore him from my grip. I shoved her away, and she pointed at him. "Call me that again, corpse, and I will make sure those teeth never again break flesh!"

"Mortal!" he said.

"Corpse!" she spat back.

I held out a hand to keep Pythia from coming at him again. She glared at me. "He brings disease with him. Look at him. He should accept Extinguishing over this . . . this . . . disgusting visage."

Ophion glanced at her and began snarling right back. "You Alkemaran sow, with your lies. She knows who I am. Ask her, brother, go on. Ask the spit of Merod."

I began laughing, and Pythia shot me an acid look. "I don't know him," she said. "But I can smell him from here. He's rotting. He stinks of old meat, left in the sun, swarming with flies."

"Old meat? Left in the sun? Flies? Did you hear that? Did you hear what she said, my brother?" His skull began tottering side to side as if ready to fall.

"Why do you call me brother, Ophion?"

"Because we are . . . oh, not brothers of the flesh," he said, keeping a snarl for Pythia. "You are another kind of brother. I, too, am Maz-Sherah. I am like you. I came before to fulfill prophecy."

"Lying jackal!" Pythia shouted.

"Fanged whore!" Ophion screeched. Then, calming quickly, he said, "I was Maz-Sherah so long ago. Many moons, as they say. Millions of moons, I suspect, although I am not certain."

"You're a ghoul," Pythia said. She pointed her finger at him as if laying a curse. "I smelled you in Nezahual's prisons. Your stink was everywhere. You wanted the mask for yourself. That is why you followed."

"I admit it." He nodded, and picked at a scab along his bony elbow. "I did seek the mask. But only for its . . . its healing properties."

"It does not heal," I said. "It leaches."

"To some," he whispered, "oh, my brother, to those who have leached, it leaches. But to those who have healed, it brings healing. To some, it brings immortality. It is a fickle mask, and takes and gives, and gives and takes. It is ruled by old laws of old tribes, old as the birth of the moon."

• 3 •

WE spent most of the night speaking, although Pythia refused to stay to hear his lies. She went off hunting, and Ophion and I sat along the mountain ledge. He told me of his escape from Nezahual's clutches, for he had been there many centuries, forgotten in an airless chamber "where I drank the blood of scorpion and snake, and small crawling things that chanced through the slits at the door and cracks in stones. His kingdom had many shiny beetles, my brother, many, and their blood was sour and white and nearly extinguished me. Nearly."

"You followed us for the mask?"

"When my prison was destroyed by fire, I escaped, and drank of mortal blood for the first time in many years, brother. I followed because I smelled Maz-Sherah on you. Your stream is strong and cannot be lost. I am weak in many things, for I do not have youth as you, or sorcery as your"—and here I was sure he would use some rude term for Pythia, but instead he chose—"lady. The mask had called to me for many years, and I also could feel its fingers reach for me, even across the seas."

"Why did you run from me on the ship?"

"Oh, my brother, I was ashamed of how I looked. Ashamed of much. Ashamed I had drunk of too many mortals that night. Ashamed of these bones. I did not know if you would harm me, for vampyres do not like me. Many have tried to destroy me. The priests themselves wished my end, and yet I had come to fulfill their prophecy. I failed in my quest to heal the Veil and destroy Ghorien."

"Ghorien?"

"You must know him. Oh, but you have not yet spoken to the Myrrydanai? For if he has you in his clutches, he will make himself known to you."

"He is not among the Myrrydanai. They are shadows—and take on the skins of the dead. But none seem to have a person within them."

He grinned and it seemed like a lizard's smile, for the long, sharp teeth extended as he did so. "Oh, there *is* a person within them. Ghorien controls all Myrrydanai, for he is the only mind they have—they are like locusts gathering around honey. When Ghorien goes, so go the shadows. I know him well. He hides among them, but will reveal himself only when it is safe. He can be destroyed, though I did not have weapons to do this."

His rictus grin faded, and for a moment I was sure he would weep. Despite the rotting of his corpse and the bone and sinew revealed through that leathery gauze of skin, I found something almost endearing about him.

He spoke eloquently enough, and had no love of my own enemies. "He did much to cast me into this sorry state. For it was in the Myrrydanai prisons of Myrryd I—Ophion—*Maz-Sherah*—was tortured and tormented and my flesh was drawn off, again and again, even while it grew in the day's sleep, so at night they tore at it with their instruments . . . This is what awaits the Maz-Sherah. This was my destiny, and is yours as well. This is what you were born to, my sorrowful brother. Oh, Ghorien will surely want you to bring this mask to him, and a staff of bone, and any other enchantments you have—to use against you, my brother, as he used much against me. Ancient sorceries are strong, and the Myrrydanai seek them always—but they must seek them through others, for they cannot find them on their own."

"I am sorry to hear you have been abused," I said. "But the staff—do you mean the Nahhashim?"

He nodded. "Broken from the white-bone tree of Myrryd, born from the bones of the gray priests themselves. Yes, gray their cloaks, and gray their eyes, and gray their conjuring. I do not know of them other than their legend, for they had been destroyed before all the priests of my early nights, though they must have held great power—for the staff broken from their tree carries old sorcery within it. It is guarded—oh, well guarded—by the swarms of those called the Akhnetur. The Myrrydanai cannot touch such magick for long, for it eats away at their souls—the treasures of Myrryd's depths are not meant for these shadow priests. Yet, they must control it. This mask as well—they cannot wear it, yet it must be in their possession that their queen might come to flesh."

"And a sword of fire?" I asked.

He nodded, but shivered before he spoke as if remembering a terrible encounter. He leaned toward me, and whispered nearly at my ear, "This . . . this treasure . . . this weapon . . . I have never seen, for I failed, oh, I failed." He drew back from me, raising his knobby hands to the skies. "As deep as the sky above, so are Myrryd's nether regions beneath the earth. In Myrryd's depths I despaired. Yes, for I have been in one prison after another since mortal man first built his cities. I escaped the prisons of Myrryd at the fall of that great city when many of our tribe extinguished, only to flee to the prisons of Nezahual. I have not tasted freedom in such a long time. Had I not felt your stream, my brother, oh, where would I have gone? For the world is much changed since last I breathed the air of a mountaintop, or saw the view from a cliff's edge. My brother, it is changed, and all I knew of it was that brother—yes, you—I felt like the pull of a tide within the stream."

"Brother," I said, for I truly felt our kinship, "will you tell me of Myrryd? Is the Nahhashim tree still there?"

He looked bewildered, as if there had been no point to my asking. "Perhaps, perhaps. It will not die, this tree, nor will it grow. Yet only a branch broke to make the staff."

"But another may be broken still?"

"It is guarded by the Akhnetur, as I told you, and their swarms will tear at your flesh. Not even the priests could approach it once the Akhnetur were called from the deep. It is said that only the Great Serpent himself may enter its garden."

"This sword—is it hidden in the city?"

"I do not know, my brother," he said with such a peculiar

tone, a death rattle at his throat. He knew more of the fire sword, and he was not good at hiding his lies without the thickness of flesh to cloak them. "Many things are hidden there, and many creatures lurk." His eyes seemed to focus on some distant star as he spoke, and his voice took on a hypnotic quality. "It is unseen by outsiders, my brother. Only those who have been within its gates may return to it. It is lost to all others, protected by a sorcery more powerful than Medhya herself. A legend, a vision to some."

"Yes, legend—and vision," I said. "Tell me of it."

"Myrryd is hidden—as if a curtain had been drawn over the cliffs above the many towers of the city. A curtain the color of fire when the sun is at its zenith, and beneath the stars, a cloak of crystal. Myrryd has remained hidden in this way, and those who get close to it, sense the poison. The ground seethes with gases from its depths, and it sucks energy from mortal and vampyre alike to light its strange fires as if the city itself has a soul and a spirit. There are many dangers for winged jackals like us. There are creatures there that have been born of Medhya's nightmares and crossed the Veil to guard the bones of the high kings."

"There are kings buried there?"

"Kings of the Blood, as there are Priests." He nodded. "Very wicked jackals they were, and tricky, my brother. But all are extinguished, in tombs that shall never be disturbed. A great sanctuary of the dead—a hall of kings and queens, and their many servants and protectors—all extinguished, all dust and bone beneath the watch of stone effigies."

"How far is Myrryd, do you think—from here?"

Ophion grinned, nearly laughing, breaking the somber mood.

"What is it?"

He could not stop laughing, a death rattle from his throat, his teeth chattering as they clacked against each other. "You must never go there, Maz-Sherah! It is a city of the dead, a poisonous gouge in the earth. It is not meant to be found, not meant to be found at all!"

But I had set my mind to this. "You will guide me there,

Ophion, for I have heard it is across this sea, in the lands of desert and sea and deep forest—far from the ancient Carthaginian port, yet not so far for one who flies. I have but seven nights to return to fight the Myrrydanai at Taranis-Hir. If I can make a new Nahhashim staff—if I can find the sword . . . the power of its magick will be with us."

His laughter ended, and he grew quiet. "Why should I do this? I never wish to go back there."

"If you are Maz-Sherah," I said. "As I am. And you are not extinguished, but have survived centuries of imprisonment and torment . . . then you will want to fulfill even that destiny denied you. I need your knowledge, Ophion. Has your existence been a waste to be tossed out with the dead? Or did you rise up, Maz-Sherah, and suffer at the hands of the Myrrydanai, never to avenge the wrong done to you? Never to destroy the shadow priests who held you in a terrible captivity—never to taste the moment of victory over those who had taken away your glamour—your youth. Show them that they did not take your soul along with such things. Lead me to Myrryd. Show me where its treasures lie. For if we are both anointed of the Great Serpent, then we will rise up against his enemies and smite them."

He remained silent for too long a time, and when I asked him of his thoughts, he finally said, "All these years, I lay in the dark and believed another Maz-Sherah would come. I believed you would raise me up from the prisons and be my brother. Then, I did not believe. Hope, I lost. Will, I lost. But you came. You came, and the city of Ixtar fell. The mask escaped the grasp of that fierce goddess. And I, too, escaped. Because you are my brother, and you came to my prison. And hope, also, found me. And now I understand. Yes. Yes, my brother. I will take you to the red city of Myrryd. We will fly swift, and we will face its haunted towers and poisoned depths."

• 4 •

HE glanced over at the corpses lying several feet away. "You are resurrecting these men."

I nodded.

"By the time the last of them rises, we might return. Do you truly believe you are the Anointed One? For I once believed this, my brother, but I do not anymore."

"I have devoured Merod, the last Priest of Blood, as was the prophecy," I said. "If I am not the Maz-Sherah, then my doom is certain regardless. But will you guide me, Ophion, brother?"

He covered his bony hands over his eyes as if blocking out a memory. "If I return . . . I will remember too much . . ."

I reached for him, and took his hand in mine, laying it over my hand. "Do you see? I am like you beneath this flesh. I will fulfill this destiny, but you, my brother, will be with me. You are not a failure in this destiny if you guide me to Myrryd. You will be the one who fulfilled your destiny within me, and those years of your imprisonment will not be for nothing. You have paid a great price, but I will offer you the reward of such a payment."

He clasped his hand to me and formed a fist around my fingers. "Yes. Yes, my brother. Yes. You are my brother. I knew you would come. I knew you would. All that I have suffered should not be lost and buried with my Extinguishing. Yes, I will guide you. Yes, my brother."

• 5 •

"That . . . that . . . ghoul . . . is a loathsome creature," Pythia said to me when I found her drinking from a soldier who had wrapped his naked body around hers in his drunken sleep, believing she was a whore of the camps come to him in the dark. I stood nearby, shaking my head. "You should send him away. Destroy him. That thing is not meant to exist."

She pushed the drunken youth away, leaving him to sleep off his fantasy, puncture wounds at his thigh and wrist as he rolled to the earth.

We walked along the trails between the sleeping soldiers and the horses tied by the knight's tents, careful of the many men who lay wounded and exhausted nearby. When we had reached a quiet place among the rocks by the water, far from the camp, I said, "How can I destroy Ophion? He is of our tribe. He is a Maz-Sherah."

"There is only one Maz-Sherah," she said. "You. The others were dreamers. Fools. The untested. You fulfilled the prophecy of the Priest of Blood. You alone. None of the others did."

"I may yet fail," I replied.

"Do not confuse what you have within you with that unspeakable vampyre. I knew it when I passed the Sacred Kiss to you. I saw it, as I had never seen a vision before." Her voice softened, and it was at such times that I trusted her least. "That beast is a blasphemy to all vampyres. Look at him—a walking corpse with wings like a mangy bat. He has no glamour. No beauty. His flesh is half-peeled from the bone, and rotted brown and oily. His teeth are yellowed and like tusks. When he drinks blood, do you see how some of it runs down his legs? It is a miracle of our tribe that he even survives with so little flesh left to him. It's a wonder he can even speak, and yet it is hard to quiet him once he has begun. We do not share many traits with this beast. He may drink blood, but what good does blood do him? It does not restore the semblance of health to this oaf, Ophion."

"When you first drank from me, I saw the corpse beneath your glamour. I saw, for a moment, the skull and bone and sinew as you tore at me. I have also been trapped in a hall of great silver mirrors. In them, I saw myself without the magick of our tribe. I knew what my body truly was."

"All illusions," she said. "It is a trick of light and of quicksilver. Nothing more."

"That is what your father suggested," I said. "But we are not so far removed from Ophion, are we? He has been called 'Anointed One,' as have I. He is my reflection in the mirror—and I am, perhaps, his."

She shook her head lightly. "You cannot look at a corpse and see yourself. You cannot look at ghouls and see what I see. You are young, and you will be eternally young.

You are a man, and you will never be rotted flesh. In your loins, there is life, where there is no life in his, nor does he have even the semblance of such life. Ophion is a betrayer. A liar. There are those who knew this creature once . . . and met their Extinguishing because of this knowledge."

"You have *never* seen him before?" I watched her eyes for the glint of a lie. She called Ophion those same things that she herself could be called—a betrayer, a liar, a destroyer of vampyres.

"I certainly knew that a creature like him lurked about the dark chambers of Nezahual's prison," she said. "Nezahual had a menagerie of monsters. A monster that drank the blood of goats and gathered up the skulls of men, a dragon that stood upright like a man and turned those who looked upon it into stone, and beasts with many long arms and the eyes of an owl. Ophion may have been among them. I felt something in the stream, but I could not be sure what it was, for the stream was strong and full in that country. But I did not know him."

"He is more like us than these others you mention," I said. "I will not seek the Extinguishing of a vampyre as easily as you might."

"If this is your will, then so be it," she said, finally. "But he would be wise not to be alone with me, for I will show him no mercy. But for your sake, I will allow him his existence."

She was not so generous when I told her that I would leave within the hour to travel to Myrryd with this vampyre—but she was wise enough not to fight it much. In the end, she said, "Do not forget the newborn tribe that will arise within two nights. These will be your warriors, and they will need to know their leader. If you truly decide to leave me here with these newborns, you risk all that you have suffered—for what? A journey to a dead place. A quest for sorcery that may no longer exist."

✦ 6 ✦

"TAKE the cudgel from the dead man," Ophion said, as we walked among the dead who lay between the smoke billows along the plain. He pointed to a fallen soldier. "This one's good and dead, brother—and look, a shiny razien, there, see? Beautiful as a fine sword, but far better for the hack and jab. See the sharp blade? Very fine work, that one."

"What do we need with such crude weapons?" I asked. "You said no vampyre exists in Myrryd."

"There may be creatures we do not know of, and others who hide." As he spoke, his voice grew small and soft as if he were remembering a dreadful nightmare and was afraid to speak of it. "It has been abandoned for too long, and it holds energy even when no mortal or vampyre sleeps within its gates. Myrryd calls to creatures that live only in dead places. It takes all energy from us. You will not sprout wings there, and there will be no strength in you. You will be as a mortal among its towers and ruins. It sucks at us—at our sorcery. It lights its lamps with our energies." Of this he would say no more, no matter how I dogged him with questions.

I crouched by the dead soldier, drew out the razien from its sheath, unstrapped the sheath and took that, also. I drew the corpse's short cudgel up, hefting it about. I strapped the razien sheath at my waist so that it hung down along my right hip, and the cudgel over my shoulder. Ophion also picked over the dead, finding the prize of a two-bladed sword that had not yet been scavenged by others. He looked at me, and at the weapons I had gathered for myself. "These should do," he said. He glanced up at the stars. "I will follow the beast who runs among the stars." He pointed to a constellation I could not see for the heavy smoke. "If followed, its tail points the way to Myrryd. We must go soon, my brother, for the night will not linger."

◆ 7 ◆

WHEN I went to bid farewell to Pythia, my heart felt heavy. She grasped me by the wrists and drew me back to her. She whispered at my ear, "Do not go to Myrryd. It is forbidden for all of us. It is a place of Extinguishing."

"I am going," I said, pulling away from her.

She drew herself close to me, her lips near mine. "I brought you into this existence, Aleric. It was your beauty that seduced me, and then it was your blood, and then your flesh. But when I saw my future as I passed the breath of immortality to you, I knew that I would have to destroy you . . . or save you. I cannot let you go with that creature."

I watched her eyes. The gold on her face moved in slow liquid waves along her brow and around her cheeks.

"You will have to let me go," I said, wishing I could tell her otherwise. "I will return. I will find you again. Five nights. I will meet you at the Akkadite Cliffs at the edge of the last of the Great Forest. We will bring war to Taranis-Hir."

"Please, Aleric," she gasped, reaching for me.

"Do not forget—you must extract the oath before feeding these new vampyres. You must lead them toward my country. You know the way. It will be but a few days' flight. Look for the high cliffs to the east of Taranis-Hir, called the Akkadites. There is a gold tree. Wait for me there, but take command of this rabble. They have sworn an oath, and they have honor in their blood and will obey you. I will not be far behind you, I promise. If it is trust you wish me to have, then remain with our tribe. When I come for you, I will have the new staff, and the sword of fire that is buried in the dead kingdom."

"Wait," she cried out, as I turned my back on her and spread my wings. She reached into her pouch, and withdrew the Eclipsis and ran toward me. She stood before me, and held the Eclipsis up.

"Take this." She pressed it into my hands, then unraveled the pouch and strap at her waist. "It pulses with life when you hold it. It is not meant for me. Perhaps its death-light will protect you in that city of the dead."

This was the single most selfless act she had ever done for me. Perhaps the mask did not just leach her immortality, but also something darker within her soul. Perhaps the child that grew in her womb had awakened this. Or perhaps she had the instinct to protect me, even when she had first shared the vision of the ritual, after giving me the Sacred Kiss. For surely, she might have destroyed me then, but instead, fled from me out of fear. I knew that within Pythia, there was an instinct for good—for what was right, within the realm of our tribe—and she too often buried it. She had saved me from a terrible Extinguishing at the jaws of Ixtar, and now might save me with this gift.

I embraced her and did not wish to let go. I accepted the Eclipsis and its pouch, and wrapped them around my shoulder. I held her face in my hands, and said, "You are a queen among our tribe. But you must not forget how vulnerable you are. If you arrive before I reach the Akkadite Cliffs, do not take the war to Taranis-Hir. Wait, and keep company with the mortals who are there and who will join the fight. Do not hurt them, except to drink, and then, only enough."

She whispered, "Do not go there. I may never see you again. Those who seek Myrryd do not return."

I touched the edge of the gold mask, feeling its ice. "I will see you again before the new moon is dark in the sky." I pressed my lips against hers, opening against her mouth, wanting to pull myself into her, never to have to—again— leave any I had loved, any I had hated. Just as I had grown afraid I would never see Ewen again, so I was sure that I might not return to Pythia, nor see my child born.

Yet I knew no other course, for I did not have sorcery to fight the Myrrydanai White Robes or the staff that Enora held in her grip. But how I wished I could do as Pythia wished and travel with her to lands as warm as summer rain and raise our child without knowledge of the damnation of the greater world beyond us. I loved her, and I hated her, and I did not wish to part from her upon that bleak mountain.

I let her go, and her last words to me did not hurt as much as she wished. "Do not judge me harshly, if I fail you," she whispered, almost as if she didn't want me to hear.

"You will not fail me," I told her, and went out to the

ledge of the cliff, joining Ophion, who had already begun the flight.

• 8 •

WE flew across the great sea that had carried me from the Italian shores to the land of the Saracens in the last days of my mortal life. South and west, we flew, and slept on a windswept island, in a chapel that had been carved into rock perhaps a hundred years previous. We closed our eyes in a windowless chamber beneath the chapel, surrounded by bones and barrels of wine. Ophion brought me a squirming vessel of blood when dusk broke—a young monk who had come to open the chapel doors and sweep the crypt. I drank greedily, forewarned that we might not find mortal blood again for several nights.

Before the sun had vanished from the sky, we sat together in the vault. Ophion spoke to me about what he had experienced at Myrryd, and though his memories seemed vague at first, once he had drunk his fill, much of it returned to him. "I was like you," he said. "Robust then, robust and full of . . . the look of health. Like you, brother. Older than you, but yet not so old. I knew of this Myrryd. Knew it like I know the bones on this hand." He held his hand up for my inspection, the small finger bones thrusting out from the tattered flesh as if it were a well-worn glove. "Knew it like I know the taste of good blood. There were armies of vampyres. Cities of them. They knew the legends about the Maz-Sherah. They knew. I was famous, like you, and I believed the prophecies I had been told of Maz-Sherah and what it might mean. Myrryd still reigned in those lands, though its energy waned in those times."

"But," I interrupted, which was made difficult as Ophion rarely took a breath when he began speaking. "But . . . wait . . . why would there be a Maz-Sherah, when Myrryd had not yet fallen?"

"Oh, yes. The kings. The priests. The Myrrydanai were not yet shadows," he said "Their flesh had not yet been torn.

And yet I tell you, I was born to the same destiny as yours, for it was prophesied of me."

"Then, what would you save our tribe . . . from?"

He leaned into me so that I could smell his fetid breath and the stink from his curdled eyes, and whispered, "Enslavement, my brother. Enslavement. Medhya reached out when the Veil was thin and tore at our tribe. She whispered secrets to mortals that they might hunt us. She had already turned the Myrrydanai into her hunting dogs."

He told the story of the centuries of enslavement of vampyres, by the priests themselves. I learned soon enough that the Myrrydanai priests had used their sorcery to bind vampyres into service. The Priests of Blood had already been expelled from Myrryd, and the Nahhashim were imprisoned in the bowels of the great Myrryd city. It was only when the Myrrydanai overstepped their own powers and broke the Veil through the use of the purple flower's juice that Medhya tore their skin from them and tossed their meat to other creatures of the city. "A horrible, horrible time," Ophion whined. "So long ago, before mortals rose up against us. But the shadow priests asked for it, for I suffered greatly at their hands. But I know little, my brother, so little. When I came here, I was ignorant and full of want. I had visions as you must—the dreams that haunt and torment. I went to find answers, but oh, when Ghorien saw me . . ."

"The leader of the Myrrydanai priests," I whispered.

Ophion nodded. "He is the voice—the throat of the Myrrydanai, the gullet, the heart. There are many in the shadows, but he is chief among them. When he saw me, he knew. Maz-Sherah is foretold, and many will come. Many will fall, my brother, my falconer."

"They tortured you in these prisons, but did they reveal any weakness to you?"

"Weakness? Myrrydanai? No, oh, none have they, but for the touch of the mask. They fear it—they fear what the Great Serpent has himself touched. They fear the Nahhashim, as well, but when these priests were destroyed, their bones bound in the tree, Myrrydanai did not fear again. My prison? Much worse than shackle and chain. Stripped me of flesh, salted these bones, and nearly extinguished me. Raised me again only to break my bones beneath great rocks, my brother. They threatened to turn me to ash in a terrible furnace. The kings watched and allowed all of this, for they, too, had become prisoners of Myrrydanai. The Fallen Ones of Medhya, our mother and destroyer, believed Ghorien and his Myrrydanai—for kings must be ordained. When not ordained by country, they are ordained by the corrupt few who convince them of their power. For three hundred years, Ghorien held me there, seeking to find a way to make what was Maz-Sherah in me die. But he could not. We, who are Maz-Sherah, may only be Maz-Sherah. We may extinguish, and we may not know what this power is that brings such fear in visions to the powerful and the cruel . . . but what is in us, is in us. Those such as these shadow priests fear us. Yet, we, too, have much to fear."

Ophion told me more of this as we soared up into the night, heading for the coast of a country that had been conquered many times, but there was an area of it that remained wild and untamed—and unknown by outsiders for centuries.

He told me of the creatures that Ghorien had called up from the Veil—of the Lamiades, which were like lizards, but as large as horses, and of creatures called Akhnetur; and in their sorceries, Ghorien and his minions forgot that Medhya's prison was in the Veil. She was using these priests to free her, though they did not know this. When she was nearly free, she reached though the Veil itself and tore at their skin, and in trying to escape the Veil, she failed. Instead, her breath drew their souls—within shadow-clouds—into that otherworld.

But by then, Ophion had gone into hiding. "In the old caves, I hid. I did not show myself. With my glamour gone, I was but a monster to mortals and to the vampyre tribes. The earth changed its course, and mortals flourished when the kings of Myrryd were extinguished. Men hunted the

Priests of Blood. Mortal hunters who had grown in their knowledge of weapons and warfare. It seemed but a night to me but the world changed over thousands of years. I did not recognize it when I returned to it. Medhya still visited me in my dreams—as a whispering darkness she came to me."

I could not help my next question, for it vexed me to even wonder. "Have you seen the Serpent?"

Ophion went silent for a moment. In that silence, I eagerly asked, "Is it real? Or is it in visions only?"

"The Great Serpent exists," Ophion said. "He manifests in . . . flesh . . . in fire . . . in many things. Though I have only heard the legend of this father of our tribe. As you have. It is the mortals of Myrryd who have seen his fire."

"Mortals? In a vampyre city?"

Ophion nodded. "Human rats in Myrryd—mortals, stupid and like vermin—living off eels and spiders and drinking foul water. They scramble to the depths to seek their vermin, but not all come back up to the red city. Many remain there . . . and die in the beneath. Some are caught by even larger rats in the deep damp below. As I spent years in prisons living like a rat myself, I understand them, though they disgust me."

"Human rats? Mortal men? Women?"

"Barely human. They were vessels bred in captivity for the population of the kingdom. Their descendants could not escape the fallen kingdom, not from its heights or its deep places. Trapped there, unable to leave, breeding for generations, yet, with short life spans. They have felt the Great Serpent, too, though they fear him. We all should fear him. It was to Medhya he offered the secrets of immortality and sorcery, and from him the priests learned of the sorceries to undo Medhya when she had grown too corrupt. It was he who showed secrets to the priests that they might destroy Medhya, who had ruled for a thousand years in that red city. She was feared in all kingdoms. It was the Serpent's magick that brought her to her knees. It is a sorcery of the earth, and of fire. But she had broken many laws, and had murdered her sisters that she might gain their power."

"Datbathani—and Lemesharra?"

Ophion nodded, grinning like Death herself. "These are our histories told to us by the ancients. These are stories lost. I dream of her sisters, and of the Great Serpent. I dream of Medhya, a storm of darkness upon a throne of gold and bone, with the pelts of wolves and jackals across her shoulders, and a necklace of the teeth of vampyres about her throat. Her raiment is the thinnest skins of flesh, and at her right, the vulture, and at her left, the raven, and entwined about her legs like the cords of sandals, asps and lizards. The Lamiades stand in wait beside her, and upon the back of each one, the dark mist of the Myrrydanai shadow priests. I dream of her, though she seeks our destruction, and I am drawn to her . . . as you, too, brother, are drawn."

I nodded. I could not deny our brotherhood, for Ophion—though crude in his speaking and stammering—expressed what I felt. That Medhya followed me, always, and that my fate and hers would be tied, as my destiny had been bound with Pythia.

I, like Ophion, dreamed of Medhya.

That night, we approached the shores of Myrryd.

BOOK TWO

THE QUEEN
OF WOLVES

I

THE RED CITY

• C H A P T E R 7 •

The Kingdom

• 1 •

MYRRYD had once encompassed land to the east, to what had once been the great city Carthage, and far to the west, where the sea poured out into the vast oceans of the world. Ophion's words returned to me as I beheld it from the sky: "Mortals are blinded at the fire-colored sea, but those who have been clever enough to shade their eyes have found the inverted ziggurats that seem to spiral into visions of Hell, and though it is not that infernal place, still it is the origins of the legends of such an underworld."

The sea was indeed a flaming red and yellow, a reflection of the structures that had fallen beneath the waters in some cataclysm.

But the heart of Myrryd was in its namesake city, hidden from the children of the earth by the final sorceries of the Nahhashim: for most mortals were blind to it, and vampyres did not dare enter it, fearing its terrible history and the threat that something slept within its labyrinthine avenues, some power of a dark magick that would overtake even the undead.

From land, Myrryd was invisible, for a fortress of rock encompassed it on three sides. A series of enormous, jagged cliffs rose above the sea below, which entered it in a kind of great bay, but a bay that was too perfect—as if it had been carved out by men over the millennia rather than by the sea itself.

From the water, the city of Myrryd was too enormous to contemplate, and a sailor might not make out the more manicured curves and angles of its steps. I knew why it was called the fire-colored sea, for the ancient structures would catch the sun's light in such a way that it would seem the waters themselves burned.

In the clouded moonlight, the jagged and spiral shapes seemed like ghostly giants guarding a frozen wasteland in the night.

I clearly saw the great red-rust color of fallen structures, bright copper in the dark light of my vision; waterfalls of a league or more in extent fell from the high cliffs above like streams of white silver to an inlet from the sea far below. An enormous harbor had once been here, and fallen pillars and long stone slabs lay in heaps. Among its sunken monoliths just beneath the dark waves were the remnants of enormous statues of kings and heroes of ancient days, though the denizens of the sea had scrubbed their faces.

The air above the sea-swept ruins was windless and bland in some way; but once we cleared the tops of the trees, the wind began to roar as it whipped along the beginnings of a deep forest.

Suddenly, I felt a searing blast of heat, as if there were some boiling springs nearby, and a strange tugging at my wings and my legs, drawing me downward. I fought against it, but quickly enough it was like fighting against the gale force of the sea. Ophion had already dropped down into the forest below, just beyond the place where the ruins of towers had once arisen from the red rock of the cliff.

I followed him downward, as my wings felt as if they

were breaking under the pressure that pulled me down. I felt a strange burning along the bony outcroppings of my wings. Some unseen force tore at them.

I retracted them, and they receded and vanished at my shoulder blades. I leapt down to the grassy clearing below.

For the first time in several nights, I felt no stream here between Ophion and myself. It suddenly went silent, and I had the overwhelming sense of the place as some lonesome wood, not meant for man or beast.

Ophion had tumbled across an overgrown path, rolling over several times until he stopped.

"What caused us to fall?" I shouted to him.

He clambered to his feet and pressed his fingers to his mouth to beg my silence. Even as he limped over to me—for he had turned his wayward foot farther inward in his fall—he whispered, "Myrryd eats our power. A great force within it, my brother. Sucks at our minds to feed it."

He pointed to the grasses, and there among them, I saw dead birds, and the skulls and bones of small animals, and as he pointed, I saw many more in the areas around us. "Mortal life is at greatest risk, for there is a *magnes* that draws out energy like a jackal sucks marrow from the bone."

"It feeds . . . on energy?"

"On life. On death, too. As we drink blood, so it drinks the life energy," he whispered, all the while his eyes wide as he looked tree to tree, bush to branch, as if expecting visitors. "Myrryd feeds on the force of the soul, for it must light its temple fires, though no priest attends them."

"From *us*, as well as mortals?"

"Do you not feel it, brother?" Ophion shivered. "Your wings will not exist here. Your strength is weakened. You are as a mortal man, and perhaps even weaker than that. It knows we're here. It has tasted our soul."

"What is *it*?"

"The dead and immortal city of Myrryd awaits us. It has tasted our energy and taken from us the sorcery that allows us to fly."

"Forever?"

"Only within its field. The ancient kings called it a *magnes*—a place that draws power from life."

"But—" I began, and meant to ask what he meant about the temple fires and how far the citadel itself was from these woods.

Swiftly, he reached over to put his hand against my mouth lest I speak again in a loud voice. His voice grew even softer, smaller, and I had to strain to hear him, for the rasp of his voice had come like a light death rattle.

"We must be quiet as the dead," he said.

◆ 2 ◆

THE trees around us were like giants, and thick around as houses; the violent wind rushed along their swaying branches; leaves scattered in brief whirls along the path and among the overgrowth of brambles. Ophion released his hold on my mouth and crouched, grasping me about the knees as if he might be blown away like a dried weed.

"Long ago I was here, and know of its treachery," he said. "I trust nothing here."

I grinned and squatted, patting his back. "Don't be afraid," I said, trying to comfort him as if he were a child. "What harm can we meet in the woods? The wind? Perhaps some thunder?"

"Tasmal, so it is called," he said. "Many spirits hunt the woods."

"Spirits of the *wood*?"

"These are not elementals, my brother. *Tasmal* means 'the Laughing Ones.' They are disincarnate, they are the cursed dead—spirits of evil men who brought war to Myrryd, and were torn apart, living, their bones and flesh scattered beneath this ground, where the forest has overgrown. They wander these woods, but cannot leave them unless within the body of another. They seek flesh. When they possess a man, they can travel great distances before they've devoured the skin—if the host has not gone mad from them. But always, when the flesh is gone, they are drawn back here as if by the wind itself. They are called the Laughing Ones, for they make a noise that is like a madman's cackle."

"I hear no laughter among these trees."

"Perhaps they have truly left, but ... oh, oh, my brother, oh, look, look." He leapt from the ground to the trunk of a tree, glancing about as if expecting some forest beast to spring out at him. He pointed first to a twist of brambles that ran—a forest hedge—through the groves of bent and gnarled trees. Among the brambles, I saw the bones of men. "The thorns of this heavy vine are like daggers, and sharp as any knight's blade. The mortals run against the thorns and die from madness rather than face the Laughing Ones." He grimaced. "But up there, look."

I glanced upward into the swaying branches above us.

"This is their handiwork," he said. *"Tasmal."*

On several branches of this old tree, as big around as a castle tower, dead men had been hanged—nearly rotted, some preserved as if they'd been pickled, and others wrapped in dried leaves like mummies. The nooses about their necks varied from thick-corded ropes to chains to leather straps torn, no doubt, from their clothes.

Still, more trees carried these hanging corpses, high up, far beyond where an ordinary mortal might climb—and if not a corpse, then the remnant of bones—a skull and spinal cord, an arm bone through a noose, a series of skulls strung together by a length of cord.

Ophion shivered. "Some of these dead men sought to enter Myrryd. Others were the mortal rats, trying to escape the red city. See the pale ones? When they are possessed, they seek their death after a time. Their flesh has been skinned, or has rotted. The Laughing Ones are done with the flesh, and have no use for it. They kill their hosts from within the body as a worm wriggles through the flesh of a fish. The mortals who are their victims are alive until the end. The spirits invade the flesh. Men go mad from it, and pain is their doorway, and death, their release."

I looked among the many enormous trees and saw many bones and many bodies swaying.

"I do not fear them," I said. "For it is true that spirits may harm mortals, but among the immortal dead, as we are, what mischief may they do? I have known that necromancers speak to the dead to learn of future events. I would like to speak with these Laughing Ones, for if they see the future, I would learn it from them."

"Do not even say this thing," Ophion gasped. "It is blasphemy. The Laughing Ones are not merely spirits. They come in vibration, and the pain of their entry is as the worst tortures devised by men."

"I hear no laughter. Perhaps they no longer haunt these woods."

Grudgingly, he nodded. "It is silent, but for the wind above us. Perhaps they sleep, or have wandered elsewhere. But do not wish to meet them. When they find entrance through your flesh, it is a terrible feeling, like a thousand invisible insects burrowing beneath the skin."

"You have felt this yourself?"

He nodded. I felt great pity for him, more now than when I had first seen him. Ophion had suffered much. He had sustained humiliations and tortures I could not imagine. "The hungry spirits invade the body, even of the immortal dead. But do not speak of them, for speaking of them may awaken their hunger."

As we walked among the trees, Ophion paused to sniff as if this would help him find his bearings and the direction toward Myrryd's red city. I began to hear a distant sound as if a seagull were calling out to its mates.

Ophion froze in his path, "Do you hear it?"

I nodded.

The piercing shriek seemed closer, and it was followed by a series of staccato bursts—a cackling laughter that seemed to fly far above us, with the wind.

"We must be silent and still. They may pass over us. If they speak to you, do not answer, for to do so is to invite them."

We stood frozen to the spot. The branches of the trees of the grove began to sway and creak. Whirling leaves spun at the edge of the path. Within the leaves and debris, I nearly made out the shape of a man or a boy standing there. The leaves flew out and landed on the tall grass. The sound of laughter grew louder—a cackling, a giggle, a loud honk of a laugh, and each sound sent shivers down my spine, for it was like listening to several people who had lost their minds, and circled around us. I felt a whir of wind so strong at my ears it was like the beat of a drum against me, and the laughter had grown deafening as vibrations pushed against my flesh.

In my mind, I heard a strange melodic voice, like a choirboy about to sing. *You are in our woods.*

"Yes," I whispered.

Your flesh smells sweet to us.

As the voice spoke to me, I felt what seemed a rough, wet tongue licking up my back as if it had crawled under my tunic.

You taste like the dead. The voice seemed disappointed.

"I am dead," I said. "Like you."

But you have flesh. You must give us some. Give us! Give us!

"Take it," I said.

None give their flesh willingly, the voice said.

"You must enter me to own this flesh," I said.

Ophion was wide-eyed, watching me. As soon as he sensed that the spirit was only interested in me, he scrambled away and slumped down at some distance, watching what would be done to me.

"Inside me," I said.

You are kind to invite us, the spirit said, and in seconds, I felt a burning heat at my back, and it seemed that small hands were there, pushing at my flesh, and moving through it.

As if a wind had crossed through my mouth, into my lungs, I felt the gusty presence of a spirit within me.

The laughter began to die down, as I became more

focused on the feeling of possession. It was as if someone had squeezed into my body with me, and pushed against my thoughts.

I closed my eyes.

Behind my eyes, I saw several misty shapes watching me.

We cannot wear your flesh, dead man, the spirits said. *For the flesh of the immortal dead is our tomb. It is living flesh we seek. Release us, and we will leave. If you do not, we will always be here within you.*

I will release you—if you tell me of the future, I said.

It is unwise to imprison us, immortal dead man.

I only seek answers that the spirits may know. You are not ordinary spirits, Laughing Ones. You must know much of the past, and more of the future.

The Laughing Ones went silent for minutes. And then, *You do not seem a necromancer, dead man. We will tell what we can, but you cannot compel us. Be quick and we will be gone. Do not tempt us to stay inside your flesh for very long, for even the immortal dead may lose sanity when we possess them. We have spent time in the worm-holes of your companion's flesh, for we smelled his rank odor as we surrounded you.*

I wish to know the future.

What future would you wish to see?

Is there more than one future?

Oh, many futures, and each in a different world, dead man. Your understanding limits you. You exist here, and you exist beyond the Veil. Or did Merod Al Kamr, the great teacher of the Priests of Blood, show you nothing? For we sense him here within you.

Does he speak to you? I asked.

Only you speak to us, dead man.

Do you know of Myrrydanai sorcery?

The Laughing Ones began cackling again, then grew silent. *Those devils!* the spirits said. *It has been many lives since they have haunted our wood. They would not return here without their Dark Madonna to protect them. It was they who cursed us, and kept us from the threshold of Death. If one were here, we would devour it. We would eat even the shadow of it.*

Is there a future of their unmaking?

The spirits went silent. I thought they had left my body, when suddenly they grew as a bright light in a pitch-black chamber.

There are but two futures of the Myrrydanai, they said. *In one, their defeat is in a ritual of the Great Serpent, which we cannot know. In the other, they bring Queen Medhya into flesh, and their plagues cover the earth, and spirits are enslaved as well as the living. In that future, even we might be dissolved into the ether, for Medhya has no place for us in her kingdom. The world will be over-taken by both ice and fire, and the sky will burn while the oceans freeze. The Veil will tear and those who have slept since the Old Times will crawl the earth again and be the devouring gods.*

Tell me of the ritual that may stop this, I said.

We are but hungry spirits, and do not know such things. Only the Anointed One will know.

I am that Anointed One, I said. *I am Maz-Sherah of the tribe of the Fallen Ones of Medhya.*

Dead man, you are no one to us, they said. *We have met other Anointed Ones who sought such as you seek, such as the one who cowers now among the tall grasses. We smell Myrrydanai in your grave. You are doomed, whether you pass into the city of Myrryd, or whether you remain with us. The Maz-Sherah is a lie from priests who have long ago been defeated.*

But there are prophecies that have been fulfilled, I said.

Prophecy is empty when it comes from the mouth of the Queen of Myrryd. For in her blood these were written upon dried skins of mortals. Yet who made such prophecy? Who fulfills it but the one that the Dark Mother seeks? Perhaps you fulfill a prophecy of your own destruction, dead man. You are doomed, whether you defeat your en-emy, or do not. Enough, for we have shown what we can.

*Release us now, or we will remain with you forever and
show you visions of that doom and you will despair of it
and never leave this place again.*

"I release you," I said aloud.

The moment I spoke, I felt burning heat, as if many hot
stones had been pressed into the flesh of my back. If someone had told me that my flesh opened up at the base of my
spine, and a creature made of thorn and stinger wriggled
free of my innards, I would not have doubted it, for it felt
just so.

I opened my eyes as a wind arose about me, and a funnel
of air filled with leaves and dried grass and twigs spun in a
cyclone about my body, ever widening. The heat was intense, and I felt small, invisible hands touch my face, as mad
laughter rose upward into the air and swiftly was silenced.
The corpses of men swayed from the tallest branches of the
trees around me, moved by the touch of the departing spirits.

Swiftly came the empty silence again, punctuated only
by Ophion's yawp as he cried out to me that I had been a
fool to let the Laughing Ones invade my body.

• 3 •

"I cannot go with you to the old city," he said flatly, once
I'd gotten him to calm a bit. "My brother, you are not fit for
this. You invite the spirits into your flesh? Ask them to possess you? They might have remained for many nights, burrowing beneath your heart. They could draw you into the
sunlight of daybreak just to smell the sizzle of your meat."
He clasped his hands to the sides of his head. "You cannot
be trusted here. We have no power here. It is madness. It is
a dangerous place, too dangerous for you. Your lady was
good to warn you of this place. You cannot be Maz-Sherah
if you take such chances as this, my brother. We must turn
back now, for I see nothing but Extinguishing ahead with
you as my brother."

"The spirits did not torment me," I said. "They answered my question."

"What did they tell you, brother? What?"

"They told me of my doom," I said.

He nodded rapidly. "I see it, too, brother. It does not take necromancy to see that your doom awaits you. The Lady Pythia knows much, and we should have listened to her."

"You were once possessed by these spirits," I said. "Surely they foretold your doom as well?"

He shot me a suspicious glance, his eyes narrowing as if trying to read my thoughts. "I do not remember."

"They are doomspeakers. That is their madness. Tell me, how long did the spirits remain in your body?"

He turned away from me and began walking ahead. "I do not remember," he said. "Hurry. The night is almost half-over, and we still have far to go. But we will extinguish here, I am sure of it. It sucks the soul force, and we will surely rot in these woods . . ."

I followed him along the narrow path, pushing through the overgrowth, cutting it with my razien when the vines grew too thick and the way was obstructed. All the while, Ophion would glance up into the trees to remark on the hanging dead, or he would crouch down near a bramble to sniff out any lingering spirits that might attack us.

The night was well more than half-gone when the landscape gradually changed. The forest gave way to grassland, and then to a rocky, dry terrain.

As we continued, I noticed that the rock beneath our feet became like shattered glass, and then a black dust. Above, the stars lit the earth with pale light that reflected on the dust beneath our feet. A silence pervaded the landscape, and I longed to hear some noise, even if it was the wind itself.

Dark forms loomed ahead of us, like giant chess pieces on a dusty grid.

"Statues," Ophion whispered, so quietly I had to ask him to repeat himself. "Statues, do you see?" He scrambled over to one of them and pointed at its feet. "Gifts from mortals. Gifts from vampyres. Honoring Medhya. Honoring Ghorien. Honoring the Nahhash priests, honoring the Priests of Blood. And the kings—so many kings here."

"What does this word mean?" I asked, as I touched the base of a fallen statue. The word engraved at the foot: *Asyrr.*

"That's what the kings were called. The Asyrr. Seven rulers of seven kingdoms, but they were crowned at Myrryd, and in their Extinguishing, are in those tombs of the city."

"Warrior kings?"

"Great kings who waged great wars and brought peace, as well. Two were female, five male, but all great warriors and with knowledge of sorcery, too, for they were blessed of the Serpent. But all failed in their reigns. Some failed swiftly, within a few hundred years. Others created great civilizations to the west and east, the north and south. These kingdoms lasted many thousand years. But in the final battles, they lost their kingdoms, and their powers waned. Floods and fires took many of their lands and people. Great cities collapsed, and what had once been theirs to guard—mortal man—brought them their Extinguishing, for all of us who are vampyre are vulnerable to the sword brought against us at dawn and the burning of fire and the stabbing of the heart. Whether it is within a hundred years or ten thousand, someone will always hunt us, and someone will betray us. See, this statue." Ophion pointed to a faceless statue made of white stone, fallen and broken in several places. "Here it says on this face, *anguis*—this is the word of betrayal. When a traitor of Myrryd was caught, a gift such as this might arrive after the death of the traitor, to show loyalty to Myrryd."

"I have seen this word before," I said. "In my mortal life." I remembered it scrawled across a gate at Hedammu when I went into that poisoned city to find my death in the towers that loomed above its hills. "I saw it at the entrance to a city of vampyres. Beneath it, a strange circle."

Ophion thought a moment, scratching the dried leather along his scalp. He crouched down and scrawled a circle that spiraled in on itself.

"That's it," I said.

"It was a warning to other Fallen Ones," Ophion said. He stood up and rubbed the drawing out with his foot. "*Anguis* means a betrayer is near. That circle represents the Great Serpent. A vampyre warned others that a betrayer of our father was within those gates. The vampyre within those gates would not be one to be trusted."

I didn't say Pythia's name, but I knew this was the creature meant in this warning to others of the tribe.

Anguis, I thought. *Betrayer.*

He drew two other symbols, with the bones of his toes. The first was like an arrow with three straight lines across its tail. The second was like a pitchfork with only two tines, and a curved tail.

"Have you seen these signs, also?" he asked.

"No."

"We will see many of them below, in the city," he said, somberly. "The first means a place is forbidden. And the second, is a sign that the Akhnetur gather there."

"Akhnetur?"

"I warned you of them. Small, bitey creatures," Ophion said. He held out his hand, the white of his bones thrusting from the dried flesh around his fingers. "Not much larger than this. Denizens of these dead cities. They thrive on the juice of the Flesh of Medhya, which grows among its templed gardens."

"They drink from the Veil flower?"

"Its nectar gathers in the small cup of its petals," he said. "It is honey to them. Wings like a locust. Tail like a scorpion. Claws like knives. They nest in the dark and the damp, in high places and low. They swarm when they are disturbed. Should we disturb such a hive, we may be picked clean of flesh in minutes. Remember, we have no special protection here. Do not assume you are a match for such creatures. I have seen what they can do."

He erased these two symbols with his foot, and we went on through the darkling plain with its rubble and idols.

Each statue was crudely carved, and some were simply giant heads of gods and goddesses. Some were of monsters with three heads, others were doglike creatures, and several were of dragonlike serpents, wings extended, talons spread wide.

Hundreds of them littered the ground, and we stepped over and around them.

Ophion fell back to walk beside me. "My brother, you must feel it. Myrryd is sacred. Sacred and eternal. Do you feel it?"

"It feels like a city of tombs," I said.

"Ah, yes, brother, there are many tombs in the city. Kings and priests extinguished and rotted. Many bones have taken root. Sacred and profane." He whispered this with that trembling in his voice, and I wondered at his fear. "Many gardens of the dead. Temples of worship, and more, so much more."

"The tree of the Nahhashim?"

"The Nahhash tree, within which the conjurings of the Nahhashim live." Ophion nodded. "It stands at the center of a sacred garden, surrounded by the vines of the Flesh of Medhya. This tree holds much power, though it does not bring forth leaf. Impossible to touch, brother."

Beyond the statues, we came to a ledge. There, before us: an enormous rift in the land.

Looking upon it, it seemed that I looked down at jagged mountains that were pointing away from the sky, toward the earth.

There are great canyons in the earth that I have seen since, in the Americas and within the African continent, but in that century I had never seen such a thing—it looked to me like a pit that was hundreds of miles long, and deep as an empty sea.

Ophion crept to the edge, crouching on his hands and knees to look across to the deep gorge.

"There," he said, and something in his voice betrayed a kind of pride and hope. "The red towers of Myrryd."

◆ 4 ◆

THE moment before he said the name, I saw the shapes of the giant towers below—miles down in the gorge—they looked small from that distance, but I could guess how enormous they must've been.

The kingdom seemed the richest on earth, and far grander than the kingdoms of the Saracens or of the Romans or of Aztlanteum, which seemed poor by comparison.

I caught my breath as I looked at the red towers, and those of ghostly white, and the darker monoliths that rose as if carved from the mountain wall. The moon-cast light painted opalescence across the shining towers, the statues of gods and goddesses that rose, the temples, the basilicas.

The streets were laid out on a huge grid that was off center, and for every intersecting street, there were circles with temples and statues. It seemed the fires had been lit there as if heralding our arrival.

"It is our energies, stolen from us," Ophion whispered as I peered across the great chasm that held this endless kingdom. "It fuels these fires. Myrryd knows we are here."

♦ CHAPTER 8 ♦

Temples of the Fallen

♦ 1 ♦

THIS was an advanced civilization beyond any other. The architecture alone seemed confusing in its variety and magnitude. It was like looking at the greatest treasure and feeling the shock and shiver of knowing that few of my century had ever gazed down upon its grandeur.

"All this," I gasped. "What could destroy such a place and leave it like this?"

"In one season, all vampyres were wiped clean of this place and the gods cursed it," Ophion whispered. "Mortal rats, only, tunneling here, and not many, I am certain. For how many thousands of years could they breed here with so little food beyond beetle and worm and eel and with so little hope? Friend, this was a magnificent citadel in those times before much was forgotten. A kingdom of undead kings, and priests who held magick in their words, and in their blood."

"It's not just a city," I said. "It's a civilization. Gone."

I was impelled to bow down before the great kingdom

below me. *Merod, and the Priests of Blood and of Nah-hash, and the great kings of this land, I am here to honor you and those who have come before me.*

"What are you doing?" Ophion snapped at me.

"I am praying for the blessing of this place," I said.

"Vampyres do not pray," he said.

"You told me this was a sacred place."

"Anything sacred here," he said, again glancing about the ledge as if expecting something to appear, "vanished, my brother."

◆ 2 ◆

WITHOUT our abilities of flight, we had to take rock steps, carved into the rock wall and through caves, down to the city. There were miles of such steps, and at each landing, a doorway into a cave opened up to us. When the night began to wane, Ophion drew me into one such cave.

It was a chapel of sorts, this to some unknown god, with drawings of his form upon the walls—an underworld creature with the long horns of some native deer—and all around this, paintings of various priests of this god.

Ophion lay beside me, although his stink had grown intense on our journey—yet I could not deny him friendship or comfort, and his fear seemed greater now than even among the Laughing Ones.

In a deep recess of this carved chapel, we slept, and I heard echoes of the Laughing Ones in my head as I drifted off for the day's rest. I dreamed of my doom at the hands of the white-robed Myrrydanai.

◆ 3 ◆

IT took another quarter night of climbing downward to reach Myrryd's base.

We stood on the flat rooftop of some outer chambers, and before us, the city gates were broken and fallen. Beyond this, a series of galleries and courtyards, and we crawled down from the roof and stepped onto the road toward the city's center.

Beneath the overhanging rock of the cliffs above, an entire city of many such flat-roofed buildings arose, created in a labyrinthine series of zigs and zags, a puzzle of public buildings and houses beneath. As we moved across the rooftops, crouching until the rock face above us widened and arched upward, I began to see farther and farther along, until the sky seemed to erupt from beneath the earth.

The city rose in the gloom of night, tower upon tower of shining red. These shot straight upward, built no doubt through sorcery, for I did not know an engineer so great as to design and implement this. Strange angles of the towers jutted to the left and right, like the claws of eagles, and these connected to new towers, born from these dark claws, shooting upward toward the stars.

"The ancient sorceries brought much knowledge," Ophion said, as I drank in this fantastic place. "The architects of Myrryd were many, though their wisdom did not pass into the world of mortals. These are designed to reflect what is around them, as a mirror might. Mortals who stumble upon this place do not leave, nor do they live long. I was a captive of this city before its fall, and even I could not find it by sight, nor would I wander its boulevards as dawn approached, for there are dangerous creatures here that have not found their ways into the world above."

Waterfalls spilled from the heights of cliffs surrounding the many leagues that defined the ancient city, and poured into pools and lakes that were surrounded by many temples.

These were not ruins, but looked as if they had been abandoned only recently by a population of millions of people. The temples of the Serpent dotted the landscape—reminding me of Alkemara's walls and its Temple of Lemesharra—but each temple was larger in scale than Alkemara itself. Carvings of muscular youths bearing swords and spears and strange clawlike instruments were carved in relief along the smooth pillars of these buildings; and maidens, too, naked with full breasts, carrying darts and arrows in their hands, with serpents entwined in their hair.

It was as if it were many great cities drawn together by its interconnected walls—and it had the look of no city of my time, or those that existed before. It was more like the great cities I would see more than eight hundred years later, with skyscrapers that seemed to reach the heavens when viewed from below. These shiny towers had been built on the grandest scale of any in the world, and in remembering this, I felt then—as I know now—that there were great civilizations long before mortals built farms and cities and came out of the caverns and hillsides and into the valleys to begin the first mortal cities.

As we passed one ruin of a temple, its walls fallen inward, its pillars broken, I saw a wide and long crack along the stones of the floor. When I crouched, I saw beneath the floor what seemed another building—even more ancient. Glancing about the dark chamber below, I beheld broken stones piled along the edges of the floor, leading to yet other chambers under this one.

Beneath this city, another—and beneath that one . . . still some other depth. I remembered Pythia mentioning a deep place, below the kingdom of Myrryd.

"Yes, you see the chambers beneath? Myrryd has resurrected many times," Ophion said. "One city was built atop the other. Even before there was Myrryd, there was the Asmodh."

"Asmodh? Another city?"

"Nameless. The beneath, not a city at all. The Old Kingdom was built before the vampyre, when Medhya ruled in her flesh. Only after her fall did the New Kingdom grow from the ruins of the Old. Flood and fires destroyed much, and when it was rebuilt, again roads rose above the old city. Far beneath, it was called dark earth—the ruins of a city far older than all memory. The elder vampyres who survived the rule of such terrible queens as Namtaryn the Pestilent and kings such as Sarus the Immolator and Athanat, the Lord of Slaughter—these remembering ones spoke of Asmodh in the quiet and gloom before dawn, at the burial chambers of the ancient ones. It is covered over by the vaults built of the Old Kingdom, and those that support the New. At best, it lies beneath the sewers that flooded underground lakes and flowed to the river beneath the rock called Aranzas. In the caverns and the old vaults, the dark earth ruins still exist, far below the deep nests of those mortal rats that shun both midnight and noon. Nameless it remains—as are the things that move along its trenches and wells."

"Beasts?"

Ophion nodded. "Creatures that have not yet crawled into the upper world, and those who were banished in the wars before time. Some still are there. Fire creatures, and slimy white salamanders the size of cats that devour mortals if they stray too far below the city roads. In the crags and crevices, down the inverted rock towers, through the halls and passages formed by eons of subterranean floods, they live. Infinite tunnels cut through the rock and filth, below the subterranean canals, into which the waste and water from old Myrryd flow. Beneath this city, built upon the Old Kingdom, there lie the deep places. Some of these monsters wriggle and crawl, and others . . . others may be like men, but without the faces of men, on all fours, white people as none you have seen."

"Have you seen such men?"

"Seen them? Seen them? I was thrown down among their filth!" he shouted suddenly, as if anger tore through his bones. "I looked into their wormy faces! I survived the foul canals and swam across the black flood of filth! Escaped the clutches of the faceless men, although men they may not be, for their jaws are like crocodiles'. The priests of Ghorien took me deep into the Asmodh Well—seven wells beneath even the deepest well of the city—in those nights before they filled it in with rocks and ruins to keep others out. Ghorien told me that I hunted—the hunchbacked stair—a stair of spiked steps that rose across a stony arch from the lowest of the deep to heights within a mountain cliff that could not be reached from above. I had no more than this as my goal, for they would not tell me of markers or paths—

they did not know where to seek it, and their sorcery fell mute before it.

"Ghorien whispered—before I was released to the well—that I would sense the stair when I neared it. 'Do not linger there, nor steal the treasure for yourself,' he warned me with that whisper that was like steam escaping a boiling pot—with his red eyes and narrow lips, his long fingers at my mouth as if he would tear out my tongue in a moment if I spoke to him. 'Find what we seek, and you will be set free, Maz-Sherah.'

"They tossed me, and I plummeted into sludge and offal. Down through the Asmodh filth I went, thrown beneath the old city. Dead was I to the world above, and dead I felt in the world below. The stink of mortal rat and the smothering stench of the infernal gas that permeates the canals nearly suffocated me. Fires of a deeper kingdom burned there. These flames—ignited from stone and vapor—gave off blue light and no heat, cold as ice to be near such fire."

"How far is this place?" I asked. "For it sounds as if it would take you many months to reach such depths."

"In the deep, a year is a month above, and a month is a week above, and a week below is one night lost on the earth where we now stand. Nowhere else upon this earth does time shift as it does in this underworld. I will tell you how long I stayed, for though it seemed a month, only six nights passed before I returned to the New Kingdom far above. How far is it? It is quick to descend, but easy to lose one's way, for there are no guides for such a journey. I followed the stink of mortals, who would know of the treasure though none would touch it."

"What treasure did you hunt?"

"When I am done, I will tell. I will not tell of all I saw, for no language have I for it, nor the stomach, no, my friend, my brother. Unspeakable and unknowable, without fathom and without understanding that nameless place is. Into wormholes I crawled, and saw the eyes of demons in the great spaces that opened beneath the earth. The bones of the mortal rats piled along subterranean streams that smelled of death and mortal waste. Lost I was, in the dark earth beneath the Asmodh Well. As I crept through a ribbed cavern, I heard the growl of one of these tenebrous creatures and saw its slick pale skin as it moved toward me.

"I had stumbled upon their colony, and the larvae of their offspring, formed like huge fly maggots along the gully and trough of the cave. Wriggling children, head to belly, wrapped in fish-pale skin, waiting to be born. This unspeakable man—yet not man at all—leapt upon me, for he was guard of these monstrous progeny. His jaws snapped and spread, and I felt the terrible wind of his breath on my face. My last moments, I was certain, and I knew the smell of oblivion. Yet I fought him, and scarred him—drawing his puslike blood from deep in his skin. I lifted up one of the squirming larvae and threw it into the mouth of the canal below. The other creature dived into the water to rescue the child, and I escaped—but not before I tore into many larvae that they might not be born. When I found a passage upward, I scrambled toward it.

"Yes, I had felt the tug of my prize—and saw the footpaths of mortal and monster here, for the stair was known to these denizens. The hunchbacked stair, the Myrrydanai called it, though they would not deign to venture up its many spikes. Yes, these steps were like spines of a lizard, thrust up from rock, and rose upward, carved into the arch of umbric rock by the underworld sea that had worn away the inner hills before time knew light. I thirsted much for blood. I dreamed of the taste of the mortal rats in my teeth, dreamed as I slept on the ragged teeth of that stone stairway. Slept, but did not know dawn from dusk, for all was dusk. Slept and prayed, my brother, to Ghorien himself—for I had no other god then.

"Over long nights, I scaled that arch with its spiky stair that seemed to go to a greater height than the red city itself. At its highest peak, there a statue stood, formed from brown amber.

"A knight in amber, a lord of some old kingdom in

ancient armor, and this barely covering his naked form. What infernal sculptor had made this statue I cannot say, though it was an expert craftsman, no doubt, my brother. His shield leaned at his knee, and round it was, with spikes and claws carved along its curve. His helm lay at his feet. A sword, broken below its hilt, clasped in his right hand. The head of a Gorgon in his left, grasped by her snaky scalp, her eyes wide and terrible. There, I found the treasure the priests sought. A treasure that stung me as I touched it.

"It was this treasure that drove me into madness, and began to tear at me, my beautiful flesh, which was once as comely as yours. It stole the glamour I held, and left me this mirror of death, my brother. It is a terrible treasure, a cursed treasure. I was certain I would extinguish there, upon that pinnacle of steps that went all the way to Hell's height. In the nights to come, as I scrambled through damp holes and crusted windows of rock and filth, I came upon one of the slick white salamanders as it tore into mortal flesh. Mortal rats had come here, and I knew I could sniff their trails. When I found a nest of them, I drank deeply from three, draining them to a flat pulp. I followed the stink of those who ran from me up into the blue fire caves. I felt the stream of our tribe as I rose again through the great lakes of sewage. From there, the Asmodh Well's great bottom curved and rose at a crooked angle from the depths. I climbed up its rough-hewn stones with the treasure in my mouth—at my teeth, my brother, stinging what little flesh remained at my lips—that I might leave the depths forever. I desired too much to please the Myrrydanai, who I believed then would release me, my brother."

"Did they?" I asked.

He shook his head, his bony hand reaching up to cover his eyes. "The treasure I brought them was stolen even from their grasping claws. Who was blamed for that? *Ophion!* I, who had risked all to find it for them."

"What did they do to you?"

He shivered, looking out from between his fingers. "To tell of these things is to live them. Do not ask, my brother."

He pointed down into the crevices. "What lies beneath us is Hell itself. All legends of Hell come from this place. All men know of it, though they do not find it. But I have known Hell in the grasp of the Myrrydanai priests, and in the creatures they called from the Veil."

"What was the treasure Ghorien desired?"

He turned away from me and began hobbling over to the steps of a temple nearby. He pointed to its marbled black and red statue of Datbathani. She rose thirty feet into the air, a girdle of serpents at her waist, her wings at full spread, her breasts small and high, and her face broken as if some king of this city had taken a cudgel to the statue in an effort to obliterate this sister of Medhya, the Lady of Serpents. "It was hers once. And you have seen it. It is the golden mask upon the face of your Pythoness."

◆ 4 ◆

"Do not ask me more, my brother. I do not know what thief took it. Stolen by someone who had gained Ghorien's favors, and through many centuries was bought by Neza-hual in trade for some other sorcery," Ophion said. "But do not ask me more. My memories bring pain. I know so little of these things."

"You went to Aztlanteum to retrieve it," I said.

"Foolish of me," he said. "For who am I to these gods? To these priests? I was Maz-Sherah. I had a fire in me to seek my destiny. I believed it, as you believe it—even when my youth and flesh had abandoned me. Ghorien told me he would find and destroy me if I did not get it back. Nezahual worked strong magick, and held me fast in his prisons. There, I languished, until his sorcery failed. Until I knew the mask left his kingdom."

"So, you followed."

"I followed the mask. But I felt the power of the stream in your wake."

I went to him, and put my arm over his shoulder, embracing him. "You suffered greatly, my brother," I said. "You are truly an Anointed One to have endured this."

He let out a strange yawp that was part cry and part gasp of joy. If he had tears to cry, I have no doubt Ophion would have shed them. He drew back from me, and thanked me for understanding his torments. He warned me again of Myrryd's many traps and terrors.

Ophion pointed out the Kamriad, beyond the temple where we stood. It was a building of a thousand columns and deep chambers, which contained the prisons and places of torment.

"Before Ghorien took the kingdom, it was the center of the Kamr priesthood. But the Myrrydanai hunted them, and turned what had once been a place of beauty into a pit of unspeakable torment." Ophion warned me against the doorways of this enormous structure for fear that the residue of the sorcery of tormentors still remained there. "The Myrrydanai inquisitions lasted many lifetimes, and mortal and immortal dreaded its arched doorways." He whispered of the machineries of the Kamriad as if these were living creatures, which made me remember the Red Scorpion. I felt I knew who had stolen the gold mask and sold it to Nezahual—that architect of destruction and torment, Artephius.

Ophion led me to the great water clocks, with their tipping bowls and shifting gears. These were like fountains at the center of various districts between broad boulevards. Fueled by the falls and the underground canals, they still kept time for the near-empty city. He showed me the nests of sleeping mortal rats within the ruins, for these men and women and their offspring were still terrified—generations after the last vampyre had abandoned this city—to sleep in the temples or the public houses.

All along the streets, the torches burned bright as if expecting us. Despite the fact that Ophion told me of the energies that the city drew from both the living and the dead, I still could not help but feel apprehensive—for it was as if Myrryd were a living entity, waiting for us to step into her jaws.

We passed by dome observatories, the basilicas of palaces, and the obelisks that rose above the halls of the kings. Myrryd held secrets that would not be unlocked by the world beyond it for many centuries after my visit.

I counted twenty-five towers, roughly half of them were of rust or copper coloring, but many were black, and others white, and the gray of stone temples and the brown and yellow of the gorge walls themselves, carved out into winding streets of what had once been homes and tombs and grottoes, all brought the color red to the forefront. Beneath each tower, a city unto itself, and within the walls of each towered city, grand boulevards, and crooked alleyways and great octagonal public buildings with columns the height of ten men and their girth, as well. On the avenues, the torches burned bright, drawing on the energy that still existed here.

He led me to long rows of temples to Medhya, adorned with enormous statues of the goddess with her hair braided for war, and her wings spread as wide as a great ship from end to end; her feet were talons; her hands were covered with jewels that caught the starlight and glittered red and green and blue in the darkness.

Clutched in those hands, a sword with a lit torch at its tip; or what seemed to be a panpipe; or a bull's horn; or a scythelike instrument; or an eagle; or any number of other animals and weapons and instruments. With each temple, the statue was slightly different, but all of the statues had been vandalized and disfigured, generally by chipping at the faces as if wishing to obliterate all memory of the Dark Mother's features.

Following Ophion, I wandered along the broad boulevards paved with a slatelike stone, cracked with age, the roots of vines reaching up through it. I marveled at the strangely organic structure of the towers and temples and to see the places where this great civilization had flourished, and then apparently vanished overnight. The flickering lights, within globes, seemed like lightning caught by a sorcerer's magick; tombs were everywhere, for this being a city of the undead, its people had worshipped those who resurrected—the children of Medhya.

Many of the tombs were raised high onto terraced steps,

overflowing now with musky plants with heavy dark leaves, and around some of the great stone tombs, ziggurats thrust upward. The markings along these sarcophagi were similar to the tattoos I had seen on Merod's body.

"Were these priests?" I asked.

Ophion gave that strange wheezing death rattle of his, as if it pained him to respond. "No, my brother in suffering, these are not priest pits. In here"—he pointed to one of the tombs—"a sacrifice. Sealed in, you see. To bring fortune to the city. Great fortune to Medhya's cities, for those sacrificed became doorways for those exiled to the Veil. They let in many creatures from that other world, many, many creatures. Like . . . like the Lamiades. Oh, nasty beasts, the Lamiades. They are large and brownish green like moss, and scaly. Poisoned spines ridge their crests and the backs of their necks and tails. They came from the Veil once, brought when the Myrrydanai hunted lost sorceries. They move swiftly, and can crawl up walls and even run across the surface of water. Many Myrrydanai trained them with magick that they might be ridden and follow commands— but when the Veil tore and Medhya reached through, she tore the Myrrydanai priests from their skins, and the Lamiades slipped back into the Veil, as well, with their riders. Oh, it is sacred and unspeakable to call an Old One from the Veil." His left eye watched me, while his right moved independently about in its socket, as if watching for the Lamiades.

"And what else? The Akhnetur, the Laughing Ones, the Lamiades . . . What else lurks?"

"Else? I know of other creatures, too. Some . . . some may still linger . . . in these great halls," he said, glancing about. "Some are magnificent, and others are small and vicious. We must keep watch for movement, for there may be unnaturals here, even in this empty place. Or perhaps . . . perhaps these creatures vanished when the city died."

As we passed a long, narrow alley, full of pools of water along its curved stones, I heard a scratching noise and thought I saw some movement. I stopped, watching the alley.

Ophion drew away from me. "Mustn't linger," he whispered.

"What is it?" I tried to focus on the shadows of the alley, but could see nothing more than gray shapes moving between the building's walls and the street.

"The rats," he said. "Mortals."

Curious, I slowly stepped into the alley, and moved along the building, hoping to catch a glimpse of these beings.

As I passed one temple building, then another, I saw the standing walls of a fallen structure and, peering around it, watched as two of these mortals crouched down, feeding upon something.

They were naked, and their skin was pale as the moon. Their hair also was white and thin, and at first I thought they must be old. And yet, when I made one slight move toward them, one of them glanced back in my direction.

She was a young woman, and her glance meant nothing—her eyes were without color, without the sense of seeing. She sniffed at the air. She resembled mortals of the upper world only in basic feature, for her forehead seemed too high, and her jaw extended outward, while her chin receded into her wattled neck. A light down of white hair grew along her face, and she made a strange chattering sound.

When she opened her mouth, her teeth were dark red with blood and bits of meat and small gray feathers.

In her hands, the remains of a bird.

Her partner, a boy, raised his head up, sniffing also, and began to chatter with her. The noise was like a series of tongue clucks.

As disgusting as they seemed, still I had grown thirsty from the journey, and decided to drink. The boy seemed a better prospect—younger, and his flesh was firm.

I slowly moved toward them, quietly as I could. Their chattering increased, and yet they did not run. They sniffed the air, and it was easy enough to grab the boy—a strapping lad of seventeen, perhaps—and drink from his throat while the woman, next to him, sniffed the air, and yet did not scurry off.

While I drank, the boy remained still as if stunned. As soon as I set him free, he howled in pain, and then went skittering off across the rubble of the fallen building, with the woman chasing after him as if suddenly aware of the threat.

His blood was weak, but satisfying. I felt Ophion's presence, and turned around to face him. He stood at the open window of the standing wall. "I would rather die of thirst than drink from them," he said. "They are vermin."

"His blood was fine," I said. "He was an easy catch."

"They were bred for us," he said. "Rats. Nothing but rats."

I glanced at the small dead birds they had gathered. "I feel bad for them. This is their only existence."

"They would die up there, beyond Myrryd. Oh, but do not weep, lord of all vampyres, my brother," Ophion said with sarcasm dripping from each word. "There are few of these human rats left, I am sure. These are the only two we have seen. Yet when I was in this city, they were bred by the thousands, and slaughtered after the breeding age. Let us hope we run into no more."

"Aren't you thirsty?"

"A bit. But not for them. Not for that . . . taste."

"And we are heading for the garden where the Nahhashim tree grows?" I asked, for I had asked periodically as he took me along.

"We will pass the tombs of the kings before we come to the garden," he said.

◆ 5 ◆

IN a hall of gold, with a great domed roof, upon which were painted scenes of fish-tailed men and harpies and Gorgons, devouring mortals, as well as depictions of ritual and mating and what I assumed must be the commerce of

Myrryd—there was a giant statue in red stone, reaching nearly to the dome of the roof.

It was the only statue of Medhya where her face had not been chipped away. Yet the gems that had once been the statue's eyes had been removed. Painted on her forehead, the third eye I had seen in my vision of her.

Her jaws were parted as if to bite, and her fangs were ivory tusks, polished to perfect sword points.

Beneath her left foot, she trod upon the Great Serpent, father of our tribe. Her right hand was raised to the dome as she pointed to a series of glyphs. She wore a cloak of human skulls, and upon her breasts were tattooed the sun and the moon. A stone tablet, covered with etched writings had been laid—at a later date—at the border of the statue's feet. As I approached it, I felt a slight vibration from the Eclipsis, but ignored it, for something else had caught my eye in the great chamber beyond the colossus:

The effigies of the Asyrr—the rulers of Myrryd—and their great tomb chambers, filled with the funereal beds of their servants and their warriors. I went swiftly from one chamber to another, marveling at the beautifully carved statues of the great kings and queens of the kingdom.

"A tomb and an armory," I said. I drew a spear from its place against the wall of one of the chambers. I hefted it in my hand. "It is a good weight." I glanced about and saw the crude bows along the walls, hung carefully as if never used; and long swords and double blades stacked without care in piles.

Near these were bronze helmets, piled high; and then a series of armor unlike any I had seen. These were of leather and bronze and some heavy black metal unknown to me. I went to one suit of armor that had been placed upon a metal rib cage. Its helmet had scales upon it, and at its crest, small spikes that went down the back of the neck like the shelf-scales of a dragon. The leather underclasp was like a corset in some respects, and the rest of the suit was of that black metal that shone nearly as reflective as some dark mirror.

I set the pieces back where I had found them, and followed Ophion as he scrambled along the narrow hall, down a stair, beside a long flat pool, still as ice. As we passed twin columns, and went beneath an archway, we came upon a temple without roof—above it, a shaft of light from the night sky, and the stars themselves far above in a rift of the rocks.

I saw the moon's light—full now—the solstice was close.

I felt a dull ache in my body, thinking of what I had not been able to fulfill, and felt the urgency return.

"Where is this tree of the Nahhashim? For I must cut a new staff from it now."

Ophion pointed ahead, beside a round fountain at the center of the roofless temple. Beyond, in what seemed a garden thick with purple flowers, and through another doorway, into what seemed a great red-domed basilica, I saw at a distance what might have been a white tree.

• 6 •

IN the doorway to this strange garden, Ophion pointed to the swarms that moved along the upper hollows of the dome overhead.

"They are the Akhnetur," he whispered. "Long have they guarded this sanctuary. Small biting terrors, from a demon-haunted earth."

I heard their movements—a *sh-ch-sh-ch* sound from the beating of their wings and movement in their swarms. I had assumed at first there were a dozen or so of them, but as we progressed inside the garden, the noise grew deafening.

"There must be hundreds!" I shouted.

"Thousands," he said. He glanced about the rounded ceiling and along the painted scenes of the high walls.

He looked along the high, jagged columns that supported the structure. He pointed toward the monstrous faces carved at the elephantine base of one of the pillars. Dark swarms gathered at the ledges below the ceiling.

"They were here before Medhya and her sisters had come. Before Myrryd was Myrryd. Before the crystal caverns below were torn by flood, and before the golden mask was forged. The Akhnetur guard this place from the likes of you and me, my brother."

"They protect the tree?"

"The Nahhash tree, and the flowers," he said. "I would not raise a hand to them, and neither will you. I have seen a man run from them, and within seconds they attached their claws, and their stinging tails, oh, like razors against the flesh. Still running, he was—the flesh and tissue torn from him, a blur of bones dropped to the earth." He reached over and with his fist tapped at my heart. "Their only work is to protect the Nahhashim."

The Sang-Fleur, which held the juice of the Veil—grew along the trunk of the white tree, and from it, its vines had wandered out and entangled among bone and skull like a vineyard of Hell.

These were not the small purple blossoms I had seen in Alkemara—these flowers were as large as a hibiscus, and within their purple petals, deep crimson stains.

I glanced at the thousands of Akhnetur, stirring but not moving far from their swarming hives. I could not make out any single one of them, but I imagined they were the size of my hand. My sword could not stop them if they wished to attack, nor could my cudgel hammer more than a few of them away.

I stepped forward cautiously, not wanting to disturb the swarms above. I drew my razien from its sheath, but as I did the buzzing sound of the creatures grew louder.

"Touch the tree, or a petal of the flower, and the Akhnetur *will* attack us."

I watched the ceiling, but our presence did not do more than agitate them. Their noise increased. None moved down to seek us out.

I ran for the tree, drawing my razien up, and was about to hack at one of the low branches, when the humming burst into a sound like thunder at my ears.

The great cloud of Akhnetur approached swiftly, flying scorpions whirling around me, buzzing at my scalp, forming a perfect outline of my body, right up to the tip of my razien. I saw them more clearly now—their tails dripping with some liquid, their pincers snapping, their black wings fanning the air. They whirled around me, an army of these creatures, and I knew that if I made one more move toward the Nahhashim tree, they would tear at me. And I had no power to stop them.

Yet none touched me, nor did their poison harm me, nor was a single claw drawn across my flesh. But when I made a slight move toward cutting the tree's branch, they drew closer until I felt their heat upon my skin.

I drew the blade back slowly, sliding it into its sheath at my hip. I reached for the Eclipsis, hoping to draw out its deathlight, but nothing came from it. I slipped it into the pouch again.

The Akhnetur pulled back in the air, and as I stepped backward through the flower vines, they, too, retreated until I was again at the doorway with Ophion, and the creatures, in their swarms at the corners of the domed garden.

As we returned toward the great tombs of the Asyrr—the great kings of Myrryd—Ophion whispered at my ear as if afraid someone might hear him, "Another man they would have torn apart. But you have the scent of the Veil flower in your blood. I smelled it all the way from Aztlanteum. But had you cut the branch, or harmed a twig from that tree, do not doubt that they would have spread your flesh across the garden until your Extinguishing was relief."

"There must be a way to disarm them," I said, and wandered back through the temples and tombs, remembering the vibration of the Eclipsis.

• 7 •

WHEN I came again to the great red statue of Medhya, I asked him about the language of the stone tablets by her feet. "When I draw near to this, the Eclipsis moves in the pouch."

Ophion shrugged. "It is some poem, though I do not read, my brother."

I felt the Eclipsis pulse against my waist, and drew it up from the pouch. I lifted the small globe into my right hand—its gentle but insistent throbbing shot a spike of warmth up my arm. I held the Eclipsis to the stone tablets, and the deathlight came up in a shadow-glow.

Despite its dark illumination, there was a brightness to the deathlight as it touched the words in the language of the ancient ones. From these ornate scrawls, a green light projected into three dimensions within the light's penumbra.

From that light, a voice spoke as if from within the strange green light as the script raised outward from the tablets. It was a woman's voice. That of a Priestess of Blood, who had extinguished in some forgotten millennium of the city's birth.

She spoke in my own language, maddeningly slow, as if she were dying as the words came from her mouth:

> Beneath this temple, terror reigned
> When she upon her throne cast down
> The Serpent into endless flame,
> And set new shadows at her crown.
>
> The Queen below, the Queen above,
> Stolen was her blood and bone
> Into the Veil, imprisoned she—
> Beneath the city, lies her throne.
>
> Above the door, her face engraved
> Her Gorgon sisters with tongues sublime
> Golden youths in silence serve
> Within the chamber of her crime.
>
> In nameless depths, the burning sword
> Makes hostage of the winding stair
> But he who comes to heal the Veil
> Must break the stone and find the lair.

Him for whom these words were writ
Will take the Nameless to his sheath:
The conquering Queen commands above,
The vanquished lies in wait, beneath.

The voice stopped, and the green light receded into the shadows of the deathlight.

I repeated the words, for I had memorized them as she spoke, afraid I would forget them. I slipped the Eclipsis back into its pouch. Ophion looked at the tablets with horror upon his face. "'The Queen below, the Queen above,'" I said. "The Old Kingdom and the New. 'When she upon her throne cast down . . .'" I repeated more of it, slowly, and tried to understand the significance of these words.

"Tell me what this means," I said. "What is the Nameless? Are these the Asmodh depths? For I believe it is this burning sword I must find, more than even the staff. Where is Medhya's throne?"

"Do not make me tell you of this, my brother, for it will be your end."

"Tell me," I said. "For I did not come here to be misled by you. If you are truly friend and brother, you will not withhold from me."

After several minutes of his whining and warnings, Ophion said, "In the rhyme, she speaks of a throne. Medhya's palace remains below us, and sealed is the throne room of it, for it is cursed."

"Have you been to her throne?"

"Never seen, though I was taken there, blindfolded. Tormented . . ." he said. "It is where the priests attacked her long before you or I existed. The Kamr and Myrrydanai and Nahhashim all held her while they skinned and bled her and cut her bones apart from her flesh, that she would have no entry to this world except through ritual. She was banished to dream and vision, exiled in the Veil through the ancient words. It is a torture room, my brother. The throne room should not be breached. Do not listen to this voice, these words, for it is a priestess of the Myrrydanai meant to harm us, I am sure of it."

"I am not so certain of this," I said. "Whoever first spoke these words was an enemy of the Queen of Myrryd. As am I. These words were meant for the Maz-Sherah. For us, Ophion. Take me to the palace of the Old Kingdom."

"I will not, and you cannot force me to do so," he said, and he even repeated the words several times as he and I pressed our way through one of the rift breaks at a place where a building had shattered from the movement of the earth itself.

We climbed down along the arches that held up the street above, into the bowels of the Old Kingdom.

• CHAPTER 9 •

The Palace

• 1 •

BENEATH the city above us, another kingdom. Its sky was the stone underpinning of the last Myrryd, buttressed with great stone arches that seemed all of one piece, and which descended downward as if the beneath was a great well, a secret bunker, deep and endless. It was a ruined and shattered landscape, for walls crumbled, and roads had become muddy with the leaking of fountains and canals both above and below. Mosaics adorned the walls, and there was no torch that lit here, but all was dark—and yet my eyes, powerful in absolute night, saw more clearly than in torchlight.

Ophion did not wish to accompany me, for he spoke of the depths farther below. "It is a drop into a lost doom," he whispered. "Do not seek such places."

"You must show me the palace of the first Medhyic dynasty," I said.

Ophion glanced downward to the subterranean vista of

this undercity. "Yes, I cannot forget these places, for they have been pierced into my bones."

He began shouting "There!" and "There!" as he mentioned places where mortals made their nests and were easy catches in the old nights. He pointed out the temples, the strange round buildings that were called Hives, where the rituals of the Myrrydanai often took place, far from the prying eyes of the rulers of the New Kingdom. "Ghorien and his priests sacrificed vampyres—a blasphemy and a threat to us all. There were rumors of the calling up of Medhya then, but I did not believe it until I felt her presence. They hold the keys of necromancy, those Myrrydanai. It is their greatest sorcery to know the secrets of the dead and those beyond the Veil. This was in the days before *she* tore their flesh from them. Before she brought them into shade."

Then, as he spoke, nearly idly, his eyes widened, and he pointed off in the distance. "Look there, where the light falls from above—do you see it? Her palace. Magnificent in those nights. There. There, my brother!"

◆ 2 ◆

A series of stairs led downward, built upon arches that were flanked on either side by public buildings of the kind we had just seen in the Myrryd above us. This led into a galley of sorts, although it had been more of an open square in the old nights.

From this we emerged into what would have been the evening light, had the New Kingdom not been built overhead. Above us, the arches that kept the New Kingdom from dropping down onto the Old, seemed impossible in their height, though from each arch, other arches grew at angles so that there was an arch for an arch for an arch.

In certain places of this sky-ceiling, water streamed down like a thin waterfall, and bled a well-worn path across a street, forming a narrow canal as it went. Breaks and rifts above showed flickerings of torchlight, and as we passed under these, the air grew slightly fresh but cold, while in other spots without such cracks, the air was damp and smelled of mold and rot.

Below, the narrow streets led to broader ones, and the canals made by the streams of water from above became wider and longer. As we passed one of these, I saw circling ripples come from a particular spot, and then another. I was about to ask Ophion what swam in such water, when he reached over to squeeze my wrist, unwilling to speak of such things.

This city was crumbled and torn as if by some ancient war, and of it I asked Ophion nothing. The history of the Old Kingdom was written upon its fallen walls and the statues, which had been defaced and lay in many pieces on the flattened limestone steps of the temples of Medhya, which seemed to have been built every quarter mile along the narrow labyrinthine streets of that district.

While above, it was a red city, here below, the city was white; and though it was not made of caelum stone as Taranis-Hir had been built, the white stone had a similar effect upon me. It made me think of those I needed to find. The feeling of urgency again returned, and with it the sense that I was underwater as I walked on land—as if I could not move fast enough toward what I needed. Yet, I knew in that city, whether above or beneath, some secret would find me. Yet I did not think I had but three nights until the solstice would come, and I did not know if the passing of the solstice might be the passing of all hope.

The streets themselves were of a green glass, broken to bits and formed as an unintended mosaic beneath our feet. The air was thick with a heavy humidity, from the many thin falls that fed into the various canals generated over the many years from gulleys and culverts and the foundations of fallen buildings. I tasted metal on my tongue—as if there were bits of iron and copper in the moist air.

As we passed various openings into the ruins beneath the upper city, pungent smells assaulted us—from the overripe stink of human nests, to the sweetness of some aromatic flower in the stagnant pools among the tangled brown weeds that had grown tall and thin as slender trees along the canal edge.

"This is the heart of the kingdom," Ophion said as he pointed to the place farther along, where, in the light that exists in darkness, I saw a great tower rising up, broken at its flank by the arches that buttressed the New Kingdom, a burdensome heaven over the earth. "Her palace."

• 3 •

LIKE a blind whore parading her wares before the tombs of the dead, so this palace with its ornate and gaudy statues, its countless pillars holding up its rooftops which were flat and broken at intervals along its rotted mile, its bone-white steps that led to its troughs and gaps—filled with the world-robbed treasures of priests of the queen—stood beautiful and endowed and brazen among the ruins of the Old Kingdom. The statues of the queen herself were head-less here, torn off no doubt when the Priests of Blood and Bone and Flesh had sent Medhya to her exile. Thrown and battered, these statues lay on the steps, crushed to dust their hands and their breasts, and I imagined the moment when the conquering rats—from which my tribe descended—had swarmed and trampled the same art and treasure they had once polished and carved for her.

Her palace was too much to take in as we walked along its well-worn path, past the empty pools where once rituals of the priests had been enacted, past the chambers of the nobles of her reign, past the broken doorways filled with untouched gold and jewels, as if it were cursed to desire it.

Art adorned the walls in the form of friezes, and upon the ceilings faded images of wars and tribulations, of monsters that were like giant lizards upon the earth, of vampyres such as Ixtar and those of that lineage, with the aspect of jackal and bat and vulture upon their forms. So much color and movement seemed to exist in the barrage of images that I began to dread them, and then ignored them. When we found a room of gold, with chairs and tables and great long rows of golden flagons and bowls and plates and cups, I began not to want to see such things. It was a willful blindness as I followed Ophion. He spoke of what he remembered and of how little had changed. Ghorien and his priests used the palace for ritual and torment.

But no one else, not servants or protectors, nor any vampyres "but those who are fools," he whispered to me. The mortal rats did not enter this palace, for even in their memory, fear remained through many generations of such a place.

I felt its flow—not a stream, but a burning sensation, as if there were in its bone-white stones and golden rooms a smoldering ember behind, beneath, above, and around it. A fire had not been set here, and yet a fire was felt.

"I feel as if we are being watched," I said, suddenly, and stopped at the center of a room that was shaped in an oval, with several doorways. Upon its recessed wall, as if a stair, there were urns and bowls filled with ash, and at its doorway, in the corridor beyond, a large brazen bull. Beneath this animal, an empty bowl in the floor, wide and long, and beyond its rim, the bull's hooves were set.

"They put me in that," Ophion said. He went to its side and reached for a small lever, barely visible. Turning it, a creak and squeal, and as he drew the lever downward, the right side of the bull opened up. "Beneath it, they built a fire. For hours I lay in it as the metal heated. I began to moan and roar, and that is what they wish, for it is the bull roaring and not the one inside it who roasts. A mortal in such a device will die after many hours. But us . . . I roasted a night, and then they drew me out to sleep. Upon the rising of the moon, they put me in it again."

"They must have been seeking some information," I said.

"I had none. It was because I was Maz-Sherah. They wished to take away all I had."

"They could have sent you to your Extinguishing. Why not that?"

He shook his head. "You do not understand the

Myrrydanai. Their nature is beyond ours. For hundreds of years, they played such games with me."

"They were looking for something," I said. "I'm sure of it. They were waiting for something from within you." Yet, despite speaking these words, I could not understand what it was Ghorien sought.

I put my arm over his shoulder. "My brother, do not be afraid. It is many years past. It will not happen again."

"Yes," he said, but as we passed down the corridor, he glanced back at the bull as if it were alive and might pursue him.

When we had gone just past the middle of the palace chambers, we came upon a door made of stone, sealed with wax of some kind at its edges. I did not need to decipher the words written above it in the old tongue of the Myrr—this was the throne room of Medhya.

I looked at the engraved faces of the two fierce creatures, one on either side of the door—their tongues thrust out as if in some bewitchment, their hair wild and tangled and flowing in an invisible wind.

I spoke the words I had memorized of the statue above: "'Above the door, her face engraved, her Gorgon sisters with tongues sublime.' Look." I pointed at the door's arch. The stone had been chipped away. "They destroyed the engraving of her face. They did not want her here."

I reached up to touch the face of Lemesharra to the right of the door. I ran my fingers along her eyes, down her nose, to her lips.

"What are you doing?" Ophion asked.

"It's a code. In the rhyme. There is something about the faces of Lemesharra and Datbathani here. Something that matters." *With tongues sublime,* I remembered. I touched the tongue of the engraving and it gave inward slightly. "Sublime—if the word might mean . . . something other than what it seems. Yet the sorcery of the statue's words is that it would mean this . . . to me."

"Mean what?" Ophion asked as he watched my fingers press into a kind of softness in the rock.

"Beneath the limestone—perhaps the play on words—sub-lime," I said. I bade him go to the engraving of Datbathani on the opposite wall and similarly depress the softness of rock at her tongue, and he did so.

In a moment, we heard the scraping of rock against rock, and the great square door grudgingly moved inward an inch, breaking its seal without our help. I guessed that there must have been a lever and gears within the stone wall—made hollow at its center, and our pressing these spots, marked by the tongues of Medhya's sisters, had set off the lever mechanism.

The door stopped after opening less than a two-inch gap, but using our combined weights, we pushed against it, managing to nudge it forward another half inch. At which point the internal mechanism took over, and the door slid, groaning and scraping, to a wide enough gap for me to step inside.

• 4 •

GOLDEN *youths in silence serve*. The words became true as I entered Medhya's throne room.

The great chamber seemed airless, and yet as we unsealed its door, a great rush of air moved through it like a spirit—and flames came up from bowls that were held in the hands of statues. Twenty statues—golden maidens and youths with garlands in their hair—held these wide bowls, and within each bowl fire rose from oil. It was as if we had let the energy of Myrryd into a place that had been robbed of it.

These statues were not on pedestals, but set into the black marble of the floor, and were of varying heights as if modeled directly on specific mortals. The walls, also of black marble, caught the light through the door as we opened it. The torch in my hand reflected along the smooth, shiny marble. Something about these statues reminded me of the mounted bodies of vampyres I had once seen in Alkemara when I had first entered the hall of the Temple of Lemesharra.

The place had a great sense of emptiness upon entering, and I felt that it had been sealed from fear rather than care.

But now, with a hundred golden bowls lit by flame, and the smell of sulfur and burning incense in the air, it felt as if some living queen would enter it at any moment. I half feared that I had stumbled upon an entry to the Veil and that this would, itself, bring Medhya into flesh.

Yet, despite this fear, I walked down the aisle between the many statues. I had an unsettling feeling as I looked from youth to maiden. Their golden arms so perfectly imperfect. Their nakedness so well wrought, each detail seemed too lovingly created. Each golden young man seemed an individual with nose and eyes and chin and shoulders that spoke of a specific life. Each maiden, too, was different from the other, and perfect in the casting of feature and form.

I withdrew my cudgel and, with as great a force as I could muster, smashed it against the shoulder of one of the youths. The gold was more fragile than it seemed, and after a few such hits, the thin outer layer of gold crumbled, and beneath it, I saw human bone.

"Medhya did this to her own subjects," I said.

Ophion, a few feet behind me, touched one of the maidens on the elbow. "Dipped in gold," he marveled. "Molded. So beautiful and terrible."

I turned back to face him. "You have been in this room?"

He shook his head several times. "No, my brother, not as it is now. Not like this."

At the end of the room was a series of steps, bone white against the dark floor. Twenty steps upward, a platform, and upon it a great throne made entirely of gold, designed with serpents with their jaws parted, fangs jutting, as well as a dragon motif that encircled the throne and rose up to become the backing of its seat.

It reminded me of the many-dragoned doorways I had seen in the Temple of Lemesharra, at the heart of Alkemara itself. I knew whose throne this was without Ophion's words.

"Medhya," he said. "Before the priests took the kingdom and raised up new kings of Myrryd. She built this. She consecrated it. They used to say that in the walls of this temple, children were buried alive to protect her. Beneath the throne itself . . ." He hesitated, and covered his mouth like a child afraid to use a blasphemy.

"What is beneath the throne?"

"Poison, and those who had died of it," he whispered. "Do you not smell it? Beneath the burning incense of the fires? I know of one thing there, but only from what I heard in the prisons of Ghorien. A flooded place, my brother, that is all. Sewers, where the human rats drink foul water and throw the bones of their dead." His voice grew more quiet as he added, "The nameless depths with its underworld sea and dark earth."

I sniffed the air—again, a trace of sulfur, and some other odor. "As the old pythonesses would sit above the vaporous cracks in the caverns," I said. "They would feel the inspiration of their gods. So she sat here, and the breath of this dark earth arose to her." I crouched down, and felt along the hairline fissures that ran like the too-slender roots of some tree—these cracks were barely noticeable, yet it was from these that the odious scent emerged. *It is why they sealed the chamber,* I thought. *That no one would breathe in the air that Medhya had tasted. Yet, why do this? Why not destroy the throne or take it to the New Kingdom? Why leave these gold statues here? Why preserve this place if it offended Ghorien and his priests?*

"She built her throne on poison, and her sanctuary with the bones of children," Ophion said as he glanced from the floor to the ceiling.

"Poison will not hurt an immortal," I said, as I began to see the many cracks along the floor and the steps up to the throne. For a moment I had a strange flash of insight—for something about this chamber reminded me of the tomb of Ixtar, in which I had briefly been held captive. I did not know why that thought came to me, but the more I looked at the steps and platform that upheld the golden throne, the more I became convinced that it had been built as a kind of tomb. *But to what? To whom?*

"You know of the depths below," I said. "Have you been beneath this chamber, beneath this palace?"

He nodded, but shivered.

In his eyes, I saw something—more terror there than when he had seen the brazen bull, or the various sites of his imprisonment. "It is the Asmodh Well," he whispered.

• 5 •

"HERE? Beneath her throne?"

"We should not be here," Ophion said as he paced along the black floor. "There may be a trace of her left behind. You should not come here. Maz-Sherahs extinguish. Only those ordained by the priests may be here. Only those whom Medhya has blessed, for to all others, this is poisoned. We have no ritual to hold it back. None at all."

"Tell me, where beneath us is this well?" I asked.

He would not reply until I had dragged him to the steps up to the throne itself. "Show me the Asmodh Well, where it exists. Beneath the throne? One of these statues?"

"These steps," he said, shivering and barely able to get the words out. "These steps, my brother, are much changed. When I was brought here, these rose up at the center, and all around the throne, the depths of the Asmodh Well— more a deep gouge of earth, a sinking chasm, than a well— with its poisoned vapors like yellow smoke, rising from the beneath. Mortals were cast into it, sacrifices to those below—to the breath of the Asmodh, which lingers."

I set him free, and tried to imagine it—the steps had originally gone straight from the floor, suspended as if part of an arched stairway, with the throne at its low peak, and on either side . . . the deep well. "They dropped you?"

Ophion had grown angry—I had forced him to remember what he most wished to forget. "Oh, my brother, there are ancient stairs beneath this world in all lands and under the oceans as well. These are the ruined lands of the deep ones who never know the sun or wind or moonlight. Why

don't you join them? Dig your way to that flooded mouth
of Hell if you wish." He wiped at his lipless mouth, as if
the words themselves disgusted him.

"What is the source of these fumes, and of Medhya's
prophecies?"

"I do not know," he said, and spat upon the floor. "I was
cursed to bring you here. I hoped to keep you from your
own doom. But I see that is impossible! You hunt the dead,
Falconer, and your oblivion will find you."

"Something powerful exists in this beneath," I said.
"For Ghorien would not go there, nor would the priests.
What could they have feared? What could they have
known?"

"Feared? They? Oh, the Myrrydanai fear the Asmodh
Well, my brother. Why do you think they have not returned
to Myrryd? Why do they send their plagues from the bogs
of your homeland and not their true kingdom? It is the
power of it that reached its tendrils up from the deep and
tore their flesh and threw them into the abyss of the Veil itself, to be jackals to their lost queen!" He shouted as if
taken with an explosion of memory. "They feared what lies
below, as I fear it, and as you must fear it! It is beyond sorcery, beyond magick, and would make Medhya bow down
in pain if it ever reached the upper lands. Do you think
Medhya's reign ended because of the uprising against her?
No, it was the rituals of the priests, who called a fearsome
sorcery from the throat of the dark! From this throat, such
a horrible breath came, and burned all it touched! Even
they could not control such terrible power. All feared these
depths, and when they brought me here, I feared them. I
feared what whispered in the fetid air of the Asmodh Well!
My mind flew apart when I crawled along those narrow
passages below us!" When he calmed a bit, he covered his
face with his hands, and said, "Brother, I cannot lead you
down into that place. Remember the rhyme that the statue
spoke. It will be your guide, not I."

The words of the statue returned to me again, and I
spoke them aloud:

"'In its depths, the shattered sword makes hostage of the winding stair. But he who comes to heal the Veil must break the stone and find the lair.'" I was at a loss to understand much of it. "Is it a sword? In the Asmodh depths?"

"I have never seen such a sword," Ophion said, clambering back behind the statue of a maiden, as if trying to hide. "Nor a winding stair."

"These are not the spiked steps you spoke of?"

"Those did not wind, but grew like spines on the back of an arching beast of rock," he said. "It is a many-chambered heart, the Asmodh Well. There are stairs of stone and steps of dirt and bridges into the dark, but I do not know this winding stair. I have never heard of it, nor seen it. Perhaps it was destroyed long ago. Perhaps it is a lie."

"Tell me of the sword. Why did you not retrieve it, for surely Ghorien demanded it of you?"

"I could not, my brother. No, I could not. It whispered to me from its tomb. It whispered that it knew of me. Of my coming for it. It whispered . . ."

"What did this sword whisper?" I shook him too hard, and regretted it, for the poor vampyre had nothing but terror in his memories, and had returned for my benefit.

"It whispered *your name*," he said, his eyes narrowing and his teeth gnashing. He *spat* out the words, "*Falconer*, it called me, but I knew. I knew I was no falconer! It did not want me, so it would not *let* me find it!" He stomped around and raised his fists as if cursing gods and mortals and his own mother for his birth and existence. He cursed the vampyre who had given him the Sacred Kiss, and the night he knew he was Maz-Sherah and sought to prove it. "Ghorien knew when I returned. When he lowered the ropes for me, down, down, down in the stinking swill of the Asmodh Well that I had scaled like a spider! I brought him the mask, but it was not enough! He had believed I was the Anointed One, he believed I was meant to take the sword from its wound in the earth, but no, it was you—even in those ancient times, it knew you, long before your birth, Maz-Sherah, it knew you would come! Ghorien has ever since known of your coming. He has waited in the dark world of the Veil to be released. You—in fulfillment of prophecy, your existence, your entering of the Veil through the venom of the Serpent—let loose these Myrrydanai dogs. I am no Maz-Sherah, although I had believed it. All my existence, for nothing, and now you will extinguish below, my brother, if you enter the Asmodh Well."

I could not help myself, I hugged him close and whispered at his ear. "Do not allow the trickery of these memories to harm you, Ophion. You are my brother as sure as any vampyre may be." I did not press him as to why he had not mentioned before that he knew the name I was called by many. It did not matter—for here we were, and I would seek this sword of fire. I owed Ophion much, and it pained me to feel his wounds of those years of captivity.

He recoiled from me and slunk off across the chamber. "I will never go to those depths again," he said. "It is a terrible evil, that place. It lies, and tricks. It is the arms of doom. Do not go there. It is the tomb of many who have explored in the Asmodh lands."

"Who are the Asmodh?"

"Before time, before name, this name given them by those who came after. In the old tongue Asmodh means 'the Nameless.' They were delvers and forgers who fed upon the dead and dying—and could not exist even in starlight, for all brightness blinded them. With their burning forges—which the blue fires below fueled—the Asmodh made weapons that could not be defeated. It was the mask that they had made, and the sword, though I do not know who held it in his hands. The delvers cut the bridge of Myrr, and tore apart the Asmodh depths to channel power from far below where the eternal fire rages in the earth. Some believe their race died out, but those white creatures I have seen, with their slick bellies and jaws, I believe those are the descendants of the Asmodh, though they no longer delve or work the forge, for their race has been cursed by their own sorcery." He told me more of these creatures, and more of the sorceries unleashed from beneath—but what interested me the most was the terror of the Myrrydanai at the mention of the Asmodh, for their power was greater than even Medhya's.

"If you are afraid, you may go. Wait for me beyond the palace walls," I said to him, and as if having waited for my leave, he turned and scampered off.

At the doorway, he glanced back, and called out, "Do not go to the depths, I beg of you, my brother! If you see the bridge of Myrr, within the vast beneath, do not cross it, nor dwell upon the foul waters!" Then he cried out, "The Maz-Sherah is a lie! A lie of our tribe! It is a wish for Extinguishing, that is all! Do not suffer as I have suffered, my brother!"

When he had gone beyond the chamber, I heard the echoes of his moans and pleas as if he argued with himself as to whether or not he should abandon me entirely.

• CHAPTER 10 •

Medhya's Throne

• 1 •

I reached for the orb, clutching it. I felt no pulse from it, no life. *He who comes to heal the Veil must break the stone and find the lair.*

I approached the throne, walking up each step, but feeling uneasy after Ophion's outburst. I had a greater sense of the vanity of the Dark Madonna. She was vain and cruel, and represented the worst of vampyrism. She was the opposite of the Great Serpent—and his servants. Merod Al Kamr had spoken to me of guardianship, of protection of the mortal realm.

But as I stood before the gold throne of Medhya, I inhaled a ruinous scent. I knew she would destroy all, for she herself had the seed of destruction in her thoughts. She had left Ixtar in some past eon, and with her sisters, Datbathani and Lemesharra, had come to this place, and in building this kingdom through power and war, she destroyed her sisters and drank their power from them. She took their faces to fool the priesthoods with aspects of justice and mercy and benevolence—visages she herself did not possess. She stole her immortality from the Great Serpent and subjugated even that god to a place at her feet.

This city, this kingdom had been built for her vanity, for her control and enslavement of others.

The priests had rebelled and overthrown her for her actions. The Myrrydanai had grown corrupt, despite their rebellion. They had returned to their former roles as slaves of her will.

I touched the golden serpent entwined on an arm of the throne. It was as cold as frost.

A shock went through me, from the icy gold through my flesh and nerves. I was shot into a Veil vision:

A snowy landscape, with ash falling from the sky, and the white towers of Taranis-Hir in the milky distance. In the sky, falcons moving in circles, as if on some hunt. Merod Al Kamr, his body alive with tattoos. In his hand a sword with fire emanating from its blade. His eyes were shiny and black like the iridescence of a beetle's wings. His flesh was alabaster, and the tunic at his waist, a deep crimson.

"You have failed, Falconer," he said, and he took his sword and thrust it into the earth. The fire of it spread from blade to snow, and the flames ran along the surface of white until it formed a ring all around the Priest of Blood. "Your children bleed, and your tribe will extinguish. The Dark Mother comes through, for you have strayed from your path. You have forgotten much. But look." He reached out with his right hand, and upon it was a heavy glove made of leather, wrapped around his forearm with thin strips of cloth. He held this gloved hand to the sky, and a falcon dropped from a great height downward, coming to rest upon his arm. "The falcons hunt the skies, Maz-Sherah. Do you still hear them? Do you know them? They are vigilant. They are your strength. You are here, you exist, because you are the Falconer—the Maz-Sherah—and you must lead those who ride the storm of war. You have held too long to your preparation. It is time, although much has already been lost."

The falcons hunt the skies.

As he said this last word, he released the falcon, which shot off into the darkness, with a piercing cry. The flames around Merod leapt toward the sky, and all I saw was fire itself like a dancing, twisting creature.

Then, I saw her, though she did not look as she had in my earlier vision. Medhya sat on her throne, dressed in ceremonial armor so that she was like a dragon itself—spines came out of her helmet and thrust like daggers at her arms. The armor was of metal that shone like the black night beneath a full moon, and was segmented so that it gave her the appearance of a serpent. I saw her as she had been once in the flesh—her skin was pale and thick, and her eyes were small, but had been painted black and red and gave her the appearance of great beauty. A third eye was painted at the center of her forehead. Her lips were reddened, emphasizing the bone white of her skin. When she opened her mouth, I saw the dark onyx teeth I had seen on Nezahual, with elongated fangs and sharpened edges to all the teeth in her mouth.

In each of her hands, she held the head of one of her two sisters by the scalp, each more beautiful than the other—Datbathani, whose golden mask remained upon her face, and Lemesharra, within whose mouth had been thrust the Eclipsis, stolen from Death's handmaidens. There, leaning against the throne, the sword I had seen that Merod had held—the sword that burned. Medhya had stolen these things herself.

All her power had been drawn from theft and slaughter. All her magick from the Great Serpent.

In my vision she stood up from her throne and lowered her helmet's visor to cover her face. All that could be seen of her were slits for her eyes, and a gaping open wound for her mouth. She seemed a creature who was nothing but sharp teeth, swallowed within a serpent armor. The mouth surrounded by metal opened and closed, its teeth like the sharpened tines of gates as she barked to those who were beneath her. She was no great goddess, but a vampyre as Nezahual had been—a daughter of Ixtar. How had she gained such power? Such might? How had she been able to murder her sisters and steal from Death and immortality?

Was all power a great theft? Yet—who had made the Eclipsis? Who had endowed the mask with its energy to draw out immortality?

She shouted orders to those I could not see, for I was unable to turn in this vision and see the room itself, nor could I hear her voice, yet I detected her intent. She stood before her throne in serpent armor, a creature of metal and teeth, judging and condemning those brought before her.

As I watched her, I saw what seemed a movement along the throne's gold surface.

But not precisely movement—a reflection of movement.

The throne reflected something in the chamber that I could not see, but it twisted as if it were some giant form. I saw the distortions of soldiers with spears alongside it.

I heard Merod's voice. *You have been seeking the wrong power, Falconer. Just as Medhya fooled the Serpent, you have allowed her to fool you. Where is your path? Why are you not on it? Why have you come to Myrryd when it takes you from your path?*

Priest of Blood, within my own blood, show me what I need to understand, I thought.

This I cannot do, for the way is closed to me, Maz-Sherah. But you must ask yourself: Whom do you seek here? Who lights the fires of Myrryd when its queen is beyond the Veil, and its kings lie extinguished in the tomb, and the priests are devoured and destroyed? Who draws your energies and keeps you from flight here? When you answer this, you will know what you seek. And you will find your path. Do not look at the power of Medhya, for like the she-wolf among tombs, all she has was stolen from the suffering of others. The Queen of Wolves cannot create a kingdom like this, nor can she be a source of her own power. She must steal what others have created. She must suck the energy as our tribe sucks blood for sustenance. But who is the source of this?

And then I heard no more of him.

It was as if a lightning bolt had gone through me, for suddenly I myself could answer those questions now. It was as if a door had opened, a door for which I held the key.

I knew who lit the fires of Myrryd when no vampyre or mortal human ruled in that city.

There could only be one answer.

One source.

The Great Serpent.

The conquering queen commands above,
The vanquished lies in wait, beneath.

♦ 2 ♦

I realized what I saw reflected in the throne's gleam: it was the moment when Medhya had conquered the Great Serpent. Her soldiers held the Serpent beneath her throne. I remembered those statues in the chapel at my home—of a saint with his foot upon the serpent.

Medhya had done this—she had put her foot upon the Great Serpent, and stolen his treasure, which was immortality and those objects that—somehow—absorbed it.

The mask. The Eclipsis. Even the sword. Though I did not see the Nahhashim staff in this vision, I knew this object held some secret of the immortal world.

I knew now why I felt drawn to seek Myrryd.

I opened my eyes, thrown from the vision.

"The Great Serpent is here," I said.

I began cutting away at the white stone, at the fissures that ran through it, using cudgel and blade until I had drawn back chips of stone. Using great force and industry, I opened a hole beneath the floor.

Fumes of sulfur and steam came up from beneath the throne, yet though I felt weakened by this, they did not seem to contain any terrible poison. Through this opening, I saw the throat of the Asmodh Well, a scarred and jagged drop. I did not have a rope as Ophion had once had to be lowered to it; nor could I draw on my wings to journey there. I would have to crawl as best I could along its pitted walls.

Within a few hours I had made the opening large enough to fit through, and I slipped down into the gap. I swung myself down to a slender ledge, but when I reached for a dent in the rock wall, I slipped and fell. It was a long drop, but soon enough I landed in a large pool of black water, lit on all sides by the strange blue fires that burned upon spurs and spikes of rock. The water was icy and deep, and I felt strange movement along my body as I came up to the air. Swiftly, I swam to the shallows, and then stepped upon the cavern floor, which had been built by men, for it had flat stones laid across it to create a ledge.

Above me, I saw the crevasse that was the well—it must have stretched the length and breadth of Medhya's palace. It was a wonder to me that the palace itself had not fallen into its depths.

As I walked along the ledge, I saw a honeycomb of chambers opening up before me. The blue flames flickered along each corridor, and I heard noises both terrible and curious from these entrances, but at some distance. I remembered the creatures that Ophion had spoken of, and I did not wish to encounter them on this journey. I reached to my pouch for the Eclipsis, and held it forward, bringing out the light from it. *Where is this sword I seek?*

The deathlight moved like a ghostly black shadow along the rough cave walls, and through the natural vault ahead, where the waterway twisted along.

• 3 •

OPHION'S words came back to me: *The delvers cut the bridge of Myrr, and tore apart the Asmodh depths to channel power from far below.* The stonework was intricate along the ledge, and each triangle of stone fit into the next, and within the lines I saw a design of sun and moon and stars—a mosaic of gray and white and yellow stone. As I looked across the vaulted arch of rock, I saw the burned drawings of these ancient people, high above, of lizards and lions, dragons and harpies—the cultural remnants of the Asmodh. I followed the water farther—the canal was broad, and bounded on the other side by another ledge, like the one I walked, and beyond this, arched entryways into deep chambers.

The water itself was of a dark, rusty color, as if metals rested at the bottom of it—a dumping ground of the materials used to make the red city itself. I saw piles of human bones on the opposite ledge. I even heard the skittering of what I feared might be the strange white creatures at some distance, but only saw shadows as they scampered through various tunnels along the canal. I feared them, but did not turn back, nor was I precisely sure how I would rise from these depths with no power of flight and no grip along the smooth walls of the bottom of the Asmodh Well.

Overhead, the vaulted ceiling was low so that I had to crouch as I made my way along the ledge. The humid steam of a filthy waterway assaulted my senses, and I began breathing through my mouth to avoid the awful stench.

I felt the pulse of the Eclipsis, and held it ahead of me—and this time, a feeble deathlight came forward, and then died out. As I went I was faced with various twists and turns, and the canal forked, but every time, I held up the orb in each direction and followed its weakening pulse along these waterways. As I followed its vague directions, feeling like a hound without the knowledge of the prey, offense in the form of some rank, moist air covered me like a glove. The sulfurous stink increased as I bent down to follow the ever-narrowing vault above me. I heard a strange sound, like a distant roar of the sea far beyond, or of a forceful wind blowing from some shaft high in the world above.

From behind me, I sensed the source of the stench that moved nearby.

I paused, glancing back, narrowing my vision to bring up the light that existed within the dark. There, crawling along the low, arched ceiling above—and just a few feet back from me—was one of these white slimy creatures. It was a female of its kind, for her many breasts hung downward as she pivoted her lower body toward the wall of the vault, while keeping her hands somehow glued to the arch of it. Her face reminded me less of human or alligator, but more the mouth of a fish of some kind, elongated was the jaw, but small the mouth as it opened and closed as the thing breathed. She made a hissing noise as she saw me turn, and a strange rattling sound came from deep within her throat.

I froze, not knowing how this encounter might go. She drew her entire body down to the side of the wall, and if she had wanted to—in a fraction of a second and a short reach—she might have leapt upon me. She slowly parted her oval lips wider, and I could see the jagged sharp teeth, shown in a threat as she hissed, and that strange rattle sounded again. Behind me, the constant roar of water—from the place toward which I assumed the canals flowed. The creature then moved toward me without moving an arm or leg. Instead it was her neck that came forward in such a way that it reminded me of a snake swallowing its prey. Her face was so close to mine—and her stench as well—that I grew afraid to move. Yet I wondered what harm she could do me, for I was more than three times her size, and my teeth were longer and grew sharper.

She sniffed at my face, and I saw that her eyes—which had seemed white and invisible to me at a short distance—existed there in the translucent tapeworm slickness of her face as two small, shiny black dots nearly covered over by the folded white flesh. The rattle grew louder, and I felt she would strike at any moment. I lifted the Eclipsis up, and its darkening light shone as I thrust it between her face and mine.

This was enough to make her draw back, into her body, and then she gave out a loud squeal. Suddenly, I heard the slithering and splashing of other creatures as this she-beast retreated. Within seconds, a dozen or more of these underworld throwbacks were moving down the dark vault toward me. The Eclipsis light was not enough to frighten them.

Keeping the orb in my grasp, I went running down the vault, seeing light along its distant curve.

As I came out from under one of the low archways, the ledge along the canal ended, and I nearly went over the edge of a cliff below me, a great crevasse in the earth, which seemed as large and wide as the New Kingdom of Myrryd had seemed from the cliffs far above it. The roar I had heard was the sound of a distant sea far below. I nearly went to my knees, for I had been prepared to step off the edge without noticing that the canal poured in a waterfall downward.

My grip on the Eclipsis was not tight enough, and it fell from my grasp.

I watched it plummet far below. I dropped to my stomach as if I could reach down into its fall and grab it again. But I had little time—the creatures behind me were clambering along the vault, and some had just emerged onto the cliffside. I glanced to the left and right, and there, down a series of ledges, was the naturally formed arch bridge that must have been the Bridge of Myrr. I leapt ledge to ledge downward, certain that at any moment I would fall to distant rushing waters, but finally landed upon the bridge, which was as thin and old as rock might be and still span the great divide between the Asmodh depths I had left and the farther depths on the other side.

I glanced back at the creatures, and saw that none of them followed down the steplike ledges. Rather, they watched me in their blur of white undulations, as if daring me to return to face them—or knowing that I faced a worse fate at the other side of the bridge.

I did not want to wait to find them chasing me after all, and so I glanced forward—on the opposite cliff, water also poured downward from channels of some kind. Because of the narrowness of the bridge, I had to run across it nearly on all fours to maintain my balance—one slip, and I would fall. On the other side, I climbed up the series of carved steps, left there for the ancient Asmodh race no doubt. Yet all I could think of was the Eclipsis, and how it was lost—for how would I find it far below—and if the dark sea beneath ran swift and strong in the earth, where would I hunt for it again?

Lost. The Serpent's Eye. The Deathlight itself. My only guide in this place.

As I walked, the canal opened onto what seemed to be an underground lake, and from the rushing sound I heard, it emptied at some distant dam into a waterfall. The water produced foam at the point where the canal emptied into it, and its water was darker than the canal's, although I could see areas of rust and scum at its outer edges.

At the center of the lake, a small island stood. I crouched along the walking ledge and dipped my fingers into the water. It was warm, like a well-drawn bath. I saw what seemed a small, elongated, dark fish dart from where my fingers had broken the water's surface. It shot quickly farther out into the water. Beneath it, tightly packed stone with some filling between the stones that kept them from leaking water. The entire construction had been designed and built by some architect of the city, and supported much of city above with its heavy pillars and vaults.

Something caught my eyes—a strange light played in zigs and zags along the water, closest to the island.

As I scanned the island at a distance—no more than the size of a small courtyard at the center of the water—I noticed there a monument of some kind just beyond its shore.

Water enervated vampyres, and although I might bathe with a sponge and a bowl, immersion would weaken me further. I still did not know if there were creatures in this lake that might attack me. I had to go to the gently curved island at the lake's center. I had trudged the filth-filled marshes of my childhood enough, and yet something about the light in the water disturbed me more than the thought of a lamprey maiden did.

The island could not have been more than a quarter of a mile from where I stood. How deep was this water? Could I walk there? I did not have any special vampyre power in Myrryd, so what more could be taken from me?

I stepped down from the gray-stone ledge, into the

water. The bottom of the lake was also stone. It had been constructed all around, a container for something or someone.

I took a few more steps. The floor held, and the water came only to my waist as I walked through it. The lake was warm, and a light mist of steam came off from it. However, the vapors grew stronger here, and I felt a strange pain in my gut as if I had ingested bad blood. I glanced up to the curved ceiling of packed stone that lay beneath the throne room and the streets of Alkemara.

Built to hold this in. Called poison to keep the priests away.

To keep Medhya's foot upon it, even after her soul had gone—through ritual—into the Veil.

I felt something at my foot, a slimy heaviness moved against my ankle. I looked down but saw nothing. Then, as I stepped forward, something thick and long wound around my knee, then swam off.

I watched the water, and as my eyes grew focused, I saw hundreds of eel-like creatures, swarming around each other, and me, great masses of their shiny bodies. As they moved over and around each other, I saw small white sparks come from them, leaving trails of light.

This was the luminescence I saw along the island's shoreline. These eel-creatures. They rubbed against each other, creating the light. Did they live off the meat of the dead mortals? Each other? They were Ophion's rumor of crawling lamps.

Yet, they did not attack, nor did they impede my journey. I reached down and grabbed at one. It slipped from my fingers. Again I reached with both hands, and caught a wriggling eel in my hands, and brought it to the surface. Its open maw was filled with a ridge of tiny gray teeth, sharpened to perfect points.

I felt a surge of energy go through me as I held it, examining its smooth and slick form—no ordinary eel, this. It had spines along its back that raised and lowered as it breathed through its swampy gills. I could not find an eye anywhere on its head, but its teeth were small, perfect razors as it tried snapping at my hand.

I dropped the creature, and it dived beneath the surface again, joining its swarm within the brackish water.

As I began moving forward, the water barely reaching my navel, I drew out my razien, prepared for an attack from the eels. Yet, though they moved around my legs and waist, never breaking the water's surface, they did not bite me or hinder my progress.

As I drew closer to the island, the eels here grew more numerous and larger, until some of them, in swarming, rose into the air, their great tubular forms crossing over other swarms. I felt no fear from them, nor threat, yet these were of a size that, if they chose to attack, they might easily disable me.

I had to rest upon the rocks as I reached the shore. After I had recovered strength, I went to the statue at the center of the island.

I touched its words, but they were written in a language I did not understand. Yet, I saw the coiled symbol of the Great Serpent.

I looked around the lake. I tried to call Merod within me, yet all was silent. No vision came; no insight.

I spoke the words of the statue aloud, and my voice echoed:

> *In its depths, the burning sword*
> *Makes hostage of the winding stair*
> *But he who comes to heal the Veil*
> *Must break the stone and find the lair.*
>
> *Him for whom these words were writ*
> *Will take the Nameless to his sheath:*
> *The conquering Queen commands above,*
> *The vanquished lies in wait, beneath.*

I had not yet seen a winding stair, nor a sword of fire. All that remained before me here was a stone statue.

Was it what I must break?

This statue, worn by time and water and with features barely visible upon her face, only the rudiments of breasts and hair, and a rounded belly that indicated a child within her womb.

The form of a woman, and yet no woman at all.

Who was this woman?

The statue was ancient, and looked as if someone had spent time chipping at it. When I touched it, it wobbled slightly, although it seemed rooted to the spot by some anchor at its base.

I glanced over at the rubble of rock beside me. It was comprised of chips and bits of the stones that had been used to build here—at the base of the lake itself and the ceiling above and the ledge whence I had come. Someone had built this place in some faraway time. I lifted a few of these greenish gray stones from around the statue's footing. As I did this, I saw what seemed a glimmer of colors in stone beneath my feet.

I picked up more rocks, tossing them aside. As I did so, I began to make out the island itself beneath the rubble that lay upon it.

The carefully constructed mosaic tile had been laid out in blue and turquoise and jade and yellow and white, the surface of this curved upward, until the peak of the upturned bowl was the statue. It was no island.

A flooded place.

I glanced at the statue again. As I looked at the timeworn surface of the face, I saw the third eye engraved in her forehead. *Medhya*. It was she, I was certain. And in her belly, her children, born from union with the Great Serpent.

She had placed this statue here, a monument to her conquest of the Serpent and theft of his powers.

I spoke the lines, "The conquering queen commands above, the vanquished lies in wait, beneath."

Just as beneath the New Kingdom of Myrryd, there had been the Old, but beneath the Old Kingdom, whose domain was this? The Asmodh? The Nameless? As I wondered at this, the answer nearly coiled at my feet.

What great king of a world before Myrryd had once built a vast kingdom, that now lay in ruin beneath the red city above?

It came in an insight that was nearly like a sharp pain.

I looked across the lake to the stone shore, and up to the curved ceiling, and then back down to the island upon which I stood.

An island that was no island.

I stood on the rooftop of the original temple of the Great Serpent.

• 4 •

MEDHYA had stolen immortality from him, and had put her throne and kingdom above the place of his worship. She had buried the temple beneath stone and water, but had not buried the Great Serpent.

She could not destroy it, for it was the energy that built her kingdom. The same energy that created my tribe.

Medhya was the Queen of Wolves—she did not create her power, but stole it as Pythia had stolen the mask of Datbathani. But the mask was older than Datbathani. Older than Medhya. Older, perhaps, than Ixtar. I knew it now— the Asmodh were the people of the Great Serpent, before even the Serpent had come to them. They had forged the mask and the sword in these depths, and their sorcery was greater than even Medhya's. But they had been vanquished—as the Serpent had been vanquished—by trickery and stolen ritual.

I stood upon—not an island—but the basilica of a sacred structure. Medhya had buried the Serpent, but had not truly conquered.

And the Serpent's only defense was what was in his blood.

The call of the blood itself to raise up an Anointed One.

But he who comes to heal the Veil must break the stone and find the lair.

I slammed more rock at the statue until I had chipped it to nothing, and then began clearing the debris. At its base, it was joined to the rounded rooftop by an ornate bronze plug of some kind.

I used my hands to sweep away the last of the rock debris from the broken statue. On my knees, I leaned close to it, for I felt a strange vibration from it. It was little more than a few inches above the roof, jutting upward, a perfect center to the circle of the dome.

On it, there was ancient script and scrollwork. When I touched it, I heard a strange hum from it, as if it stood above a nest of Akhnetur. The scrollwork was in the same language as I had seen written in Alkemara itself. The words I read from this, I had seen in a vision of a statue of the Serpent:

Also, I am here.

I realized this protuberance was a sword's grip, and I tugged at it, though it was well lodged in its place. I felt a sting as I touched it, and let go quickly. My curiosity was intense enough to have another go, but this time the sword felt like ice, and I released it without it budging one inch. In frustration, I kicked at it with my boot and nearly went sprawling.

"You *will* come out of there," I said, as if it could hear me. I squatted again and wrapped my hands about it, feeling the strange stinging sensations along my fingers. But I was unwilling to let go. I knew the old stories of kings who had drawn swords from ancient pagan mounds, and I did not intend to let this moment pass.

I held on tight, and tugged at it, trying to saw it out of its resting place.

I spoke the words from the rhyme, "'In Asmodh's depths, the burning sword makes hostage of the winding stair. But he who comes to heal the Veil must break the stone and find the lair.'"

I gripped the sword ever more tightly, and still it would not give.

"Damn you, come out of there," I muttered in frustration.

The sword slid upward slightly, rising in my hand, its hilt emitting a squeal as it scraped against stone.

· CHAPTER 11 ·

The Sword

· 1 ·

I drew the Asmodh blade out completely.

The sword did not burn, nor did it seem to hold any great threat as a blade. Broken, it was. There was nothing beyond its hilt, for it was shattered and jagged as glass less than a hand's length down from the crossguard. I held it up to try to read the ornate writing engraved upon the hilt.

In frustration, I shouted at it as if it could hear me. Surely, if it had whispered my name to Ophion, it would speak to me. It was just a damaged weapon—perhaps its centuries in this place had dulled it. Perhaps this wasn't the sword I sought. I stood up, furious that I had come all this way—and had lost the Eclipsis in the process. I raised my arm and was about to toss the sword into the lake, when I felt a tingling at my fingers as I had when holding the Eclipsis for the first time.

A strange blue flame emerged from the broken edge of the blade and grew outward into the air, outlining the sword itself. It was as if the igniting of the fire had re-created the broken and missing blade. The fire-ghost of the blade extended out, curving slightly. The fire died out quickly, leaving the gleaming metal of a full sword.

It was long and curved, sharp at both sides of the blade. It was closest to being a scimitar in its shape but with inset curved teeth cut by some fine machine along its outer surface. Designs of serpents covered its length, and it held a reflection of blue fire in the shine of its metal, as if the fire still existed within the blade.

"Do you make hostage of the winding stair?" I asked the blade as if it could answer. It did not, of course, and I felt foolish—but with such sorcery, anything was possible.

I turned it over in my hand, and on each side of the sword, I saw markings that seemed to move as liquid on metal, as if the broken sword itself had life—like the life I had felt in the Eclipsis. Something pulsed in the grip, and I began to feel as if the sword had taken root in the palm of my hand. I felt a burning beneath my own skin, and the fire shot up my forearm.

At my shoulder, a shock of pain, and then a general warmth simmered beneath my flesh. I felt as if I were mortal for that moment, and had, again, stepped out into the sunlight.

Beneath my feet, the roof of an ancient temple.

All this time—millennia—the Serpent's temple had been under Myrryd, in the Asmodh depths—the nameless places of dark and mystery.

The sword of fire had been thrust into the roof, as if it held the Great Serpent in his lair and cut off the source of the Serpent's greatest powers. The kingdom overgrown above it, a subterranean sewer flowing over what had once been the sacred home of the Serpent, and destroying the last of the Asmodh civilization that had once existed in these depths. The spirit of this nameless place could not be held, nor imprisoned. Its power was a great threat to Medhya—and the priests of the Kamr and the Nahhashim had learned the old rituals of the Asmodh. It was in this deep

place where the true sorceries—the source of all energy—
of our tribe had originated.

Beneath even the secret places of the earth, there was another world.

All conquerors must bury the vanquished, I thought.
*And yet, the conqueror will one night fall when the van-
quished rises up again.*

I looked down at the mosaic tile with the slender crack
in it where the sword had rested. A strange vapor of smoke
drifted up from the crack at my feet, and as it moved past
my face, I smelled a scent like bitter incense.

The mosaic showed the image of the Great Serpent himself, not a snake at all, nor a dragon—but the figure of a
man. A sword gripped in his hand, and its blade entwined
with serpents. His face resembled my own, though he wore
a suit of scaled armor with what appeard to be talons thrust
out at his ankles and along his shoulders.

"Also, I am here," I said aloud, glancing back up at the
sword and seeing my reflection in it—not the reflection of
a corpse but of another me—a youth, a vampyre, looking at
me as if he knew me too well, a stranger.

His eyes were translucent black but with liquid red
within them—like a thin layer of obsidian with the red of
blood pulsing beneath. His lips parted, his fangs long and
curved, ready to strike.

"I am here," the Serpent said as I watched my reflection.
My eyes had darkened as the eyes of Merod had been. I
had passed some test, though I did not understand it yet.

I felt heat at the grip, and I nearly dropped the sword, but
the blistering at my hand only made me clutch it more tightly.

A sword of fire, Merod had told me.

Yes, a voice whispered—the reflection in the blade.
*Medhya and Datbathani and Lemesharra turned these
gifts against me. A sword of fire. A mask of gold. A staff
of power. Meant only for one. Throw the sword and see
who is its rightful owner.*

I did not wish to throw the sword, but it burned at my
hand, creating a fever up my forearm.

Throw the sword, Falconer. The thought came to me again in a whisper.

I flung the sword out across the water, expecting to lose it with a splash several feet away. Instead, the sword shot out from my hand as if taking flight. When it reached the point where I believed it would stop, it changed direction and flew back at me, as if thrown by some invisible swordsman. In an instant, it was in my grasp again.

The thin blue flame renewed, erupting along the teeth of the sword. The sword seemed to split at its middle, becoming a double blade, and then re-forming into its scimitarlike shape. As I thought of another weapon, so it molded itself to my will, and was a double-ax. It lengthened, and thickened, and drew back again, curving upward into the sword that I came to think of as the Asmodh, for the people who had forged it in the ancient fires.

The burning at my fingers had cooled, and I found I could no longer drop the sword—it had become embedded in my palm, and my fingers would not let go.

Holding the blade up, I went to the edge of the temple rooftop, where the filthy water lapped gently along rocks.

I plunged the blade down into the lake, hoping to cool the fire. The eels that swarmed about seemed to thicken and wrap themselves about the sword. The fire did not die, but instead spread—a blue flame—along the surface of the water.

The flame grew, and the water roiled as the fire spread farther. I thrust the sword deep into the wriggling eels, and could not let it go. Fever overcame me, and I shivered as I watched the entire lake erupt in flames as if it were made of oil. Yet from this fire, no smoke came. The eels continued to swarm around each other, even as the fire burned across the lake.

I felt a coolness at my hand, and two eels wriggled up the blade, within the fire, and I knew that this was the presence of the Serpent—the fire and the eels and the sword.

I looked out across the lake of fire, and the swarms became one great slick creature—a serpent with the jaws of a vampyre, its scales burning as it reared its head.

This proved to be an illusion, and what seemed a man without feature—an orb of light shaped as a man—stood in the fire and called to me, "Also, I am here, Maz-Sherah. I am within you. I am in the blade itself, through you. I have been with you since first you drank of my venom in the flower that is sacred to me. But there have been others like you—and it is not up to me to know you, Maz-Sherah, for it is your path that finds you here. The Azmodh blade recognizes you, and the Eclipsis knows its master."

There, in a twisting path of fire, a voice spoke to me. "It is not I who ordain you." Within the movement of fire, the turning of the serpent—a blue and yellow line through the burning lake. "It is you who make the crown of your tribe, and who follow a path of thorn and bramble that is yours alone. You have drawn my sword, stolen by Medhya, murderer of her sisters, destroyer of her children. She thrust it into my temple to bind me, but she has known that you would come to draw the Asmodh blade, to wield the Nahhashim staff, and to know the rituals unheard of by any born of vampyre or mortal, rituals known once to Merod, and to Ghorien, and to the priest of the Nahhash called Aryn. But once spoken, the ritual burns the mind and is lost again—for none who breathes the air above is meant to possess such power for long. But you, Maz-Sherah, will know these words of unraveling the Veil, for you will need them in the nights to come. You have found the mask used to take immortality from me. You know the Lamp of the deathlight, called Eclipsis. It is within your grasp. You know of the Staff of the Nahhashim, formed with sorcery to bind those who would destroy Medhya. No creature of this earth has moved the sword since Medhya herself pressed it to my heart."

"Tell me of the staff," I said.

"Bones of the Nahhashim and the bones of Medhya, drawn by sorcery together," said the Serpent. "Bones that bind the Nahhashim. Bones that drive the Dark Mother back into the depths of the Veil."

"And the orb?"

"The Eclipsis calls the deathlight. It will show you what you seek in the darkness. If you are its master, you will fuel the Eclipsis, and this will call up those of your tribe who have fallen—for it stores its power, though it may weaken if used too much. There is no Extinguishing for you if the Eclipsis remains whole and in your possession."

"I have lost this orb, deep in the seas below," I said.

The voice did not respond to my words, and I did not wish to repeat them. For I felt ashamed at having lost such an important sacred power.

"This sword, what power does it hold?" I asked.

"It was forged in the fires of Dolmyr, in the white-hot deep below the seas. A relic of an older age than the age of the Asmodh. Medhya stole it from me—the only weapon that can be used against me, for it is made with my blood. But it can be used against them, as well, for it carries no ordinary fire in its metal—the fire is my blood, and the fire sends the soul to the Veil. You must not let it be used against you, Maz-Sherah. For if it is taken from you, all will be lost—and you will be sent into the Veil itself, from which few return."

"Do you exist in the Veil?"

"In many worlds have I existed, but I have been imprisoned here too long. Watch the sword, Falconer. It is shattered, but forms in your hand. If you throw it at an enemy, it will always hit its target, and return to you. But this does not mean it cannot be stolen from you. Yet it will only bring its flame for a master, and once it is thrust into stone, it will take root there until its master returns to it. It breathes fire, and shapes its blade to the necessity of cutting and fighting. Above all things, it has only one other master—and that is Medhya herself. She cannot touch it beyond the Veil, but if she comes in flesh to this world, she will want the sword above all other possessions. You have more power than you know. The power does not come from bone alone, nor from the sword of fire, nor from the Eclipsis, Falconer. The power is within you to ignite them. It flows from you into them, a key that unlocks what they hold. You must know this. You ordain the sword and the staff. You ordain the Eclipsis and the mask. But the question you must ask, Anointed One: Will you ordain what is to come, or leave it to the Myrrydanai to do so?"

"But I am ignorant of what I seek."

"Do not tell me your weakness, for though I protect you here, I cannot defend you on your path. It is yours alone. If you are ignorant, it is because you have not yet opened your eyes, Maz-Sherah. If you are unsure, it is because you have not awakened. Open your eyes now, or forever they will be closed. Your children will suffer. Your loved ones will extinguish. The world itself will grow dark with Medhya's sorcery. If I live, I live in you. If the rituals of the Asmodh exist, they will exist in your lips to speak when the time comes. There have been other Maz-Sherah, and they, too, have closed their eyes to what is within them. You may be no different. The Myrrydanai will destroy you. Medhya will devour you or keep you as her slave. She fears you, Maz-Sherah. Many fear you. They fear the deep sorcery you bring. Why would this fear exist if you had no power?"

"It is prophesied that I will bring war."

"You are afraid of war? Mortal and immortal—the bloodthirst is the arena of this earth. Your vampyre blood is born from darkness, and only you can journey into the heart of Medhya herself—and destroy her. All life devours all life. But even life must have its protectors, and to protect this life—this earth—you must find the fury and rage within you. She is the Queen of Wolves, and only a Master of Wolves may destroy the Wolf Queen. You must be the falcon who hunts the wolf. You must be the Maz-Sherah because all others have failed."

"Medhya defeated you," I said. "Who am I against her?"

"She did not defeat me, so long as you hold the sword in your hand. It is called the Asmodh—the Nameless. This weapon you hold causes suffering, even for he who possesses it. Her mind had turned to the sword's sorcery, and she used it for destruction rather than justice. As the eons passed, much was lost, much forgotten. But you have felt me, as others have. The fires of the red city burn because I exist. The stream you feel between your brethren exists because I am here. Where you are, I am with you."

"Why was I born to this?"

"Each man is born to destiny. Most avoid it, and many fail in its pursuit. You are here. There was no Maz-Sherah the moment before you drew the sword from my temple roof, though many believed they were the Anointed One. All failed."

"Will I fail?"

"She may destroy you and all your tribe. What is this to you? Will this fear dissuade you from what you must do? Do you fear war? Do you fear her? Burn your fear. Unleash what is in you. You have drunk of my venom and survived it. You have the Veil within you. You have the blood of the Serpent in your veins. War is not enough. Do you think the Dark Mother of your tribe does not love war and its spilling of blood? Prophecy is not enough. Medhya's blood and bone and flesh gave the prophecies to the priests. Were they strong enough to resist her? When the Myrrydanai were skinned alive by her reach beyond the Veil, could they resist? When the Nahhashim were bound into bone, and planted in the Garden of Flesh, could they resist? The Veil sorcery that Medhya knows is beyond what her priests understood. But you have crossed the Veil and returned. No Priest of Blood has done this. Even the great Merod was destroyed and captured, freed only by you. You are the match for the Queen of Wolves, the Dark Mother of your tribe. When the Priests of Blood were destroyed, and the tribes of the Fallen Ones driven out from their kingdoms to be slaughtered by mortals as they slept—where was their power? The Asyrr rulers who lie entombed within this city—what power did they have against the spirit of Medhya and her shadow jackals? Do not talk of prophecy and sorcery, Maz-Sherah. The greater power is within you now, for the Asmodh depths offer it to you. It is not the thieving alchemist's seed planted in your mother's womb that brings this. It is you—your essence—now. You are my son. As Medhya has sought flesh to escape the Veil, you are my flesh. And your path is your power. You are here to overcome the Extinguishing itself. You are here to be guardian to the mortal realm. Though the Fallen Ones were born from an act of thievery and violence, you will redeem your kind."

"In sacrifice?" I asked.

"To sacrifice yourself is to leave others to do what you would not," the Serpent said. "You must gather courage and intention around you. For you are not here because of prophecy. Nor are you here because it is your fate. The winds of existence do not blow a man to darkness or to light. A man reaches and finds his shadows, and he remains with them—or he crosses through the shadows to find the fire that will light his way. You are here—you are Maz-Sherah—because you have come to claim this and are here, where no one vampyre or mortal has done so."

The fire of the river seemed to explode before my eyes.

I was thrust into a vision of burning cities along the coast of my homeland, and then taken to palaces of the kings of the earth, where the sky rained fire upon mortals; in a blur of motion, I was drawn to Rome, and watched as the cathedrals and fountains were torn apart by the White Robe priests who had multiplied in number. The sky was red-gray with smoldering ash, and I saw Myrryd rise up from the gorge, its towers looming toward the heavens, and upon the throne of the dead and the damned, there sat Medhya—and in the flesh of Pythia herself, no longer imprisoned by the golden mask.

Her eyes yellow, and her skin blue, and my son Taran, his skin blistered from his face, a knight of her dark kingdom. Mortals were enslaved in every land, and the burnings of Christian and pagan and Jew and Muslim who had not renounced their faiths lit the night sky. I saw my daughter, Lyan, as a young woman, being led to a pyre, and doused with oil. Just as the flame was brought to her hair—

The Serpent drew me back from this vision—

I stood in the subterranean chamber of Myrryd, and the river of fire in the pit below continued to burst upward in waves.

"This is the future if you renounce your path," the Serpent said.

"I did not choose this path," I said. "It was forced upon me. Pythia brought me to this existence. I would rather I had died."

"Death was never for you, Maz-Sherah. This is the existence that you yourself have reached for, and you must hold it in your grasp. You must become what you intended to become. You had power as a child. Do you not remember . . ."

A vision swept through me, and I was there in the Forest with my grandfather, as I called to the ravens to come and nest, and then later as I trained the falcons to hunt with mortals. "You are more than seed and egg, and more than blood, and more than vampyre, Maz-Sherah. I am within you. I am part of you. You have always known this, and yet you have denied me. As you devoured the Priest of Blood, you began to unravel what was within you. I am you, Maz-Sherah. I am you. You must now be the Serpent."

As he said these words, I felt the realization shoot through my veins like the Veil juice itself.

I felt myself soaring above the cavern walls, above the earth, above the stars themselves.

I remained there, on the roof of the temple, before the rising flames.

The voice of the Great Serpent was within me, and the fire itself went out, suddenly, doused by this understanding. *We are guardians of this realm. The blood of mortals is their sacrifice to us. We are not meant to be part of senseless slaughter, Maz-Sherah, though many of your tribe have brought this to mankind. We are the watchers of this earth, and we guard it from those of the Veil, and those who would unravel this world. We have been demons and angels to some, and we are hated by the very mortals we guard. Yet this is why you were born, and why I have existed since the first mortal rose from his haunches, and called to the gods for aid. There is a will to this universe. You have come to its center, and you have found the path meant for you and for you alone.*

I felt as if every bone in my body cracked. I dropped to my knees, and fell down hard on to the rock ledge.

The voice of the Serpent within me. *I am with you. I am you. You must find me within your soul. You will understand the power of those objects of the Priests when you call me forth from your own depths.*

What must I do? I asked.

In my temple, there is my skin, sloughed, in the form of a tunic. Beside it, a sheath for the Nameless. Near this is a suit of armor called the Raptorius. Take off these mortal clothes and wear my skin. Once you put it on, it will become part of you, and you may draw it beneath your flesh. It will protect you in times of danger. Wear the Raptorius, as well—it, too, is from my flesh and bone. When you draw the visor of its helmet closed, you may walk in the sun, for its burning light will not harm you. Of the Garden of Flesh, the Akhnetur will not harm you if you wear this armor. Break off the branch of the white tree, and make of it a new Nahhashim staff, for these priests' souls are within the tree, not one staff carved from it. Call the Eclipsis. It will answer to you alone, and will find you though it has been cast to the deep. Your energy will bring its life, and the deathlight will come from you, focused upon its lamp. With this, call the ancient kings from the Extinguishing. You have the power within you, and no city, alive or dead, may drink of your energy now. But, Maz-Sherah, be cautious with those you raise from death or Extinguishing. There is no being of the earth that has not been tempted by great power, and few may resist its call.

I am tempted by it, I said.

With great power, what would you have the world be?

I do not know, I said. *I am no different than any other vampyre. I cannot say that I would be a great hero, for I have left many to die when I journeyed to Ixtar's country.*

All heroes are tempted, the Serpent said. *But I have been with you when you drank the blood of your prey, Anointed One, and you did not bring brutal deaths to them. I have felt what was in your heart when your friend lay in your arms in a deep prison. I have read your soul when you knew of your children. You are not a vampyre as any other. You are one with me. What you do, I also do. Now, the time is short. Nights will pass before you will return to Taranis-Hir. Set right your course. Resolve yourself to these things.*

· *Will I go to my Extinguishing through what I am about to do?* I asked.

Prophecy is for fools, the Serpent said. *You are no longer subject to the whim of priests and mages. Put on the cloak of my skin. Wear the Raptorius and let your flesh drink from its strength. It is more than mere armor, and holds the greatest powers given to you. Yet, be cautious with it, for the same sword you wield may be used by the possessor of the staff to burn the skin away from your body, and destroy its armor. All sorcery may be undone, and you must not rely upon it alone. Yet I have great faith in you, for you have freed me from these depths where no one has before you. In you are my blood and venom, for you have drunk from the flower that is sacred to me. Call the Eclipsis and draw your energies into its deathlight. Raise the kings. Find your powers. Be Maz-Sherah to your tribe.*

Then, he spoke no more, within me or without.

The fire burned off across the lake, and what had seemed a lake was now dry, as if it had never held water or eels. I stood upon a stonework plateau, and off the edge of the temple roof were steps downward beneath the plateau, that wound around and around along a strange spur of rock and wall.

The winding stair, I thought.

> *In Asmodh's depths, the burning sword*
> *Makes hostage of the winding stair*

But he who comes to heal the Veil
Must break the stone and find the lair.

I eagerly went down these dampened steps, and long-dead blue flames lit, of a sudden, along the curving wall. When I reached the bottom of the stair, I stood at the entrance to the temple itself. Jeweled mosaics depicting ancient Serpent Wars covered the walls. Friezes depicted an earthly paradise, as well as the depths of Asmodh, with furnace and forge and a spiraling terraced cliff, and the images of thousands of people, some with the wings of dragons, and others with wings like angels.

At the center of this rounded temple, a suit of armor had been laid across an altar made of black rock. Beside it, on the floor, a nearly transparent pile of cloth, so thin that when I lifted it, I could see my fingers through each layer.

I undressed, leaving my shirt and trousers on the floor.

Naked, I drew the cloak of the Serpent's skin over my shoulders. Within moments, my own flesh had soaked it within.

I went to don the suit of armor—the Raptorius.

It had shiny copper-colored metal plates upon it that seemed like the scales of a reptile, and was no heavier than ordinary cloth. Just beneath the scales was a leathery skin-like material. Beside the suit of armor, a helm of leather and bronze, with flares along its skull so that it had the semblance of a dragon's head with bony spurs in waves along the back of it, while the visor itself became the upper jaw.

I drew the helmet over my face—it felt light. Yet, when I touched it, I also felt its contours, like the hardness of solid rock. I drew the visor down over my face. It had only slits for my eyes, and yet I was not impaired in vision as I looked about. After a minute of wearing this helmet, I felt as if I wore nothing at all on my head.

I drew the coat of armor upon my body. As with the helm, this felt light upon my flesh, but I had a strange sensation that it had small feelers touching my skin. Digging into my flesh. I felt a nausea at the pit of my stomach, and tasted the Serpent's Venom at the back of my throat.

The armor moved beneath my flesh, a new skin of the Serpent passing into mine. A white-hot pain shot through my back, beginning at the base of my spine and moving upward to the back of my skull.

The scratching into my flesh grew too intense, and I dropped to the floor. I felt as I had the first time I died—as my vision darkened, I saw a brief spark of blue, as if from a flame that had only just been lit, and then this went out.

No voice of Merod entered me in this dark place, nor did I feel great power from the Serpent. My extremities tingled, and I lay there with my arm outstretched, watching my fingers twitch as if controlled by some source other than my own will. Across the stone floor, I imagined an emerald-green snake twisting its way toward me. Nothing more than a snake, not a god or a messenger, but a creature that haunted such abandoned temples.

I stared at it as I felt a kind of death come for me, and the snake moved toward my hand, and then over it. As it traveled, I felt a prickly heat across my fingers and palm where the snake moved.

It slowly traveled along my arm, and when it was at my wrist, it opened its small jaws, and bit down on the flesh where my forearm and hand connected, into a vein.

A frozen numbness shot through my arm, and in an instant I no longer lay upon that temple floor but had crossed into the Veil itself.

The entry of the Veil was a mist across water, and rising from the depths of it, Medhya stood, her body a mass of writhing scorpions and flies and milk-white maggots.

She brought her hand to my face. I could not move as she touched my chin, and then leaned into me, bringing the swarm of her lips to mine. As she kissed me, she whispered, "You have freed the snake, Maz-Sherah. But you tear the Veil as you do this, and I am also freed. Your children will die. You will extinguish. But first, you will give me life, and this sword you hold will be mine, for I am its true mistress. When I have you, I will flay the snakeskin from within your flesh, and you will greet the dawn, spread-eagled, upon the dust."

She drew back from me, and like a cobra striking swiftly, lunged for me, her teeth slicing into my throat and tearing at it. It felt as though it was not my blood being taken from me, but my breath.

◆ 2 ◆

I awoke sometime later, alone in the temple.

I rested, feeling in need of blood. As if sent by the Serpent himself, one of the pale human rats from the city crawled along the floor toward me, muttering in his gibberish. As he drew closer, I saw that he was the same boy from whom I had drunk before. The wound had only barely healed at his throat.

He chattered at me, as he sniffed the air. I realized he had memorized my scent, and I wondered if he had followed it down into the depths.

I pounced upon him, and drank enough for strength. He howled when I let him go, and went scurrying off out of the temple. I heard his footfalls echo on the steps back up to the subterranean passage.

Then, there was more chattering of these mortals far above, and I was sure when I glanced up to the crack in the roof that I saw some creature looking down at me.

I stood, feeling a surge of energy in my arms, and I raised them to the ragged cavern ceiling. All the energy of Myrryd, all that had been stolen from vampyres and mortals, all that had been used to fuel the lamps and torches of the city, seemed to flow through me, in me, upon the surface of my skin.

In an instant, I had become a mass of wriggling locusts, and moved with one mind into the air, breaking apart and re-forming again.

In solid flesh, I brought the Raptorius armor out from beneath my skin. I felt the tickling pain, as of light, sharp razors. Yet once the armor formed—a skeleton of metal plates and talons over my skin—all sensation on my skin's surface deadened. I went over to my clothes and drew out the broken sword.

As I held it before me, I willed the fire to come from it, and form the curve-toothed sword. I then emptied it again so that only the shattered sword hilt was in my hands.

Call the Eclipsis, the Serpent had told me.

I held my left hand out into the air, palm upward. I thought of the orb, as it had lain in the pouch that was tied about Pythia's waist.

Come to me. Come to me, Lamp of Death, come to me, for I am the Maz-Sherah. I am your master now, and it was from the Asmodh fires you were born, broken from the glass in the Veil, born again from a stem in those furnaces of old, formed perfect and dark and alive. You were never meant for the handmaidens of Death's children, but for this hand—and from you, I will have power over the dead who have not yet crossed the Threshold. As I thought this, my mouth opened and words spilled forth in a language I had never heard, that sounded as a ceremonial chant.

Within moments, a dark light moved like vapor through the door of the temple, and as it brushed against my hand, it formed into the round Eclipsis. Up from the great subterranean sea's depths it had come, moving like a bird that flew by instinct toward its home.

I grasped it, and went outside the Serpent's temple, and up the steps.

I shattered my being and all I held, and re-formed myself as a flight of ravens, which poured into the air, through the subterranean depths. My flock went upward, past the white creatures, past the vaults and Medhya's throne room.

Seeking Ophion, I re-formed in the flesh upon the golden throne. Fear seemed to overshadow him. "Do not fear me, brother. For had you not brought me here, I would not have seen the face of the Great Serpent himself. I will not harm you, for you are the instrument of my ascent. I am as the prophecies spake, but even prophets may be blind to what will come," I said, and I saw fear overshadow him. "The Serpent lives within me. I am also here."

"You are truly the Maz-Sherah, my brother. You were not before, though many saw it in you. I was never Maz-Sherah; this I see now. I only existed to bring you here, that you might find your anointing. I see it in your flesh. In your eyes," Ophion gasped, and got down on his knees before me. "You are the Serpent, reborn."

II

VAMPYRE MESSIAH

• CHAPTER 12 •

The Tombs of the Asyrr

• 1 •

MY mind had grown strong in the Asmodh depths, and the sorcery of the Serpent had brought new power to my body. I felt as if I had gained the wisdom of many, and had lost the uncertainty of mortality completely. No longer was I thinking as Aleric, chained to mortal memories.

I had entered a realm beyond even vampyre, and had touched the face of an eternal fire and brought it into my soul. Never would I let anyone take such fire from me.

• 2 •

"UP, Ophion." As I touched him, I felt a strange shock. "I do not wish your destruction, but your knowledge of these avenues and alleyways. I want you to guide me to the hidden tombs of the vampyre kings—the Asyrr. Let us not waste time. The war begins."

• 3 •

I walked along the paths of the Garden of Flesh. The purple flowers had entangled themselves around the trunk of the white tree, as if holding it to the earth. The Akhnetur hummed at a distance, but I ignored them. When they swarmed and came toward me, they stopped in the air, inches from my flesh. The Serpent skin protected me. They buzzed and snapped at each other, but parted like a great molten sea before me. I had no fear of them, for they were creatures born of the depths, as I had been reborn within them.

I took my sword and I cut the tree of the Nahhash in two. From one half of it, I carved a staff. It was not jeweled or covered with the symbols as was the Nahhashim staff Merod had passed to me. It was crude and simple, and when I raised it in my hands, it seemed more of a war club than a mage's wand. Yet I felt a surge of power shoot from my arm through it. A glimmer of light shone from the staff itself, and as it did so, the swarms of Akhnetur seemed to form into almost human shapes.

One by own, these swarms in the form of men, seemed to bow before the staff, then reconfigure into greater and greater swarms until finally, they flew at the staff itself, against its now-fierce glow. As they touched the light, it was as if the Akhnetur vanished into the staff itself, sucked in by the light, held by sorcery.

• 4 •

I found Ophion beyond the garden's temple, and commanded that he help gather up the human rats.

"We will raise the dead tonight," I said. "But they will be thirsty."

• 5 •

CHASING down these pale inhabitants of the ruins and depths of Myrryd took but a few hours. We gathered forty or so, and they were docile and meek when caught. None expressed fear, though they howled terribly when taken to the tomb chambers of the kings. These mortal vessels would be enough to slake the thirst of the kings, though I did not know if the others we raised that night would find enough blood in them.

I stood at the entry down into the great tombs of the seven rulers of Myrryd, and their hundreds of warriors and servants and followers, and held out my hand, calling to the Eclipsis.

Within seconds, it flew at me as if it were a rock shot by a sling in an expert's hand, and yet when it reached me, I grasped it easily. It felt warm in the palm of my hand, and its pulse was like a hand beating rapidly on a drum. I looked into its depths and sensed its life.

I raised the Eclipsis up until I saw that shadowy light emerge from its source.

I held the staff forward, pointing to the piles of bones among the biers of the extinguished kings. "Come to me, you who lie in your Extinguishing! For I am Maz-Sherah, and have ransomed your souls through the fire of the Great Serpent! For you, this long sleep is done, and your life force will return!" The staff burst with a crackle of lightning that ran from it to my fingers, and reached my spine. As I spoke, my words were translated from my lips into those ancient languages of the early tribes, and I felt more than my presence here—Merod spoke from deep within me, and the words that came were unknown to me—a ritual that had been kept secret by the Nahhashim, now released within the staff of their bones.

I held an image in my mind of life coming to each of them, of endowing the Eclipsis with the ability to draw them from the Extinguishing as Death and her handmaidens drew the mortal soul from the body, or returned it to the body. From the orb, the deathlight shot out among the tombs, and many of the lids of these biers smashed and fell, and great lights seemed to burst from the deathlight.

The power drawn into me, and torn from me, brought me to my knees, yet I held fast to the staff and the orb, and though every ounce of my being felt as if it were shattering, I did not let go, nor did the voice of the ancient priest quiet from within my throat.

At first there was silence in the great hall, and then a strange pounding from within the tombs as if the bodies of the kings were smashing against the stone as their bodies began to form from the dust and bits of bone.

"Wait!" I shouted. "I will raise you from your Extinguishing. But you must swear an oath to me that you will fight against Medhya herself, and her minions, the Myrrydanai, and all those who protect them. If you wish to rise up again, and claim guardianship of the mortal realm, swear this oath to me—and to this staff, and to the Serpent. If you call me Maz-Sherah, and will follow me as both your leader and your Anointed One—then I will bring you forth from these dusty graves, as it is the will of the Great Serpent himself! If you do not, the ancient sword of Asmodh will send you into the Veil itself!"

At first bones arose as if in flight from the tombs.

Then sinew and veins formed upon the bones, like vines rapidly moving a tree branch.

Skin raveled as if being knit by a demon, thickening about the muscle and veins and nerves that had sprung along the bones and muscle.

The seven kings of the vampyric world, the Asyrr, stood before me. Some were female, some male. Some had the pale skin of the entombed vampyre, yet others were dark, and none looked to be from the same continent, for each had features of a distinct tribe of mortals. Their servants, who also rose from the urns in which they had been placed at their Extinguishing, drew their tunics and robes around them. Other guards of their tombs also came from the extinguished tombs, and the gathering numbered in the hundreds.

"You are thirsty," I said, and went over to draw the rope that bound the mortal rats. "Let these sustain you."

• 6 •

AFTER the regaining of strength, when the last mortal
had been drunk and held close, I raised the staff up to draw
their attention.

"Zoryas! Namtaryn! Illuyan!" I shouted off the names of
the kings as they stood beside their tombs. "Sarus! Setyr!
Athanat! Nekhbet! Kings of the Fallen Ones! Fallen since
the last nights of Myrryd, when the Veil had thinned, and
the Serpent stirred, and Medhya had reached across the
darkness to destroy you! Born in the generations following
the prophecies of the Words of Blood, found by Merod, of
the Kamr priesthood! Defenders of the guardians of the
world, and drinkers of mortal blood! The Veil again has
torn, and the Great Serpent calls you! The Extinguishing
you have suffered has been taken from you that you might
serve as guardians of the earth again! That you might taste
the blood of the enemy! That you might align yourself with
the Serpent and again know of the pleasures of the night
and of Myrryd itself!" I spoke to them of all that had come
to pass, and all that must be done.

I told them of the buried kingdoms that they had once
ruled, and the guardianship of the mortal realm. "For this
is why we exist! It is not to raise the cattle of mortality that
we might drink and plunder! We drink that we might survive, but these mortals are no cattle! They are our children!
They are what we once were, and though they see us as
demons and devils, still we must protect them from forces
they cannot understand! Once, our kind were jackals, feeding from the weak, chasing the herd to catch the easy prey.
But now, a new age of the Blood begins! A new age of
Myrryd, and of the Serpent! Monsters though we are to
mortals, still the earth is our field, and mortals, our sheep.
And as shepherds also feed upon the sheep when the season comes, so we must protect them from the wolves
among us, who would slaughter them outright, then turn
against us, as they have before! There is a great Queen of
Wolves at the edge of the forest of life! You know her, for

she has haunted your Extinguishing! Medhya, yes, our mother—our Dark Madonna who seeks to scorch the world with her damnation! To the north and west of here, there is a city born of the tearing Veil—and another Queen of Wolves, an earthly queen, holds the first Nahhashim staff! Ghorien and the Myrrydanai gather there, and plagues ride the night and weaken the mortal realm. Yet, it is there I must lead you—for the mysteries of the Great Serpent bade me. You are my army, you are my strength! It is to this fortress, called Taranis-Hir, that we must go when the night is reborn. Are you with the Serpent, or are you a servant of Medhya?"

To a vampyre, they shouted, "The Great Serpent! The Serpent!"

In ancient tongues they praised the will of the Serpent and the power brought to them that night. Their cacophony of language was dazzling—some sounded like sonorous music, and others like the clucking voices of the human rats that dwelled in the red city. Yet, within moments of their speaking, I understood every nuance of their words, as they had understood mine—as the Great Serpent was the creator of the first language.

"Which of you is Illuyan?"

A vampyre thick of chest and strong of arm, his hair shorn close to his scalp, looked up while his servants dressed him. "I am Illuyan, King of Myrryd!"

"I have met a descendant of yours—a namesake, Illuyan-ket, who is the wisest of men and carries prophecy in him!"

"I am glad to hear of it," he said, and then grinned.

"Yes," cried another. "He has many such descendants, for he did not fancy vampyre women, but sought out those who might bring him children!"

Illuyan nodded, looking embarrassed as he glanced at the others. Then, when he looked at me, he said, "In those years, my Maz-Sherah, some could bring new life into the wombs of mortal women. I am just honored to know my name is remembered among men, for I guarded that realm until my Extinguishing."

"As we all did!" shouted one of the two females among the Asyrr.

I pointed to this ancient queen, and signaled for her to approach me. "What is your name?"

"I am Queen Nekhbet," the dark-skinned vampyre said, as she stepped close to me. Her arms were covered in gold bracelets of serpents, and her hair drawn back and oiled in what seemed the ancient Egyptian style. Three servant-warriors stood at her side, crouching to their knees before her.

She held her hand out for me to take, which I did, leaning to kiss it. "I ruled during the time of the drowning, when the old cities fell to the seas, and when mortals cried out for our help. We raised them up to the mountains that they might find dry ground. I reigned for six hundred years, before the wars of the priests began. I am your servant now."

"I thank you for your oath," I said. "You honor me."

"We have lain in torment in dust and bone." She drew my hand to hers and kissed it. "But we dreamed of the Maz-Sherah, and in our dream, we did not lose faith in the mercy of the Great Serpent. I see him in your eyes, Maz-Sherah, as I saw him in dreams."

She turned slightly and pointed over to another—the king called Sarus. "You will need to speak with Sarus. He was beloved of Medhya, and he is the most ancient of us. It is through him that she reached us, and tore the Veil when she had first been exiled to it. You must spend time with him, for he knows her weakness, though he himself is weak before her."

Sarus had the heavy muscles and thickness of a gladiator, and his face seemed coarse and unkingly—like that of a foot soldier in the wars. I liked him on sight. "Do you see Queen Namtaryn? I only knew of her in legend, yet she also was early to our tribe, and was the mother of Merod's many daughters." I glanced in the direction of that queen, whose servants had placed a great crimson robe upon her form. She was tall and pale as the moon, her hair fell in tresses along her shoulders, and there was something deeply disturbing in her glance. Centuries later, I would see images of her in various snake goddesses of Persia and India, for she had been worshipped much in her first existence. This was the mother of Pythia. The lover of Merod. She had already drawn a small double-bladed dagger from her tomb and thrust it into her hair as if it were a comb. As she did this, I almost was certain she knew that Nekhbet was speaking to me of her. "You must beware of her, Maz-Sherah. She has taken oaths before. Many of her children were cursed by the Great Serpent because of her many betrayals. The legends of deceitful women descend almost directly from her existence and her rule of Myrryd—mortals have written of her under many names and guises, for their tribal memories of her run deep. She is known as Lilit to the desert people, and Namtareth to those who speak to the dead. When I was queen, she was the cautionary legend of the bad ruler among our tribe. I only know of these things from what was passed down, but it is good to be careful with her."

I could not take my eyes away from Namtaryn as Nekhbet told me of her. Namtaryn had the beauty of a lost world in her flesh—she was more radiant than her daughter, and she glanced over at me, smiling as if to invite me to her lips. The roundness of her breasts was outlined along the crimson robe, which opened at her throat, creating a line of soft white flesh down the front of her body, beneath which were red tattoos and—further—a ruby-pierced navel, and a silk cloth wrapped tight so far below her waist that I could see the light thatch of hair of her pubic region. I looked back up at Namtaryn's face, and saw her smile had broadened, and her small pearly teeth—sharp as any blade—showed where her lips drew back from them. She was enjoying the fact that I watched her and took in her sexual beauty.

"She was the first Queen of Myrryd, many years after Medhya was destroyed by the priests. In her mortal life, she was . . . a whore to kings of the earth. Many of them ended with poison in their eyes or down their gullets. Even Merod was beguiled by her, and she was his doom. A few believed that it was her doing that the Veil began to tear at all, for it was whispered that she was secretly a priestess of Medhya."

"She will fight against Medhya now," I said.

"If she does not betray us," Nekhbet muttered, and then laughed as if she understood some desire of mine. "Does she already have you in her spell, Maz-Sherah? Do not think you are stronger than Merod, who could not resist her. Do not believe for a moment that she does not wish to own you. But she has her uses. She is a powerful ally, when it suits her."

"Then we must make sure it suits her." I almost smiled, thinking of my Pythoness. "I do not believe she will betray me."

Nekhbet looked at me curiously. "You seem to take this too lightly. None of us became rulers of these kingdoms because of our loyalty and kindness. Namtaryn may be the worst of us, but I slaughtered many Nahhashim priests that I might take Medhya's throne and taste the power at her breast, and at the jaws of the Great Serpent. You must be cautious in all things, for it was the want of absolute power that was our weakness during our reigns. You will be offered such a prize, Maz-Sherah. Medhya will offer you more than she could offer her beloved. When you take that prize, you will be in chains and will never again have freedom. I have seen what Medhya and her shadow priests can do, Maz-Sherah. The earth has gone through many bleedings. Once, many serpents filled the continents, but when the Veil tore, a sun fell from the sky and destroyed them. In another age when the Veil grew thin, the stars seemed to fall from the heavens and took down many kingdoms of men and those ruled by the great women of the earth who were wiped from it within a genera- tion. In those nights, mortal kind was of various tribes and races, and they warred against each other until entire mortal species had been slaughtered. This was another plague of Medhya, for she could not stand to see mortals raised to the position of the gods. In my time, it was the great floods of the world. In your time, it is Medhya herself, for the Veil has torn and has not been mended. You must be careful of all these kings and queens of Myrryd, for each of us betrayed our guardianship for want of greater power—and went to our Extinguishing for this deed."

"You confess this to me now—to earn my trust?"

"I confess it," Nekhbet said, "because I cannot pretend otherwise if I am to serve you."

"How did you betray the Serpent?"

She closed her eyes, and smiled in a way that signaled sorrow. "It was Ghorien."

"The great priest of the Myrrydanai."

Opening her eyes, she snarled. "He is a master of hounds. He devoured the souls of his own priests through Medhya's whispering to him, and he is their source. They are without mind, without reason, without power if he exists. I knew him when he had flesh. It is an old story, Maz-Sherah, and all who were once mortal have played a part in it. You do not need to hear the details of it, for you know of such betrayals. I had grown complacent in my reign. Mortals loved me and sacrificed their finest, most beautiful to me. I ruled with an open hand, and did not punish unless it served justice. There was no famine, and hunters gathered the riches of the woods and field, and crops were plentiful. My cities grew beyond Myrryd, and my namesake city, Nekhbet-Luz, thrived in its sea trade across the great oceans. I was called Nekhbet the Merciful, for my counselors were wise and fair. Yet Ghorien gained my trust and confidence, and I passed kingdoms to him that he might relieve me of matters of state and use the sorcery in the scrolls to bind those who meant me harm."

"You were powerful. Who could do you harm?"

She looked at me as if I were a fool. "When the crown is upon your head, Maz-Sherah, everyone is your enemy. Do not forget this. You can trust no one. I trusted Ghorien . . . and he brought a silver blade to my heart and laid me in my tomb while I remained conscious, knowing I could not fight him. Knowing I had lost, and I would spend eternity staring at the stone lid of my own grave, ever thirsting, ever longing for all existence to end." She tilted her head slightly, and I glanced in that direction. The Asyrr king called Setyr had raised his arms to shoulder height as his servants placed a lapis robe upon him. "A man from the northern cities had raised an army against mine, and with the magick of Medhya's scrolls, and my Extinguishing, he had destroyed the city of Nekhbet-Luz in a mortal generation, and had established himself as ruler of Myrryd and the Alkemar territories. No one knew of what Ghorien had done, and when I felt Setyr's Extinguishing in the stream, I knew that he, too, had been betrayed."

I reached over and lifted her chin that it might again be proud as a queen and a warrior. "I raised you and these others to right the wrongs done to you, and to others. To destroy Medhya, or drive her beyond the Veil where she cannot return again to this world. Do not let the crimes of thousands of years become the punishment of this present age. In the stream, we are one. There is no separation between any of us here."

"Yes," she said. "Do you feel it?"

I nodded. She meant the stream. It no longer seemed a spider's web strand, or a lightly flowing current. We were in the ocean of it, here, all of us, a heavy and yet unbearably light feeling.

"This is what Myrryd was like during my reign. The stream was everywhere and flowed through many."

"The raising of the Asyrr has strengthened it," I said.

"No," Nekhbet said. "The stream comes from a source. And you, Maz-Sherah, are its origin. You are the Serpent in flesh, and the stream is your wake. The blood of Merod is also in you, and the venom. Your existence is tied to ours, and, though you must not trust any here, know that none here will raise a sword against you, for our own breath depends upon yours."

Then, abruptly, she changed her tone, and loudly called out, "On your knees, Anointed One!"

I stared at her, and then saw that the others had begun gathering in a circle around us, and their servants and soldiers, too. Nekhbet wore a mischievous smile upon her face.

"On your knees!" the Asyrr shouted.

Nekhbet's servants brought her a vial of oil, and a sword.

She wore a half smile as she said, "You must bend to us now, for we must recognize you as our leader. Even the lord of all vampyres under the Great Serpent and the Dark Mother must present himself in humility to those who have come before."

I got down on one knee, and she took the vial and spread oil mixed with aromatic herbs upon my head. My scalp began to tingle with the warmth, and some of the oil dripped down over my brow. Then, she wiped it down my face. She crouched down at my feet, her servants removing my boots. She rubbed the warm oil into the tops of my feet and along my ankles.

Then, taking the sword, she pressed the flat of its blade to my lips. "Bless our swords, Maz-Sherah, Anointed One of the Tribe of Medhya, son of the Great Serpent for whom we have long waited. For we bring war to our mother, Medhya, and seek the blessing of the chosen of our tribe! This is the time of the Great Crossing, when Medhya seeks to return to power upon this earth—to destroy us, and enslave the mortal realm. But she is her own destroyer—for no being can exist whose sole aim is power that will not be sent to oblivion. We are oblivion, and you, Maz-Sherah, are the scourge of Medhya!"

The others gathered around repeated this in various languages, though, to me, all sounded as one tongue. They shouted her words, and the phrases "Scourge of Medhya" and "We are oblivion!" became like a roar.

I kissed the blade, and she withdrew it.

"Show us the instruments of your anointing!" she shouted, raising her sword into the air.

I held up the crudely cut staff of the Nahhashim tree. I drew the Eclipsis from my shirt, and set it on the floor.

Then, from my belt, I unsheathed the shattered blade. When I held this up, all went silent.

The blue fire grew from the jagged edge of the hilt, and the curved, toothed blade emerged.

"What do you know of this sword?" Nekhbet asked.

"It is a sword of fire, forged by the Asmodh, a weapon of the Great Serpent, stolen by Medhya, and used against the Serpent to imprison him."

"It is called the Nameless, Maz-Sherah. It is a sword of the Nameless nights of the solstice when the membrane of the Veil is thin, when the Great Serpent first breathed the fire of life into the dead. Many kings and queens of Myrryd attempted to tear it from its resting place, yet none could. Many were driven mad by its whispering. But the sorcery of the Nameless is greater than any other sorcery upon the earth. None may take it but its master," Nekhbet said. "If an immortal wields it, it will curse him."

"And so, I am cursed," I said, as I held the blade aloft.

"All who hold the Nameless blade will suffer," she said.

"The Nameless," I said, looking at the blade. "Asmodh."

"Asmodh! The Nameless!" they shouted. "Eclipsis! The Staff of the Nahhashim! These are the signs of the Maz-Sherah!" They called out other names—those vampyres lost to history, those battles remembered from their kingdoms, the wives and children, the heroes and the fallen.

Amidst the throng, the tall, gaunt vampyre king called Athanat trudged along, pushing the other vampyres out of his path. When he came to me, he gave me a look of disdain. "There is among the missing, a mask. A sacred golden mask. It holds great power within it. Drawn from many immortals. If he is the anointed, where is the mask?"

"The mask of Datbathani," I said. "The Lady of Serpents."

"If you are Maz-Sherah, then you possess it," he said. "Why do you not have it?"

"It rests upon the face of a vampyre called Pythia," I said.

"Pythia, daughter of Namtaryn?" Athanat spat on the floor at my feet. "She sent me to my Extinguishing, Maz-Sherah. She is no better than the Myrrydanai. She should not wear the mask."

Namtaryn came rushing forward, drawing the twin-bladed dagger from her hair. She held this at eye level with Athanat. "Do not speak of my daughter this way, coward, unless you are willing to tell how you stole her from her rest and bound her and laid her out upon a desert that the sun might immolate her at dawn!"

"She did not burn, Light of Namtar," Athanat snarled as he drew the sword from his side, ready for a fight. I heard the clank and squeal of swords and other weapons being drawn by the others surrounding us.

I reached out, grabbing Namtaryn's wrist, and drew her blade-wielding hand downward. "What I have brought from the dust, I can return to dust."

She shot me a feral glance, and I saw where Pythia had gotten her fury. If Pythia was a tiger, her mother was a dragon. She glared at Athanat, and when she returned her attention to me, muttered nearly under her breath, "You are a fool."

"Sheathe your sword," I said to Athanat. Then, looking out at the gathering. "All of you. There will be no battles between us, not while Medhya threatens to destroy us all."

Nekhbet glanced at me as if about to warn me of something, but thought better of it and disappeared into the crowd, her servants trailing her.

Namtaryn set her blade back among the tresses of her hair and reached over to touch my throat. "Are you my daughter's lover?"

Her fingers created an intense heat as they stroked my neck, then went to my left ear, touching it lightly.

"You have great sorcery in your touch," I said.

"She has kissed this throat, and whispered in these ears." She smiled, and combed her fingers through my hair. "She had a fondness for the young. It was she who brought the Sacred Kiss to you? Ah, she must have enjoyed your dying."

I reached up and grabbed her hand, pulling it away from my scalp. She drew it back from my grasp. "I thought you would be concerned for her."

"She does not need her mother's concern," Namtaryn said. Her eyes narrowed as if she were trying to understand what I meant. "You have been told to distrust me. That liar—Nekhbet—oh, but you must know about the jealousy of women, for I am sure many fought for your attention, pretty one."

"Nekhbet spoke true," I said. "I know of your deeds, Namtaryn. I want your solemn oath that you will not betray any here. For with the Nameless, I will slice off that beautiful head of yours and hang it upon the highest mountain that you may watch the eternity of this world in your second Extinguishing."

Her mood changed quickly, and a flood of radiance burst across her face. It was as if she had shapeshifted from a haughty queen to a young maiden who knew nothing of the world. For an instant, she looked exactly like Pythia. "Believe as you will, Maz-Sherah, but I am so filled with the joy of movement and freedom from my cage, that I would do nothing to threaten you or bring your wrath upon me. So, I give you my oath, solemn or not, as I did when you asked it of all of us in our tombs. Now, tell me, how is my daughter?"

"Across the sea, traveling with an army of vampyres toward the castle where the Myrrydanai rule."

"And the mask? Has it yet . . . has it . . ?" She could not bring herself to say the words.

"Yes," I said, wishing I could tell her otherwise. "It has leached the eternal from her."

She shook her head as if dismissing some minor grief. "She deserves this. She is wickedness. Filthy." She waved her hands as if sweeping a thought aside. "Those who do wicked deeds deserve their punishment."

I grabbed her by the throat and felt a growl in my voice as I whispered at her ear. "You are not worth one ounce of her blood, Namtaryn. If it weren't for your daughter, you would still be in your tomb, rotting through eternity."

Her warriors—oiled youths of muscle and too much beauty—leapt upon me, but I shook them off too easily. I felt astounded by my strength, but also inspired by it. I let go of their queen and grabbed one of her servants, holding him with his face to her. I took the Nameless from its sheath, and thrust it into his heart, all the while watching her face. I felt a fire go up my arm, and a painful vibration at the grip of the sword. Then, it was as if a great gust of wind—from the vampyre's own flesh—burst outward. His eyes sank into his face, and his jaw slackened. Within mere seconds, the last of him fell in a pile of dust and bone at my feet.

I stared at the sword in my hand. I did not feel cursed by it, but invigorated. Something within the Nameless made me want to use it again. A surge of power shot through me, and I looked at Namtaryn, wondering what it would feel like to thrust it into her throat.

"You cannot be brought back twice!" I said in warning to her, raising the shattered blade close to her face. She flinched as she felt its warmth. "You will honor your daughter Pythia, for she has saved me from the destruction you see before you on the floor. If I hear one word from you—from any of you here—against Pythia, daughter of Merod, daughter of Namtaryn, I will do the same to you without a moment's hesitation!"

I felt nausea and revulsion from my words and the thoughts that inspired them, and quickly sheathed the shattered blade. *It is like the mask. The mask seeks a face. The Nameless seeks the grip of flesh. The sorcery of these things corrupts. They are not to be played with, not to be used lightly, for with each use, they prey upon the mind.*

Namtaryn snarled at me and reached down to brush the dust of the extinguished youth from her feet. As she crouched there, she looked up at me as if wounded.

"Do not look at me with false pain," I said. "For you have done such things to many. You would do them again if you thought you could steal this blade from me and use it against those who would grant you your freedom."

"You have extinguished one of our tribe," she said with bitter fury. "If you cannot control the Nameless, do not wield it. It is not meant for demonstrations of your power."

I turned and walked away from her. Athanat joined me, and whispered at my ear, "Show no mercy to the vampyre queen. She should not have been raised from damnation at all."

"I did not want to kill the servant," I said. "I wanted to threaten Namtaryn. I wanted to show her . . ."

"The Nameless knows your thoughts," Athanat said. "In the nights of my five hundred years, I tried more than once to take it. I crossed the sewer lake, and stood atop the roof of the temple. But when my hand drew close to the hilt, I began to hunger for it as we thirst for blood. But it was a hunger of one who would destroy others just to hold the Nameless once. Oh, of such great things I might do if I held it. If I wielded it. Of becoming the Maz-Sherah—a king, and a savior. But even touching it, I felt its sting. Many dawns I went to my rest with terrible thoughts of it, as if just wanting it had cursed me." He reached over and touched my shoulder lightly. "It will be a burden to you. There will be those among us who wish to steal it. It will call to you—to do terrible things. But what is within you will also temper it. Fear it, respect it—but know that it is meant for you alone."

"I do fear it," I said. "I will use it, when necessary. I will bring Hell itself to Ghorien and all the shadow priests—and to the defenders of Taranis-Hir. And to any mortal or vampyre who betrays the Serpent."

"As it should be," he said, then suggested we search for a vessel for renewal. "The shattered sword has exhausted you—it is in your eyes, this weariness."

After we had drunk from a mortal—and allowed her to scurry off to her lair—he told me of the others, and some of his tales differed from Nekhbet's recounting, and others supported what she had told me. Both of these rulers had warned me of Namtaryn, but Athanat added, "But she is not as terrible as she seems. For she loved Merod in both mortal

life and during her rule. Perhaps I am the only one to understand this, for I also loved Namtaryn in my young nights.
Her daughters also, she loved until they turned against her.
Her Extinguishing was not at the hands of Ghorien or a
usurper of her throne. It was that daughter you know of—
Pythia—who betrayed her mother to mortal armies. Pythia
set a trap, and her mother was easily caught as she went to
her morning's rest. They bound Namtaryn, and set her out in
the blazing sun. Those who witnessed it later wrote on stone
tablets that she did not cry out when the fires of the heavens
burst across her flesh. Even mortals wept when they heard
the news of her passing. I was a mortal general of her army
then, not yet vampyre, and it was centuries before I would be
king. But I remember her justice—fierce, and swift, yet not
unjust. She was a great queen, and did not deserve what her
daughter did to her. You must be careful of the Pythoness.
She has brought disaster to many. I would extinguish her before any of the others of our tribe—if it were up to me."

I did not wish to argue against him, for I knew Pythia
well enough. My first knowledge of her was that she had
bled a child—the boy named Thibaud, whom I had felt
close to in the mortal wars. She had deceived me, and had
destroyed her father's kingdom, and cursed her sisters. She
had brought Artephius the Medhyic scrolls, and had further heaped destruction on our tribe.

I knew her now as a mortal. I knew her now as the
woman within whom my third child grew. I knew her for
her tenderness and fears.

Yet I could not completely ignore the centuries of her
existence that told a different story.

◆ 7 ◆

OPHION accompanied me to the throne of Medhya,
with dawn but an hour away. In fury, I went to the golden
statues and hit them with the staff, cracking them open, the
bones of the dead falling in fragments to the marble floor.

I broke apart into a swarm of rats and raced up to the
throne itself, re-forming upon it. I sat there, looking out at

the fallen statues, at Ophion, who stood at the center of the room. "On this throne, Ophion, Medhya began a destruction that has not yet ended."

"You are here to end it, my lord," he said.

"Is it worth stopping her? For you see them—they are not kings and queens. They are as brutal as she. I, too, am like her. Her breath is in me. Her blood, my bloodline."

"Do not say that, my lord," Ophion said. "I have seen the works of Medhya, and she does not have the Serpent within her. You possess it. You are no son of mortals, nor are you a son of Medhya. You are the progeny of the Great Serpent, and none other. They fear you in that hall of the dead, and they will follow you in battle. In the stream, you are known to them, and the stream is their guiding star."

I rapped my hands upon the gold serpent of the throne's arm. "Why should I risk myself—and my unborn child— for these creatures? They would destroy me if I did not have the awakening power of these objects. If they could wield the Nameless, they would—and do to me what I did to that poor servant."

Ophion drew his hands together, and would not look at me.

"What is it? Ophion?"

"I cannot say, my lord, out of fear."

"Fear of me? You have nothing to fear from me. Come forward. Come, now. Tell me what is on your mind."

He glanced up, but would not move. "It is Medhya, Maz-Sherah. She is here. In some way, she is here. It is not like you to have sent that servant back to damnation. Not like you at all. The only law I know of our tribe is not to send a vampyre to Extinguishing. You are now the law, and yet you have broken it. Here, you sit upon her throne. The Asyrr also have sat upon it. All knew her voice, whether they admit it or not. Her power is seductive, Falconer. It traps many. When I was imprisoned here, the king was Setyr, called the Conqueror, and Medhya influenced him. The Myrrydanai had grown corrupt, but it was Setyr who signed my fate—my imprisonment here. My torments. He was a good king when he first ascended this throne. Like you, who would be a good king. But she whispers in power and the draw of the Asmodh sorcery is strong when it is in your blood to have it. This is why none may wield the Nameless but you. None wish to, for she always exists in the sorcery of our tribe."

"I will rid myself of the blade," I said.

"It is the only weapon against her. Will you leave it for someone else to hold? Some thousand years from now? After she has cut you down to your grave, and held you there in chains? No, you must wield it, and the staff, and the Eclipsis, though the grasping of them will destroy you. Medhya and her hounds do not destroy from wounds and fights, but from this—from the want of power. Your appetite for it will grow, as I have seen it grow in mere hours this night. You are now the source of all this, Maz-Sherah. The fires of the city have gone out, for you have this energy within you. You must use it."

I pushed myself away from the throne and drew him into the corridor beyond it. "I will fight such influence. We must leave when night comes. The waning crescent comes, and within two nights, the sky turns dark, and the solstice will have begun. I would leave now, even as the sun rose, but for those who I must lead back. Yet, I have wasted much time."

"In you, the Serpent lives," Ophion said. "And all I suffered has been cleansed. The solstice will not come before we return. Your staff, your sword, bring us the power of Myrryd itself."

"How do you know this?" I asked.

"Because it is before me, in you, my brother," he said as solemnly as I had ever heard him speak. "No one will destroy us, so long as you lead the tribe. The Asyrr have bowed before you. The Great Serpent is within your blood, yes, my brother, within you—and the door to the Veil as well. I feel now as if you were with me in those years of my captivity, for you were my hope though I did not know your face. You were my sustenance, though I did not taste your blood. Into the deepest prison of the Asmodh I would follow you now. The Asyrr and their warriors, also, would take this plunge if you asked it of them."

I went to him and clapped him upon the shoulder, and embraced him. When we separated, I said, "Let us go sleep among the tombs and rise at dusk to begin this war."

WHEN the sun fell like blood beyond the cliffs of the red city, with the thousands of stars in the darkening sky, I led the kings and queens of Myrryd upward, and brought blessings of the staff to each of them, and to their men and women who would fight, and their servants who would guard.

"Our way is written upon the wind!" I shouted to the host gathered there. "To the cliffs beyond Taranis-Hir we fly—and if we go with the winds, it will be two nights' journey, I am sure of it. But none must lag behind, nor must you stop to gaze upon the earth for long. We will not drink blood until we are at the Akkadite Cliffs, for we would waste precious time otherwise! Now, with the blessing of the Nahhashim staff—fresh-cut from the bone of the priests who were cursed by the Queen of Wolves and full of the power of their ritual—let us follow the path of stars that point north and to the west!"

To the north we flew, swiftly, and from below, we might have looked like a great flock of giant falcons moving toward the lands of bitter cold, more than three hundred strong, toward the birthplace of the plagues of the Veil.

Beside me, Ophion, who knew the markings of the stars, for it was an old magick learned in his travels.

I told him our destination, he led us across the heavens.

The stream grew strong and thick that night, and dark angels, within it, we soared.

◆ CHAPTER 13 ◆

The Akkadite Cliffs

◆ 1 ◆

FROZEN was the great sea along the straits of Iberia, with leviathans dead along the frosted shore, come up from the deeps of the western sea, unable to survive its chill. The fires of men burned below, and the smoke of many wars rose to greet us. Towns had grown dark beyond the fortress walls of cities, and cities themselves had hundred of guards, and in those hills, the pitch fires smoked to ward off the breath of ice. Famine stretched its fingers to many lands, and the wars between town and fort, between neighbor and kinsman, were signs of this lack.

The plagues brought by the Myrrydanai had done their job too well over the years, and the Disk dream had silenced the cry of human need. Within the stream I felt the fury of the warriors who trailed me, for they knew the power of the Dark Mother and saw her handiwork in this sorcery. Many spoke with their minds, yet I ignored them, for I had no answers for their complaints and their anger. They saw the handiwork of Medhya in the ruins of once-great citadels, and in the strange silence of the night in those places where once fires had been lit for warmth rather than war.

Snowcapped mountains passed beneath us, and we were nearly thrown off course by a storm that raged from every direction with rain like spears of ice. The wind howled like the wolves of the north as our company came to high mountain caverns for rest—though we did not see the coming sun for the tempest that had descended, we felt its heat in our bones.

But I needed no rest, and the sun would not harm me with the serpent skin beneath my flesh. I drew Ophion out to the morning sky and asked him if he knew the constellation to my home. He looked up to the fading stars and told me that there were several that headed north and west, but he would not know these cliffs if passing over them. He pointed out one of them. "See it? The great coiling cluster," he said. "In my youth, the seers called it the Uriz—the gyre of Ur—for it turns over and over upon itself, like the ancient creature of the mists. There, do you see? Oh, but it is hard to find in this lightening sky. I know this ancient forest you speak of, and its third cluster ends not far from it, my brother."

"We have made good time, for even the storm has not impeded us, but it will as we venture over these mountains. The cliffs are but a half night's journey, if this fierce wind ends, a full night if not. Where the plagues have been many, where the snow gathers thick, these cliffs are miles from a white-towered city," I said. "The Myrrydanai haunt this kingdom, and you will sense them there. But you must not go near it, for we must meet others at the Akkadite Cliffs. You must be cautious, for there are vampyres called Morns under the guidance of the White Robes, and they will not recognize you or our company as their tribe, for their minds have been destroyed, and they hear only the Myrrydanai. I will keep watch for you and draw your stream toward our lair."

I passed him the Eclipsis in its pouch.

He looked at it in his hands, and then at me. "My brother, this is for you only. My touch does not bring its deathlight." He tried to pass it back to me, but I folded his hands around it.

"Tie it at your waist," I said. "Wrap it as tight in its pouch as you can. When you are near—and I will keep watch, for if you stay on course, it will be but a night at most—I will call it. It will come to me, but hold fast to it. It will guide you to the spot where I stand. The others will follow. Do not let anyone touch this, and pass it to no one."

"You will fly . . . during the day?" he asked.

"I wear the skin of the Great Serpent," I told him. "And from my skin, I may call the Raptorius armor. The sun cannot burn me while this exists in my flesh. Now, my brother, sleep, and at nightfall, lead them north and west. When you feel my strength in the stream, I shall also feel you. I will call the orb to my side, and you shall come with it."

We embraced, and I left him and the company to their rest.

Tired though I was, I drew out the cloak of skin from my flesh, and from it, the suit of armor with its helm. Raising the staff, I moved through the sky at sunrise feeling the heat of that great burning chariot upon my face for the first time since my nineteenth year. Yet the storms continued, and the sky grew dark before midday, and what was not a tearing at the clouds of light and thunderclaps, was a gloom of snow and ice, pelted from the roiling black clouds. I moved more swiftly as I shapeshifted into a flock of ravens in the sky, as I did not wish to be recognized as a demon returning to Taranis-Hir's towers. The wind blew at my back, and my shifting was difficult, but I held fast to it. The sorcery of such shapeshifting is intricate, for I felt like nothing other than myself, with the Nahhashim clutched in my fist and my wings drawn out from that scaly armor. Yet, at the same time, I was aware of the multitude of forms I had become—I was infinite in this form, and I saw from every raven's vantage point, and felt their many wings beat against the whistling wind. It was a pleasure to shapeshift now, and I felt a glorious upsurge of energy from it, for

I was a multitude, and I was a single being. It was as if the boundary of my flesh had expanded to include many within one movement forward.

The whirling storm did not abate until I saw the trees of Brittany, and the ancient wood of my ancestors, after nightfall.

Much of the Forest had been burned in the past few weeks, and the fires of Taranis-Hir were blinding along its towers so that it seemed like daylight there—made more brilliant by the heavy blanket of snow that covered all, thicker than any winter before, for even trees groaned under the ice, and many fell to it, and the white of the land could barely be distinguished from the white of the city itself.

I remained far beyond the sight of its towers, and flew low into the Forest from the east, rising up to the Akkadite Cliffs, then leaping down onto a ledge, weary and exhausted.

◆ 2 ◆

WITHIN the intricate series of steps, beyond the cavern vault, I expected to hear the sounds of mortals, or to find the dark chambers of rock where Pythia and the soldiers we had raised from the battlefield might wait among these warrens of dirt and stone. Instead, silence greeted me in the cool, damp shadows, and the need for rest overcame me, though I did not desire it.

I lay down in the green shadow of the roots of the Akkadite trees themselves, thrust into the rock of the cave, and there in the earth, I slept several hours.

My dreams were disturbed by a whispering at my ear, and I recognized the voice as that of Enora herself, as if she had sent her spirit form into my soul. *Come to us, Falconer*, was all she said.

Someone pushed at my shoulder, and I awoke suddenly. My eyes adjusted to the shadowed dark, and I recognized the woman who stood over me.

• 3 •

CALYX sat down beside me. She called out a name, and an elder woman dressed in the brown cloth tunic of the Forest dwellers came in, limping as if she had damaged her left leg. I tried to speak, but my thirst left a whisper to my voice.

Calyx drew back the woman's sleeve, and offered the stranger's arm to me to drink. Neither of them spoke, nor did they have to speak, for I read sorrow upon their faces, its veil drawn away, the plague beneath her skin a glow of amber.

When I had drunk my fill, leaving the old woman sleepy, I asked Calyx of the army that had been raised among the mortals.

"Hundreds dead," she said. "Fewer than a hundred left."

• 4 •

CALYX led me up the hidden paths of the cliffs, and within those quarters she shared with her fellow mortals, she showed me the wounded, the dying, the ones who had not survived the night. Many men lay with broken bones and bodies. Their sunken eyes told me a tale of hopeless battle, and women, bound with bloodied rags at their shoulders and waists, who had fought with valor against an enemy with none. Their faces all seemed of one face— despair and loss, for none of them were untouched by the horrors of the Myrrydanai, the scratches of the Morns, the bites of the Chymer wolves.

Calyx told me of the fight. The armies of the Akkadites—raised within weeks by a knight called Per Ambler who wished to destroy all who served the Disk—rose in a thunderous host to besiege the city. Their spies within the walls of Taranis-Hir would open the gates, and the mortal warriors would cut down all who opposed them. "But the spies had already been found out, and their heads hung across the high gates, as if in a necklace. The White Robe priests flew like spirits as they rode creatures like dragons, and drew swords, quickly leaping upon the knights and foot soldiers. Their mounts devoured our horses, tearing them at the spine, grabbing them in their jaws like jackals running down deer. Enora rode out upon her white horse, and raised the staff—and from it, a gray mist came, and all who breathed this poisoned mist fell to the snowy ground, and their skin bubbled and dissolved as if the blood boiled from beneath the skin."

Fallen knights and soldiers lay on straw mats near a roaring fire at the cliff's ledge. Several did not even look up as we passed by, for they stared intently at the flames as if willing their minds to escape this place while their bodies could not.

"When did this happen?" I asked Calyx.

"When the moon died."

"One night past?"

She nodded, and did not show me any kindness in her glance. "You have much to answer for, vampyre, for you are too late for us. Taranis-Hir holds power beyond what I even believed."

"It is not yet the solstice night," I said. "You should have waited. One more night."

She had been pushed too much in the past several weeks, and I saw in her anger the buildup of years of waiting for such battles. Calyx snarled and snapped as she told me of the bloody battle—the wolves, the phantoms, the fires that came from the staff and burned men alive on horseback. "We could not wait. They came to us. We had no choice. We did not know if you would ever return. No one believed you had survived."

I could not fathom this—I asked her how many had died, what had occurred, why could they not have waited another night?

She shot me a fiery glance. "Another night? How many days should pass before their Chymer wolves came to us? Enora astride a white horse that breathes smoke, raising that staff—that was stolen from you—to tear apart the flesh of many men? We waited for you. They *hunted* us. It was not a battle, but a capture—a hunting party. The hunters had skill and sorcery on their side, and all we had were men and women willing to fight for what they believed. My sisters and I called up the Briary Maidens for your safety and to find out what delayed you in your search for this mask, and those sisters of the brambles told us you had a whore's legs wrapped around you. Even those elementals have fled the wood, for too much has been uprooted, too much burned, and the bog sorcery has gone to something deeper of the unknown world. All is a wasteland, and Enora, its queen. From other lands, other kingdoms, more soldiers come to fight for her—for the Disk dream has torn their reason from them, and replaced it with faith in this cursed Virgin of Shadows. The solstice no longer mattered! You left us to this!"

She quieted as she glanced around at the wounded, who stirred, and several looked over at the two of us and began murmuring among themselves.

"Look at them," she whispered. "They are mortal men and women. They are in pain, and our healers cannot take away many of these wounds. Some burn within, and some without, and others have bones that will not set to heal. They are not like you blood-drinkers. The White Robes broke bone and spirit down along the Forest floor, and used such magick as I have not seen before. From the bogs, they called up their infernal lizards to ride, and from the art of their alchemists, they made poisons to tip their arrows. A single shot, in the arm, in the thigh, might fell a man and leave him in burning agony. The Morns dropped down like vultures, and drew men and women up in their arms, and dropped them from the clouds that they might break against the ice of the canals and sink below into the frozen water. The Chymer wolves tore at others. Few of the Disk knights fought at all—for why should they, when such monsters did their work? We fell by the hundreds, and Per Ambler was the first, for he led the charge. The bravest of men I have known, and he raised his sword against Enora herself—but his horse was brought down by the monsters, and when he was on foot, three White Robes gathered around him and with great pleasure tore off his armor and, with his own sword, eviscerated him that the steam rose from within his fundament. His cries shook all who heard them, and it was not until his blood had soaked the ice, like some new dark bog coming from the deep, that the priest stopped their torture of that goodly knight. By then, many had gone to the arms of Death, and of those who remained, all scattered. I, too, fled upon a horse, though I wished to turn and fight to my death. But the screeches of the Morns, and the howls of the Chymer wolves—it was the mouth of Hell itself. Why did you not return before this? If you had but been here . . ."

I told her of what had occurred, but she told me she did not care for my stories. "We had to attack, Falconer. We had to attack, for Per Ambler, the renegade knight, had gathered an army of hundreds of men—all loyal to kings far and away, and some from the Aquitaine, others from Cornwall, and others from the mountains to the north. Pagan and Christian fought side by side, for these warriors did not fall under the spell of the Disk dream. Too many of our people were caught and tortured and burned, and we could not wait for a flying devil to return to save us."

"How many died?" I asked.

"I do not know an exact count," she said with fury in her eyes. "They had come from every kingdom to fight against her, called by Per Ambler, called by those of distant Christendom, called by the pagans of the endless groves. Some who didn't die in battle were captured. Others, in terror at the sorceries and horrors of the wolves, surrendered. We are abandoned by all gods here, Falconer. We could not even save many of the wounded, for the Chymer wolves tore at those who fell, and others were speared as they lay upon the ground. Of those who surrendered, their heads appeared this morning upon the pikes of the city gate. There was nothing . . . nothing . . . we tried all we had," she said. "We waited for you."

"Did *any* escape?"

She glanced about the room, to the men and women

who lay in pain, watching us. "These are all we could manage. There are twelve of us who are able. Seventy or so wounded." She glared at me. "Old women stood with staves in their hands, attacking the Chymers as they rushed them in their wolf forms. Old women with nothing but their prayers and their fury. Torn down in moments."

"I am sorry, Calyx. Forgive me."

"The time for such sorrow is past. I waited and I told these knights and men to wait more. Two more nights, I said—one night! No, an hour. But the wolves came to us, and their queen, upon her horse, her staff drawing unearthly light—and where she touched, fires burst across trees and rock. Since you left, the White Robe sorceries have grown stronger, and the bogs have given up new poisons to them. And yet, none touched me—no sword, no priest, no Morn. My weapons, they stole in the struggle, but no one would cut me down when I had no defense. The plague within me made me untouchable to them. Even the Chymer wolves shied away from me, for they fear what lives beneath my skin. And yet, I cannot release it, though I have cut myself. I cannot send it out to attack them." She held up her arms, and drew back the cloth to show me the newly formed scars. "What is within me, I tried to pass to them. But it would not go. This plague that lives in my flesh and marks me—a plague maiden—brings no power but protection. And I would rather die than live beneath the towers of that city. But I thought you would come. I held my hope, Falconer, when none did." She began weeping, and covered her eyes with her hands.

I wanted to go to her and hold her that she might feel some comfort, but I held back.

She told of the horrors of the battle, of the men who were skinned alive by the White Robes, of the women set afire as they fought, of the shrieking of human and animal. She spoke of the blood-eagle, the cutting and tearing of a soldier's ribs, pulling them out of the back so that they resemble crimson wings—done while the victim was alive. "Their dragons—large as horses—drawn from rituals of the bogs, creatures with spines and scales who obey the White Robes who ride them."

"I have heard of these," I said. "They are the Lamiades—and have served the Myrrydanai before."

"They devour men and poison with their spines," she said. She talked about the howling of the Chymers when they were in wolf form. "The White Robe sorcery has made them larger than wolves of the Forest and mountains, and their jaws catch many of our men and women, for they run faster than our horses, and only a spear or arrow aimed for their hearts will stop them. They have a piercing howl, and when it is heard by the man standing near them, he will lose his hearing—and the world will spin, for the sound drives us into madness. The Chymer women—when not in their wolf forms—call the dead from skull and bone beneath those Tomb Gardens of Taranis-Hir. Enora's staff brings some substance to these underworld spirits, and they are drawn into the living through rituals of the Myrrydanai. From the Barrow-Depths, the ancient dead come—spirits of fury and war from an ancient age of evil—and they possess the living soldiers who have been blessed by the White Robes for such duty. To stop them, they must be obliterated by sword and spear, for a single blade to their hearts will not end their lives."

"Possessed? All?"

She shook her head. "Only a few dozen spirits were drawn up from the dredge of the Barrow-Depths. But these leap from body to body, so that when one knight falls, the soul called up by the necromancers flies into another. And another. Our wounded believe that Enora herself creates nightmares in their minds, for she speaks to them in dreams. Her sorcery has grown stronger as the solstice approaches. And the atrocities of Enora's guard . . ."

She drew me out along the narrow rocks, where a crumbling window looked out on the distant towers. She pointed beyond the Forest, to great torches that lit the Forest roads that led to the gate of Taranis-Hir. "Those are prisoners, covered with pitch and straw, set alight. Many were alive when the fires began to burn—human torches to light the road into the Forest.

"The world will be ravaged, and the plagues will come again. Enora will swallow other kingdoms, for many fall under her spell. I have even felt the pull of its tide." She pointed to the staff I held. "You hold this now."

"It is a second staff," I said. "But as long as Enora holds its brother, she will have much power, for it contains some magick of the gray priests of the Nahhashim." I turned the staff lightly in my hand. "Even I do not fully understand the depth of this sorcery."

"They call Enora their Queen of Wastelands, and the Queen of the Great Forest, and the Lady of Wolves. She is the end of us. When we saw another vampyre come from the south, we thought you would be with her. I held that hope as I watched the creature soar across the sky. Yet, even one of your tribe has gone to Taranis-Hir, a traitor."

Pythia, I thought. "Were there others with her?" Even as I asked this, my hope began to die. She and I had raised many men from the crusading warriors, and made them take oaths to us. Yet, had none returned with her. Had she left them among those mountain caverns? Had they simply extinguished soon after rising, for they had no mortal vessel nearby to drink? Would Pythia do this?

Yes, I knew. She would. She was capable of cruelty beyond imagining, and yet I had come to believe the mask had changed her. I wanted to believe that she had a spark of love within her—not for me, but for her child's own future.

Why would she go to the Myrrydanai? What would she gain?

And yet, I knew: the safety of our child, the protection that Artephius might give her.

Perhaps even the alchemy that would remove the mask from her face, and the essence of immortality that the alchemist had extracted from my tribe in his torturous experiments.

Part of me still did not believe she would commit such

treachery against me. Not with our child growing within her. Not with the mask upon her face.

"It was not a Morn, you are sure?" I asked.

She offered me a look that approached sympathy. "She flew low to the earth, and I saw upon her face that mask of gold that you sought. I was certain then that she was a messenger sent by you. A message of some hope. And yet, she did not come to me when I called out to her, but soared like a dragon toward the great white towers. You may ask Mordac who watches the skies from the height of our cliffs. His eyes are sharp and strong, for he is part wolf. He saw her cross the towers, untouched by Morns, and descend toward the tower of White-Horse itself. She is a traitor to you, if she was ever other."

• 5 •

I sought the boy in his stony watchtower, and he told me of the flying devil whose "face like sun. Beauty. Devil wings." Mordac was the boy I had once seen in a vision of Calyx before I knew she was more than an ashling. He was a bastard of one of the Chymers, but did not have the taint of their evil in him—he was feral and smart, but with trouble expressing his thoughts, for the wolf in him did not trust speech. He told me much through growls and grunts and snarls, and I knew it was Pythia for certain when he said, "Golden hair and golden face," again and again as if he could not forget how she had looked down upon him as he sat among the rocks at the peak, as if she were marking the place of the Akkadite Cliffs in her memory.

My mind reeled as I tried to imagine reasons for Pythia's betrayal—perhaps she had a plan, perhaps the army of the undead we had breathed vampyrism into was just a night's flight away . . . and yet, for every reason, every excuse I gave, the word written in the old tongue haunted my mind:

Anguis.

Betrayer.

Betrayer of the Serpent.
Betrayer of Merod.
Daughter of Namtaryn.
Lover of Artephius, of Nezahual—of those who held great power.

Yet, I remembered those moments on the *Illuyanka*, when we danced and she hummed the tune of her mortal life. I remembered the passion in her arms, and her pleading voice as she begged me to go with her to some deep forest to escape the doom of this city. But I also bore the memories of her greed, her fury, and her need to best whoever held her in their arms. I remembered how she had helped bring the downfall of Alkemara, and how she had murdered the boy, Thibaud, in the tower of Hedammu, and had drunk from me until I was her mortal slave—and until she brought me the Sacred Kiss.

How many times had I been warned of her duplicity? How many had told me that she could not be trusted? Nezahual himself, though enraptured of her, did not believe her lies. Ophion, who had proven himself and suffered greatly, had not believed there was good in her.

Despite this evidence, I did not believe that Pythia would betray me—betray us—nor would she have abandoned those resurrecting vampyres to their fates along the mountains beyond Hedammu. I did not believe the woman who had passed me the Eclipsis that I might have guidance would go to my greatest enemy and the source of my destruction.

I remembered her fear, her terror at our shared vision—of the sacrifice upon the altar, of the maiden with the golden mask, of the ritual that I would perform.

My heart wished to believe that she was a victim of this sorcery of the White Robes. But my mind knew otherwise—for her thousands of years of life had taught her to save her skin before thinking of any other.

Unbidden, the memory of her words came back to me, from my first death until my last sight of her. Her voice seemed fresh in my head as she had once whispered,

While you live, you are mine, you are my love, you are the dirt of my grave, you are the flesh that is my bed. And the sound of her voice grew haunting. *If I could destroy you now, I would. If I could tear you limb from limb* . . . In Aztlanteum, Pythia had told me, *When I saw my future as I passed the breath of immortality to you, I knew that I would have to destroy you . . . or save you.*

Then, her words to me when I left her at the cave mouth to journey to Myrryd. *Do not judge me harshly, if I fail you.*

I raged within myself, thinking of how I had trusted her, and how foolish I had been, for she had been unworthy of trust. She knew she would betray me at that last moment, and she had told me many times in many ways how she would stop me from the solstice ritual.

I had wanted to believe some goodness of her, yet she had become as Enora herself—as Medhya, too—a Queen of Wolves, a betrayer.

Anguis.

For the first time since I had abandoned Taranis-Hir and the Akkadite Cliffs, I felt the heaviness of absolute despair. I had lost my children, and my companion, and Pythia herself—for I could not deny the love I felt for her. Yet love became ice in my blood, and in moments, I was numb to these feelings. I even cursed the child that grew within her, if that had not itself been a lie, as well.

• 6 •

CALYX, waiting for me, led me down into the valley below, out to the night sky, along a ledge and down a stone stair. We came out beneath the shadow of the mountain, where Taranis-Hir was unseen, and the Forest beyond the snowy meadow thickened again. Here, below the cliffs, was a long paddock made by hedging stones along the field that ran through the Forest. In the paddock, nearly a hundred horses, tended by three Forest women who brushed and hayed them. These were all that had returned from the battle from the hundreds that had entered it, carrying knights and warriors who had come to the Akkadite cause.

I turned to Calyx and put my hands on her shoulder. "Soon, hundreds of my tribe will come to these cliffs. We have not lost the solstice."

"Do you think the guardians of Taranis-Hir have not been honing their skills with your kind? Since the night you left, they have tormented those of your tribe. The vampyres that were not tortured into becoming Morns are put out at sunrise as examples to other such demons. They are spread-eagled and staked, and the sun burns them slowly throughout the short day so that by nightfall, many are blackened bones. We have heard their cries of anguish. Those who survive one short day are brought out again the next until they are roasted. Their ashes are gathered and put in silver boxes, as a reminder that the demons are not invincible. A few, they have made examples of—your friend. The one with whom you shared your long years in prison at the bottom of the old well."

Ewen, I thought, but could not say his name.

"I was there," she whispered, her eyes downcast. "I stole into the city, for I did not understand why they did such things to the devils, rather than torture them until they had become Morn. I watched from a culvert beneath the foundry tower. Even I felt the suffering of this winged devil."

"Tell me of this," I said, feeling a burning at my throat. "Who did this?"

"Do not make me remember, for I carry too much pain," she said.

"I must know. For I will have my vengeance against the one who destroyed my friend."

"They made a show of it. Seven of them, heroes of the arena, their wings drawn out and pinned down with spikes. Torques at their throats, attached to wooden slats to keep their heads just so—their faces upward to the noonday sun. At dawn, they lay there, and Enora and her White Robes stood by, while the prince of Taranis-Hir, who is called Quentin—though he once was known as Corentin Falmouth—supervised this torment."

I began to curse when I heard his name.

"You must tell me," I said. "For I want to know what this man did to my friend."

"I will not tell you this," she said. She reached up and touched my brow. "You have a fever."

"It is from the gall in my throat," I said. "My want of vengeance burns. Tell me of his Extinguishing. I want to know every detail, so that when I have Corentin in my hands, I will know what to do to him that he might feel what Ewen felt."

"It took three days for your friend to pass. I tried to rescue him—and others. But the White Robes guarded them, and I found no entry. They stripped him, and led him in chains before dawn across the bridge, to where the arena opens to its Game. They tied his wrists and ankles to four black horses, and upon these horses, four knights of the Disk who goaded their mounts to frenzy until his bones popped and his flesh tore. Yet when this was done, they drew him to the center of the arena. There, they cuffed and shackled him with silver, and painted him with quicksilver that he should not grow strong. Around his throat, a torque of silver-painted iron, and in his mouth, a silver coin. Then, they staked his ankles and wrists, and waited for the sun to rise . . ." Here, she stopped speaking, unable to look me in the eye.

"And when the sun rose?"

Her eyes welled with tears. I could not help but put my arm across her shoulders and draw her close to me.

"Please," I said. "I want to know. Recall for me everything, for I must know what suffering he endured."

Her words were hesitant and slow, and she stopped here and there, but I asked her to continue. "His skin began blistering. Oozing. But he did not cry out then. Not until the fire began to spread along his arms. His cries . . . his cries . . ." She pressed her face against my chest. I had no more tears for anyone, only a growing sense of what must be done. Yet, this news—even though I had anticipated the worst—shook me to my core.

"What did he cry out?" I asked.

"Your name," she whispered. "'Aleric!' he cried, a bleating lamb more than a devil. 'Aleric!' and then from this he cried, 'Maz-Sherah!' and finally, to the Serpent he shouted his last and his voice went silent. He sounded like a boy who had been chased into the Forest by wolves and sought the hunter. Crying out for someone who would not find him. On the third day, though the sun was not even in the sky more than a handful of hours, and the bitter cold wind blew gray snow from the sky, even so, his skin turned to ash. Before the wind could draw the motes of dust and ash upward, his skull and soot were swept up into one of the silver boxes. Others of your tribe were not so fortunate, for their ash blew along with the winter winds, whirling ash taken up into the gloom, and their skulls—of those that had not turned to dust in the sun's glare—were tossed to the wolves and dogs, and other were thrown through the breaks in the ice that thickens the canals."

I covered my face with my hands, and felt on the edge of my own destruction. Why had I been so long? Gathering these Asmodh sorceries, rather than fighting for Ewen's life—and the lives of so many others?

Yet, within me, I felt the Serpent stir—and what had been despair turned to rage, and what was rage became a white-hot fury.

"We will bury them in their filth," I said, feeling calm suddenly. "And if I find the silver box, I will yet raise him from the dead." I placed my hands on her shoulders. I looked her in the eyes, though she tried to avoid my glance. "No one could help him? Not these mortal knights who fought here? Not anyone?"

The strange ashen glow of her face dimmed as she said, "Mortals do not want to help your kind. I could not rouse them. I could not make them fight that day for the life of a vampyre."

"Then it is good they died in battle," I snarled, releasing her. "Why do I care for mortals if they would see one of us suffer like this?"

Enraged, I went to the rock wall at the mouth of the cave entrance, and smashed my fists against it. Again and again, until my hands had bled enough for me to feel something again. I held the staff and brought it down hard with a crack against a pile of stones, and the rock itself caught fire, though it quickly died out. The staff sent off a vibration through my body as if it were a warning.

I called to the Great Serpent in my blood, and to Merod, but was met with silence.

I looked over at the plague maiden who watched the fire go out along the stones. "Calyx, do you fight for us?"

"Yes," she said. "Many have died for this cause."

"For *us*? For my tribe?"

"No mortal will protect a vampyre," she said.

"But will *you*?"

After a moment, she answered. "Yes. I will fight for you, and your tribe. But how? With what army do we match these White Robes and their queen? We have fewer than a hundred men! How many of your devils come before this night is through to avenge us?"

I touched the edge of her face, its mottled opalescence nearly translucent in the darkness. "Is the plague beneath your skin one that can be used against them?"

"I do not know," she said, reaching up to cover her mouth as if it would let out some secret. "I dream of what will come."

"In your dreams, is your plague released?"

She nodded.

"What else is there? What is in your fever dreams about the plague in your blood?"

"I see her," she barely said these words aloud, but her lips formed them.

Medhya. She sees Medhya in her plague.

The final plague of the Veil.

"I must drink from you," I said. "Now. I must know this plague."

She pushed me away. Calyx went out among the bramble circle, between the standing stones of the Forest women, the rocks of the ancients that had been there since those who worshipped in the old religions had come to this land. She touched the tip of one of these upright stones, and when she looked back at me, she said, "Do not do this. Your drinking may bring you the plague itself."

"I will risk it," I said. "Come. Give me your blood. Do not fear this, Calyx. I am renewed from my journey. I have strength and sorcery within me that can match the White Robes' bog conjurations. The plague will not touch me, I promise you."

I held my arms out, the Nahhashim staff lowered.

She cocked her head to the side slightly, her eyes narrowing. "You are much changed, it is true," she said. "In all those days since you left us, I had begun believing that there was no hope left for us—for my Forest—for the world. It is a place of ravaging wolves and not meant for those who may become prey. But you are a predator, yet not a wolf at all, Falconer. You truly are a hunter of those who hunt."

Then, she came to me.

◆ 7 ◆

I took her in my arms, and gently nipped the tender flesh above her collarbone. It was like slicing through soft cake, and the rush of blood flooded into the back of my throat.

I was beyond the Veil in the moments it took for her blood to enter my own bloodstream. I stood beside the plague maiden, her face a hollow of emptiness, its flesh shattered. The earth around us was burned and red, corpses of men and women and children littered the barren ground. At a distance, I saw what seemed a path of fire shooting out along a plain of the dead.

It formed into a woman, and I did not need to see her face to know who she was. But in the next instant, Calyx herself was Medhya—her face plumped into flesh again, stinging insects crawling across her eyes and nose and lips. The painted third eye was upon her brow, a sign of her constant watchfulness.

"I am the Virgin of Shadows that the mortals of the Disk

have dreamed of," she whispered, a playful grin on her face, and began laughing at me. "Anointed One, how will you keep me from this world? For in your blood, the Veil burns, and through your blood and the plague of this Forest woman, I have my doorway. But several doorways exist, and you will open them all."

In the next moment, I again stood with my arms around Calyx, drawing my lips away from her throat.

She had fallen into a deep sleep. I watched her face to see if Medhya truly was there, but all I saw was the glow of the plague beneath her flesh, pulsing a yellow-blue.

I took her to the highest point of the cliffs, away from the towered city, where the air was cold but fresh, and the distant fires of Taranis-Hir were hidden. I sat down upon the crumbling rocks, near an outcropping of trees, and laid her down so that her head rested in my lap. I searched the night sky, hoping to sense Ophion and the company of vampyres who would fight with me.

When Calyx awoke, her head in my lap, she said, "She means to use me, this dark goddess."

"She is trying to terrify us," I said. "You once told me that I had seen what I was meant to know."

She looked at me, confused. "I do not remember."

"When my mother was to burn, at a crossroads, you and Mere Morwenna passed by as I rode along. And you told me—the words have haunted me for these years. You said that I had seen a demon myself once. That it was what I was meant to know. How did you know such a thing? How did you know I would become a vampyre, as was the creature that was drawn up from that well? And in that well, one night I would be cast down and imprisoned? What vision did you have of such things to come?" When she didn't answer, I whispered, "This is not the time to withhold from me. Your people are nearly dead. Taranis-Hir destroys your kind as it does mine. Tell me what you know that you have not told me yet."

"Mere Morwenna forbade me from mentioning it again. She made me take a vow."

"She is dead, and her soul has moved elsewhere. This vow must be broken."

I could tell that she fought within her own spirit to decide whether to tell me her deeply held secret, but after a bit, Calyx said, "Since I was born, I have seen what some consider unseen. And you—the first time I saw you, I knew that you would bring a terror into this land. I knew that you were meant to some terrible fate. And when you drew up the winged demon from the well, when I heard of this . . . I saw you trapped in that same well, as that creature had been. I saw you also, with a blade to my throat one day."

"You have been afraid of me?"

"I have learned not to fear death. But I do not give it instructions on how I am to die, if I can keep this secret."

"But you are afraid," I said. "You're afraid that the Dark Madonna will come through your flesh. That in the Disk dream, you are the Virgin of Shadows. Your final plague is her—Medhya. Yes?"

She closed her eyes as if fighting the thought, and nodded.

"This cannot be true," I said. "For what is our nature now, will always be in our nature, no matter what curse comes upon us. In all my existence as a vampyre, I have learned this. I have not become a worse man from the nature of vampyrism that has revived me from death. What monstrous deeds I have done, I did no less monstrous ones as a mortal man. Neither will you become other than Calyx, raised of the Forest women. For though your plague may be a door to Medhya, you will not be her puppet. I have met many devils and many men, and some were blood-drinkers, and others drank the soul. And none were made worse for their fates, though some gained power from such destiny." Even as I spoke, I thought of Pythia, and deception. Was that her nature? For many thought so, yet I did not truly believe it; for all she had shown me of herself—though cruel and self-serving—she did not seem the great traitor Pytheness that others believed. To Calyx I said, "We are one night from the solstice. If the ancients were right—if the priests of my tribe understood the nature of the Veil—there is yet a chance to end this."

"It is the day of the long darkness, and soon the beginning of the ember days. The Veil is thin, this is why the Forest folk call to their dead—and to our goddess—on this day."

"Do not fear the shadows you see in your dreams," I said. "For I am also here. I was born in the ember days of the year, and I will not meet my Extinguishing before they come."

"Yes," she said, her eyes brightening. "There is a difference in you. Something flows in your blood."

"As a plague flows in yours," I said. "Like your plague, what is in me brings me strength. Do not be afraid of Medhya, whom you see in blood visions. She is Queen of Wolves like Enora herself, and has no throne or crown, and she will not gain a foothold through you, or anyone. Call those of your folk who still remain. They must offer their throats to my army. None of you shall die from the bleeding, but the strength of the kings is important, and of their fighters. I will bring healing through the staff to those who suffer here, if they will fight with us in the coming night."

◆ 8 ◆

AFTER several hours, during which I brought the Nahhashim to many of the wounded and saw a gray-white light emanate from its spine, and pressed my hands to their flesh that they should heal, I felt a tugging in the stream, and went out to the cliff's edge.

A storm brewed at a great distance, and the clouds above were black as pitch—but I felt Ophion in the stream. And then it became so strong, and was like a throbbing pain at the base of my skull.

I spread my wings and rose up into the sky. I held the staff out to the wind, and called to the Eclipsis that it should find me.

As I looked southward, across the great expanse of Forest that had not met Enora's torches, I saw the great dark swarm of my tribe moving fast through the murk.

As they descended toward the cliffs, a new snow began to fall from the skies, and lightning split the clouds with its white fire.

When the Eclipsis was in my hand, I embraced Ophion and brought the others into the caverns that they should drink from the healed mortals, and rest—for we would wage war against the white towers by the following dusk. I lay down among the warriors, and slept, as well, for I needed all the strength within me for the battle to come.

A crash of thunder awoke me at dusk, followed by the earsplitting horns of the white towers—they blew their alarms along the hills and valleys of the wastelands. From the many towers, and the city gates, the horns called to all who served the Disk, and Enora, the embodiment of the Virgin of Shadows upon the earth. The misguided and misled, the merchant-soldiers who followed gold rather than truth, the weak-spirited and the enslaved, all would gather beneath the White-Horse standard. Many would bow and scrape to the White Robes and swear allegiance to their new queen—for yes, Enora was no longer baroness; she had claimed and taken lands that her armies had burned and pillaged, and nearby territories long abandoned from famine and pestilence.

These dreaded sounds were followed by the piercing howls of the Chymer women as they shapeshifted near their grotto at the Forest edge.

I lay there and felt the heavy burden of the night ahead of us.

III

TARANIS-HIR

CHAPTER 14

Before the Battle

• 1 •

BEFORE rising, I closed my eyes and went deep into the dark of self. *Merod, where are you? Serpent, be with me. It is the time of the war, and though I do not know its outcome, I wish for your spirit in my blood. You have given me many visions, and much guidance. I call you in humility, for though the weapons of the Asmodh are with me, and the soul of the Nahhashim priests in the second staff, I do not know if this is enough to defeat the enemy. I do not wish the death of the innocent, nor of those who are blinded to truth, nor those misguided by the plague dream. I ask for the safety of my twin children, and even for Pythia, though I cannot fathom her reasons for betrayal. In the vision of the ritual I am meant to perform as Maz-Sherah, it is with the Pythoness upon an altar stone, and it seems a sacrifice, although I do not understand why this should be. Yet, when the time comes, inspire me with the ancient Asmodh words—the words before language—that only you can offer. Keep safe our company, and those who aid us in this fight to close the Veil and to send the Myrry-danai to their rightful oblivion.*

These thoughts were met with silence. I no longer felt the guidance of Merod within me, nor did I sense the Great Serpent as I had in the Asmodh depths.

I rose from my day's tomb and went to those who readied for battle.

◆ 2 ◆

THE air had grown more chilly. I heard the sounds of others in the depths of the caverns, coughing off the day's rest, calling out to each other. The nest of vampyres went deep in the earth of the Akkadite Cliffs—several chambers snaked below the rock and cave. Though protected with blessings from the Briary Maidens, I knew that the Myrry-danai would seek out those who existed here if there were one more day, and using their mortal soldiers, slaughter the vampyres.

I wondered that the mortals here who protected us had not died from fear, or had not been tempted to stab us in our hearts themselves while we slept—for I could see upon their faces they still thought us devils.

Calyx approached me with a man of twenty, who—shivering with fright—offered me his wrist for drinking. I calmed him with words and those seductions known to my tribe, and told him that the pain would be swift and would heal soon after—and with it, lingering pleasure. I was careful with him, and did not drink more than a cupful, for I knew I would drink from mortals that evening whom I could drain. When it was done, I raised his face and looked into his eyes, which were battle-worn and despairing. "For the strength you have given me tonight, I will bring much slaughter to those who have offended you and your kin."

Afterward, Calyx took me by the hand and led me out to the mouth of the cave. "Upon three white steeds, three riders dressed in the robes of the Knights of the Disk rode out of the widening gate of Taranis-Hir at middle day. Beside the ice canals they went, and through the drained marshes, across the Forest floor. Along the burned path they rode, and several of us watched them come, drawing our blades and axes to meet them if they sought to climb the worn steps and brave the western and southern ledges, to attack us in our lair. But they brought their horses to rest down by the rumblerock, among the snowdrifts where the shallows of the bogs had been covered with brambles. One of them called a challenge to us, while you and your tribe slept. He shouted with angelic voice for us to have faith in the Virgin of Shadows, and to sharpen wood or heat our blades, and to thrust them into the hearts of the devils we harbored. 'Bring their heads to the tor of the ancient saint who lies beyond the Chymer grotto, and drive them upon your spears for the heavens to see!' He drew off his helm, and showed his face.

"I went to the ledge that overlooked the deep fall below, and I recognized him as a youth called Robin Carverson who had once been kind to me in the foundries. He was fair and gentle, and he told me of the White Robes' mercy. 'If you and your people do this—destroy these devils from Hell—and will come now, and lead your Akkadites to the city, you have the word of the Queen of the Forest and of the Wastelands and of the Jeweled Sea, the earthly saint of the Disk itself, Enora, the Lady White-Horse, that none will be held responsible for any acts committed prior to this day. You may bury your dead who still lie upon the frosted earth, and celebrate the victory this day—with us. And you, ashling, Calyx of the Forest women, will be allowed to return to these woods and their spirits, for our great queen acknowledges your innocent nature, which is like that of a fawn in the forest, despite the crimes you have committed against her, against Taranis-Hir, and against the Disk itself.'

"And to him, I answered, 'I am no fawn, I am the plague maiden whom you should cower before. When the night falls, you shall have your answer, and not a moment before. But I also offer you and your companions something, for I remember your gentleness from days long past. If you would join us in these cliffs, and swear allegiance to our company, and fight those shadows disguised as priests who rule the city with plagues and bog sorcery—and their queen, who is no queen at all, and only a baroness by the murder of her family . . . then you, also, will be spared, and will be forgiven.'"

I could not help but laugh as she told me of her response, but she maintained an aura of gloom about her.

"They did not think this so amusing," she said. "The boy I had once known as kind began to curse me—and curse all who remained in the Forest. He told me that he and his riders would find me when the battle came and make me suffer such torments as devils—and women who worshipped at the Forest fountains—deserved. I grew afraid that my challenge had doomed us all, for they could have scaled the cliffs had they wished to and sounded an alarm that the city might hear. But they did not. They rode back to their towers and left us. We have watched the paths and roads and narrows since then, for fear of their return— and of others the White Robes might send."

"They do not need alarms for what they are about. These Disk knights are afraid," I said. I gripped the staff. "They have much to fear from us. And tonight, their fears will come to them, for the devils are here, and we will ride to them on the wind and upon the backs of horses."

Snow had continued its blizzard onslaught all the day long, and lightning flashed. The towers of Taranis-Hir— small at this distance—but still like the upward-turned fangs of a jackal, blazed with torchlight along the battlements and the turrets.

I saw the faint blur of dark movement at the top of the walls and gates as many men prepared the weapons that would be thrown from above to those of us who attacked the city gates from below. On all sides of the walls of the city these soldiers stood, though they seemed smaller than ants at such a distance.

The drums began, and pounded out a slow but regular beat. These were answered with drumbeats along the canals, and the drums at the towers, and in the brief interval between this dooming noise, thunderclaps burst from the clouds. The booms grew softer as the last light of day was no more, and the deepening shadows of the storm clouds—rightfully called ravens by the pagans of the wood—darkened even the white snow.

"The day passes too swiftly," Calyx said. "The long night begins. In years past, I would be here with the other women of the Great Forest, and we would call the Briary Maidens to aid us, and give offerings to the Lord and Lady of the Wood. But now, I feel the Veil's torn caul, as I feel the plague in my blood. The rage of the Old Ones grows, and the fires of the heavens split the skies. Enora's army burns the canals and the woods at the edge so that we must enter fire to meet them in battle. They know you are here. They are prepared. If we do not take it to them in a few hours' time, they will ride to us—but a thousand riders of the Disk, and not three."

"We will end this at their gates," I said. "I will take the heads of many. I will find those who have offended you and your kind, as I will find those who have harmed my tribe among them. Corentin Falmouth will feel the suffering he brought to Ewen and those vampyres of my tribe. The alchemist, and Pythia—the betrayer of her tribe—if she is with him, will find no escape from the sword I bring to the gates of Taranis-Hir. Before dawn, Enora will beg for the mercy of the Great Serpent, but I will cast her down into the Asmodh fires before I allow her breath to cloud the air for one more night." As I spoke these words, I no longer felt Aleric within me. Falconer I was, and Falconer I would remain, son of the Great Serpent and no other.

The storm of falcons would fly with me to the gates, and tear them down, and when the city had been taken, we would burn it to the earth, and salt the earth that such a city should never again grow from the Barrow-Depths.

She turned to me, grasping my arm lightly, leaning in to me. "Their sorcery is powerful. The White Robes have called many men from provinces and towns, offering them wealth and the promise of Heaven for their loyalty. The minds of so many are polluted by the Disk dream. How do we fight the world?"

"This is not the world," I said. "I have seen other lands in my journey, and the plagues have touched them, but not all mortals cower before the Disk dream. These White Robes are the hounds of the Veil, the shadows of priests, and the one who rules them. Our aim is for closing the Veil itself. This is the time of the Great Crossing, and Medhya uses the tears of the Veil and the blood of many to break through. An aspect of Medhya herself—in the form of Datbathani, her sister—told me that one of my children will mend the Veil. The other will tear it. That one was made of fire and one of blood, though I do not understand these words. They are both flesh and blood, of me. I must take my children beyond the grasp of the White Robes. They will not be pawns in this war."

One of the mortals came out from the rock opening, and told Calyx that there was not enough blood among them to satisfy the hundreds of warriors who had come from Myrryd.

"I will tell my tribe of this, for they are bidden not to harm you. But they shall drink deep tonight, in battle," I said. I reached for Calyx and drew her close. "Will you join the fight, ashling?"

"Everyone here will join it," she said. "For we still have weapons and will. And now that you have brought healing to the wounded, they, too, will take up arms and return. We will fight to the death."

"Good. Have your men gather nine horses from those in the paddock. We will descend the cliffs in three hours' time, and the Asyrr and you—and I—will ride into battle as kings of this earth, while our warriors cover the skies as hunting falcons."

"But we can have the horses ready within the hour," she said. "For they are rested and watered, strong and able for battle."

"I have something I must do first," I said, and would not tell her my intention. I found Ophion, and drew him aside. "While I am gone, you are in charge of our tribe."

"Do you leave us now in these first hours of dark?" he asked. "Oh, my brother, do not do this. I cannot command this . . . this rabble."

"It will be a short while," I said. "You must make sure they do not overcome the mortals who offer blood. And here, you may hold this"—I drew out the Eclipsis—"as a symbol of your power."

"I cannot do anything with it," he said, turning the obsidian-black orb over in his hands.

"They will not know that," I said. "And they will see you as my representative here. You led them from Myrryd with your knowledge of the stars. They trust you, as do I."

Then I returned to where I had slept the day, and donned a simple tunic and breeches and boots, borrowed from one of the mortals. Over this, I drew a hooded cloak. I sought Calyx, who walked among her people and brought them strength and comfort for the coming battle. "Where in the towers do they keep my children?"

"There are rooms in the tower of White-Horse—they will probably be locked in their chambers," she said, but cautioned me, "Though you seek your twins, you must know that the boy, Taran, is as cruel and bloodthirsty as his mother. It is Lyan who is gentle and has learned lessons of humility and suffering from watching the kingdom's evil."

"They are both of my blood," I said. "And if the boy is a monster, it is the Myrrydanai who have made him so—and their mother, whom I saw within the Veil bleeding him over the bogs to call up the dark spirits that have invaded this land. He is innocent, though he may not seem so."

"I wish I could say that the nature of a child is so changeable," she said. "But I do not believe it from what I have learned of life."

"You will not speak of my children like this," I said. "Tell me, is there no other place they might be kept?"

"None that I am aware of," she said.

I was not angry with her for her opinion of my son, for I did not know either child except at some distance. Yet I could not blame either for the lives they had led to this point. I was determined to save them from the tyranny of their mother's darkness.

After I spoke with the Asyrr and settled their impatience with strategy, and warned their servants and warriors to drink no more from our mortal hosts, I leapt from the rock face of the cliff and flew out into the darkening night.

• 3 •

THE blizzard had grown thick, and battered at me as I went. Lightning flashed, followed by roars of thunder, and the constant beating of the war drum from far below. I flew high above the trees, into the storm clouds, where the temperature nearly froze me, yet I did not wish to be seen by Morns, who would surely be patrolling the skies.

In moments, I focused my mind on falcons, and felt the tingling of the Serpent's skin along my body as I burst into many forms—and became several falcons flying in formation, together, moving as a mass of blurred wings. In the centuries since, I have understood the molecules of the body, and the influence of the mind over them—their shapes, their separations, their joinings. The shapeshifters of my early life somehow had a key turned within their blood and flesh and minds to shift like this, though most could not control their shifting.

It is something in the mind that can be tapped to re-create the form of another species, but it requires the strongest of minds not to lose one's self in the creation. The molecules connected to the shifter also go, and become part of the new creation—so my cloak, the Nameless wrapped at my waist, my clothes, all became the skin and feathers and talons of the birds. The Chymer wolf-women were victims of a plague particular to them—and their shapeshifting was not within their conscious control at all, but came upon them from the will of Ghorien and his Myrrydanai. But my mind had become touched with the greater Asmodh sorcery, and I felt a great surge of life with each shift of my body.

When I shifted into the birds, it felt no different to me than drawing my wings from my shoulders. It was a pleasure to do so, and I felt an utter freedom and a desire to leave the cares of the world of mortal and immortal behind me, and become the creatures to which I had changed my form. I descended—a flock—from the roiling clouds, and the snow felt fresh upon my being—for just a moment I felt the presence of that greater self within me—the Serpent.

As I swooped the towers of the city, I heard the shrill cries of the Morns, and glanced downward to watch a mottled-skin Morn, her head half-shaved, looking up at me, her eyes narrowing as she watched the flight of birds.

Her milky eyes seemed to take me in, and although I only glanced at her for a second, I knew who it was from her shape and her face, despite the scarring and the absence of personality there: it was Kiya.

She had been turned into one of the Myrrydanai slaves, slave to the staff, to the Queen of Taranis-Hir, to the will of the alchemist Artephius.

I flew past her, wondering if she would follow me, but she did not. The Morns had no thought of their own, but were merely the hunting jackals of this city. In a whirl, I flew across the tombs of Taranis-Hir, and toward the towers of White-Horse itself, past the hundreds of soldiers who mounted great pots of boiling fire, and timber cut from the Forest to be used to pummel those who came beneath the city battlements. In the loopholes of the castle walls, archers stood at the ready, and many lined up with bows between the crenel spurs above the gates themselves. At the conical spires of the towers, still other lookout guards watched the skies for vampyres; but none noticed the birds that flew just beneath them, as falcons might, though not on such a stormy evening.

When I found again my daughter's bedroom as I had seen it once before, I dropped through its narrow window and re-formed myself once I touched the floor.

• 4 •

IT took a moment for my re-formation—I felt a shimmering of my body as the many birds came together. The staff drew from my fist, and I felt at my waist for the sword. I drew the hood of my cloak over my head, and brought the glamour to the cloth that it should resemble that of the White Robes.

The chamber was empty, but when I went into the hall, I saw the servant Constantine there.

"Do not be afraid," I said. "I am here to find my children."

He looked at me, eyes wide, and would not speak. I saw a bandage at his right wrist, and his hand was missing—cut off, no doubt, as punishment for his part in my escape from the clutches of the Red Scorpion. He shook his head, his eyes downcast, and I understood from the gesture that my children were no longer in the tower.

"Where then?" I asked.

He tried to talk, but strange raspings came from him. *His tongue. They had cut it.*

He pointed at me as I approached him, but I realized quickly that he pointed through me—to someone who had come out of one of the chambers down the hall.

I heard a noise—a slight whistle of metal—a dagger, flung in the air? I turned swiftly, raising the staff, and the blade that had been aimed for my back broke against the Nahhashim.

Behind me, the consort of the lady of the castle drew his sword.

• 5 •

"CORENTIN Falmouth," I said to my half brother. His face had grown gaunt over the past weeks, but he wore the look of royal smugness he had always cultivated. His hair was cut short, a fashion of the knights of the Disk, and he wore the robes of a king, though he was born—as was I—in the marshes at the edge of the Forest and field. He reached for his sword, and I heard the whine of its blade as he drew it out. I pulled the Nameless swiftly—it formed a short sword with the flicker of fire upon it—and flung it at him and willed that the blade should find his sword-bearing wrist that he might feel the punishment meted out to the elderly servant.

The blade struck bone, and seared his flesh, then was in my grip again, for I was its master. Corentin's sword dropped to the floor, clattering. His hand was still wrapped tight around its hilt as it fell. He leaned forward, clutching his wrist, crying out in pain.

"You're fortunate," I said. "You will not bleed as you have bled Constantine, for the the fire of the Asmodh sword sealed your flesh and blood as it cut you."

Corentin looked up at me, fury in his eyes, sweat pouring from his face. "You bastard son of a whore! My wrist burns now, but you will burn in the sun eternally!" He shouted for guards, and I leapt upon him, wanting to drag him then and there out to the walls and drop him to his death. But I heard the whisking of cloaks, and the sound of approaching guards and knew I had no time for him.

Instead of soldiers, the Myrrydanai in their flesh garments arrived, though the skin had begun rotting as it hung from the shadows beneath their robes. A dozen White Robes moved swiftly along the corridor toward us, and several more came from the opposite direction. I lifted Corentin by the throat until his legs dangled. "Would you like to lose both hands? For your crimes, I should tear your heart out now."

He snarled and groaned in pain, but the White Robes moved closer, their capes and robes drifting across the floor as if they had no feet, their skin drawn and battered as if they had not changed the skins of the dead for many weeks.

"Maz-Sherah," they whispered, a hundred maddening locusts tickling my ear. *"Come to us. We know you, and wish for your safety. Do not believe the lies of the Serpent, for it is the Dark Mother who seeks your blessing this night."*

I tossed Corentin to the side and glanced at Constantine. The old man crouched on his knees in fear, covering his face and whimpering.

The White Robes drew swords from their long, heavy sleeves, and their fleshly gloves held them tightly.

"You fight as men now," I said. "Your magick must be waning as the fire of the sun wanes at this time of year. I call to Ghorien to show himself to me."

"Maz-Sherah," they whispered as one. *"Come to us, and we will take you to our Dark Mother that she might delight in you."*

The priests lunged at me, and I willed myself to shift into a burning swarm of wasps, swirling around them, and through them, feeling their thoughts as my wasp forms bit their flesh, while they swatted at me—I felt among them for Ghorien, for I sensed the winds of their minds, and moved through them to find their master. He was not among them. It pained me to be the small creatures, and I could not shift again to another form quickly. I found cracks in the walls, and went through them and in the courtyards flew down, and had to re-form swiftly into my own body again, for the cold would have killed the insects I had manifested in but a few moments.

I shifted again, and brought much pain into myself as I sought out my new disguise. I had not expected to suffer from the shapeshifting, but I was sore as I re-formed myself, and my skin seemed to unravel as I did this. In seconds, I became the figure of a White Robe, feeling the slickness of rotting flesh on a form of shadow, and thus dressed, passed by many guards and the commotion raised by Corentin's alarm. Within, I felt jabs and stings, as if I had abused this new sorcery and demanded too much of it.

Many more guards had come to Taranis-Hir since the weeks of my journey had passed. Mortals were fooled by the false piety of the White Robes, and by the magnetism of the Nahhashim staff that Enora held close to her. Their sorcery blinded men, and tempted them with rewards. The

courtyards and the tribunes and the steps up to the battlements teemed with soldiers at the ready, and hundreds of
squires held horses for their knights, who sought blessing
among the chapels of the Disk. Soon, a new alarm sounded
as men shouted from the towers that there was an intruder
within the city walls. Horsemen rode by, fully armored,
their vigilance wasted as I walked by them in disguise.
New blasts of horns sounded along the towers, and shrieks
of the Morns pierced the night. I saw three of the creatures
soar above, then a howling of the wolf-women began out
beyond the castle walls.

The streets were empty of all but guards, and each nodded to me as I passed, for they revered these foul White
Robes as emissaries from the Virgin of Shadows. I pitied
them in their ignorance at the doom they had brought upon
their own kind. Many of these soldiers would fall in battle,
and would serve as vessels to the Asyrr and their warriors.
Many were young men from distant lands who had come
because the plague of the Disk dream had taken them over.
I saw the Disks hanging by thin straps about their throats or
dangling from their wrists, or wrapped about their scab-
bards. Pitied them, yes, but I could not save them from
what hell would come to them that night.

They had willingly walked into shadows and abandoned
their own kings and queens and lands and gods to follow a
plague dream's command. There had been those who did
not love this city, and did not revere its baroness as a "Queen
of Wastelands," a blessed saint of the earth. But these soldiers and knights had come, as had the alchemists
and foundrymen who worked the furnaces and the laboratorium, and assisted Artephius in his tortures and experiments.

I would have hunted for Pythia among the white towers
where she might be feted as a foreign princess for her
grand betrayal . . . but I knew that it was to Artephius she
would return.

So, as a Myrrydanai priest, I sought out my father's
workshop.

• 6 •

DESPITE the noise and cry above, the Barrow-Depths of the city were nearly silent, interrupted only by the dripping and gurgling of the vaulted rooms between the canals that ran below the city itself.

I followed the slender low corridors, through the vaults and passageways, across the laboratorium floor that had been abandoned by its workers. I closed my eyes, seeking the stream, for even Artephius existed within it, an immortal who did not have the breath of the Sacred Kiss within him. I followed along the niches and passed the foundries, and finally reached the study where I had been taken and bled one night during the arena games.

I touched the arched wooden door, and in the stream's vibration, I felt him, like a colony of termites in the wood of the door itself. Locked was the door, but as I brought the staff to its keyhole, I heard the click and turn of the mechanism, for no lock could keep out the one who held the Nahhashim.

I entered the alchemist's study with the Myrrydanai hood drawn down to conceal my features.

At the room's threshold, I shifted again to myself, the rotting skin and shadow giving way to the solid flesh, staff held beneath my robes, and hand on the grip of the Nameless should I need it.

The armored man stood near a bellows and a fire, while two grimy assistants—one wearing the Phrygian cap that was popular among alchemists of the time, and the other a skullcap—worked the flames as red liquid shot through a clay trough, and spilled down into a fat round crucible that sat upon a wooden tripod. Skullcap turned and saw me first, and called out to his master. Phrygian Cap dropped his crucible full of green liquid, and as it crashed to the floor, a vapor came up from it that seemed nearly in the shape of a small beautiful woman—a spirit that dissolved in the air.

Artephius turned from the high table where he pored

over pages of his grimoire. I knew this book well, for its scrolls had once been buried in an urn, and when broken, the words had escaped and found Merod Al Kamr. I had no doubt that all of Artephius's power was generated by this grimoire. If I had it in my possession, I would destroy it.

His visor was closed, and I could not see his eyes through the slits of the metal of his helm. He dismissed his workers quickly, admonishing them to return to the furnaces for their continued labors. "You will tell no one of this," he said to them, brusquely. "Or you will be back in the foundries working with the ashlings again."

After they had passed by me at the door, he said, "You will want to shut the door behind you, my son. You risk much to come here."

• 7 •

"I do not have much time, for many search the towers and streets," I said, as I drew the staff out from beneath my cloak.

"Ah," he gasped, and reached his gloved hand forward as if he might touch it from across the room. He held his palm facing outward. "I feel the power of the gray priests of Nahhash in its warmth. This is fresh-cut, not the old staff Enora keeps at her side."

"It is from the earth of Myrryd, a place you know well," I said.

"How did you keep the swarms from tearing your flesh?" he asked. "For when I walked in that garden, I was much abused by the Akhnetur. They guard the bones of the gray Nahhashim with their lives. Yes, Maz-Sherah, I saw much in the red city." He waved his hand toward the thick, rough-bound book. "But did not learn of its secret until I spent many years studying the scrolls. It has been too long since I visited the temples and palaces. The tombs of the Asyrr. The Asmodh Well."

"You have been in the Asmodh depths?" I asked, for I did not believe it. Artephius was someone who allowed others to suffer that he might find his knowledge. Though he himself had lost his youth and humanity over many centuries, still I did not believe he had suffered in the way that he had made others writhe in pain.

He did not answer my question, but took a step toward me, his hands upraised as if feeling for some invisible field between us. "You have the Serpent in you now. I can smell him." He seemed to take in a deep breath, then slowly exhaled. "You stink of the Asmodh, as if you still are there beneath the flood."

"From those depths to these, I have drawn great sorcery."

"Yes. Yes," he said, as if confirming some suspicion. "For you were born to this. You are Maz-Sherah." Again he pointed to the grimoire, and whispered a few words in a secret language, and the old book began to flip its pages, unfolding ragged edges of skinlike paper. "It is written on her flesh, the words of blood. If you would read what is there, you will understand much, little falcon. It is for you I have spent these years in study, seeking the marvels above the earth, and the prophecies of the ancients. It tells of your future as well as your past."

A page ripped out of the book, its paper yellowed and veined, and stained with the brown of old blood. It flew on an invisible wind, as if carried by some unseen demon, to float between us. Upon it, a thin line of fire scorched words of the old language. When the fire went out, the blackened words became the image of the sword of fire, and around it, a hand gripped it, and from this hand, an arm grew, and from the arm, a body, and a face. I did not have much trouble recognizing myself in the art that he had conjured.

Suddenly, the arm tore from the body. Almost instinctively, I clutched my arm as if it were mine that tore from its socket.

The page burned away, dissolving in a flash of flame, becoming blackened bits that floated downward to the floor, and yet the torn bit with the arm and the sword remained intact and flew swiftly to Artephius's hand.

"I know of this sword," he said as he glanced down at

the bit of paper. "If you explored the Asmodh Well, it must have called to you. It has known your name since it was first thrust into the Serpent's temple by Queen Medhya herself."

I drew my robe to the side, to show him the Nameless in its sheath. "It has found its master," I said.

"The treasure of the Asmodh, falcon. It has more than one master," he said, but in his tone I detected a shift, as if he had not expected the sword to be in my possession. "Medhya once wielded this, and she will call to it if you do not grasp it tight. Have you read the words at its hilt?"

"They are in the ancient languages, and I do not understand them," I said.

"Ba-yil-ir set-isil," he said, as if from memory. "It means 'In Veil, I burn.' For cursed is the one who grasps the Asmodh blade. Medhya was cursed, for she held it too long. How many nights have you kept it at your hip, little falcon? Has it brought you its dreams of the Asmodh terrors? For they were not benign sorcerers who delved and forged in the subterranean climes. They cursed the Great Serpent, and Medhya, and any to whom the blade calls. These ancient weapons were a damnation for the world above."

"Let me be damned to Hell then," I said. "The Nameless has had few masters. But all have had great power." I drew it out with my left hand, holding it in the air, parallel to the staff in my right. "If I were to thrust it into your plating, alchemist, no sorcery would keep it from burning your heart. Will it hurt, I wonder, as much as the Red Scorpion does? Or will this burn too fast, and will your suffering be too short?"

"In the scrolls of Medhya, this Nameless is spoken of," he said, no fear in his voice. Was he tempting me to attack him? I wondered. Did he wish for me to come closer that he might use some magick of the grimoire to trap me? Still, I stepped forward, the broken blade pointed at his chest.

"Have you studied the Art of the Nameless?" he asked.

"Its Art is in my blood," I said.

He laughed, and in scorn said, "It is not merely fire at its broken hilt. Do you understand what it can become?"

"The Great Serpent guides me in this weapon of the Asmodh," I said.

"Ah, well, then, you do not need the Medhyic grimoire," he said, contempt in his voice. "Though within the bound book lie recipes and rituals for making another master of the blade. There have been many Maz-Sherah, and many that have failed. You have not—yet. But you may fail, my son. You may, and then another will take the Nameless as his own. For, was not the Nahhashim staff cut for you? And yet, who owns it—a mortal woman, a new queen, hailed by many for the staff has ordained her, as have the White Robes."

"A Queen of Wolves, she is, like Medhya," I said.

"Will you use the sword of fire against her?" he asked, almost a challenge. "For you must wish to see what it can do to mortal flesh."

"I would test its metal now," I said, and lunged toward him. He did not step back, nor did he tremble in his armor. He held no fear of the blade. "In all your torments of my tribe, in all your plans for my birth . . . did you ever think there would come a moment when your own son would come to send you to the Veil itself?"

"Show me its flame," he said, a whisper that echoed from the chamber of his visored helm. "For I long to see it."

I heard labored breathing beneath the visor, and felt his excitement as I stepped forward, toward him, and drew out the sacred fire from the sword. It grew straightforward, thickening at the tip, and separating there into a trident of burning.

"Do you control this yet, or does the sword decide its form?" he asked, his hands nearly approaching the flame itself as he sought its warmth.

"From my thought it comes, though it takes its own path."

"After all these centuries on this earth, to go where the fire would take me," he said. "It has been my greatest desire, to explore the Veil—to seek that place of the exiled gods, where such creatures exist. You do not understand even now, my son. You have fulfilled more than prophecy. You have fulfilled every dream of my deepest soul. For I spent lifetimes learning the Asmodh ritual. I baptized myself in the filth of its underworld sea. To its gods, I gave worship and paid the tribute of a thousand human sacrifices—children and maidens and beautiful sun-kissed youths who had never yet stained their souls with lust or lies—in that lonely deep where the spirits of the Asmodh moaned and roared. In my seed, they brought you—in my loins you were formed from the prophecies of Medhya, and from the sorceries of the Asmodh. And to your mother I came, a knight in armor to the lowliest hovel, in the filthiest marsh, for that was prophecy. But she was a daughter of the Druid priests, a priestess of nature and of hidden talent, whose knowledge came from the upper world, and was not of Asmodh. Into her, I brought the Asmodh prophecy, and from her, a son was born with the instincts of his mother's tribes, and the destiny of his father's desire. You have become everything—*everything*—I have lived for during these centuries. And all this—the torn Veil—is from your existence. If you were to stab me with that Asmodh blade, I would go to the Veil and leave this wretched earth to my son. And to Medhya and her shadow priests, for I have spent too long a time in this wasteland of the earth, of the small and foolish mortal mind that has no memory beyond its puny lifetime. To you and me, my son, the mortal realm is a vast colony of vermin, and the monsters of the Veil would be a blessing here."

His words filled me with a shivering cold, for I did not want to believe that I was a tool of his making. But when he went silent, watching me, I said, "My true father is the Great Serpent. The Asmodh have fooled you, for even immortal, you, too, are vermin, alchemist. You sacrificed innocents in error, for the Asmodh deep had many fallen gods

who sought such bleak places. You are no god, and the exiled ones of the Veil would rip you and devour you, and still
not allow you to die. You will not get your wish, alchemist.
You neither have a son, nor will the Nameless be raised
against you. You are not deserving of an honorable fate, and
though none may destroy you, you will walk the earth until
the end of time, knowing that what you desired most will
never come to pass." I did not wish to waste another moment with him, for I knew that soon enough his assistants
would speak to the guards if questioned, and I would need
time to return to the cliffs where my tribe waited.

"Where is the Pythoness? Tell me now, old bones!"

"The one who carries my grandchild?" he asked. "She
is safe. She does not desire to see you, though she felt that
you would harm her after she came to my bed."

My rage exploded at this, and I lunged forward, closing
the gap between us. I brought the staff to his throat, and
drew off his visor. I expected to see the bone and gauze of
the mummy he had become, but instead, flesh had begun re-
forming, and beneath it, muscle and fat.

I stepped back, gasping.

"Yes," he said, smiling. "The essence. I have distilled it,
at last. Immortality and youth eternal. Your friends offered
me this in their pain."

I thought of those vampyres I had known who had gone
to their fates in the pincers of the Red Scorpion, that infernal machine that plucked and cut and tore and pierced
those of my tribe to find the essence of immortal youth.
The glamour of our tribe, which we had thought was sorcery. But it was something in the blood itself. He had destroyed many of my tribe that he could bring back flesh to
his bones. His lips had not re-formed, and his face was
pink-red with the striation of muscle and the thinnest of
flesh across only half of it.

Summoning every drop of fury that was within me, I
smote him with the Nahhashim staff, and in mere seconds,
a swarm of yellow light emitted from the staff's tip, and
flew through the cracks of his armor, and covered his face

where the visor had been drawn up. The light became the Akhnetur, obliterating his features, their infernal buzzing raised to an unearthly pitch.

I shut the visor and held it, while Artephius screamed as if his skin were being torn. He reached for my throat, and I held the visor shut despite his strong grip upon me—for I was the stronger, and he would suffer as he had made others writhe in agony and lose their minds and souls.

I held him there until he was on his knees, and the sounds from his throat were mere gargles of noise. I nearly felt pity for him until I thought of Kiya and Yset and Midias and other members of my tribe who had been pierced and flayed in the infernal machine the alchemist had invented. He would not die, but he would lose what skin had begun forming on bone. He would not gain what he sought when so many had suffered at his hand.

"I, your son by birth, but no longer the son of a wolf father, am your Red Scorpion," I said as I released him.

I glanced over at the hefty book, leathery and falling apart. The scrolls were bound into it, with the blood of Medhya upon its pages. Her sorcery would be there, and all the art that the alchemist possessed existed there.

I ran to it and drew it under my arm. As I did so, I felt the same kind of pulse from its binding that I had felt from the Eclipsis. The grimoire had great magick in it, and—in my possession—would offer insight into the rituals of the solstice, I was sure.

I left the alchemist writhing in his armor upon the cold floor of his private study. The swarms of the flesh eaters would destroy the growth of sinew and skin he had brought to himself—but they could not murder him. Immortal he would remain, but without the essence of youth, without the freshness and beauty of skin and muscle to disguise the corpse he had made of himself.

Hiding the staff beneath my robes, I went out along the corridor of the furnace and foundry, and when I came to the causeway that crossed a canal, there I saw guards rushing to search for me.

There was no time left to find my children, or to seek Pythia. I had failed in what I sought to do before the battle began. I prayed that they would find protection from us, and from their own ruler. Tempted though I was to seek out Enora and take her life before the battle, I did not trust Ghorien or the first staff—and did not want to clash with them until I had weakened their army.

I returned to the form of several falcons, drawn together with one mind. As I did so, the old book, bound with sinew and leather, dropped to the floor, and did not shapeshift with me—its sorcery would not allow it to come under my command.

One of the falcons among the flock grabbed it in its talons, and we flew up from the arched vaults of the Barrow-Depths into the swirling storm. I heard the shouts of guards, and even the terrible call of Artephius from some nether window, a garbled scream for his grimoire.

Bowmen at the battlements shot at the flock I had become. One of their arrows hit a falcon beneath the wing, and it dropped, a part of me, onto the road below.

I felt an excruciating white-hot pain, though I did not know from which part of my body, for I was one within the many.

Yet, a falcon looked down at the road, and saw that the bird that had fallen had become a human forearm with fingers that still twitched in the hand as it landed upon the earth.

Beside it, the grimoire, its pages open and fluttering as the wind blew across it. A rider came out from the gate, and moved swiftly toward where my arm had fallen, and when he reached it, he stabbed the arm with his sword and drew it up, and then leapt from his mount and hefted the grimoire in his hand.

My falcons watched him ride back to the opening gates, two prizes beneath his arms.

It was only later, when I crested the peak of the cliffs, and resumed my form, that I felt the pain at my elbow. I lay there, with the wolvish boy Mordac staring in wonder at me. Moments before, several falcons had soared up to him, and now, the flock had become the winged devil. "Like me," he said, as if he had never before seen anyone shift other than his Chymer mother and her sisterhood.

I lay on my back, with the staff in my right hand, my cloak spread out beneath me, but my left hand and forearm were gone, sealed off with flesh as if I had been born that way.

I remembered the page of the grimoire, torn out and floating—with the sword arm cut off.

Artephius had known this would happen. He played with me. He had known I would steal the book, although his ability to see the future had not included the Akhnetur swarm beneath his armor.

I lay there in agony, and drew the staff over to my left shoulder, and closed my eyes that the regeneration of the limb would return. Pain shot through my neck, and the muscles of my biceps bulged as if bearing great weight. It felt as if someone were drawing the bone from its socket at my shoulder. In a sudden sweat, I blacked out. When I came to, a few minutes later, my arm had restored itself, my hand and fingers moved normally, but with a deep blue scar around the flesh just below my left elbow.

WITHIN the hour, the Asyrr stood before me in the lowest entrance of the caves. Calyx and her people had brought horses from the paddock, well rested and ready to return to battle.

◆ CHAPTER 15 ◆

Taranis-Hir

◆ 1 ◆

THE horses had been dressed in the bards that would
protect them in battle—and on the greatest and dark-
est of these, I would ride, with the kings and queens of
Myrryd and their mounts behind me. Mortals would ride
after, on the remaining mares and stallions, and some would
ride double, then dismount as we approached the gates of
Taranis-Hir.

I drew Ophion aside, and asked him to lead the flying
vampyres—for they would first need to attack the Morns in
the sky before descending to those of the earth. "And if
you slip past the gates, seek the Barrow-Depths. Beyond
the foundries and furnaces, there is a study of the alchemist
called Artephius. The grimoire of Medhya is there, those
scrolls that carry her blood sorceries. It is of value, my
friend, and I have lost it once. Be cautious, and watch for
the alchemist, who wears a suit of armor like a bronze
basilisk and will not want you to find the book."

"I know those scrolls, and I will find the alchemist's lair.

Shall I seek this at the cost of the fight?" he asked. "For, my brother, I do not want one of our tribe—or these Akkadites—to fall without another of us avenging him."

"Yes," I said. "Once the Morns have been extinguished, seek the grimoire. The alchemist will stay near this book, for it is of great value to him. You will feel the stream of him, and the vibrations of it at the arched doorway of his study."

"I will do this, my brother. And the Morns—will we not show them mercy, for they are like us?"

"What is merciful for them is their Extinguishing," I told him, and clutched his shoulder in brotherhood. "I wish the staff or the blade could return them to their former glory. But they are merely the flying teeth of the Myrry-danai. My only hope is that the souls within them passed into a dark sleep long ago. Now, go, brother, lead the vampyres of the air, as I lead the kings and queens on horseback."

To Calyx, I said, "If I fall beneath blade or staff, take up *this* staff, and the sword, though it may burn your hand. And be the plague maiden in truth, and destroy those who oppose you."

♦ 2 ♦

NAMTARYN sat proudly upon her mount, wearing her golden breastplate, greaves at her shins, but with little else to protect her body but a tunic so fine that I could nearly see her sex. She refused the furs that were brought to her, and complained that she missed such deep winters and longed for ice on her skin. To her, I said in private, "Your daughter has betrayed us here, and waits within the towered city. If you find her, do not take your wrath out on her, for she carries my child. Though I would seek her imprisonment for her crime, I do not wish for her to die, for she is mortal, and the child that has only just begun to grow within her, also."

She bared her fangs at me. "She has always been a snake. Kill her and be done with her, Maz-Sherah, for that child will be no better."

"I do not believe this," I said. "And I wish you to watch for her, so that others do not harm her."

"You ask me what I cannot do," she said, coldly. "For my daughter deserves death, or worse."

"Then, I command you," I said. "For you know her, and will see the gold mask of Datbathani upon her."

"The Gorgon Mask," she said, and her mood changed. "She has gone far in the world to have obtained it."

"At the price of her immortality," I said. "And you shall not harm her, but if you find her, capture her, and bring her to me, unharmed. Do you understand?"

Namtaryn cast a look upon me that was equal parts fear and confusion. Her eyes went to my staff, and the sword in its sheath. "As you wish," she said.

Athanat was in the full armor of his kingdom—including a crowned helm upon his head, with its dragon wings sprouting at each side of his face. Nekhbet wore leather armor, with an unvisored helm. Illuyan and Setyr had no armor to speak of, but wore the ceremonial dress of their ages, looking every inch great kings of the earth. Sarus, his enormous muscles bulging, gripping an ax in one hand, and a double-bladed sword in the other, wore only a half tunic. He had complained to me in his half grunts and mutterings that it was shaming for a king of Myrryd to fear the blade of a sword or the smack of the ax. He did not like being horsed, either, and complained about this while settling onto the back of his steed.

"Vampyres and horses don't mix," he grumbled, as the dark horse reared and whinnied until finally Calyx was able to calm him with her words and petting.

"We should fly. All of us," Zoryas said, equally unhappy to have to ride a horse.

"You are kings," I said. "And you will bring this war to Taranis-Hir as kings of the world."

"I am more agile on foot," Illuyan said, adding to the grumble.

"Listen to the Maz-Sherah!" Athanat shouted. "For he must have a reason for us to ride."

"Yes," I said, holding my hand up to silence them. "Your warriors will take to the night sky—led by Ophion but guided by their kings below. They are our falcons. But they will look to us for leadership! We must attack from below and above. We must be relentless in this, and slaughter all who cross our path. Once we are inside Taranis-Hir, abandon your mounts. Fight as you wish with the skills and training of your lifetimes. The Myrrydanai ride the Lamiades, and some of you know these creatures well. They no longer fly as shadows, but have rooted in the flesh of the dead. We must come at them from both the sky and the earth. We must be on mounts to fight them."

"It is not like a king to do so," Setyr said. "We can lead from the sky."

"If you wish, abandon your steed now," I said. "All who wish to follow Setyr, and Sarus. Spread your wings, and be with your warriors. But those who wish to follow me, remain where you are. Know that you will provide not just leadership, but a symbol that you are ordained by the Great Serpent, that you are a great king of both mortal and immortal. And that you bring the battle to Taranis-Hir not merely as the flying jackals, but as kings of the world gathered to fight Medhya herself!"

I pointed across the last of the Forest, to the fires of the furnaces of Taranis-Hir. Its white caelum towers seemed to have brightened in the distant torchlight. "What was once a great forest has been eaten away by this kingdom! What was once simply a barony has become a harbor for Medhya's shadow priests and thieves of the first Staff of the Nahhashim! Plagues have come to the earth and spread out upon it, bringing drought and death to the mortal realm!" I shouted. "But these are not your concerns! For what does the tribe of the Fallen Ones of Medhya care for mortal woods? For plagues? We do not suffer such things!" I glanced from Athanat, his head shaved in the manner of the Priests of Blood, his eyes fierce with bloodlust. "You! Ruler of Myrryd after Medhya herself! Athanat—called Thanos by the vampyres who once swore the oath of allegiance to you!

Founder of Pergamos! Scourge of Hedammu! When you ruled, did you burn the forests of the world for your power?"

His eyes narrowed as he watched me, and he grinned, his sharp teeth shining in the torchlight. "No, Maz-Sherah!" he shouted. "Mortals who bowed to us were kept safe. We gave them kingdoms, and to us they made sacrifice!"

"Did you go among them with wings spread to terrorize them? Or did you ride into battle on the back of a horse?"

"In those nights, it was the Lamiades I rode," he said, and a roar of laughter went up from the others. "For they are fearsome beasts in battle, and easily trained. But no, we guarded the mortal kingdoms, for they protected us, and gave us tribute."

"In war, did you swoop down from the skies to attack your enemy?"

"My warriors did, for I was on the ground, riding with foot soldiers into battle."

"As befits a king of Myrryd!" I shouted. "To ride upon a noble stallion into battle, to show the mortals you protect that you are among them, and fight for them, and will not abandon them—and to guide your warriors in the sky, as well, for they must have guidance upon the ground to look toward! Though we do not have Lamiades here—though if some are willing, you may steal them from the Myrrydanai if you can . . ." The Asyrr roared with laughter, Nekhbet shouting that she would own one of the Lamiades for herself before dawn. "We have these mounts—beautiful and noble creatures that once carried the knights who fell in the battles before we came here. These horses know this terrain, and they will carry us from these cliffs, down into the territory of the old Nahhashim staff. They are blessed with the Nahhashim staff, and are used to battle. You are kings. You need mounts. And you need to lead those in the night sky."

"Do we fight merely for the sake of mortals of one castle?" Illuyan asked. "I do not mind riding a horse to battle, but whom do we save in this fight?"

"You do not ask such questions, king of Myrryd," I said. "For you have sworn this oath to me. You will do as I say.

You will follow where I lead. Only those who wear the Disk—a medallion smaller than your palm, Illuyan—will be cut down. Only those who oppose us. You will protect these mortals who ride behind you as your children, for they are descended from the same blood that once you drank and protected in your first kingdoms! And to me, your loyalty will be, and well repaid shall you be from this, though your resurrections from Extinguishing and those of your servants and warriors should be enough—yet you will draw up those old kingdoms that you lost—and guard the mortal realm again when the battle is through! If you are the falconers to your warrior falcons, then I am your falconer—and you will come when I call you!"

"I do not care whom we fight, or whether on horse or lizard," Namtaryn said, her sharp teeth glinting in the torchlight. "I long for the taste of the blood of battle. And when it is over, I want to find the most handsome youth and take him for my pleasure." The others laughed as she said this, and she, too, began laughing. "How can we lose this fight?" Namtaryn asked. "For we follow the Maz-Sherah who has been foretold since the scrolls were written upon with Medhya's blood! How many are against us in this city? It is one thing for mortal knights to have fallen to this scourge, but I have dealt with the Myrrydanai before. Mortals are easy kills."

"I have seen their warriors," I said. "They outnumber us by the hundreds."

"Mortals." She laughed. "I have drunk from thousands of them."

"In one night!" Nekhbet shouted.

"You know the sorceries of the Myrrydanai, made strong when their flesh was torn from them and Medhya pulled them into the Veil. They return with much knowledge of the Medhyic Art, and their earthly queen holds the Staff of the Nahhashim that was once held only by Merod, the Priest of Blood. These White Robes will not be satisfied to fight merely with sword and fang. They will use all they have against us. You know what Ghorien can do—though I have not yet met him, he is their heart. If you can destroy him, the others will fall. You know what these shadows, disguised now in skin, can call to their service. They can abandon their flesh and possess any mortal they wish. They have powers we do not even understand. But I tell you, before this night is through—many of them will be destroyed, for it is Ghorien I must have—and with this sword and this staff, and with the power of the Eclipsis, I will send him into oblivion that he may never return again!"

The Asyrr shouted and cheered, and called out to the Serpent for strength.

"There are mortals we must protect here. I have two children, who may be within the towers, or deep in the Barrow beneath. There are others here who do not follow the White Robes. Yet they are slaves to this kingdom. Only fight those who draw sword upon you, and only slaughter those who threaten you with Extinguishing. We will not spill innocent blood."

"There are no innocent mortals but those who ride with us!" Sarus shouted.

I pointed to Nekhbet, with her raven hair drawn back and oiled, her helmet in her hands, her wings folded yet shivering with the anticipation of unfurling. "Nekhbet the Terror of Night! These were the words on your tomb! Yet, did you not suffer when the mortals who served you also suffered? Did you not wish for their fertility, their strength, that they might both serve you—and prosper in their lives that their children should honor you?"

She nodded, raising her arm into the air, clenching her sword in her fist, and called out to the Great Serpent for his blessing.

"And Illuyan, the Fair-Haired, were you not just to your people? Did you not show mercy to those who had been wrongly treated? I have met your descendant, from those early nights of your life when our tribe brought forth the living from undeath—a wise and good mortal this man, a namesake of yours who does honor to your name and spreads your fame throughout the world! Setyr! Namtaryn!

Zoryas! Each of you—and yes, your servants, your warriors, loyal and true vampyres in a world that once honored you. This world has changed! We have fallen—all of us—from the heights of Myrryd's red towers! We have fallen from the stream itself, for we have not honored it! Each of you— extinguished by the corruption of the Myrrydanai priests, who now call themselves White Robes and rule the citadel whose furnaces burn in the night to make weapons, armor— for a war against you, and against the mortals whom they have wronged! But we fall no more. We do not stand upon a cliff, nor do we stand beside a golden tree of some ancient legend. We stand upon the rock of your kingdoms—the or- daining of the Great Serpent is here—and it is with me, and with you. And when you remember the years of your domin- ion in Myrryd, and the betrayal of those shadow priests in whom you put your trust—recall the greatness and beauty of the earth before Medhya's hounds attacked you and extin- guished each of you! Remember what you ruled, and why you ruled, and the balance between the world of the vampyre and the world of the mortal! Remember your own mortal life before the Sacred Kiss came to you in your final moments! For we will guard the mortal realm because we are of it! I have known of vampyres who never knew mortality. Never had in their hearts the memories of a finite lifetime! Medhya is one of these! She is no goddess, no Queen of Myrryd! She is more monster than any of us here! For each of us once suckled at the breast of a mortal mother! Each of us once held a lover in our arms, and knew that we might die before we held them again! Each of us once lived as mortals live, and died as mortals die—though we did not cross the Threshold. Still, we knew that darkness better than we know the dark of night! You have each sworn an oath of allegiance to me and to this war we must wage. But your allegiance is to the Serpent himself, and it is his will—and my will—to send the shadow priests back into the Veil, to destroy the Chymer wolves, even to extinguish those Morns who were once of our tribe but whose destruction is a kindness to them! To take from the Queen of the Wastelands the old Nahhashim staff! Break her bones against the power of the gray priests of Nahhash! The war must come to them now, this night—the night when the Veil is thin, and its threads unravel as Medhya's greedy fingers reach this earth to extinguish you again, and destroy the mortal vessels who bring us sustenance! Remember your mortality! Remember your reign as vampyre! Remember Ghorien, and his priests who fell under the thrall of our Dark Mother! Remember the fall of Myrryd! Remember the Asyrr!"

The Asyrr and the warriors roared, and all raised their weapons. When they had quieted again, I cried out, "I am the Falconer! And you are my falcons! As the raptor bird rides the storm of night, so we shall all ride—and you shall be at my arm, and in the skies above, and I shall hunt with you! But it is you that will find our prey!"

I glanced over at Calyx, who had mounted her horse and trotted along the snow-covered paddock to me. She had two sheaths at her middle, and a short sword tucked into another near the blanket that was her saddle. In her hand, she carried a spear. "Will we have victory?" she asked as she came close, leaning into me to block out the roars of those behind us.

"The gods have granted us this long night that we may send those of the Disk to the arms of the children of Death," I said. Even as I spoke, I felt for the Eclipsis in the pouch at my waist. "Do not risk your plague in ordinary battle, Calyx. Let my tribe take the first sword and arrow, and I want you to guide your people in a ring behind us to catch any of the enemy who break through. When we have breached the city gates, look for me, for when they are opened I will need help finding Taran and Lyan. I do not wish them to live another night beneath their mother's rule."

Then, as I stood before them, I brought the Raptorius out from beneath my skin—its scales covering my flesh, its spurs and spines drawing outward from my elbows and along the helm. "This is the armor of the Great Serpent!" I shouted. "And it is in his name that I lead you!"

The Asyrr and their warriors and the the mortals who

fought with us roared at this, and many gasped in awe at the Serpent armor, which was like none they had seen.

I reached to my right side to unsheathe the Nameless. I held the shattered blade up in my left hand that they could see its glory. "In the name of the Great Serpent, I offer my service to this blade, forged by the Asmodh!"

I felt the heat along my arm and the blistering at my fingers as the flame erupted from the sword and the fire burned out to its length. "Those who will come from the sky, guard our descent! When we are at the edge of the Forest, then will we call you to battle! Those on mounts, follow me!"

· 3 ·

I rode swiftly along the narrow ways, with Calyx riding ahead of us, leading us through the Forest paths, out of the thickest of the woods. The snow was piled high here, but our horses galloped bravely along the twists and turns. I could not look up to the sky to watch the vampyres above us, for my senses had begun narrowing the closer we came to Taranis-Hir; but I knew Ophion led the charge from the air. I began to smell incense fire in the air, bitter herbs and a sour stench like old stew left too long in the pot. My eyes focused straight ahead, trusting my horse and the lead of Calyx.

The woods became a blur, and soon turned into open fields with canals running alongside them. I tasted bile at the back of my throat and wished that I could turn back the earth to the moment when I was a boy and had longed to go work in the baron's castle. I spat such a thought from my mouth and trusted the Serpent to remain with me through the ordeal to come.

Fires had been lit along the canals, and a strange black potion had been spread across its surface. Hundreds of soldiers on foot lined the road toward the castle, and archers stood at the ready along the walls of the city.

I held up my staff to slow the kings behind me, and those who accompanied us, as well as those of the sky, who flew down among the trees and soon stood beside the Asyrr and awaited my word.

"Wait," I said to those behind me. "For at a quarter mile, they stand for us. I will go among them. You will see the fire of the Nameless should I call you."

"It is a trick," Ophion said, as he reached my horse. "They will destroy you if you go along their gauntlet."

"I am protected, brother, but be watchful of the Morns, for I fear they lurk somewhere unseen." I bade my horse trot up the path, beyond the edge of the woods.

Across the open range I went, and within half of the hour I came to this aisle of soldiers.

Two lines of soldiers, a hundred on each side, made a path to where their queen sat upon a snow-white horse, covered with the pelts of wolves, surrounded by her minions.

I walked my horse slowly between the lines of foot soldiers, glancing at these mortals with caution. I held the staff in my right hand that they could see and fear it, for they knew such an instrument of sorcery from their own ruler. They watched me as if I were their devil come from Hell to take their souls. About their throats, the Disks on leather straps, shiny with the small mirrors that had been inset into them, believing these would ward off such devils as those I had brought with me that night. I dismounted as the lines of soldiers opened up into a wide circle, within which Enora sat upon her beast.

Enora wore a crown of silver, and her red hair had been tied with golden ribbons. Her face was alabaster, and upon it, she had painted the third eye of Medhya, at the brow. Beneath her wolf-pelt cloak, she wore a robe of deep blue and upon it, the Disk had been sewn in silver threads. In her left hand was the Nahhashim staff, and in her right, a short black sword. Upon her pommel, a black sack hung down, and I could not guess what she held there, but it intrigued me.

Growling along at her horse's flanks were the Chymer women in their wolf forms—I counted eight of them, their fur bristling, their snaps and snarls aimed only for me.

Behind her and beside her, nearly a hundred Myrrydanai priests, all wearing the white robes, and covered in the skin of the dead.

Of these many priests, who had multiplied in number since I had left the towers, twelve of them surrounded Enora and her wolves, and each of these rode one of the Lamiades. I was not surprised that these lizards seemed all sharp teeth, small eyes, brown-green skin, and spikes along their crests and backs that were similar to the spikes at the crest of the Raptorius helm I wore. At their hind limbs, I saw thornlike spurs, and their forelimbs seemed smaller than the hind. *These might be easy to disable,* I thought.

Spit dripped from the Lamiades' yellowed teeth, and one of them already had blood smeared across its snout. I watched the Myrrydanai who rode them—surely one of them was Ghorien, for he would not deign to walk the earth when he could ride such a monster. They were bridled like horses, and saddled, as well. The Myrrydanai seemed to have some trouble controlling their stillness, for the tails of these creatures whipped around as if in frustration, and several of the White Robes tugged at the reins to keep the lizards quiet.

I drew the helm from my head and set it on the pommel. I touched the grip of the Nameless with my left hand and held the staff with my right. Then, I slipped my hand into the pouch and drew out the Eclipsis.

The tingling at my fingers began, and I felt the surge of energy shoot into that dark globe. The deathlight came up, seen only by me.

As the dark light crossed over the Myrrydanai, I saw their shadows beneath the skins, but also other shades there, waiting with Enora. These were the spirits the Chymers had helped her call from the Barrow-Depths—the old evil that lay in that ground.

I drew the Eclipsis back, dropping it into its pouch. I scanned the dead faces of the White Robes with the lizard mounts, wondering which was Ghorien, as all their features were indistinct. The White Robes who had no mounts stood with their hands clutching swords, blades to the ground.

"Look at this devil!" Enora shouted, as the winds

whipped across the night and a clap of thunder deafened all. Lightning broke the clouds, and, in its flash of daylight, I saw the Morns upon the battlements with the guard, waiting for the fight to begin, waiting for the command from their leaders. "He comes to me in armor that is like these lizard skins—scaly and dirty. Are you—a devil—afraid of the swords of my fighters? Of arrows?"

"I wear the skin of the Serpent," I said. "And the Raptorius."

"Where are your lovely wings? Did you lose them on your journey?" She performed for her people, for her soldiers, that they would see her scorn and emulate it and lose their fear. I kept glancing at the sack at her pommel, for I wondered what conjuring she kept at her side. What was this? "You have been long away from us, and many have died because of your absence," she said. "Where have you gone, devil, that you let the heretics die in your place?" She placed her hand across the sack that had raised my curiosity.

I held the Nahhashim staff before me. "I have been to the red city at the edge of the fire-colored sea," I said. "I am the Falconer of the Great Serpent. I hunt you. I hunt what owns you, my lady. For your mind is too-long held in the grip of Ghorien and his Myrrydanai shadows. You have called up the spirits of the dead through necromancy, and you haunt the nightmares of the mortals of this realm, for your very thoughts take form in flesh and in dream."

"I am owned by no one, devil! Bow before your queen!" Enora shouted this against the falling snow, more for the show of it for her soldiers and her minions than for my benefit. She pointed the tip of her staff toward me. I felt a push at my ribs as she did this, but held my ground and revealed nothing to her.

"Destroy him," Corentin said, appearing from behind the White Robes, riding a muscled black horse, and wearing the armor of the baron who had once been his master. His horse was skittish of the great lizards, whose teeth ground and snapped as the animal drew near. I noticed

Corentin's wrist had been fitted with a blade, shackled at the forearm, and thrust where his hand had been.

I shot Corentin a glance, but wasted no words upon him. Enora was my quarry, for the staff in her hand was all I needed to disable her protective sorcery of the city. Looking at her face, I could barely see the maiden I had once known.

"You are a baroness. This is not a kingdom. It is not a country."

"I am Queen of the Wastelands and of Taranis-Hir and of the Jeweled Sea beyond, and even of these Akkadite heretics! I am the Lady of the Disk, and the earthly form of the Virgin of Shadows. Give me your staff, and surrender, and we will be merciful to the Akkadites."

"Just end this," Corentin said to her. He grew impatient, and it was obvious he did not enjoy the back-and-forth between us. He drew his horse away from the Lamiades and the White Robes. His mount was nervous, and moved left and right, and back and forth, uneasy around the wolves and the lizards. "Show him the peace offering," Corentin muttered, and then drew his horse to the right and trotted back behind the White Robes who stood beyond the soldiers, as if he were terrified of another encounter with me.

She ignored her consort and stroked the sack again as if it were a pet. "We do not wish war," she said. "For we have had enough blood spilled before your arrival. But you must bow to your queen."

"If you are a queen, you are the Queen of Wolves, and in your path I hear the footsteps of an even greater Wolf Queen than you, who will put her foot upon your skull and crush it. Give me the staff of the gray priests of Nahhash. It was not cut from their bones that you might keep it in your jaws. Wolves cannot carry the shepherd's staff, but must be hunted from the pen and driven back into the darkness."

"You—a devil—are not a wolf?"

"I hunt as a wolf, but my greatest prey are other wolves."

"If you hunt as a wolf, then I am your queen, and you will bow before me."

"Who has ordained you? These shadow priests?" I asked. "For I recognize you only as a sad maiden I once loved, who has abandoned the good and the pure and the true and turned to bog magick and a dark goddess for her worship."

She grabbed the Disk at her throat. "I worship the Virgin of Shadows, who saved our lands—and many countries—from the plagues!"

From the foot soldiers came the shout, "Hail the Virgin of Shadows! Blessed is the Disk and those who dream it!"

"Yes, blessed are they who dream of the Disk," Enora said, like a cat with a mouse in its jaws.

"This Virgin of Shadows—she brought the plagues, as you well know, Lady White-Horse. She is the Dark Madonna who has transfigured your wolf-women, and released the Myrrydanai hounds that you call White Robes. It is she who made you murder your brother and drink from his heart. It is she who has brought you the alchemist who seeks destruction of mortal life. It is she who has torn love from you and replaced it with the ice of winter. But I wonder why you don't have your men attack me. For I stand within your circle."

"We do not wish more bloodshed. The Akkadites are nearly slaughtered, and the Forest heresies are burned," she said. "I am a peace-loving queen. Call off your demons, and make your oaths of fealty to me, and pass me the staff and the sword you hide, which are sacred to the White Robes, and I will allow you to exist, devil. But if you bring this war to us, I will personally rip your unborn baby from your mistress's belly with my bare hands. And when I have that bloodied thing in my grasp, I will feed it to my wolves."

"Your hell will begin if these things come to pass," I said. I closed my eyes, and called to the Serpent within me: *Come now, through me, through my arm, through this bone of the Nahhashim priests.*

I opened my eyes again.

"You have held this stolen staff too long," I said. "It was broken from the white bone of the Nahhashim, who are the gray priests of Myrryd. Their bones grow as a tree in a garden, guarded by the Akhnetur. It was meant only for one—and that is I. It brings you sorcery, and strength to your shadow-masters, my lady. But to wield it—you cannot dig up that sorcery in a bog, nor call it from the dead with your Chymer wolves. You know this—as Artephius knows it. As Ghorien knows it." As I said the name of the White Robe priest, I quickly sensed that one of them had moved slightly. Not the dozen who stood nearest Enora, but one of the ones farther back. *He is hiding from me. He knows now that I know his name. He knows I have taken the Nameless, and carved my own staff from the Nahhashim. He knows I am dangerous now, where I was merely an annoyance before.* I kept my eyes on Enora, but tried to draw back in my mind and see if Ghorien would move again and reveal himself. "As with all weapons of sorcery, the Nahhashim staff calls out only for the one who is its master."

"*You* are the wolf come to us from the woods, devil. If you do not surrender to me, your children will die. All of them. In pain," she said.

I thrust the staff forward and leaned into my mount. The blast of it vibrated through my being as I felt it explode forward—a wave of vibration in the air, a heat magick. A sound like an enormous crashing of rocks boomed from it as Enora raised her staff against this assault. All of the power was invisible, but her staff seemed to catch it in midair. Then it was sent back to me in a blast that knocked me back, and I clutched at my horse to remain upon him.

"Do not use sorcery on me, devil!" she said. "Will you surrender now? Your word is good to us, and your demons will do as you wish. If you allow my guards to take you to our dungeons, we will release your demoness."

Rather than answer her, I leapt from my horse. My wings erupted from the back of the Raptorius, thrusting at full expanse along my shoulders.

I held up the staff and when I opened my mouth, words in the language of the Great Serpent came forth, undecipherable even by he who spoke.

From my wrist, I felt a snap as if a muscle had torn from bone, and the staff in my hand flew out into the air. I leapt for it, and as I grabbed it, I saw the White Robe priest whose hand had lifted in the air, as if calling some sorcery from it.

Ghorien.

I marked him in my mind—there was little to distinguish him, but upon the hand that had gone up, I saw a stain at the palm, as if the dead whom the shadow priest had robbed of skin held a birthmark that ran from his thumb to the center of his hand.

I crouched on the ground, my wings spread. In another moment, the trap might be sprung and all the fighting would begin.

But Enora had raised her staff to silence all, and from her pommel she drew the sack of black cloth, and threw it to me. "We did not think you would surrender to us before the slaughter began," she said. "So here is an offering we have made in your honor."

As the sack rolled at my feet, I saw the small curl of fair hair from beneath its opening.

I took a deep breath, not wishing to see what was within it.

Yet, I could not help looking.

I drew from it the fresh-cut head of my son, Taran.

Enora's own son.

In a heartbeat, I remembered the words of the Briary Maidens: "Only one of your children may be saved, though you will not know which until the last battle has been fought."

Another female spoke from a memory vision, the voice of Datbathani, the Lady of Serpents, speaking of my twins: "One of fire and one of blood, one to tear the Veil and one to mend it."

Taran had been the child of blood, sacrificed by his own mother and the Myrrydanai to tear the Veil.

"To the Virgin of Shadows, his blood was spilled at birth, and in fulfillment of all she has offered, he has been

sent to her in spirit," Enora said as if she were talking
about sending our son into the next room to retrieve some
tunic or cap. "To be her messenger in those shadow lands
and tell her that the Maz-Sherah has come to fulfill ancient
prophecies written upon the pages of her skin."

I dropped to my knees before the boy's head, and anything that was left of mortal feeling passed swiftly from
me. "You sacrificed your own child to tear the Veil," I
gasped. "To follow the ritual laid out upon the scrolls of
her flesh. To draw her blood from his blood. You have murdered your own son to bring destruction upon yourself!"

I leapt to my horse, and rode back swiftly down the line
of soldiers, to the army that had followed me to this snowy
field. In a quarter hour I stood before them, for my horse
had been swift and my spirit true.

"Blow the horn of war!" I shouted, my fangs long and
sharpened like daggers. "Take them! Take them all! And
leave none standing!"

The Akkadites blew the great horns, and the drums of
the towers sounded as they had before our descent.

• 4 •

THE smell of blood filled the air as our roaring company
came down upon them. Swift were the vampyres with
dragon wings spread as they met the fearsome Morns in
midflight, tossed and bludgeoned by the whirling winds
were they. Ophion and the warriors of the skies tore the
throats from those eel-skinned creatures. Many of our company were bitten and fell, but many more took down Morns
into the burning canals and emerged unscathed—but not so
their victims. Upon the white frozen ground, the kings and
queens of Myrryd brought razien and sword, spear and
claw, tooth and talon, into the horde of Disk knights who
had poured forth from the gates of Taranis-Hir at our thunderous approach. No match were the Chymer wolves for
our tribe, though Akkadite mortals they brought low. Many
horses cried out to heaven as if they had human voice, as
the Lamiades snapped at their flanks and tore their withers

and crests, as the White Robes drove swords into the Akkadite riders. Still, the vampyres of the sky fell down in a
flock of dark angels upon these robed priests, and tore at the
cloth that hid them, and scored their rotting skin with their
talons.

Foot soldiers, the fodder of Taranis-Hir, came at us with
spear and shield, arrow and ax, and I joined many in leaping from my mount and bringing a cudgel against those
who had felled the Akkadites. I looked to Calyx to see how
she fared, for we had no stratagem in this war, but merely
the will to slaughter. She had broken her lance into a
knight's visor, tearing him from his steed; and with her
sword, she jabbed and cut another who brought his ax
against her.

Namtaryn, upon her mount, chased down the wolf-
women as they scattered to the wintry woods, and in one
moment she seemed to be hunting them, and in the next,
she carried three pelts in her hand, while swinging her
double-headed ax down into a knight's back as he skew-
ered one of our tribe upon his silver-tipped spear.

Athanat had leapt from his horse, and carried several
men in his arms up to whirling winds, and there ripped at
their bodies until the earth below was sprayed with their
blood. Nekhbet led her warriors against the gatekeepers
and their guards, and I saw her slit the throats of many before the guards at the battlements above began pouring
molten lead down upon any who drew too near to the gate.

Many were heroes of this fight, and many its fallen, but
no matter whom I slaughtered, I thought only of that son I
had not known, stolen from me by the Myrrydanai. As we
fought, some of the dead Disk soldiers rose up, possessed
by those spirits that Calyx had warned me of. And to these,
I brought second and third deaths, and took their swords
and sliced them so that even if they rose again, they could
not return to combat. I felt the pressure of spirits all around
as I flew down among the White Robes. Drawing out the
Nameless, I sent many into the Veil that was their home,
but I knew this would be temporary, for the Veil was thin,

and if Medhya came through, all would be lost. I tore a White Robe from his Lamiades mount, singed him with that Nameless fire, and as the shadow separated from the robe and stolen skin, and whispered into nothingness, I glanced to the other riders among the White Robes. Ghorien was my only goal, though it felt good to take down the other whispering shadows.

Snow and ash mixed along the high walls of the city, and from the watchtowers of the North and East Gates, stones rained down upon those who stormed against the great broad doors. Knights of the Disk, their standard raised high to show the circle of their faith and its Virgin of Shadows, rode beside the canals, driving handfuls of the Akkadites who fought alongside my tribe into the oil fires. Hundreds of flaming arrows flew in graceful arcs through the snow-illumined sky.

All was lit by the fire canals that flowed between and among us. The shadows of men and horses and vampyres were like burning ghosts through the smoke, backlit by flames. There was no visible moon, but the earth itself gave up light, and those ancient kings who fought this day brought the pale-blue light of death with them.

If this were the last day of the earth, I would believe it. I felt a trembling between this world and the next, and the interplay of red and blue and green light in that terrible, dark place made me feel as if I were again in Myrryd itself, but at the height of its glory and horror.

Then it all stopped—all movement—my brethren of the air seemed to hang from the sky with their wings spread and cupped. The horses at a gallop seemed pinned to the earth through their hooves. Lances that flew in the air froze, held by invisible hands. Arrows in the sky, stopped in the arc of their aim; the fire in the canals distilled into jagged and perfect bits of yellow glass.

Ghorien, I commanded the momentary stillness in my mind. *Show yourself to me.*

In a whisper at my ear, he said, *You will find me in the place of your visions.*

Quickly, all movement returned, and I pressed my boot into the Lamiade that I rode.

The lizard screeched like a death cry, and snarled, trying to maneuver its head to turn and tear my legs off, but I kept to the saddle, and drew on its reins, and pressed the talons of the Raptorius into its shanks to go forward. I raised the staff and the sword to many—shaping it by will into the long, curved blade with its sharp teeth, or into a double-bladed long sword that cut to the left and the right as I swung it between the oncoming soldiers. The lizard wished to turn around and go with the others of its kind, but I drove it forward. When it refused to budge, I thrust the sword into its skull to stop its life. I shouted for the vampyres to take out the Lamiades—to aim for their legs with their swords, or to push the blades into the skulls as I had done. I did not want the remaining White Robes to have the creatures for escape.

Our enemy poured oil across the canals, and fires burned upward, their flames licking the roof of the sky, which in the dark of solstice night seemed white from the falling snow.

All along the watchtowers, the quicksilver arrows were shot among us, and some found our tribe and slowed them down. The best of the Disk knights found the hearts of our warriors and jabbed into them, for they knew of that method to send us to the Extinguishing. But we fought long and bravely, and Enora and her remaining wolves went into the city, protected by the walls and guard, and as I looked up along the battlements, I saw a White Robe upon a Lamiade, signaling to others of his kind to follow him. The lizards moved rapidly up the walls, crushing the crenel above as they went.

Yes, in retreat they were, for our warriors had done much damage to our enemy. Fewer than fifty soldiers remained outside the gates as we approached them, and we vastly outnumbered them. Many of these soldiers tore the Disks from their throats and fell forward into the snow, praying for mercy; but others fought us to the death, and all these fell to the jaws of my tribe and the sword of the Akkadites.

The fires along the canals burned uncontrollably, and blackened the sky, which was pierced with lightning, while many knights poured from the south and the north, having come from the farthest gates. Still we took them, and I watched good and bad fall, and what was of our side diminish as these fresh knights came at us with the courage of mortal valor. Yet they had no good in them, and many of my tribe leapt upon these riders and tore through their visors to get to the flesh at their throats.

As the Akkadite men and women raised the great rocks thrown at us and carried them as ramrods to the gates, still more riders came, spear and sword gleaming, like a blur of light and dark in the blistering storm.

There was no dawn in sight, nor did I know the hour, for time had ended here, and we could not retreat, nor could we call a truce. It was a battle to the end of all—and either I would stand with the staff and Asmodh sword raised, a beacon of fire for my tribe, and the walls of Taranis-Hir would fall; or I would be in chains, and my Extinguishing would come when the storm had ended and the sun drew its own fire from beneath the eastern Forest edge.

Fire and blood mingled between the canals and the barren snow-covered land. The clouds themselves seemed tinged with blood, and some dark magick had come to Taranis-Hir, for the light that came up within the dark was not of stars or sun or lightning, but of the horizon of the Veil itself, which sought us.

I knew what it was: a ritual of the Veil, for something was opening from the deep, and within the towers of Taranis-Hir, an ancient sorcery was being called by Ghorien and Enora, using the Nahhashim staff and the blood of my son.

I flew to my horse, which had been stolen by a foot soldier, and I scraped him from it, and rode forward toward the gates.

• 5 •

RED was the sky, and red the earth, and what was not red
was the yellow-white searing of fire and the black ash of
shadow. More knights poured in from all sides, some of
whom had been hiding in the Forest, unseen by our spies.
Others had ridden up from the quarries below the city.
From the open culverts they came, splashing the icy water;
their horses drenched with the filth of the canals, and soon,
the spattering of blood. Several White Robes came back
over the walls, their Lamiades leaping to the earth, the
creatures' jaws grabbing whoever was in their path,
whether horse or rider, vampyre or mortal, friend or foe.
These shadow priests had abandoned the skins, but held to
their robes, and the darkness of their hands brought swords
deep into the spines of Akkadites as they redoubled their
efforts at slaughter.

Horses and soldiers moved like spirits through the towers of smoke rising from the flames around us. From
nowhere, it seemed, a soldier would rush my horse. From
out of the smoke, the last Morn or two that existed might
leap out upon one of my warriors. The screams of men,
mingled with the death cries of horses and the Lamiades,
pierced the night.

As my sword hacked deep into my enemy's shoulder, I
heard a great clamoring, and shouts from my men—and I
saw the gates of the city give way. The vampyres who had
taken to the air had flown down into the city, and killed
many soldiers there. Many a Myrrydanai blade had been
thrust into the hearts of the warriors who had come from
Myrryd to serve their kings, and many of these lay extinguished along the clattering streets of Taranis-Hir.

The huzzahs and cries of victory came from the Akkadites, and like a swarm, we rode along the streets, over the
arched bridges, swiftly along, slaughtering all in our path.
Victory was sure, I felt it, and I smote many with the staff,
and by it, some were turned to stone, and others melted
at its touch. Still other mortals went to death in calm, and

more were touched by it and driven mad—such was the power of the Nahhashim. The Nameless I also used, and I rode ahead of my people, and any who showed resistance went down into the blood-drenched streets. Along the narrow and wide avenues I went, and behind me, the multitude, and above me, Ophion leading the night-flyers. The foundries exploded with fire, as the alchemists and foundrymen no doubt decided to destroy their industry rather than leave it to the conqueror. I felt the spirit of the Great Serpent within me, and held the hope that my daughter still lived, and that even the betrayer—*Anguis*—Pythia had survived the night, for I could not bear to lose any I had loved, whether they had offended me or not.

But as we reached the tower White-Horse, it was as if I had left the earth's sphere, and had ridden into a dream.

Into a vision.

You will find me in the place of your visions.

All slowed down, though I heard the cheers and cries of my men and women as they brought their merciless attack into the halls of that cursed city, and as the vampyres dropped into the pockets of resistance along the alleyways, and drank deep from the enemy who fought against them with waning effort.

Before the towers of the Lady White-Horse, had been erected a scaffolding, and upon it, a great stone that was blue as lapis, flat as an altar, and all about it, White Robes stood.

There upon the altar, the same as visions I had been given since the Sacred Kiss had come to me—and yet, slightly different, as if the visions from the Veil, from the Priest of Blood, and from Medhya herself were transmuting, and changing as I had changed. As if my becoming Maz-Sherah within the Asmodh depths had touched the truth of these visions. I felt locked in the moment, unable to move.

The vampyre, Pythia, bound to the flat-cut stone quarried from the Barrow-Depths of Taranis-Hir, seemed to wear a fierce golden sun upon her face.

Each time I had dreamed of this, seen it within a Veil vision, I had not truly understood that one day I would come to this perfect moment, when the vision became flesh and blood and fire and ash.

The sight of the altar and scaffolding; the towers beyond it, the smoke beyond the walls and the fires within the foundries; winged creatures in the red sky diving and rising and diving again like a war from heaven; below, the White Robed shadow priests, and upon her white horse, Enora.

Pythia, held by the shadow priests, turned her mask toward me. Her wings drew out from her shoulders, great spurs at their bows, the dragon wings of our tribe. Yet she could not fly, nor did she struggle.

We were frozen in tableau—my wings curved for flight, while I sat astride the stallion, my enemy in his final breath of life.

The roaring host of others, swords raised, stones at midshot, those falling to earth in death and Extinguishing and those whose thrusts tore flesh—all were still as I heard the Dark Madonna's voice:

"All is lost, Maz-Sherah, and you will see the Queen of Wolves raise the burning sword to your heart. You will know that your skin will be flayed and worn as a robe of victory as Medhya's once was worn by the Myrrydanai. Your blood will be drunk as Medhya's was by the Kamr priests. Your bones broken and thrown to the dogs, as the priests of the Nahhash did with our Dark Mother's bones. You will understand—only then—what it means to be the Anointed sacrifice of your tribe."

It was the mask upon Pythia's face that seemed to speak those words.

The sky was red with a bloody night; the towers of White-Horse lit with human torches; the armies of night on either side; the smell in the air of defeat and terror; and the cries of mortal and immortal alike as we heard the great tearing of the invisible as it birthed the Dark Madonna.

Many of the Akkadites who survived to enter this inner

sanctum had stopped fighting, and even the soldiers of the enemy looked upon the altar with awe. The three remaining kings of the Asyrr—Sarus and Illuyan and Athanat—and the two queens who still haunted the skies—Nekhbet and Namtaryn—had sheathed their swords and dropped the mortals from whom they drank. For we were in the presence of the Dark Mother's touch, and we felt it as the breath of the Veil, like the Sacred Kiss itself burned down among us in heat and despair.

The golden mask covering Pythia's face had grown as if it were a living thing. Radiant bursts off the brow formed a crown of glistening spikes, and the lower half had elongated so that it covered her chin. The ancient writing of Myrryd itself had been scrawled across its face.

She sat, roped to the altar stone. The White Robe called Ghorien—his rotting hand showing the birthmark to me as if he wanted me to know he was there—held his instrument of sorcery, the Staff of the Nahhashim, taken at last from Enora.

The mask spoke with the voice of Medhya, the Dark Madonna, mother of my race. She whispered to me, so close it was as if she embraced me as she spoke. "If you but bow to me, you will be my consort, Falconer. I will raise you up and fulfill your true destiny. You will become greater than the Serpent himself, who betrayed me as I lay in his arms. Do not fear, for you will be a god. We will give birth to gods. We shall undo all that mankind has wrought, and all of earth shall be our kingdom. All these you see will tremble before you, if you will sacrifice this traitorous creature and open the Veil."

As I looked across at the kings and the queens of Myrryd, and at their many warriors and servants who had survived the night, I saw in their faces what was in my own: they too had shared this vision, although they had not understood in their long Extinguishing.

Ghorien's skin sloughed off, dropping to the wooden planks at his robe's edge. With a dark hand, he pointed to me. "You have known your destiny, Maz-Sherah."

Maz-Sherah, he whispered in my mind. *You have lost a*

son to the sacrifice. He pointed to a golden bowl to the right of Pythia. It was thickened with blood. *You will lose a daughter to this as well.*

From among the six robed Myrrydanai, they brought my daughter, Lyan, whose mouth was covered with rope, and whose eyes were blindfolded, and her hands bound.

You were born to this, Ghorien whispered to me, and turned his free hand toward Pythia, who remained silent. *Take the Asmodh blade and tear out the traitor vampyre's heart with its fire. Medhya will come into her, and breathe life into her flesh. The mask of Datbathani welcomes her, and has drunk the immortality of this traitor that she might live in the flesh forever and walk again, a goddess among the vessels of the mortal world.*

"I was born to this," I said. "But the ritual is unknown to me."

As I spoke, I heard a scream and turned in the direction of the sound. There, held by a bloodied Disk knight, Calyx—rags and veils across her face—had been captured. Her hands were bound before her, and the knight dragged the plague maiden over to Enora. The Queen of Taranis-Hir dismounted, wrapping her wolf pelts tight about her, and drew out her dark sword, holding it to Calyx's throat, all the while watching me. A servant brought another golden bowl and held it near Enora's blade.

Enora drew apart the shreds of cloth and veil, revealing Calyx's face—beautiful as the final plague of the Veil burned beneath her skin, a red-yellow fire in her blood. Enora's blade skimmed downward at Calyx's throat, cutting through the cloth, until all clothes fell from Calyx's form. She stood there, bound at the wrists, naked, and her body shone with the deep-red light from the Veil itself.

Enora brought the blade back to her throat, and gently rubbed it back and forth against Calyx's skin. I felt powerless as I stood there, watching this obscene ritual. As the sword dipped into the cut—which steamed as it poured from Calyx's neck—all who witnessed this heard a low growl as if the plague blood itself were alive.

I knew what Calyx held within her, knew from the moment I had drunk from her. Yet I did not understand its power, for I too held it within.

The Veil itself, in the blood.

But I was immortal, and could not be the doorway of this otherworld.

Only mortal blood could carry it—if the mortal lived. And Calyx, the changeling, the daughter of the elementals, mortal and yet touched by the spirits at birth, had become a harbor for the final plague of the Veil:

The door itself, the thin caul of its skin, drawn back.

In her blood, in the steam of it.

Enora did not murder her, but bled her, and the blood went into another golden bowl.

My son's blood, consecrated to Medhya at his birth; and Calyx's blood, now consecrated by the Myrrydanai.

Calyx fought and bit, but Enora held her tight in an iron grip.

And as the blood splashed into the bowl, all felt the Veil fall back, like dark water splashed against the face, like the silence of the tomb upon the whole earth.

When she had the bowl filled, Enora dropped Calyx to the earth and brought the bowl up the steps to the scaffold's floor.

It was a hypnotic moment, and while every instinct told me to fight this, I, too, like the others surrounding us, was in awe.

And from my lips, words came—the Asmodh secrets, the language before there was language, in a series of tongues and hisses and growls and roars, I spoke the ancient ritual of those dwellers of the deep places as if I had no choice, as if these words had been written upon my soul.

And yet, Pythia whispered in my mind even as the words came through. *Do what you must to close it, for you have the blade of sacrifice.*

When I looked at her, tears ran down her golden face, and I knew in those tears that she had not betrayed me. She had gone to her fate, knowing that this moment could not be avoided any longer.

Knowing that to bring back the warriors from Saracen lands would just prolong suffering.

Knowing that I must cut her throat to complete the ritual, and wondering what would reign within me—Medhya's call, or Merod, who had given his existence to me that I might come to this moment with strength.

It was from that blood within me that I stopped up my mouth and its ritual words that had no meaning to me though I knew its aim, and I drew the Nameless from its sheath.

With the Staff of the Nahhashim in my right hand, and the sword at my left, I brought its flame up and called to Merod within my blood, and to the Great Serpent, and even to those Asmodh sorceries that I did not fathom. I did not wish to take the life of Pythia, or to end the life of that child who had not yet known birth—for I remembered my mean and shallow birth in the fields, not far from that scaffold, in those days of an innocent world that was not touched by such dark sorcery.

I did not wish this child to have less of a chance in this world than I, nor did I want the earth to darken under Medhya's rule.

I slammed the Nahhashim staff against the one Ghorien carried, and plunged the fiery blade into him, growing the fire into a conflagration along his shadow. The two staffs, as they met, cracked, and a bolt of lightning shot through my arm, knocking me backward.

But I regained my balance, and heard Ghorien—as his shadow caught fire—whisper within me, *She comes, Maz-Sherah, she comes, for the door is open!*

I glanced at my daughter, and the White Robes who held her drew blades against her and would kill her in a moment if I did not act.

I looked at Lyan, who could not see me, and at Pythia, who watched me with terror in her eyes, for she knew that

I would kill her, and I could not think otherwise for the Myrrydanai circled my thoughts, whispering among them.

I took the Nameless and curved its blade as a sacrificial dagger.

I pressed its sharp, jagged, burning edge into my heart.

• 6 •

AS I fell to the planks, I looked up at Pythia and her last look was not of the terror she had just held, but a strange excitement—in my final breaths before the fires of the Asmodh took me into the Veil I realized that I had never understood her, or what she had done. She was mystery, then, and unfathomable.

I saw gray shapes rise up from the Nahhashim staffs that had met, and broken together. I watched these figures draw themselves, phantoms, from the white bone of the staffs.

The gray priests, I thought. The Nahhashim had come, but for me? To take me to the Veil, where terrible creatures and exiled gods and monsters are held prisoners from this earth by ancient Asmodh ritual?

They carried me—or I dreamed they did—for through the Veil I went, and felt a cold, bitter wind. For in my passing, Medhya crossed a tear of the Veil that grew smaller and smaller.

Had I failed? I tried to ask the gray priests, but these looked down at me with faces of pure light, and I did not grow afraid as I felt my last breath come.

I was no longer inside my flesh, nor did I seem to be in the Veil—I floated above my fallen body, which had burned near the chest and throat. The gray priests no longer were there, but I watched as Ghorien and the Myrrydanai dissolved as rain came down, and as I moved higher, away from my body.

This was the Extinguishing itself, and I was in my body, but also watching it from far above.

Enora went to retrieve the Nameless, but from beside

me in the sky, a billowing cape dropped down—Ophion—
who had watched all of this transpire. He leapt upon Enora
as she crouched over my body, and tore her away from it,
biting deeply at her throat, for she had no sorcery without
the Nahhashim staff in her hand.

From my chest, he drew out the broken blade, still smoldering, and went to Pythia, cutting the ropes that bound her.

Lifting the two half staffs, broken at their centers, he
brought them to my ashen wound, and though I did not
hear his words, I knew what my brother—the Maz-Sherah
who had gone with me to Myrryd, brought me to the source
of our tribe, and allowed me to gain the blessing of the
Great Serpent that he had so desired—was about.

Through the staff, he raised me from the dead.

Again, I saw the gray priests in some dark and lonesome place, and realized they drew me now through the
halls of the dead. The statues of Lemesharra and Datbathani were there, their faces pure and victorious. And the
third statue, of Medhya herself, had been beheaded by
some conquering hero.

The echoes of mortal life were heard in this place, and I
saw many shades pass as they went down through the endless corridor, led by the children of Death and their handmaidens.

But the gray priests carried me along, and as we went
beneath a low arch, I opened my eyes to the corpse-
vampyre's face, watching me with wonder.

I heard the Great Serpent speak within me, words he
had told me in the depths: *You are the master of this sacred fire. It will serve you alone, but you must never let
Medhya near the sword, for she has rituals to turn it
against you.*

· 7 ·

I came from my Extinguishing like a fish gasping for air
on land, and although only moments had passed since I had
brought the blade to my heart, it seemed like hours had
gone by.

I did not hear anyone at first, but gradually, each sense returned, and I smelled the blood in the air, and heard Ophion cry out that I had returned from the dead.

I reached up with my arm and drew him down so that my lips were close to his ear. "You," I gasped. "Are truly my brother. And for all you have suffered, you will become a king of the earth, Maz-Sherah. Brother. You called the Nahhashim to bring me back to life."

❖ 8 ❖

THE burning fire of the Asmodh sorcery tore the Myrry-danai from the world into the Veil, just as I had brought the fire into my heart. Yet this fire was made of Asmodh sorcery, and could not harm the Great Serpent for long. The Great Serpent was the fire of the Asmodh, and I had taken this sacred fire into me—not a sacrifice, but a union with the Nameless itself. Through my burning heart, the shadow priests had been sucked as if by a tunnel of whirling wind and searing heat. The gray priests—the Nahhashim—had come from within the bone staff to ensure that the Serpent reborn would not be lost within Extinguishing or in the Veil itself.

But as I rose up, as the last shred of the shadow of the Myrrydanai faded, I listened for the sound of the Veil's tearing. *Medhya will come through. She will not accept this defeat. She has waited too long.* I glanced over to Calyx, who had her hands pressed to the wound at her throat as she sat among her rags. Her skin no longer burned with the plague—it had found release in a bowlful of blood. Her face was pale, and her eyes sought mine. It was as if I read her thoughts: *Enora.* Medhya would use Enora.

The maiden I had once loved and known as Alienora, now a beautiful terror, had already fled. She let her robes and wolf pelts fall as she ran across to the tower entrance. I drew my wings out, ready to find her, but was soon distracted by the needs of my daughter and Pythia herself. I saw torchlight at the slender windows of the Tower White-Horse, as Enora raced up the steps toward her chamber.

Carrying the Nameless before me, I leapt into the air, fly-ing up to the balcony at her chamber window, but just as I reached it, she shouted my name as if remembering who I had once been to her. "Aleric!"

And with that sound, she leapt from the tower, just as I reached for her.

I crouched there along the tower wall, a gargoyle of a creature, my wings covering my form. I looked down at the broken body of this terrible queen, of this lost soul.

I could not bring myself to look out over those who stood, barely moving, still in shock from the events of the night. I could only look down at Enora's face, and remem-ber the maiden with whom I had once vowed eternal love.

Had the loss of the staff brought her self-knowledge? Had the sorcery that had held her so long finally freed her?

As I watched the lifeless body far below me, I felt a shudder within, and an icy touch at the base of my spine.

Medhya.

She had not given up.

The ritual that had begun was enough for her.

As I crouched there, I saw a slight movement in Enora's left hand. A trembling, nothing more. For a moment, I hoped that she might still live. That she might somehow re-cover from this fall. And yet the dark blood that stained the snow around her did not offer much promise of life.

Then, the dead woman's eyes opened. They were shiny and black, and the moment I saw them, I leapt to the ground, flying swiftly, knowing that Medhya had used Enora after all.

"You will not have a moment's breath here," I whis-pered to her as I dropped beside her.

"Freedom," came the raspy voice from within the dead woman's lips, though they did not move. I felt something clutch at my heart as I drew the Nameless out.

I fell upon the corpse as it reanimated, holding the bro-ken body down to the earth with my knees. I looked into those dark eyes and saw the terrible beauty of that ancient queen as she sought to escape her prison. Breath that

reminded me of the stench of the canals that ran beneath
Myrryd came from her lips as she said, *"Maz-Sherah, you
will be my prince,"* and these words were her last.

"For the Great Serpent, I do this," I told her. I brought
the fire of the blade into her heart, and tore a path through
those broken bones up to her throat. As I held the hilt inside the body, I felt as if I were hanging on to the pommel
of some wild stallion, struggling to grasp the blade from
within the burning body. Finally, there was stillness. The
Veil was not mended, but it had closed, and had drawn
back its prisoner.

I thrust the blade deep into her, and left it there until the
Asmodh fires tore through the body.

"It is done," I said when I sheathed the blade.

All grew quiet, and the fire died down.

I turned to face the throng who had watched the ritual,
and the burning of the corpse of their queen.

Calyx had risen, staunching the flow of her bleeding
with strips of torn cloth; several of the Akkadites had gone
to her to tend this wound.

My daughter stood, bound and blindfolded upon the
scaffolding, and it was Pythia who undid the bindings and
drew off the blindfold that she might see.

• 9 •

SEVERAL fires were set throughout the city before
dawn, and many who still clung to the Disk and its dreams
escaped the fall of Taranis-Hir and fled to other kingdoms
and lands for shelter and sanctuary. With less than an hour
until dawn, the tower of White-Horse was the first to burn
like a great torch against the purple sky.

Ophion had not been able to find the grimoire, and I
guessed that Artephius had fled the city long before the
battle had begun. Where had he gone? That night I could
wonder this, but in years to come, the mystery grew—for I
did not trust the alchemist, nor his book of Medhyic Art.

There I stood, before the light of the world came again
from its dark edge. Surrounding me, the dead and wounded,

and the last of the tribe. "Go rest, and those who are healers, seek out those in need of care. Tomorrow night, the city walls come down, and all the towers of white caelum will burn. Those who live here must find other shelter, for the accursed city is fallen and no one—whether in tower or Barrow-Depths—shall ever find rest in Taranis-Hir. And in a hundred years, the Great Forest will overtake the ruins, and in a thousand years, few will remember this place or the Disk and its plagues!"

◆ 10 ◆

WHEN the night came, I rose late, exhausted from the long battle. I smelled the smoke of the fires in the city above. Pythia and I had gone to the Barrow-Depths, and into the study of the alchemist himself to seek our quiet rest. Upon my waking, she had already left me, and I rose through the foundries, now in ruins, and up to the streets. Above me, many vampyres flew in the night, hunting those mortals foolish enough to have remained within the city walls.

When I found Pythia, she brought a covered box, and when she drew back the leather cloth, I saw that it was made of silver.

I knew what it was, and I drew open its lid, despite the stinging I felt from that metal that is so abhorrent to us.

I could not help myself, I dropped to the earth and began weeping with joy, for within the box was ash and skull and blackened fragments of bone, broken and crumbled.

I raised the broken staff, and held the Eclipsis toward the ashes. I spoke the words silently, for I was almost afraid that I could not do this after all that had transpired.

A wind came up from within the box, and soon the ash whirled about and the bone grew as a tree might, and from the bone, sinew and muscle erupted, veins and organs and flesh blossomed as my beloved friend re-formed before my eyes, the vampyre youth he had been before his imprisonment, as if his flesh and spirit and blood had never burned in the sun.

"Ewen," I said, and went to embrace my friend.

In Alkemara, with Natalia

· 1 ·

HERE I end this tale of my first years as a vampyre—the Maz-Sherah, they said, the "One," to guide, to lead, to guard this world from the world beyond the Veil, where the demons wander, and where Medhya, in chains, sits upon her twisted throne.

Natalia turned to me as I told this tale to her, for the meaning went deeper than a mere lost century of plagues and vampyres, a history wiped clean by those who protected the demons themselves.

She was descended from vampyre blood.

"Lyan was raised by Calyx—for my daughter never overcame her terror at the vampyres and her belief we were devils. I could guard her, but I could not do more than watch from a distance. Yet, the prophecy of my daughter's life would come true one day. Calyx lived many years, teaching my daughter old ways within the deep wood. From her line arose great soldiers and scholars and explorers, as well."

"And Pythia died?" Natalia asked.

I nodded. "In our son's fourteenth year. I held her as a fever took her, a common enough way to die for mortals, but I had not expected such a slight thing to fell this daughter of Alkemara. She squeezed my hand as I saw the yellow-brown spice appear upon her lips, and I knew the child of Death had begun drawing her soul.

"Ewen remained with me for—oh, that is another history, I think, and should wait for another tale some night. The new tribe—the remaining kings of the Asyrr and Ophion and I—built new kingdoms of our tribe, based on the principles of guardianship of the mortal realm, as it was intended by the first priests before the corruption of Medhya and the loss of Merod and Alkemara. We spent many centuries together, but I am sad to report that all vampyres go to either oblivion or Extinguishing. The Eclipsis and the staff did not resurrect a vampyre from the Extinguishing more than once—it was impossible, even for the Asmodh sorcery. Even I will one day find the darkness of oblivion, Natalia, as those surviving kings of Myrryd met theirs in the centuries that followed the fall of Taranis-Hir. I am not ashamed to say that I sent one or two of them there myself, for some of them became renegades, unwilling to guard mortals. They sought absolute power over them, instead, and so Ewen and I, and others who were loyal to us, had to hunt our own kind—or enlist mortal protectors to do this.

"When the guardianship is not needed, our numbers will dwindle. Many of those who survived from those past centuries, sleep long in their tombs, awaiting the call. When the Serpent tightens his grip upon us and the Veil grows thin, and the need among the children of the earth is great, then is the time to raise up again an army of our kind. We are meant to be shepherds, not wolves, though mortals believe we have the mask of the wolf upon our faces. And within us, the bloodthirst, our curse.

"I had followed each descendant in their lives. Micahel spent his life in adventure and scholarship, living with monks when the Inquisition of Vampyres began in Toulouse twenty years after the Taranis-Hir destruction. He saved many of them, and many witches, too, and helped others escape, as he could—though he was one man against many. I had to rescue him more than once from the clutches of the ignorant and suspicious.

"He was a good man. Better than either of his parents. He wrote histories of our kind, and histories of the lost century that had vanished from other more-established history. He retained his youth for an unnaturally long period though he was not a vampyre. He had only one child, a bastard daughter, and at my son's death in his 150th year—when he looked a mere thirty years old—I promised that I would guard his child, and the offspring of all his children.

"And so I did, through the centuries, when the lies of history and the kings and monks covered the Dark Age that had fallen across the world in that Age of the Serpent and the Veil.

"I brought vampyrism to those who would protect the secrets of Alkemara, and of Myrryd, and as the hunters often did, we searched through the rubble of cities, through the ancient Roman ruins and the temples that lay beneath the cathedrals that grew over the next few hundred years."

"But you never revealed yourself to any of my ancestors?" Natalia asked me, as we sat beside the crystal tomb at Alkemara.

"Some saw me. Your mother—your great-grandfather, when he was a boy, as well. From those in whom I inspired fear, I drew away, for I did not dare risk their lives—or my existence—by showing them their lineage. But you . . . you, Natalia. Your curiosity. When I saw you at your bedroom window when you were grieving, and you looked up at me, I knew you were not frightened. Your studies—your scholarship—would find me eventually. Soon enough. You sought me, and it was only then that I felt I could reveal myself to you. I am sworn to protect you. I do not break an oath. But here, in Alkemara, there is something more for you to see. Something more than my early life."

"The wolf key," she said, her eyes showing a hint of excitement. "After all this, what does it unlock?"

I guided her along the steps to that domed room where once my companions and I had entered—a room turned upside down, with six paths leading off from it. Each arched doorway, marked with an aspect of the Serpent in its dragon form.

As I led her down the first, we entered a great low-ceilinged room carved from white stone.

Hundreds of urns stood there, and with each a lid sealed with wax.

Drawing off the lid of one, I showed her what lay within, protected for centuries there.

She gasped when she saw the old book, re-bound with a proper leather binding.

"You found Artephius again?" she asked, as she lifted the Medhyic grimoire.

"Let us say, he found me," I said, but I chose not to speak of my later encounters with the alchemist.

Then, I led her into the narrow passages that ran below even the depths of Alkemara, where the streams of black water flow.

Even there, a secret chamber had been cut from rock, and after I unlocked it, I drew the torch into it that she might see better.

All that was within the chamber was an old table, one I had bought in the sixteenth century, when Namtaryn's war had raged across two continents.

Upon the table, a strongbox that resembled the box in which Natalia's mother had kept the souvenirs passed down through the generations of her family, but this was of an older wood, a mahogany that had once been polished to a shine. Upon its clasp, a bronze wolf's head. At its jaw, I had her try the key made of the Chymer wolf tooth and bone.

Natalia held her breath and inserted the key, and turned the lock of it.

"Before you open this"—I stayed her hand—"you must

know that what I am offering you is both dreadful and wonderful. But I have learned the rituals, and I know the power of this, after so many centuries of study."

When she lifted the lid of the box, I heard a long and strange sigh come from her throat.

"If you wish it, I would bring the breath of eternity into your flesh," I told her. "For you remind me most of the children I once held and loved. And you remind me of Pythia herself, for your face is like hers, and this is what I saw in you when I first found you. I believe you have a spirit like hers, when she had learned of the sorrows of mortality itself."

"But . . . I could not drink blood," she insisted.

"It is not vampyric life I offer," I said. "It is a gift I have held these many centuries, for the one who might best use it. I have lived as a vampyre for nearly a thousand years. The Veil is never shut for long, for it rips, and those who are exiled there seek to escape to this world. Even the Asyrr were not immune to drawing sorcery from those in the Veil. The present world turns dark again—I feel it in the coming wars. My kind will not last forever, for even the hidden places are drawn into the light. Many of my tribe have fallen to hunters, and many more shall, and I am not sure it is wise for me to bring the Sacred Kiss to more of the dying. Had I given this to my son, Micahel, he might still be here with me. But he refused it. A very few others to whom I offered this, through the years, have also turned it down. But you are different. I sense Pythia's spirit in you. You have a love for the ancient studies, and a keen mind, and a good heart. I ask that you accept this gift, for it will bring you immortality, but not the decay of death."

I drew the golden mask from beneath its silk coverlet.

Natalia gasped when she saw it.

"It drank immortality from Pythia. And it holds this power within its metal."

"But it . . . it will never come off. Once I wear it . . ."

"It will own you, yes," I said. "It is like skin upon the face. You will never grow older than you are now. You will never die. Nor will you extinguish. You will be here to know of all this, until the world's end. And after, perhaps. You will be a goddess, and know eternal youth. Your children shall be immortal. And when this world grows cold and dark, as it will soon enough, for the Veil tears again—I have felt it—you will rise up against those forces that enter this world. The best a vampyre may be is a guardian of mortal life, for as you feed on cattle, so we feed upon your kind. But the worst of what a vampyre may be is a terror— a corpse of unending thirst, a wolf within the guise of a beautiful youth or maiden. But you will escape this fate. You must keep the mortal world safe, even after all the vampyres are extinguished, and all the mortal protectors vanquished. And when the world begins anew, they will follow you and your children, and create a new world, out of darkness, out of despair. And into hope."

I held the mask up. "It is a terrible responsibility I offer you. I do not ordain this. Only you may choose it. But if you accept this mask, and wear it, you will know the secrets of all."

Natalia looked at me as if I were mad, then at the mask. "All of human history," she whispered. "A thousand years in the future."

"As long as immortality exists," I said. "No vampyre or mortal may harm you."

Swiftly, she grabbed the golden mask, and before I could warn her against its abuse, she slipped it across her brow.

With the mask secured to her face, I took her hand. I brought it to my lips, kissing her warm flesh.

For a flickering moment, as I looked at her eyes and the curve of her lips, I hoped that Pythia had been reborn within Natalia.

The breath of eternity was within her, without death, without suffering, without the thirst for blood.

Within her, a new Age of the Serpent was born.